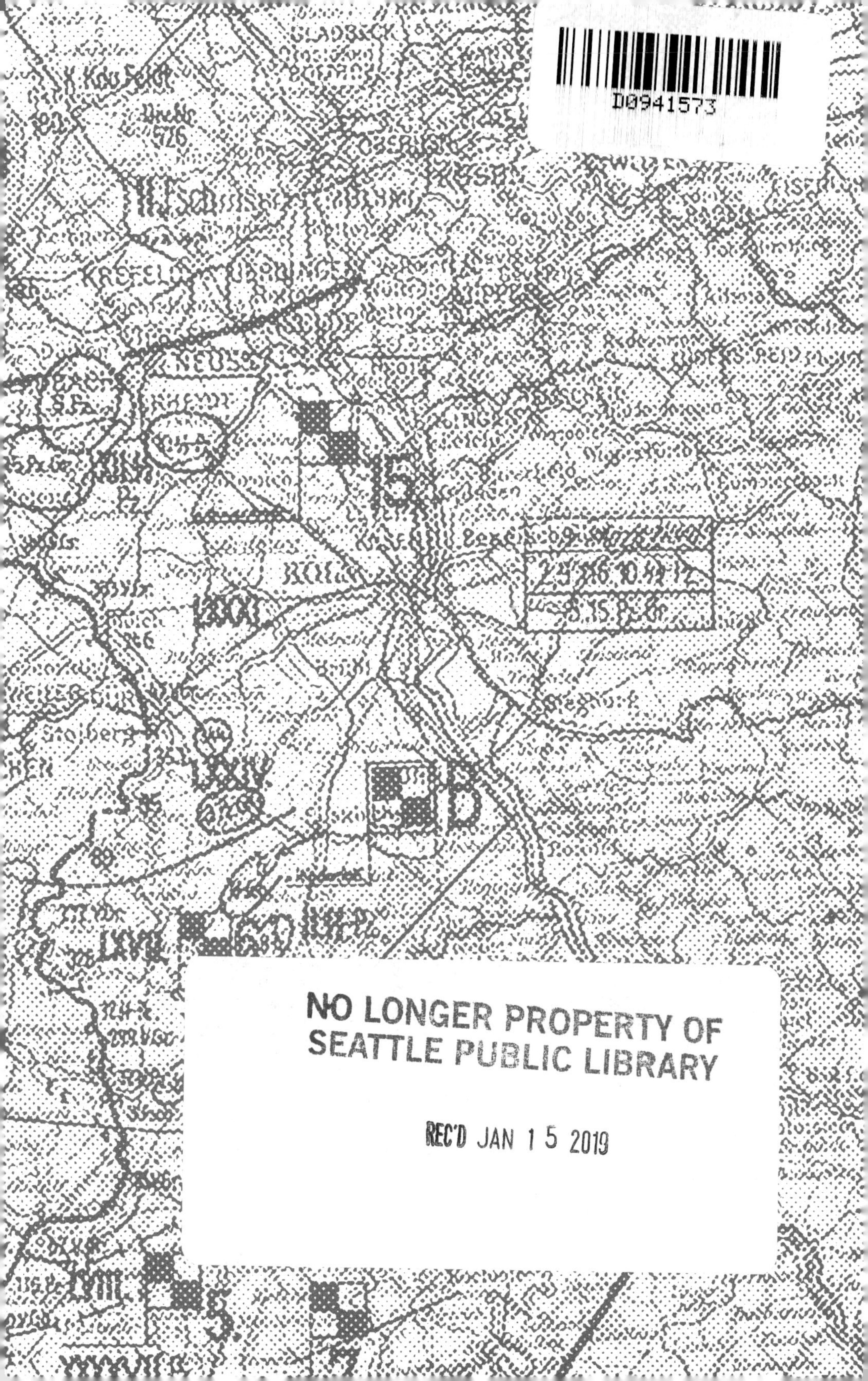

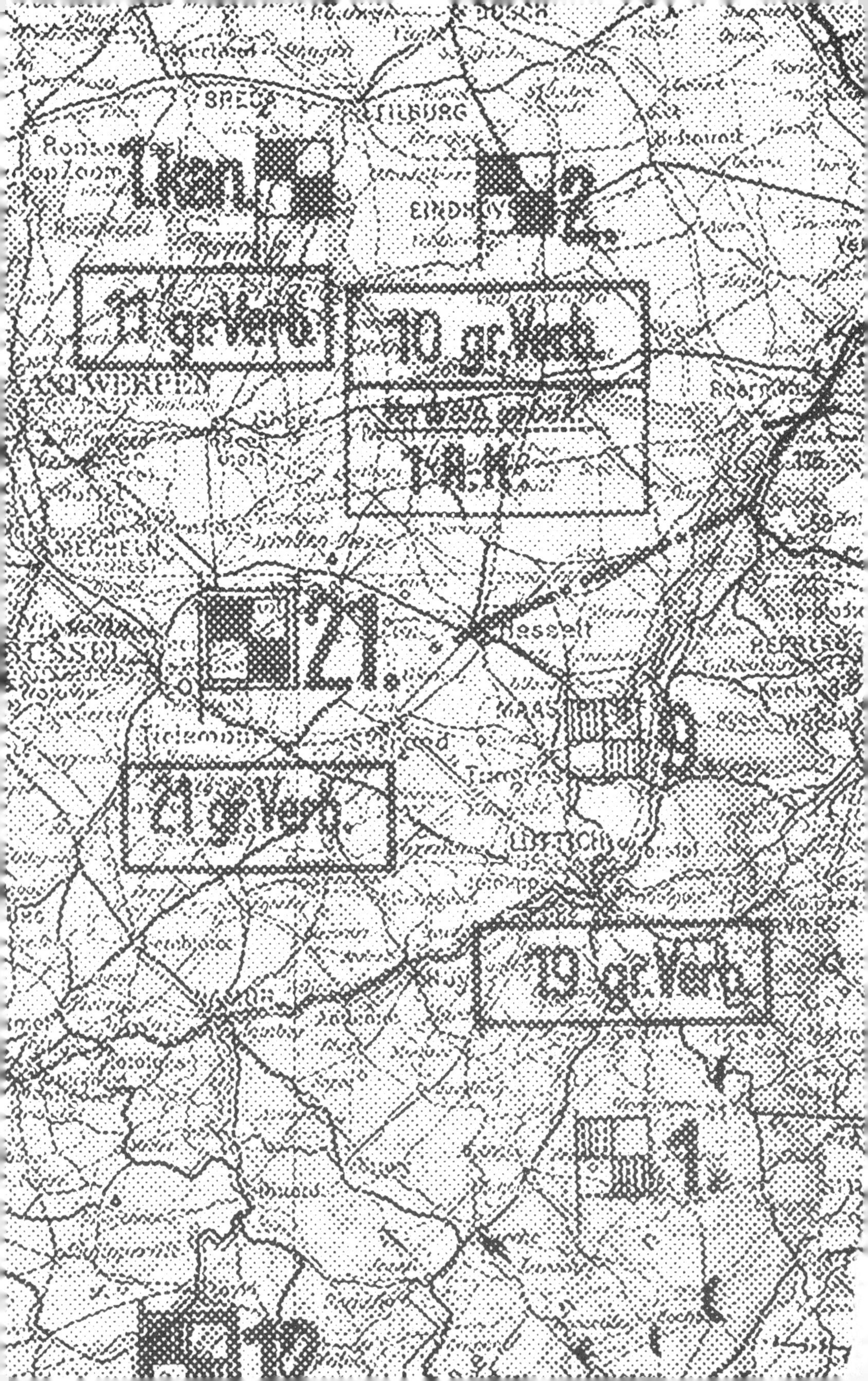
TILBURG
10 gr. Verb.
Hasselt
19 gr. Verb.

SON OF HITLER

image

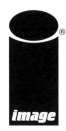

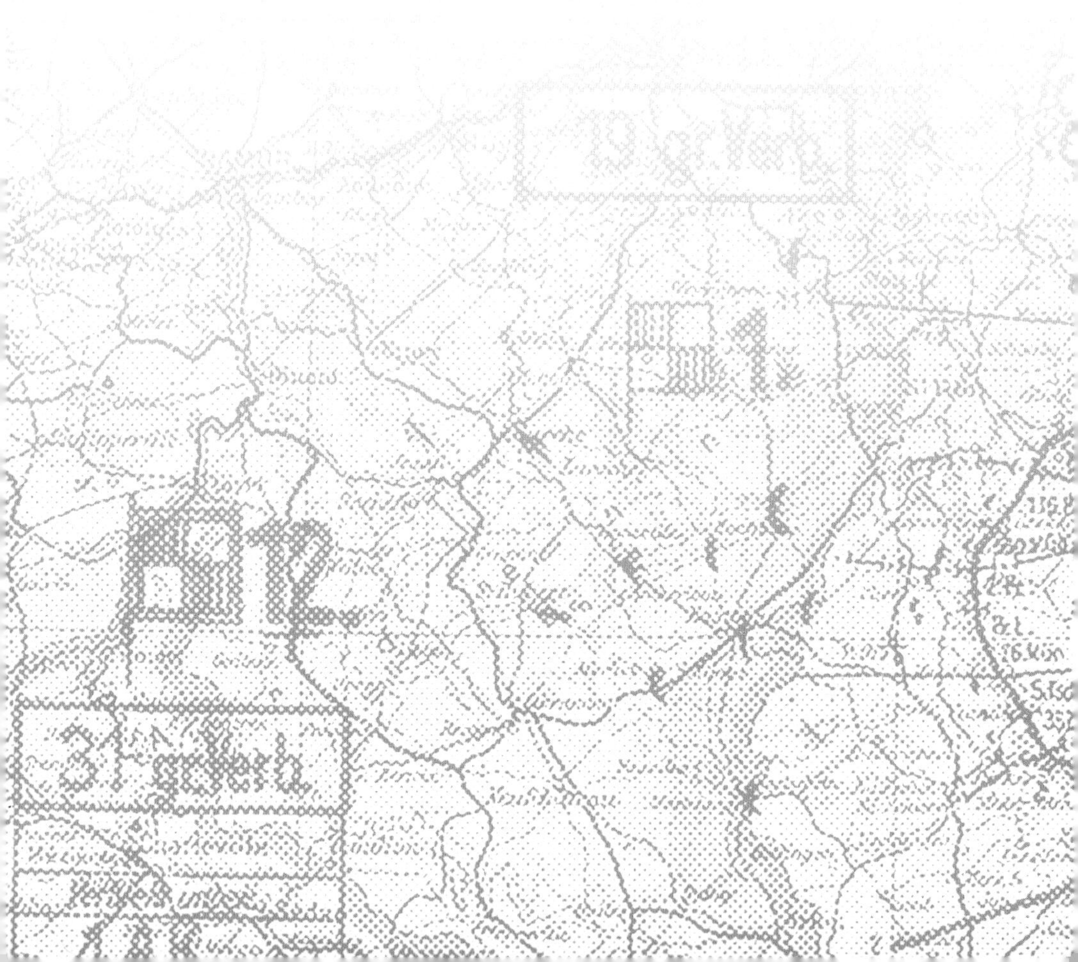
B12

"A good spy story is always about more than the operation itself, but tells the tale of the human cost, as well, and this is a damn good spy story, with echoes that from the Second World War reverberate to the present with chilling and elegant efficiency. Don't let the title fool you, or – come to think of it – let it do precisely that, because Anthony Del Col and Geoff Moore are gonna work you over with their script anyway, never mind the able and energetic assistance from Jeff McComsey's wonderful storytelling and the clarity of Jeff McClelland's letters. We need stories like this one, now more than ever before."

–Greg Rucka
(writer of LAZARUS, Queen & Country, Punisher)

"An alternate history humdinger that comes fully loaded with twists, turns and startling violence. The character work on display here is exemplary; I felt for the two leads in this book. I don't think I'm giving anything away by saying that SON OF HITLER's secret weapon is an affecting emotional core. I did not expect to feel quite so moved, quite so sad, when I finished reading it. And I mean that in the best way possible."

–Philip Gelatt
(writer of Petrograd, They Remain, Europa Report)

"Just when it seems there cannot possibly be literary ore left to be mined from World War II, along comes this book, bursting forth from cold history into hot, bloody life, a war epic that is secretly a revenge thriller that is hiding away a heart-rending family drama. Fathers and sons, you know? Damn."

–Van Jensen
(writer of The Flash, Casino Royale)

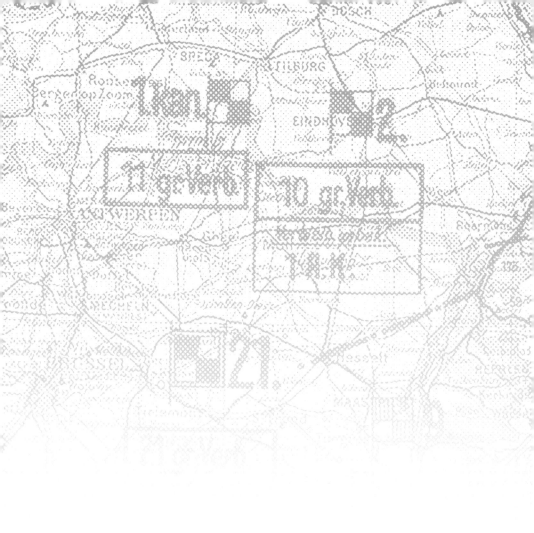

® IMAGE COMICS, INC.

Robert Kirkman—Chief Operating Officer
Erik Larsen—Chief Financial Officer
Todd McFarlane—President
Marc Silvestri—Chief Executive Officer
Jim Valentino—Vice President

Eric Stephenson—Publisher / Chief Creative Officer
Corey Hart—Director of Sales
Jeff Boison—Director of Publishing Planning
            & Book Trade Sales
Chris Ross—Director of Digital Sales
Jeff Stang—Director of Specialty Sales
Kat Salazar—Director of PR & Marketing
Drew Gill—Art Director
Heather Doornink—Production Director
Nicole Lapalme—Controller

IMAGECOMICS.COM

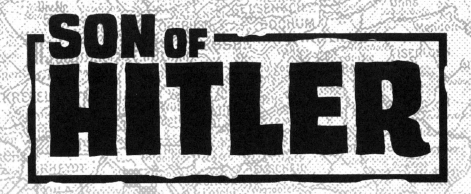

STORY
Anthony Del Col & Geoff Moore

ART
Jeff McComsey

Letters
Jeff McClelland

Cover Art
Jeff McComsey

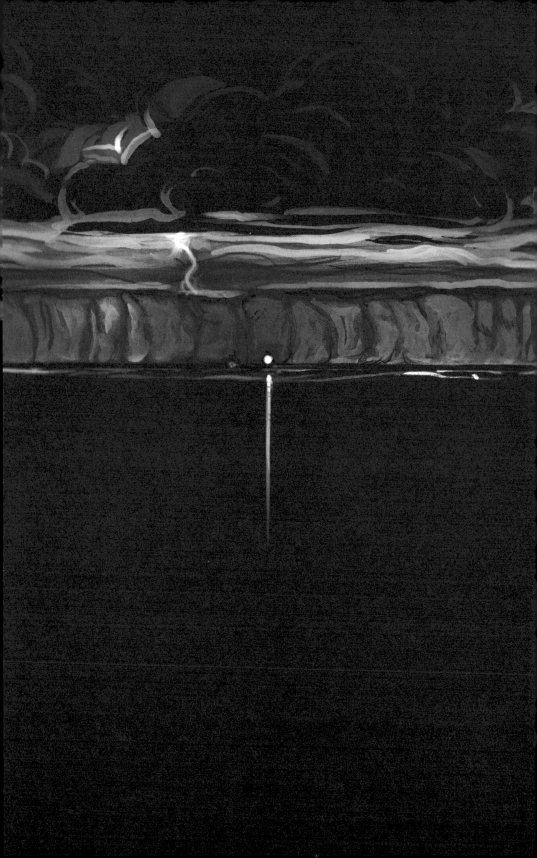

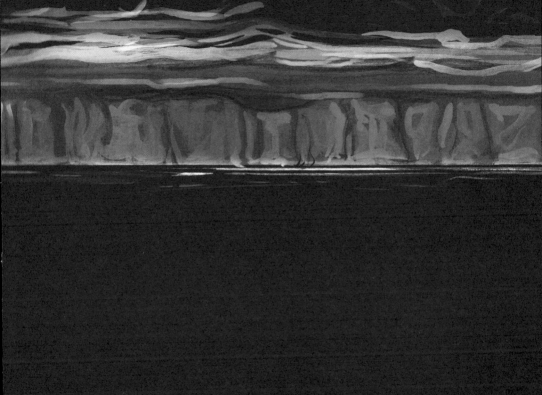

"In wartime, truth is so precious that she should
always be attended by a bodyguard of lies."

-Sir Winston Churchill

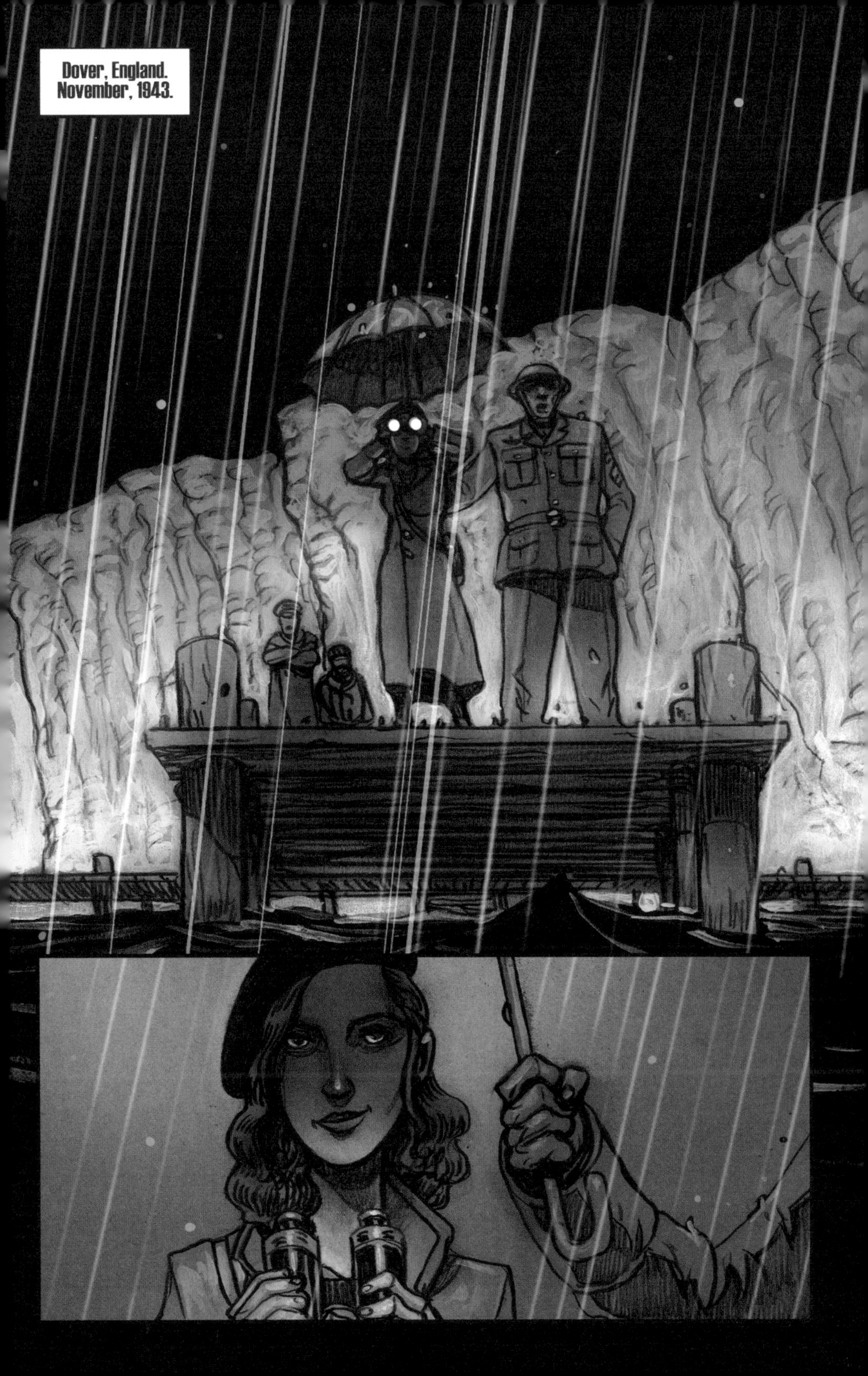
Dover, England.
November, 1943.

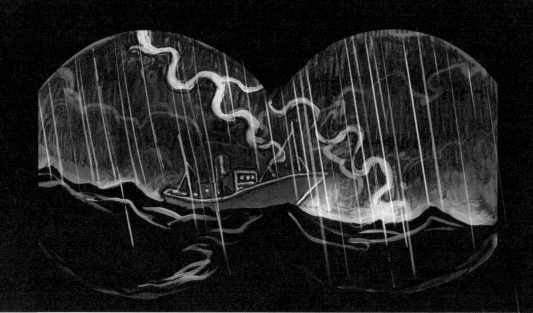

TELL THE MAJOR TO PREPARE THE ROOM.

IT'LL GIVE YOU A CHANCE TO DRY UP.

YES, MA'AM.

LET'S SEE WHAT THEY HAVE FOR US.

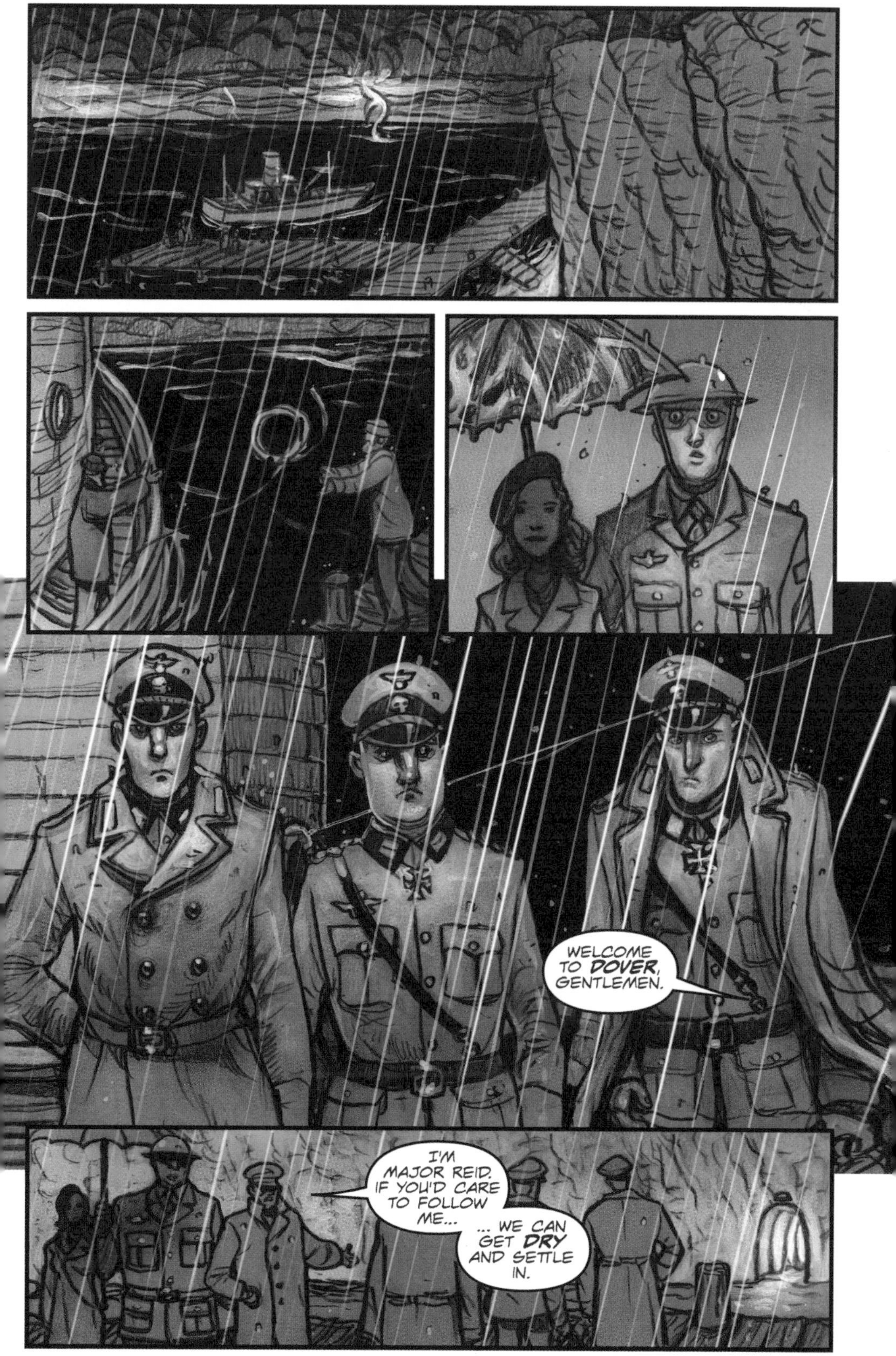
WELCOME TO **DOVER**, GENTLEMEN.
I'M MAJOR REID. IF YOU'D CARE TO FOLLOW ME...
... WE CAN GET **DRY** AND SETTLE IN.

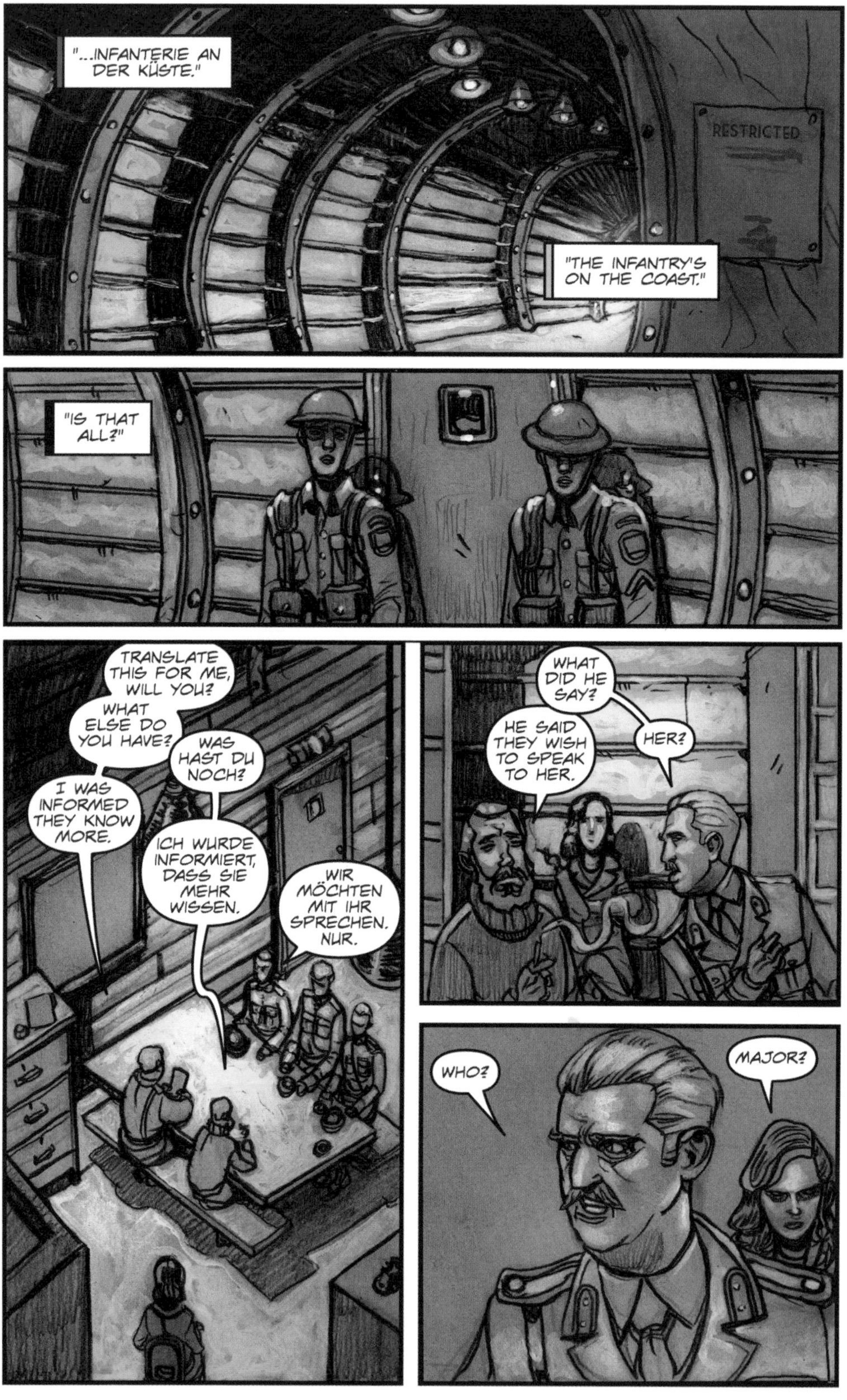
"...INFANTERIE AN DER KÜSTE."
RESTRICTED
"THE INFANTRY'S ON THE COAST."
"IS THAT ALL?"
TRANSLATE THIS FOR ME, WILL YOU?
WHAT ELSE DO YOU HAVE?
WAS HAST DU NOCH?
I WAS INFORMED THEY KNOW MORE.
ICH WURDE INFORMIERT, DASS SIE MEHR WISSEN.
WIR MÖCHTEN MIT IHR SPRECHEN. NUR.
WHAT DID HE SAY?
HE SAID THEY WISH TO SPEAK TO HER.
HER?
WHO?
MAJOR?

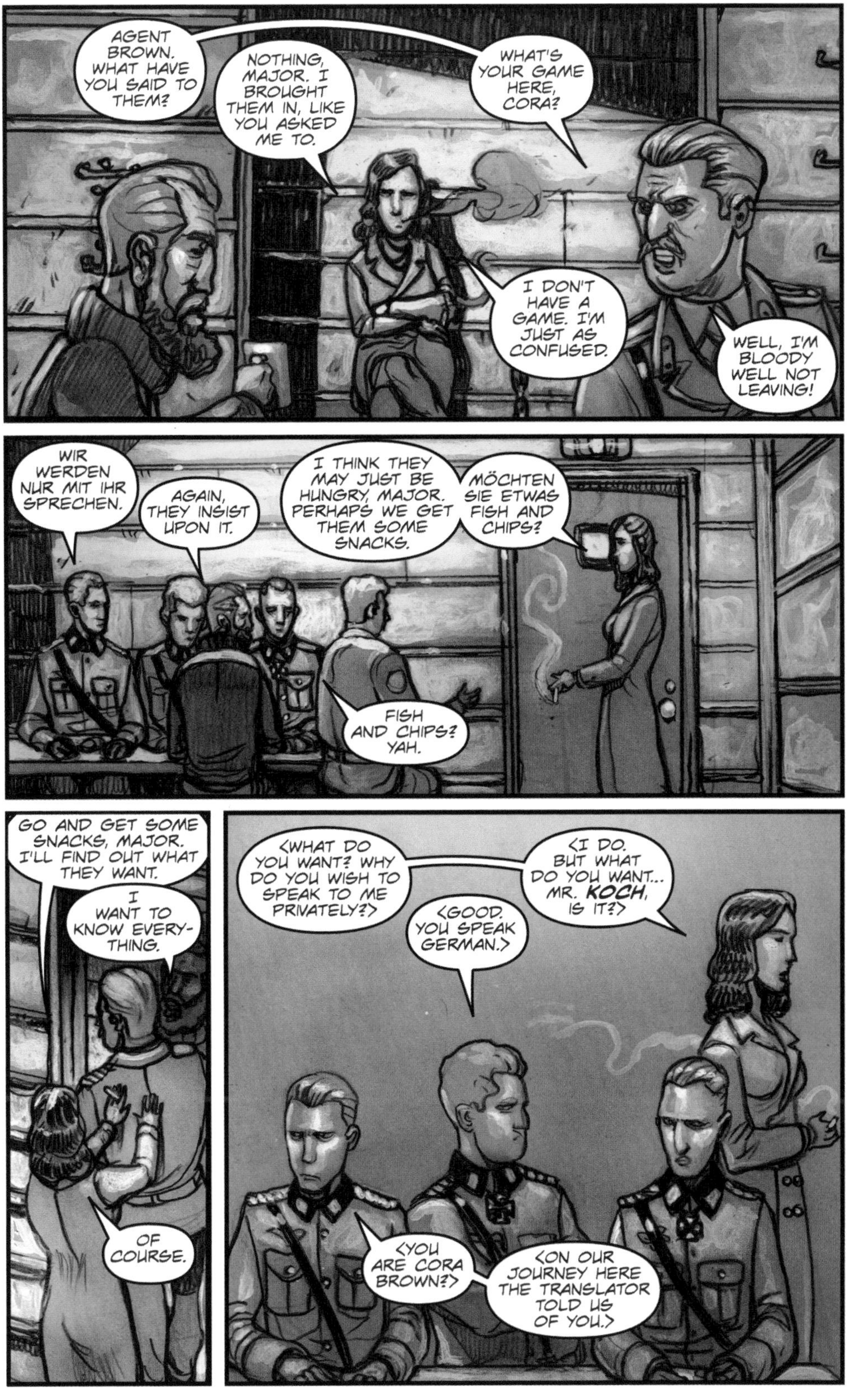
AGENT BROWN. WHAT HAVE YOU SAID TO THEM?
NOTHING, MAJOR. I BROUGHT THEM IN, LIKE YOU ASKED ME TO.
WHAT'S YOUR GAME HERE, CORA?
I DON'T HAVE A GAME. I'M JUST AS CONFUSED.
WELL, I'M BLOODY WELL NOT LEAVING!
WIR WERDEN NUR MIT IHR SPRECHEN.
AGAIN, THEY INSIST UPON IT.
I THINK THEY MAY JUST BE HUNGRY, MAJOR. PERHAPS WE GET THEM SOME SNACKS.
MÖCHTEN SIE ETWAS FISH AND CHIPS?
FISH AND CHIPS? YAH.
GO AND GET SOME SNACKS, MAJOR. I'LL FIND OUT WHAT THEY WANT.
I WANT TO KNOW EVERY-THING.
OF COURSE.
<WHAT DO YOU WANT? WHY DO YOU WISH TO SPEAK TO ME PRIVATELY?>
<GOOD. YOU SPEAK GERMAN.>
<I DO. BUT WHAT DO YOU WANT... MR. **KOCH**, IS IT?>
<YOU ARE CORA BROWN?>
<ON OUR JOURNEY HERE THE TRANSLATOR TOLD US OF YOU.>

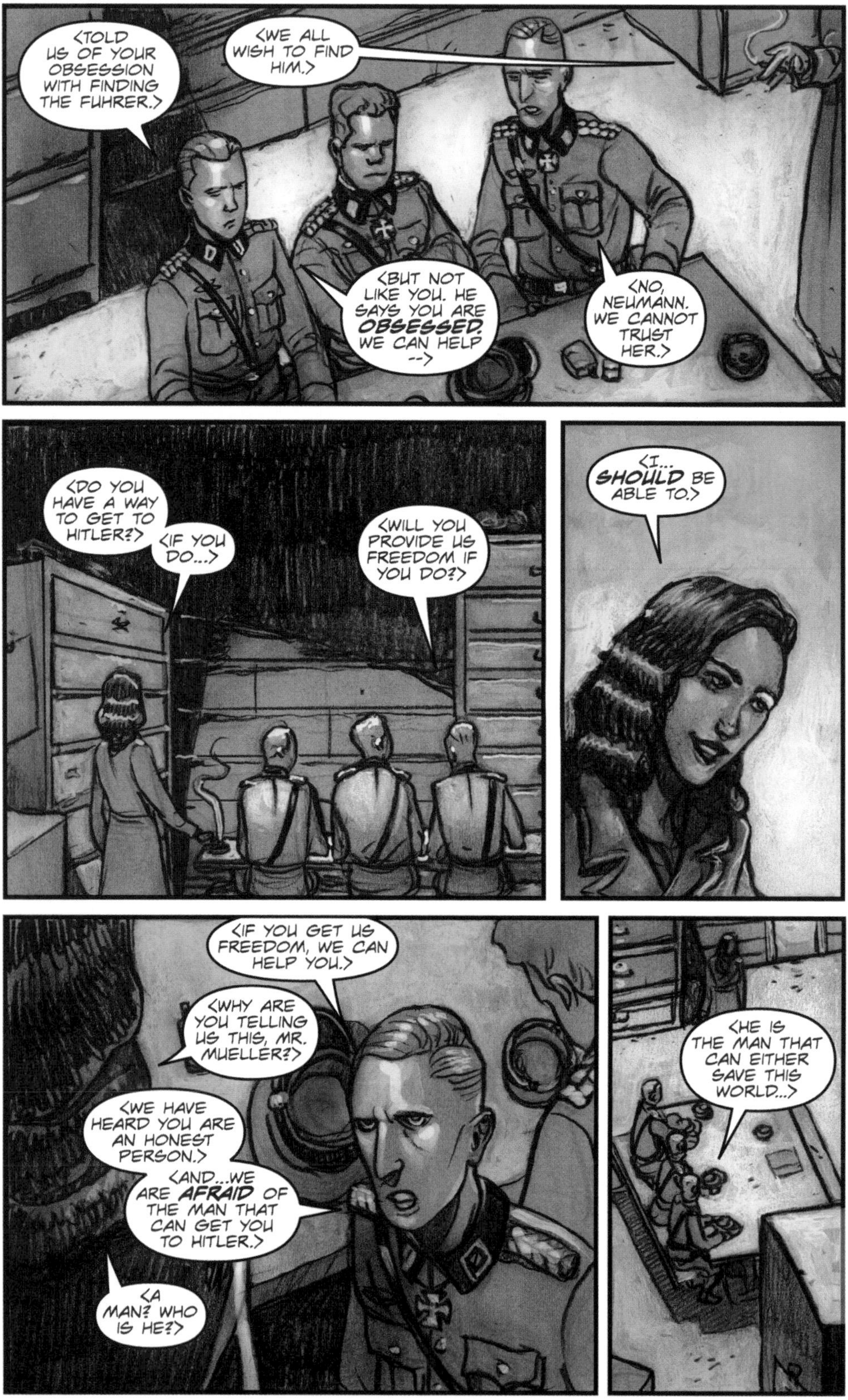
<TOLD US OF YOUR OBSESSION WITH FINDING THE FUHRER.>
<WE ALL WISH TO FIND HIM.>
<BUT NOT LIKE YOU. HE SAYS YOU ARE **OBSESSED.** WE CAN HELP -->
<NO, NEUMANN. WE CANNOT TRUST HER.>
<DO YOU HAVE A WAY TO GET TO HITLER?>
<IF YOU DO...>
<WILL YOU PROVIDE US FREEDOM IF YOU DO?>
<I... **SHOULD** BE ABLE TO.>
<IF YOU GET US FREEDOM, WE CAN HELP YOU.>
<WHY ARE YOU TELLING US THIS, MR. MUELLER?>
<WE HAVE HEARD YOU ARE AN HONEST PERSON.>
<AND...WE ARE **AFRAID** OF THE MAN THAT CAN GET YOU TO HITLER.>
<A MAN? WHO IS HE?>
<HE IS THE MAN THAT CAN EITHER SAVE THIS WORLD...>

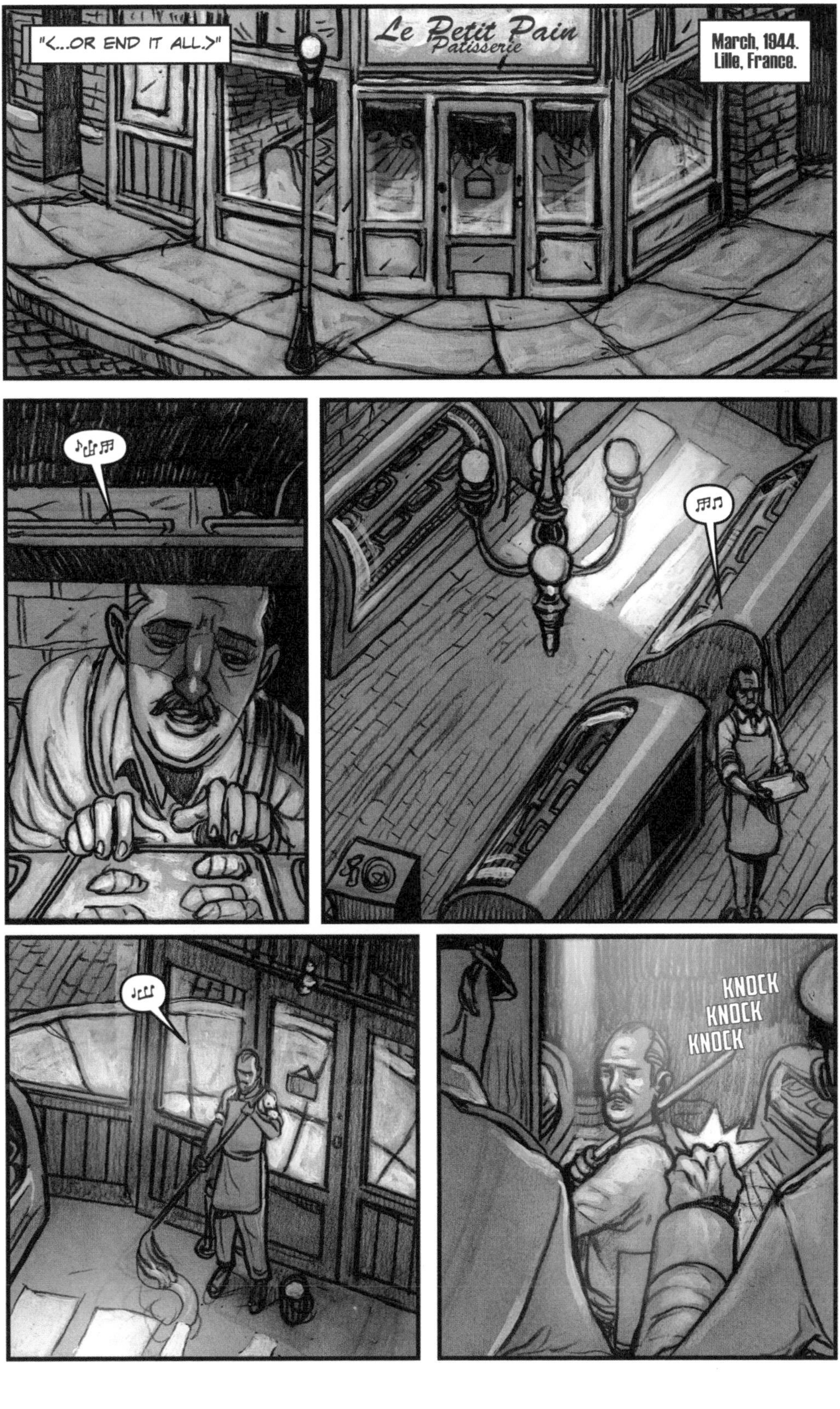
"<...OR END IT ALL.>"
Le Petit Pain
Patisserie
March, 1944. Lille, France.
KNOCK
KNOCK
KNOCK

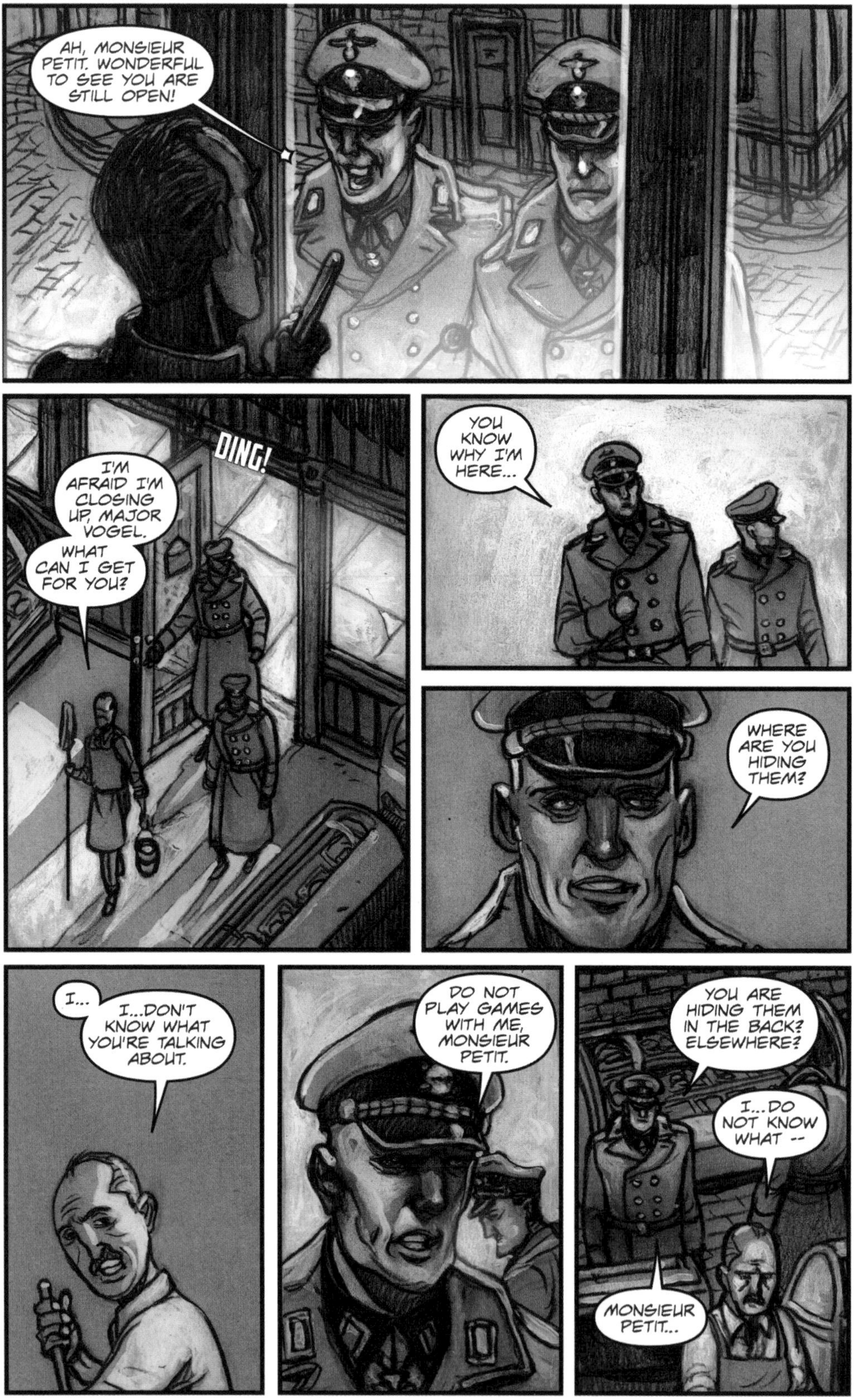

AH, MONSIEUR PETIT. WONDERFUL TO SEE YOU ARE STILL OPEN!
DING!
I'M AFRAID I'M CLOSING UP, MAJOR VOGEL.
WHAT CAN I GET FOR YOU?
YOU KNOW WHY I'M HERE...
WHERE ARE YOU HIDING THEM?
I...
I...DON'T KNOW WHAT YOU'RE TALKING ABOUT.
DO NOT PLAY GAMES WITH ME, MONSIEUR PETIT.
YOU ARE HIDING THEM IN THE BACK? ELSEWHERE?
I...DO NOT KNOW WHAT --
MONSIEUR PETIT...

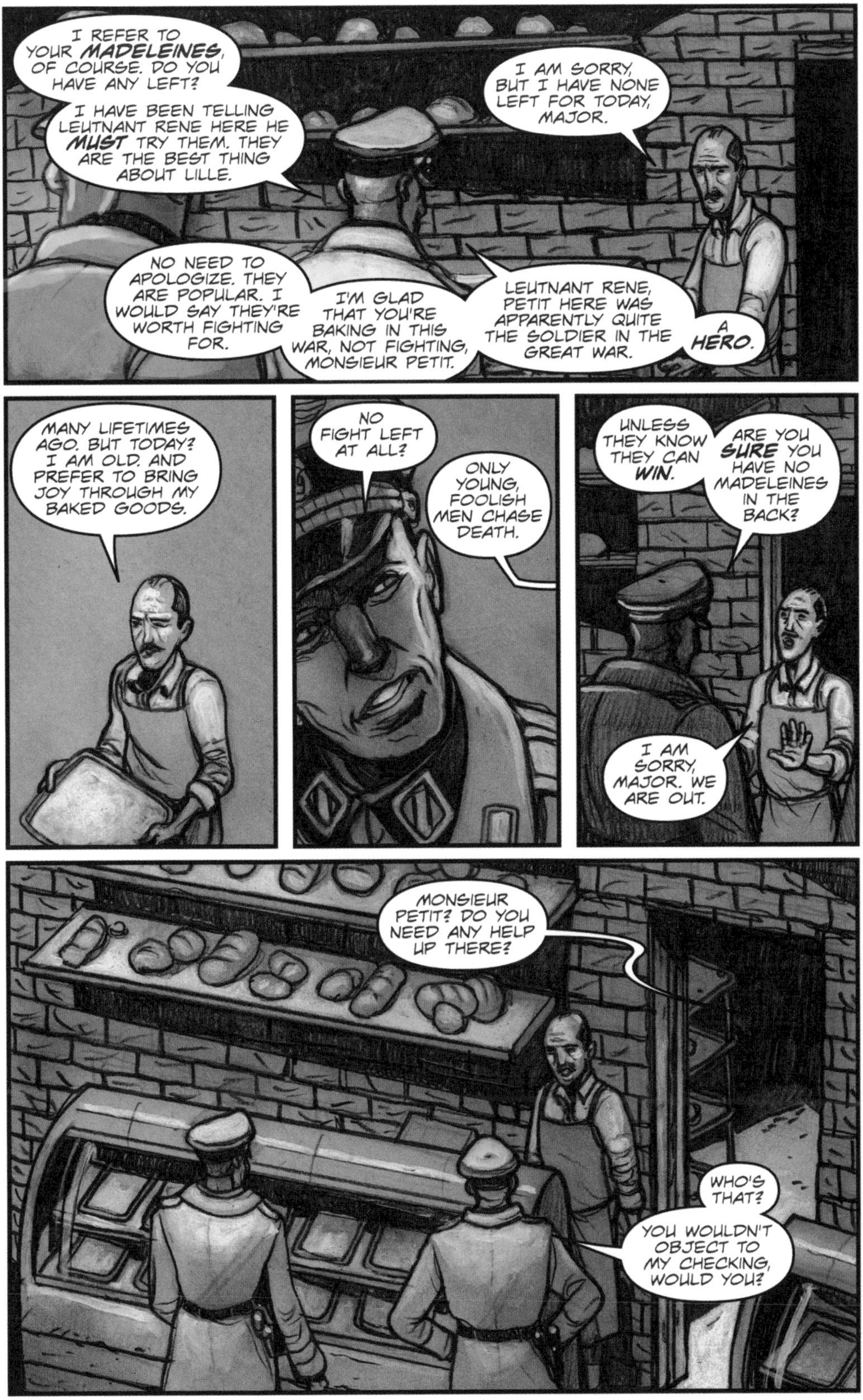
I REFER TO YOUR MADELEINES, OF COURSE. DO YOU HAVE ANY LEFT?
I HAVE BEEN TELLING LEUTNANT RENE HERE HE MUST TRY THEM. THEY ARE THE BEST THING ABOUT LILLE.
I AM SORRY, BUT I HAVE NONE LEFT FOR TODAY, MAJOR.
NO NEED TO APOLOGIZE. THEY ARE POPULAR. I WOULD SAY THEY'RE WORTH FIGHTING FOR.
I'M GLAD THAT YOU'RE BAKING IN THIS WAR, NOT FIGHTING, MONSIEUR PETIT.
LEUTNANT RENE, PETIT HERE WAS APPARENTLY QUITE THE SOLDIER IN THE GREAT WAR.
A HERO.
MANY LIFETIMES AGO. BUT TODAY? I AM OLD. AND PREFER TO BRING JOY THROUGH MY BAKED GOODS.
NO FIGHT LEFT AT ALL?
ONLY YOUNG, FOOLISH MEN CHASE DEATH.
UNLESS THEY KNOW THEY CAN WIN.
ARE YOU SURE YOU HAVE NO MADELEINES IN THE BACK?
I AM SORRY, MAJOR. WE ARE OUT.
MONSIEUR PETIT? DO YOU NEED ANY HELP UP THERE?
WHO'S THAT?
YOU WOULDN'T OBJECT TO MY CHECKING, WOULD YOU?

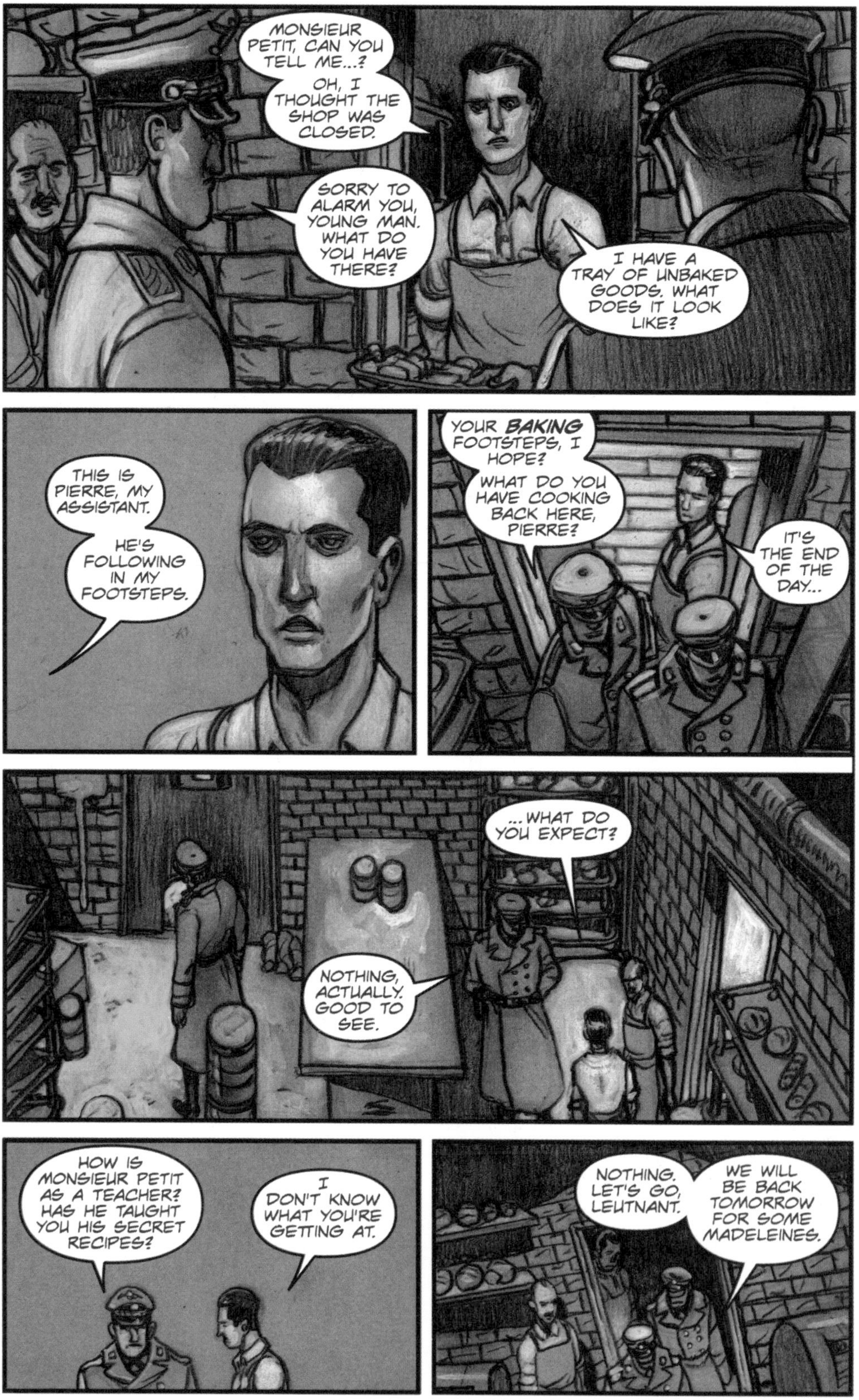
MONSIEUR PETIT, CAN YOU TELL ME...?
OH, I THOUGHT THE SHOP WAS CLOSED.
SORRY TO ALARM YOU, YOUNG MAN. WHAT DO YOU HAVE THERE?
I HAVE A TRAY OF UNBAKED GOODS. WHAT DOES IT LOOK LIKE?
THIS IS PIERRE, MY ASSISTANT.
HE'S FOLLOWING IN MY FOOTSTEPS.
YOUR **BAKING** FOOTSTEPS, I HOPE?
WHAT DO YOU HAVE COOKING BACK HERE, PIERRE?
IT'S THE END OF THE DAY...
...WHAT DO YOU EXPECT?
NOTHING, ACTUALLY. GOOD TO SEE.
HOW IS MONSIEUR PETIT AS A TEACHER? HAS HE TAUGHT YOU HIS SECRET RECIPES?
I DON'T KNOW WHAT YOU'RE GETTING AT.
NOTHING. LET'S GO, LEUTNANT.
WE WILL BE BACK TOMORROW FOR SOME MADELEINES.

DING!

WHAT WAS THAT ABOUT?

HE HAS A SWEET TOOTH...AND A SLOW WIT.

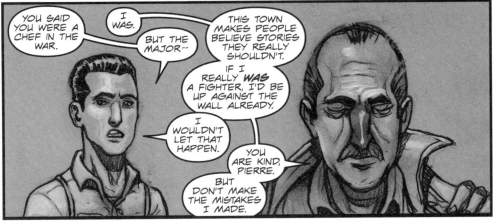

YOU SAID YOU WERE A CHEF IN THE WAR.

I WAS.

BUT THE MAJOR--

THIS TOWN MAKES PEOPLE BELIEVE STORIES THEY REALLY SHOULDN'T.

IF I REALLY *WAS* A FIGHTER, I'D BE UP AGAINST THE WALL ALREADY.

I WOULDN'T LET THAT HAPPEN.

YOU ARE KIND, PIERRE.

BUT DON'T MAKE THE MISTAKES I MADE.

I NEED YOU TO CLOSE THE SHOP TONIGHT.

YOU WERE GOING TO SHOW ME YOUR RECIPE FOR --

NOT TONIGHT, PIERRE. TOMORROW.

DING!

ARE THOSE MADELEINES?

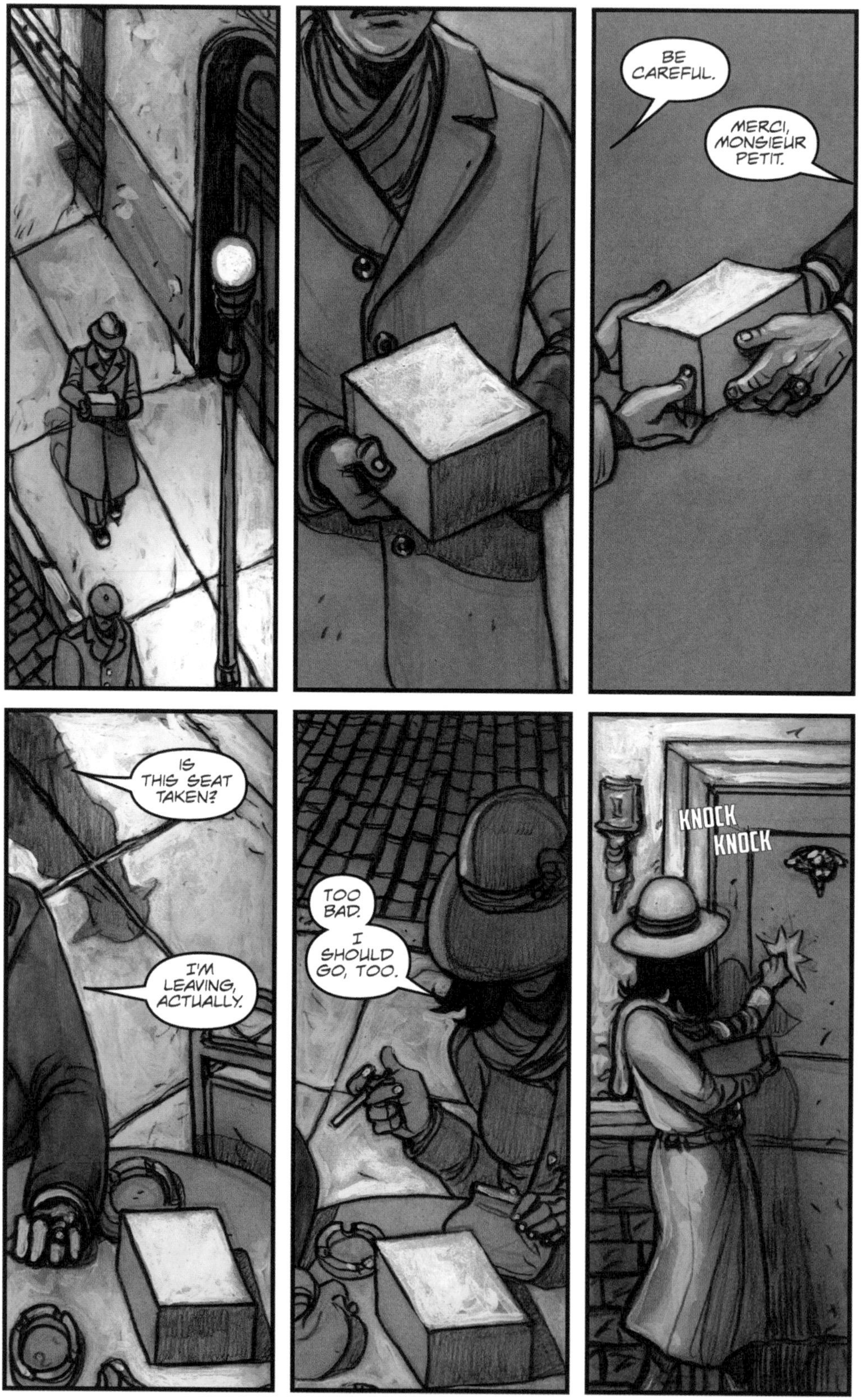
BE CAREFUL.
MERCI, MONSIEUR PETIT.
IS THIS SEAT TAKEN?
I'M LEAVING, ACTUALLY.
TOO BAD.
I SHOULD GO, TOO.
KNOCK KNOCK

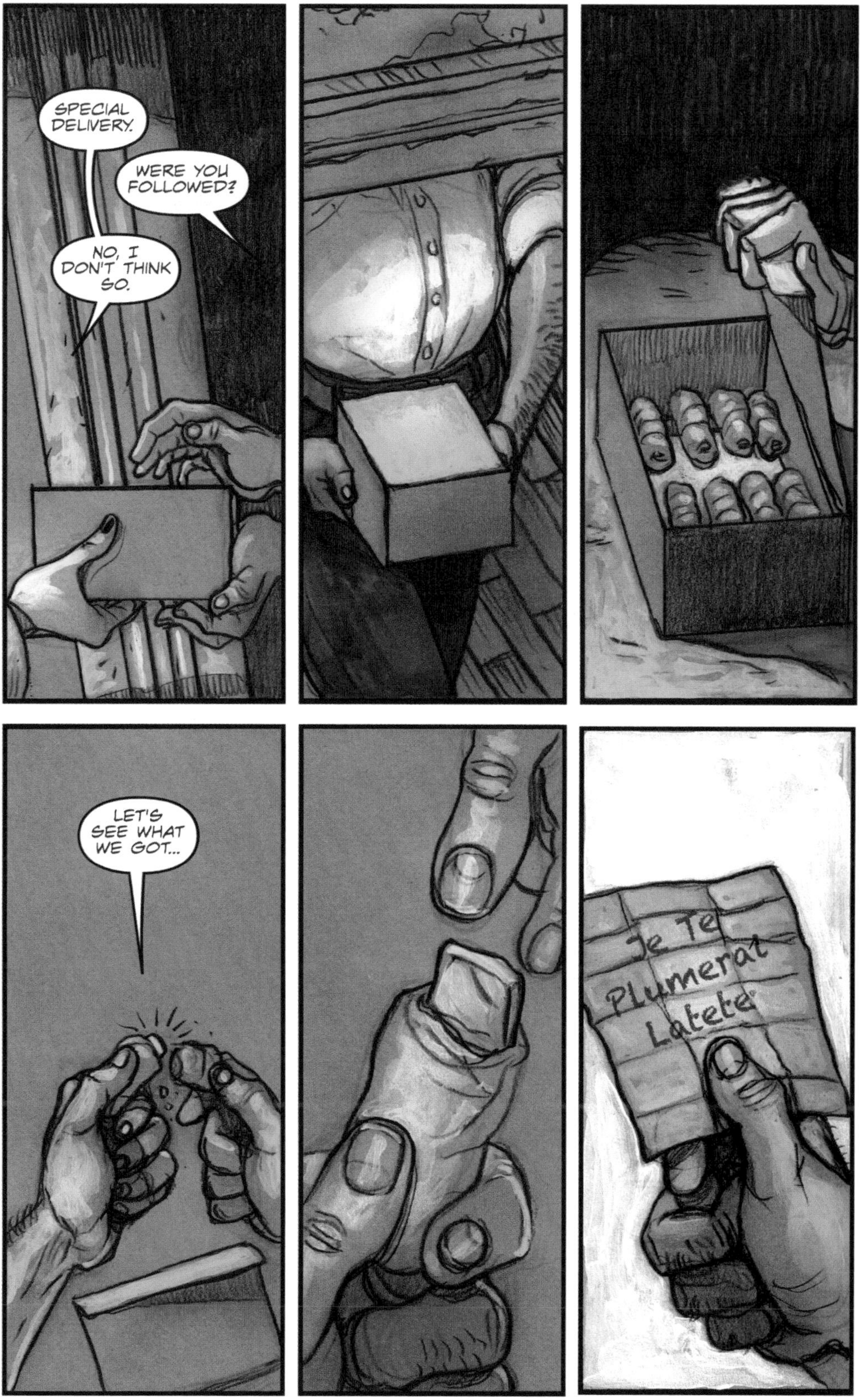
SPECIAL DELIVERY.
WERE YOU FOLLOWED?
NO, I DON'T THINK SO.
LET'S SEE WHAT WE GOT...
Je Te
Plumerat
Latete

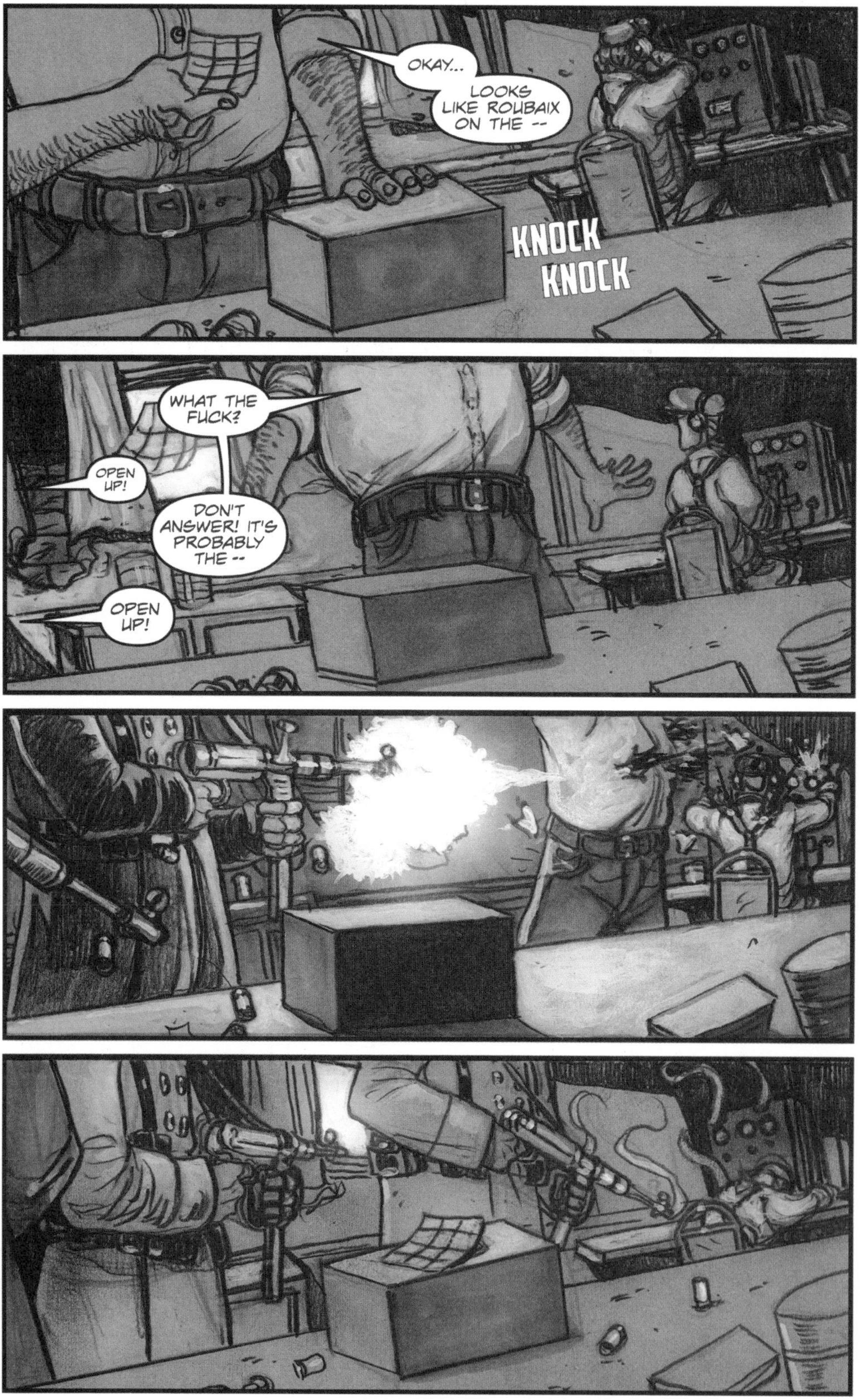

OKAY... LOOKS LIKE ROUBAIX ON THE --
KNOCK KNOCK
WHAT THE FUCK?
OPEN UP!
DON'T ANSWER! IT'S PROBABLY THE --
OPEN UP!

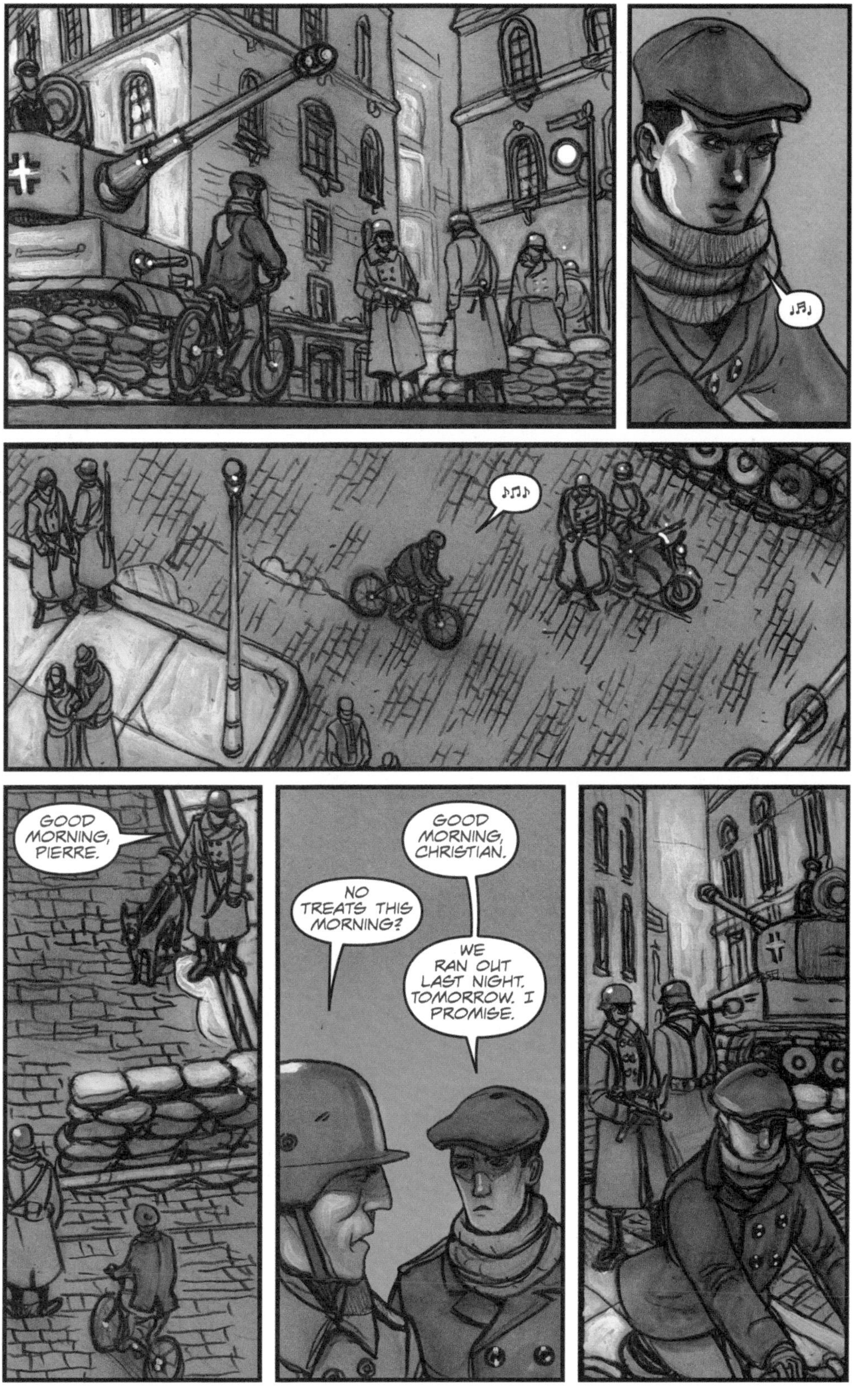
♪♬♩
♪♫♪
GOOD MORNING, PIERRE.
GOOD MORNING, CHRISTIAN.
NO TREATS THIS MORNING?
WE RAN OUT LAST NIGHT. TOMORROW. I PROMISE.

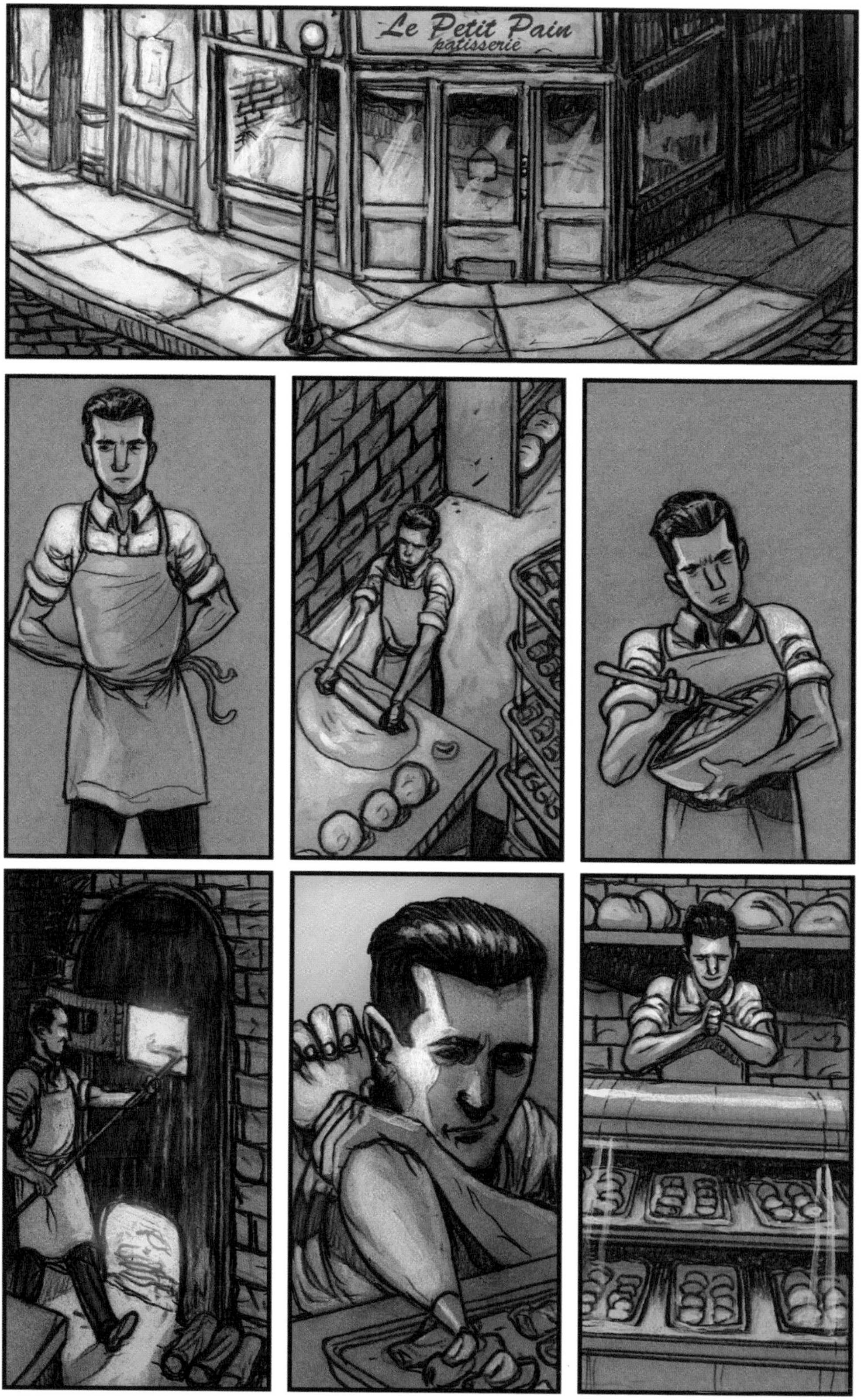
Le Petit Pain
patisserie

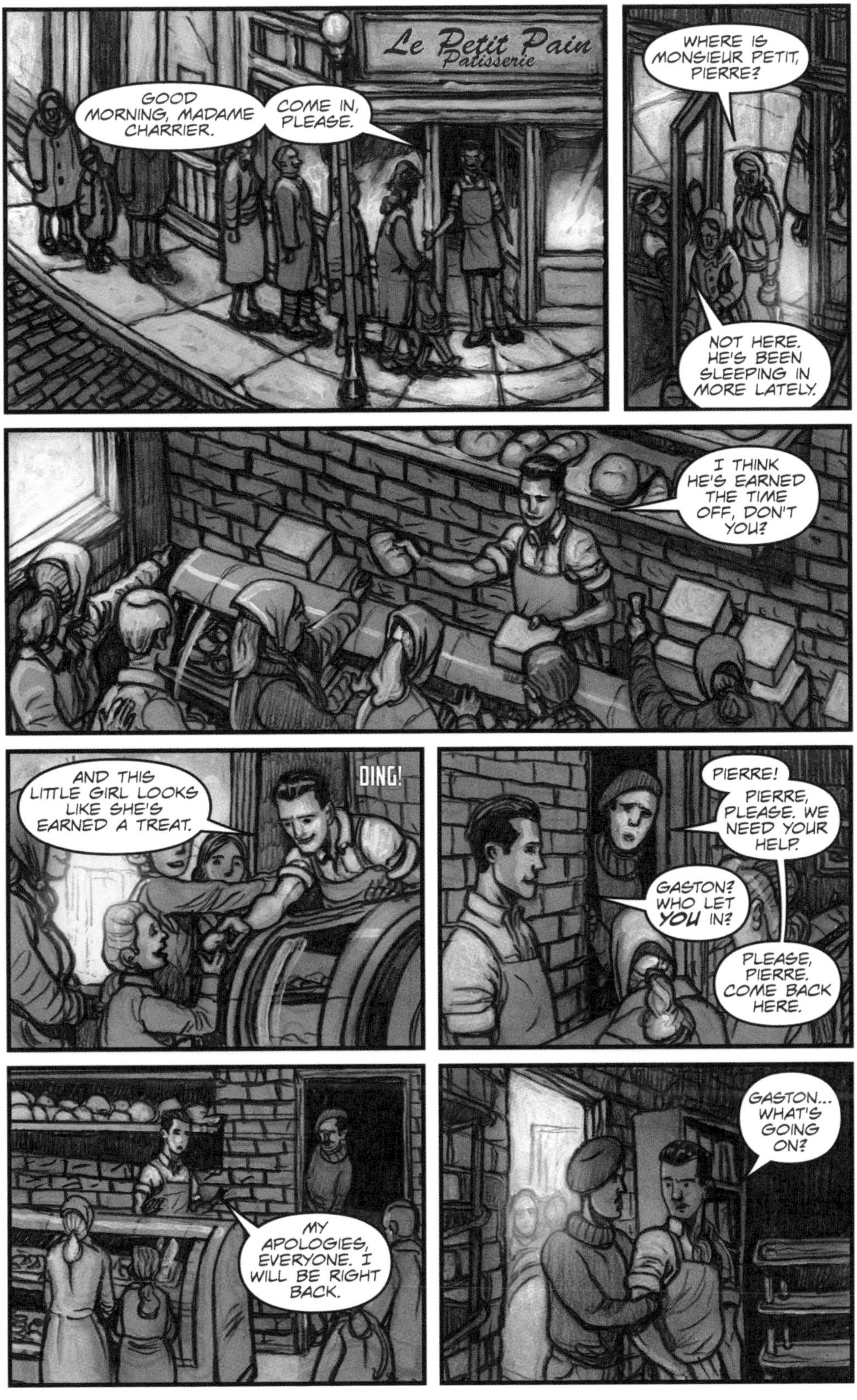
Le Petit Pain
Patisserie
GOOD MORNING, MADAME CHARRIER.
COME IN, PLEASE.
WHERE IS MONSIEUR PETIT, PIERRE?
NOT HERE. HE'S BEEN SLEEPING IN MORE LATELY.
I THINK HE'S EARNED THE TIME OFF, DON'T YOU?
AND THIS LITTLE GIRL LOOKS LIKE SHE'S EARNED A TREAT.
DING!
PIERRE!
PIERRE, PLEASE. WE NEED YOUR HELP.
GASTON? WHO LET YOU IN?
PLEASE, PIERRE. COME BACK HERE.
MY APOLOGIES, EVERYONE. I WILL BE RIGHT BACK.
GASTON... WHAT'S GOING ON?

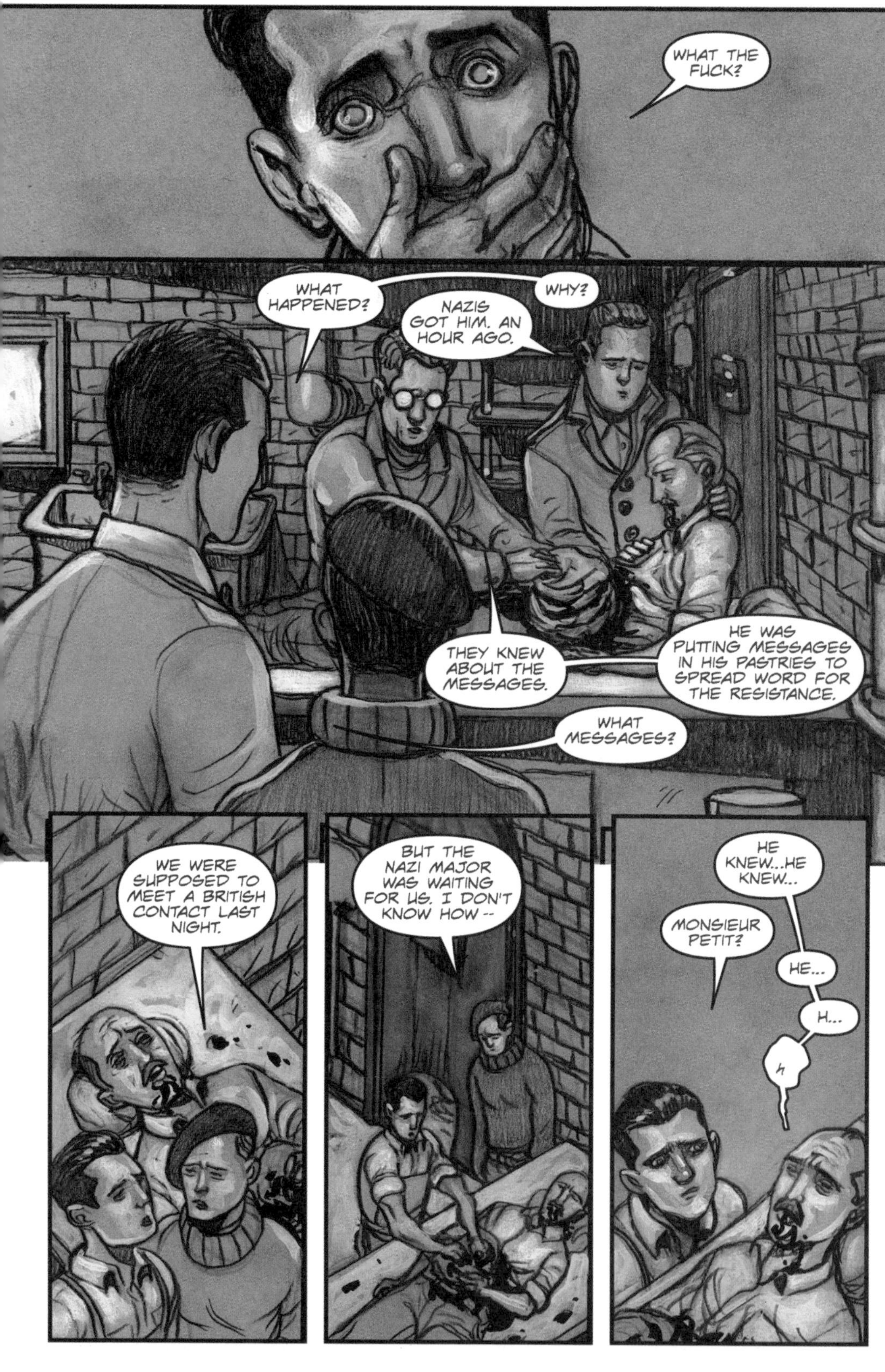
WHAT THE FUCK?
WHAT HAPPENED?
WHY?
NAZIS GOT HIM. AN HOUR AGO.
THEY KNEW ABOUT THE MESSAGES.
HE WAS PUTTING MESSAGES IN HIS PASTRIES TO SPREAD WORD FOR THE RESISTANCE.
WHAT MESSAGES?
WE WERE SUPPOSED TO MEET A BRITISH CONTACT LAST NIGHT.
BUT THE NAZI MAJOR WAS WAITING FOR US. I DON'T KNOW HOW --
HE KNEW...HE KNEW...
MONSIEUR PETIT?
HE...
H...
h

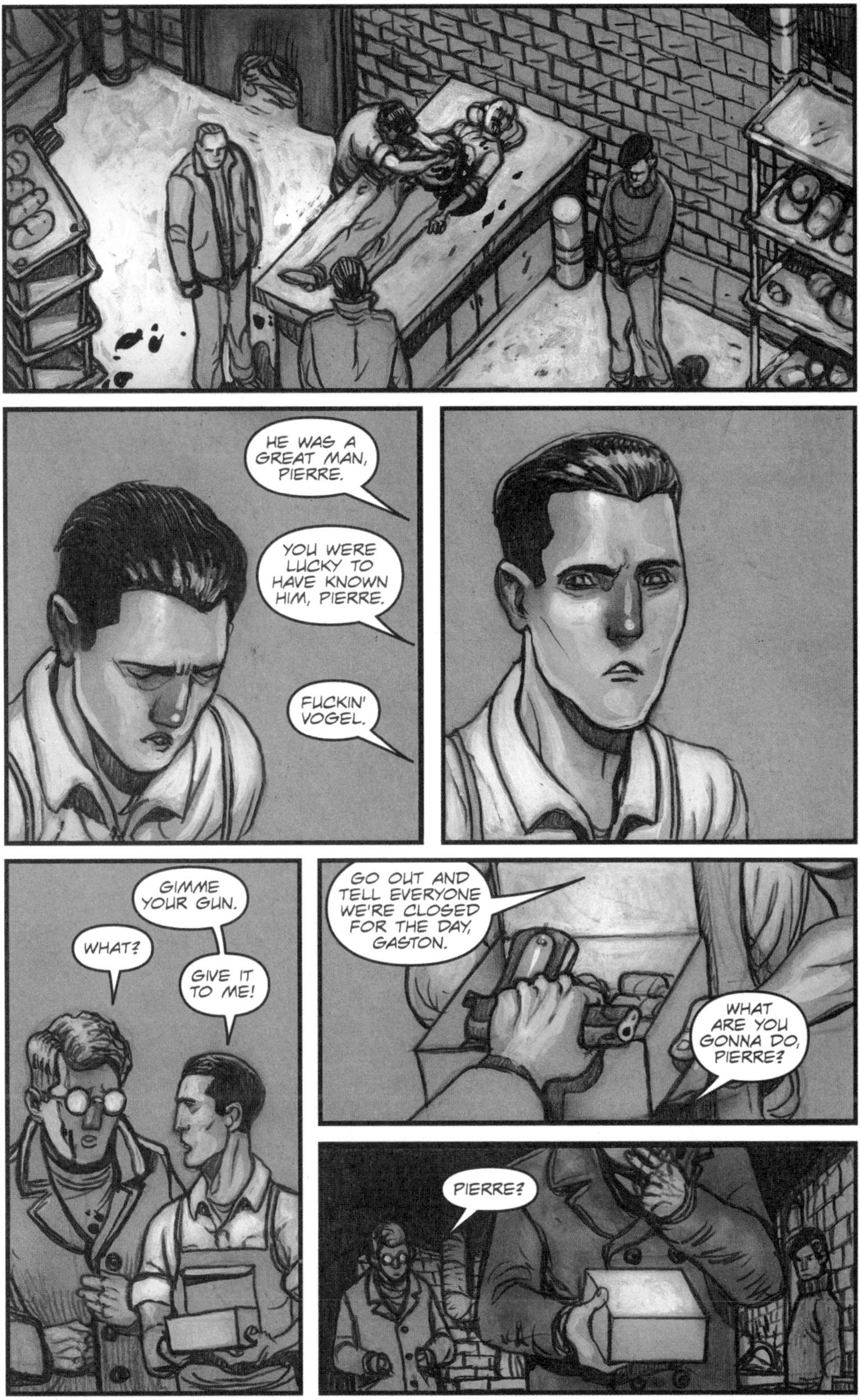
HE WAS A GREAT MAN, PIERRE.
YOU WERE LUCKY TO HAVE KNOWN HIM, PIERRE.
FUCKIN' VOGEL.
GIMME YOUR GUN.
WHAT?
GIVE IT TO ME!
GO OUT AND TELL EVERYONE WE'RE CLOSED FOR THE DAY, GASTON.
WHAT ARE YOU GONNA DO, PIERRE?
PIERRE?

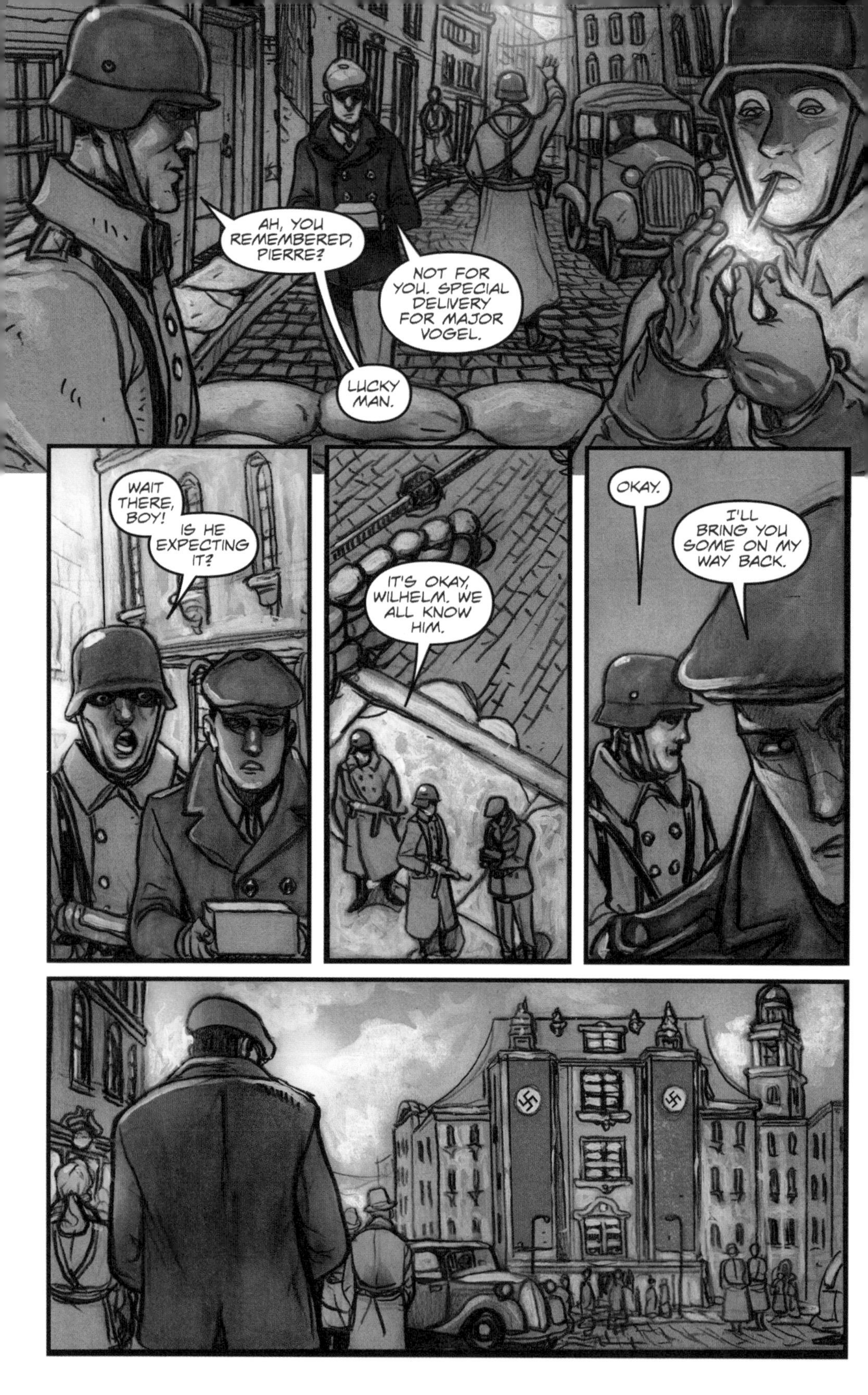
AH, YOU REMEMBERED, PIERRE?
NOT FOR YOU. SPECIAL DELIVERY FOR MAJOR VOGEL.
LUCKY MAN.
WAIT THERE, BOY!
IS HE EXPECTING IT?
IT'S OKAY, WILHELM. WE ALL KNOW HIM.
OKAY.
I'LL BRING YOU SOME ON MY WAY BACK.

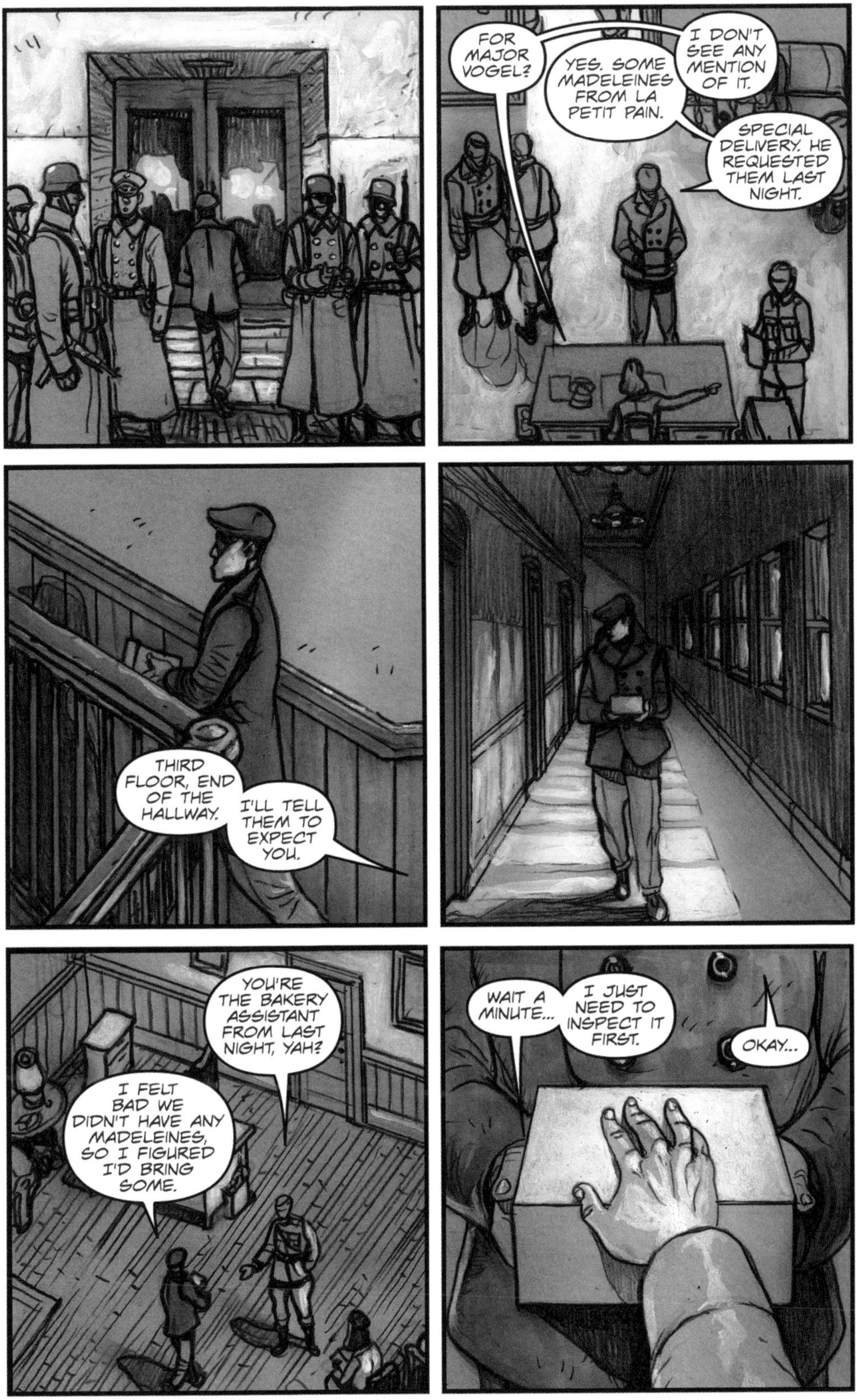
FOR MAJOR VOGEL?
YES. SOME MADELEINES FROM LA PETIT PAIN.
I DON'T SEE ANY MENTION OF IT.
SPECIAL DELIVERY. HE REQUESTED THEM LAST NIGHT.
THIRD FLOOR, END OF THE HALLWAY.
I'LL TELL THEM TO EXPECT YOU.
YOU'RE THE BAKERY ASSISTANT FROM LAST NIGHT, YAH?
I FELT BAD WE DIDN'T HAVE ANY MADELEINES, SO I FIGURED I'D BRING SOME.
WAIT A MINUTE...
I JUST NEED TO INSPECT IT FIRST.
OKAY...

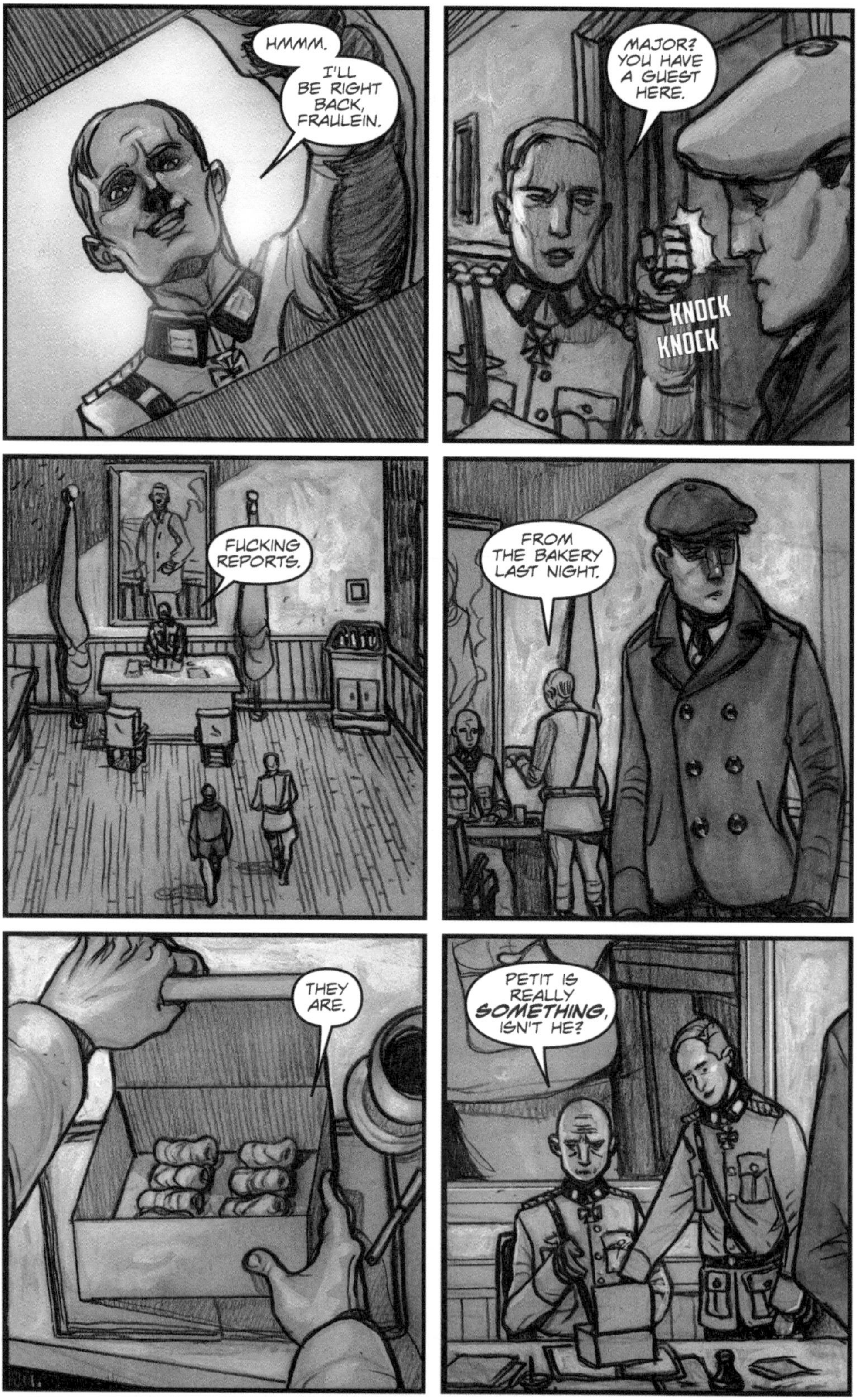
HMMM.
I'LL BE RIGHT BACK, FRAULEIN.
MAJOR? YOU HAVE A GUEST HERE.
KNOCK KNOCK
FUCKING REPORTS.
FROM THE BAKERY LAST NIGHT.
THEY ARE.
PETIT IS REALLY **SOMETHING**, ISN'T HE?

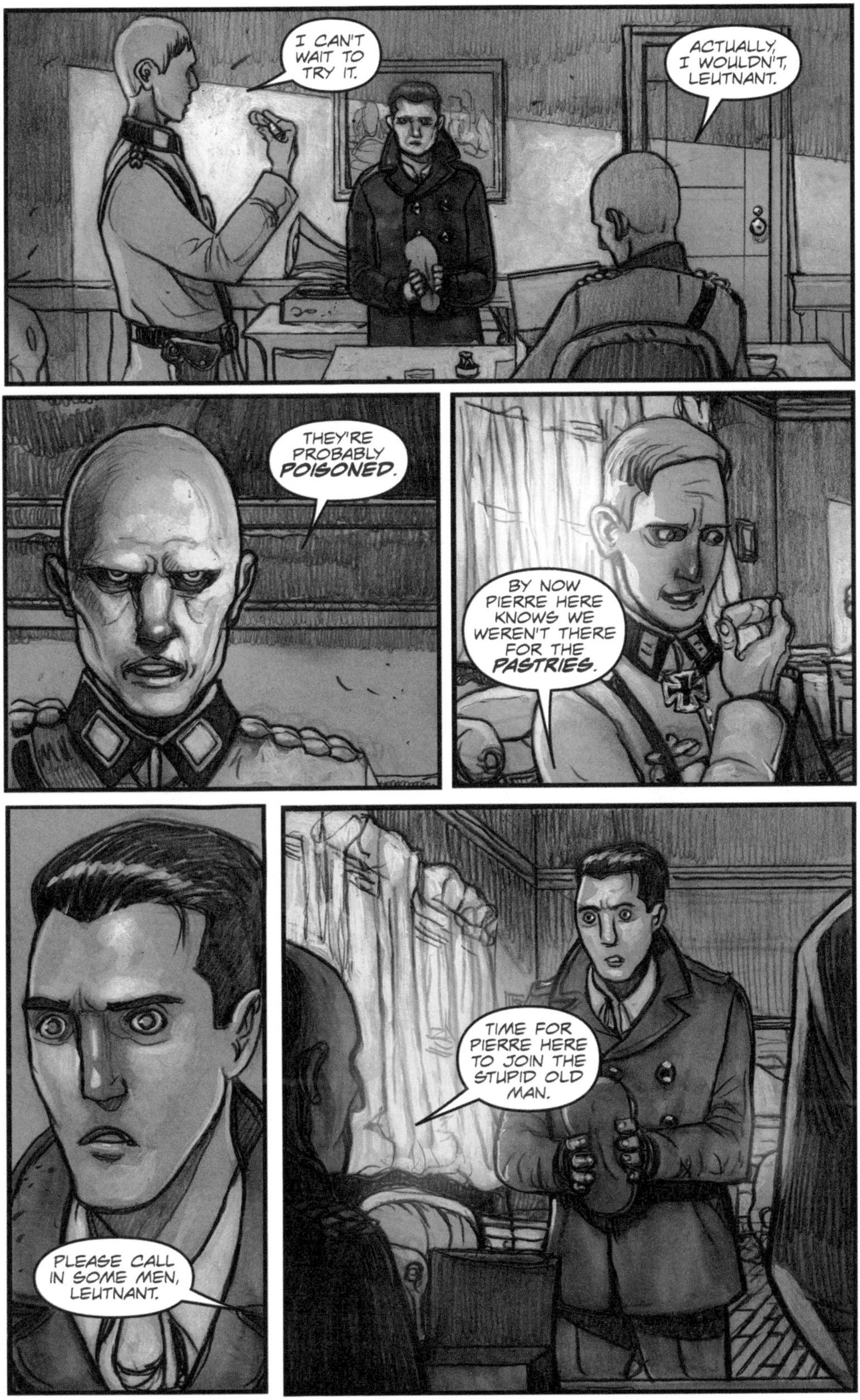
I CAN'T WAIT TO TRY IT.
ACTUALLY, I WOULDN'T, LEUTNANT.
THEY'RE PROBABLY POISONED.
BY NOW PIERRE HERE KNOWS WE WEREN'T THERE FOR THE PASTRIES.
PLEASE CALL IN SOME MEN, LEUTNANT.
TIME FOR PIERRE HERE TO JOIN THE STUPID OLD MAN.

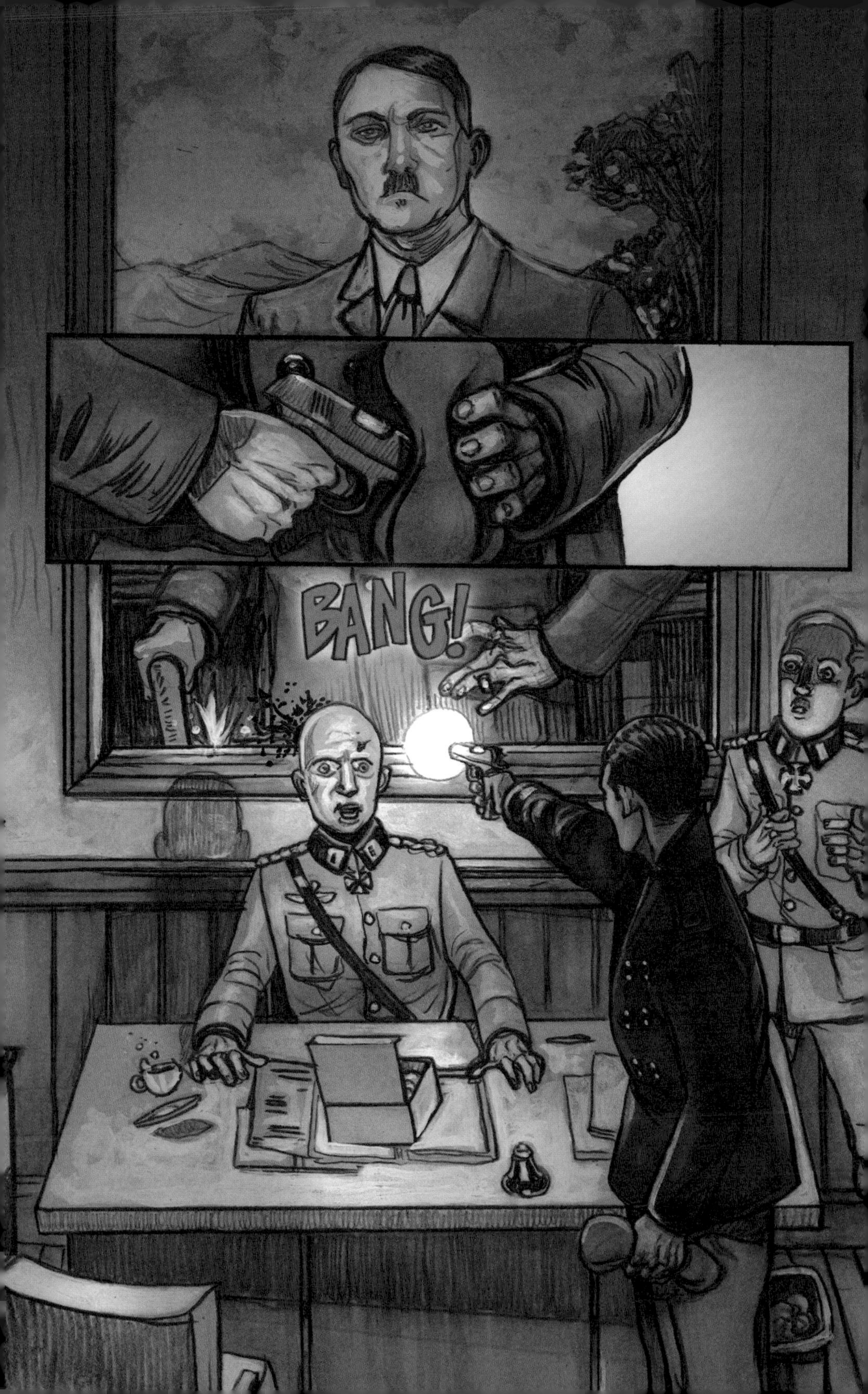
BANG!

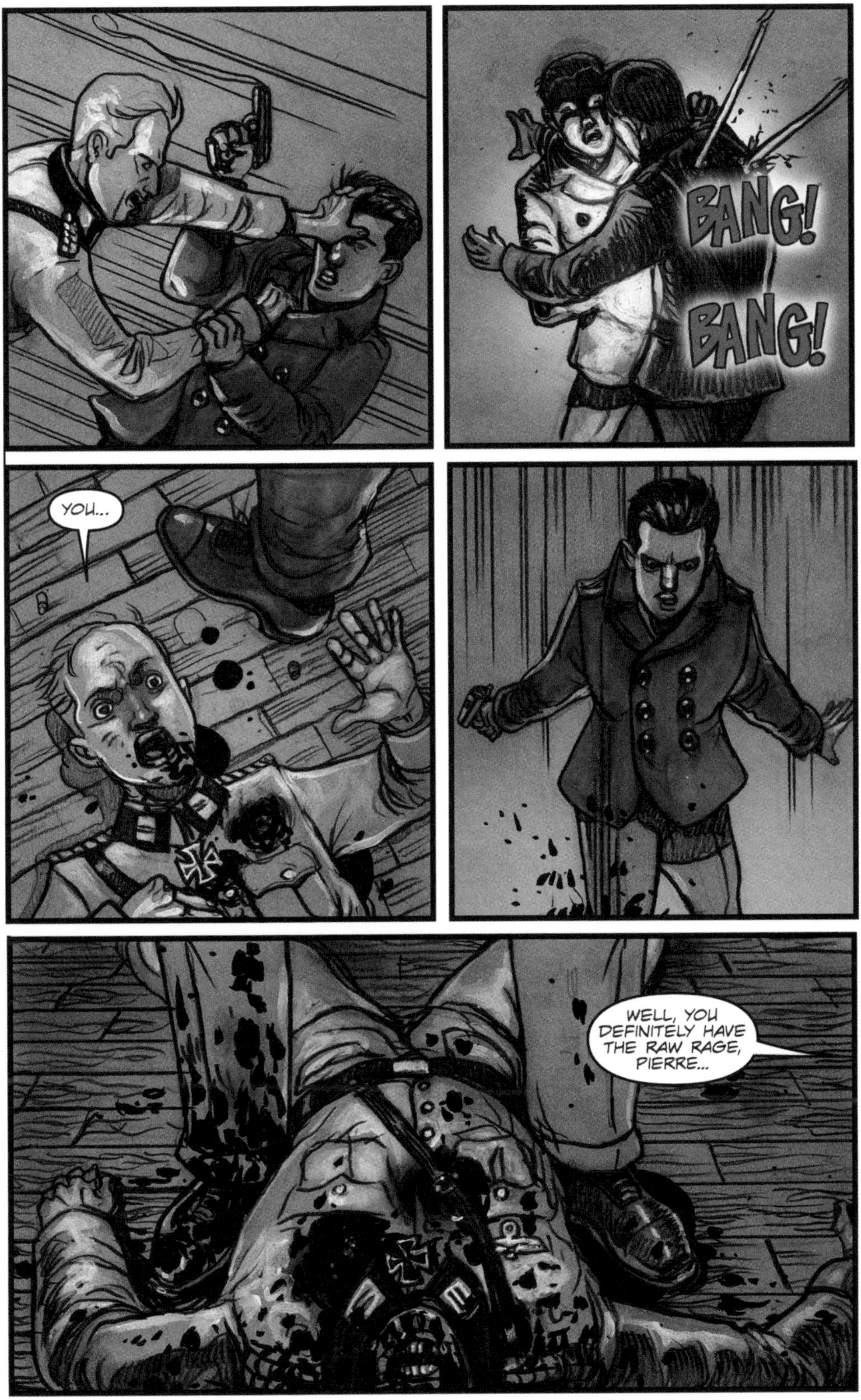
BANG!
BANG!
YOU...
WELL, YOU DEFINITELY HAVE THE RAW RAGE, PIERRE...

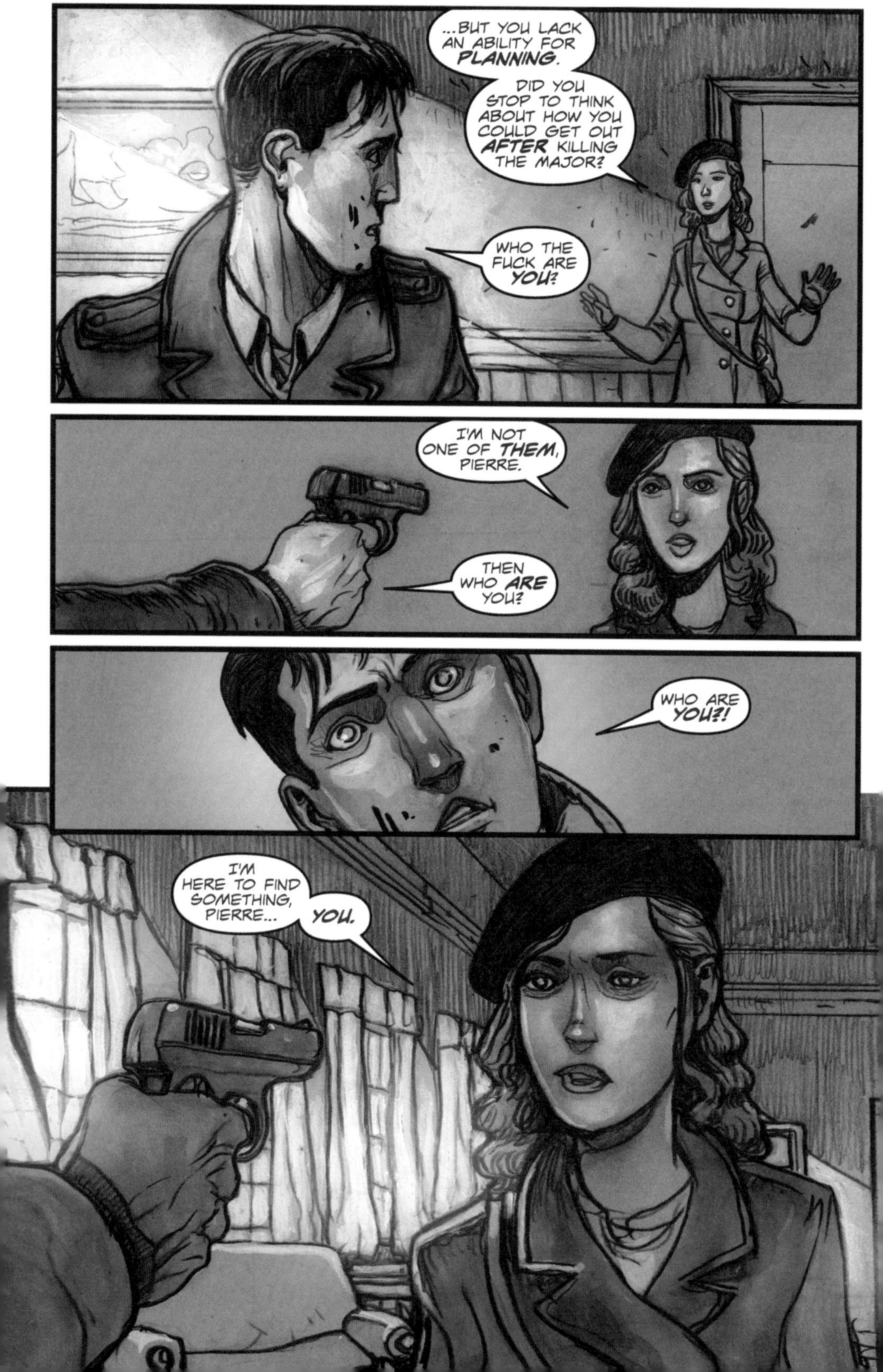
...BUT YOU LACK AN ABILITY FOR PLANNING.
DID YOU STOP TO THINK ABOUT HOW YOU COULD GET OUT AFTER KILLING THE MAJOR?
WHO THE FUCK ARE YOU?
I'M NOT ONE OF THEM, PIERRE.
THEN WHO ARE YOU?
WHO ARE YOU?!
I'M HERE TO FIND SOMETHING, PIERRE...
YOU.

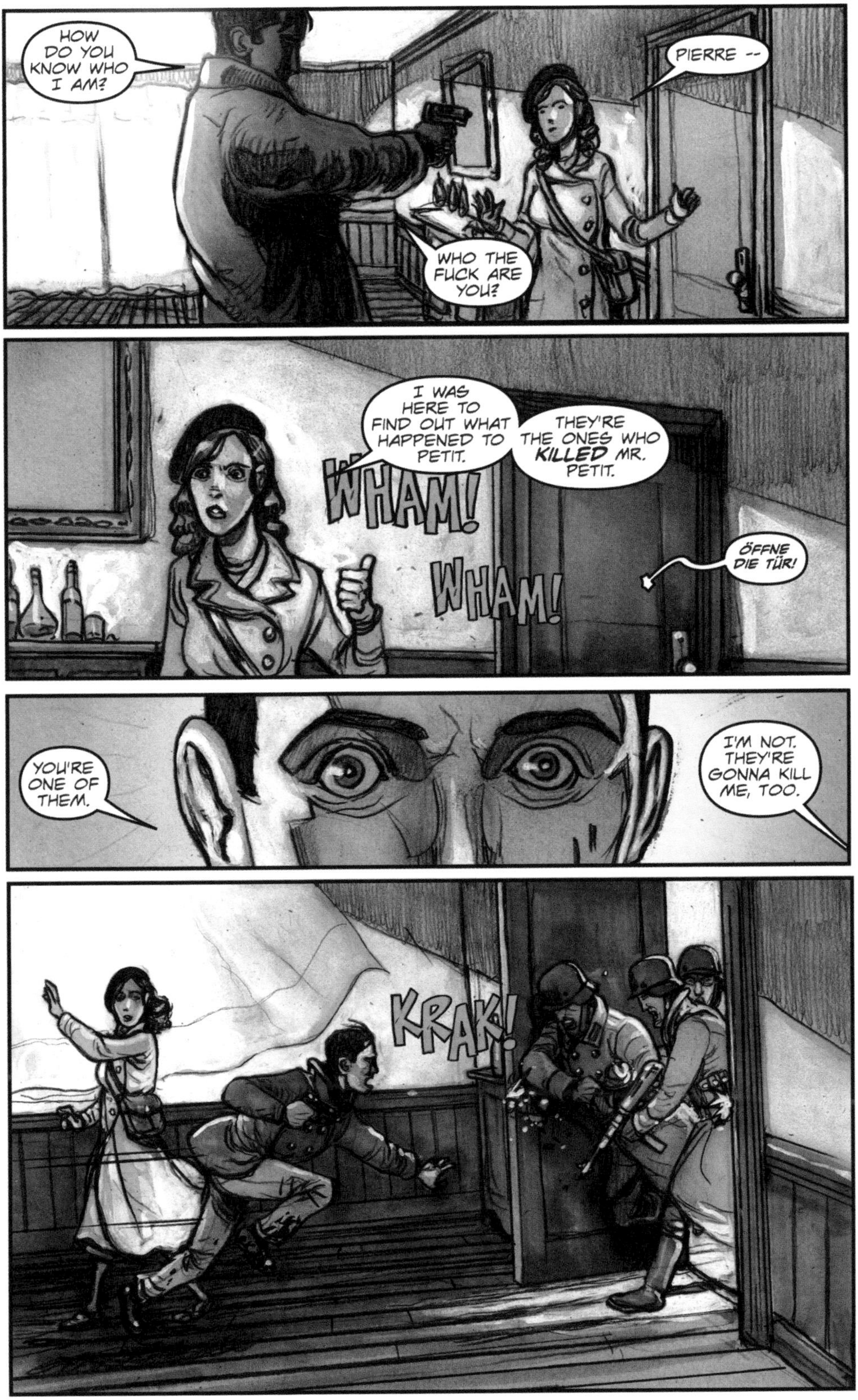
HOW DO YOU KNOW WHO I AM?
PIERRE --
WHO THE FUCK ARE YOU?
I WAS HERE TO FIND OUT WHAT HAPPENED TO PETIT.
THEY'RE THE ONES WHO KILLED MR. PETIT.
WHAM!
WHAM!
ÖFFNE DIE TÜR!
YOU'RE ONE OF THEM.
I'M NOT. THEY'RE GONNA KILL ME, TOO.
KRAK!

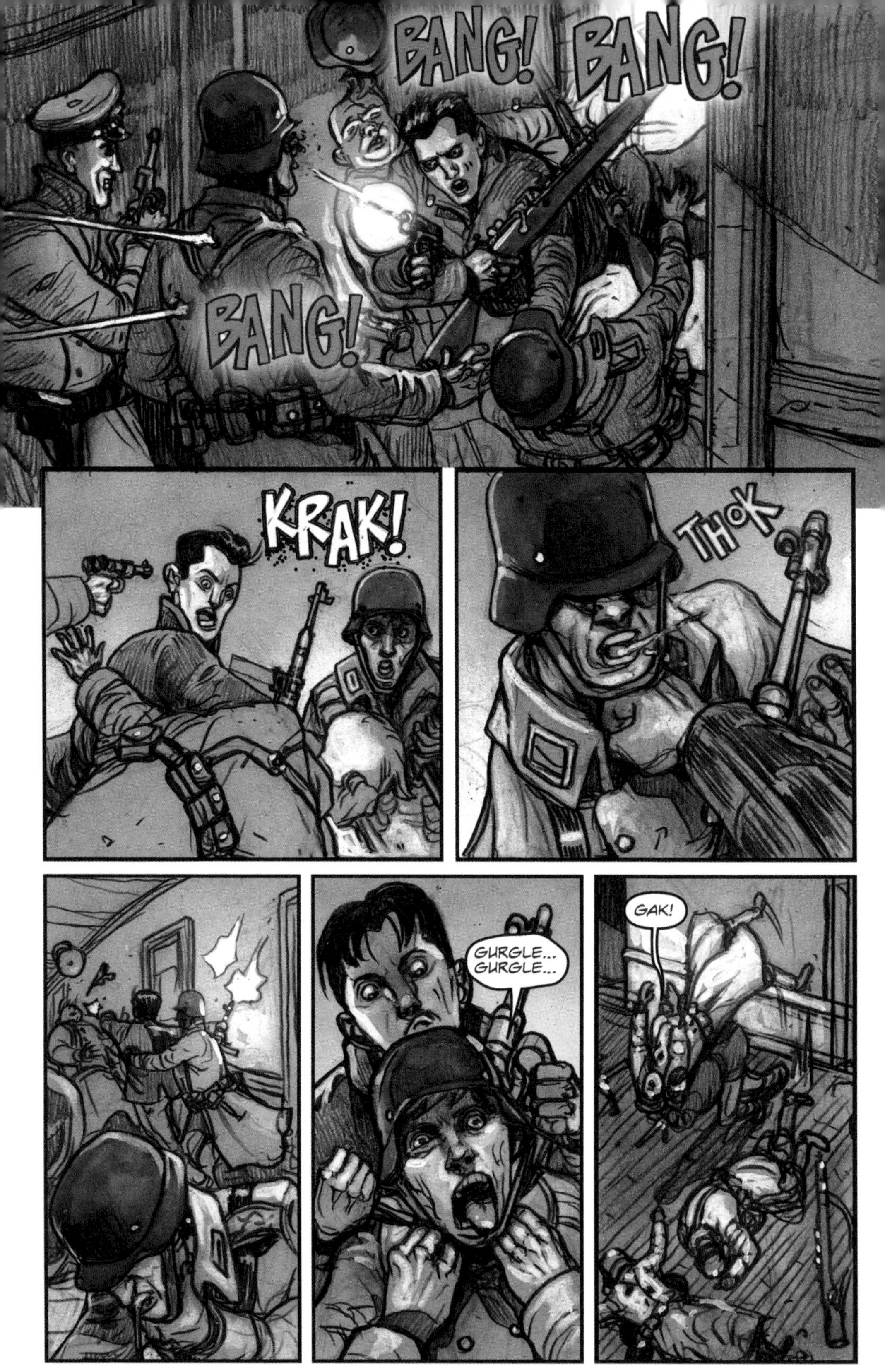
BANG! BANG!
BANG!
KRAK!
THOK
GURGLE... GURGLE...
GAK!

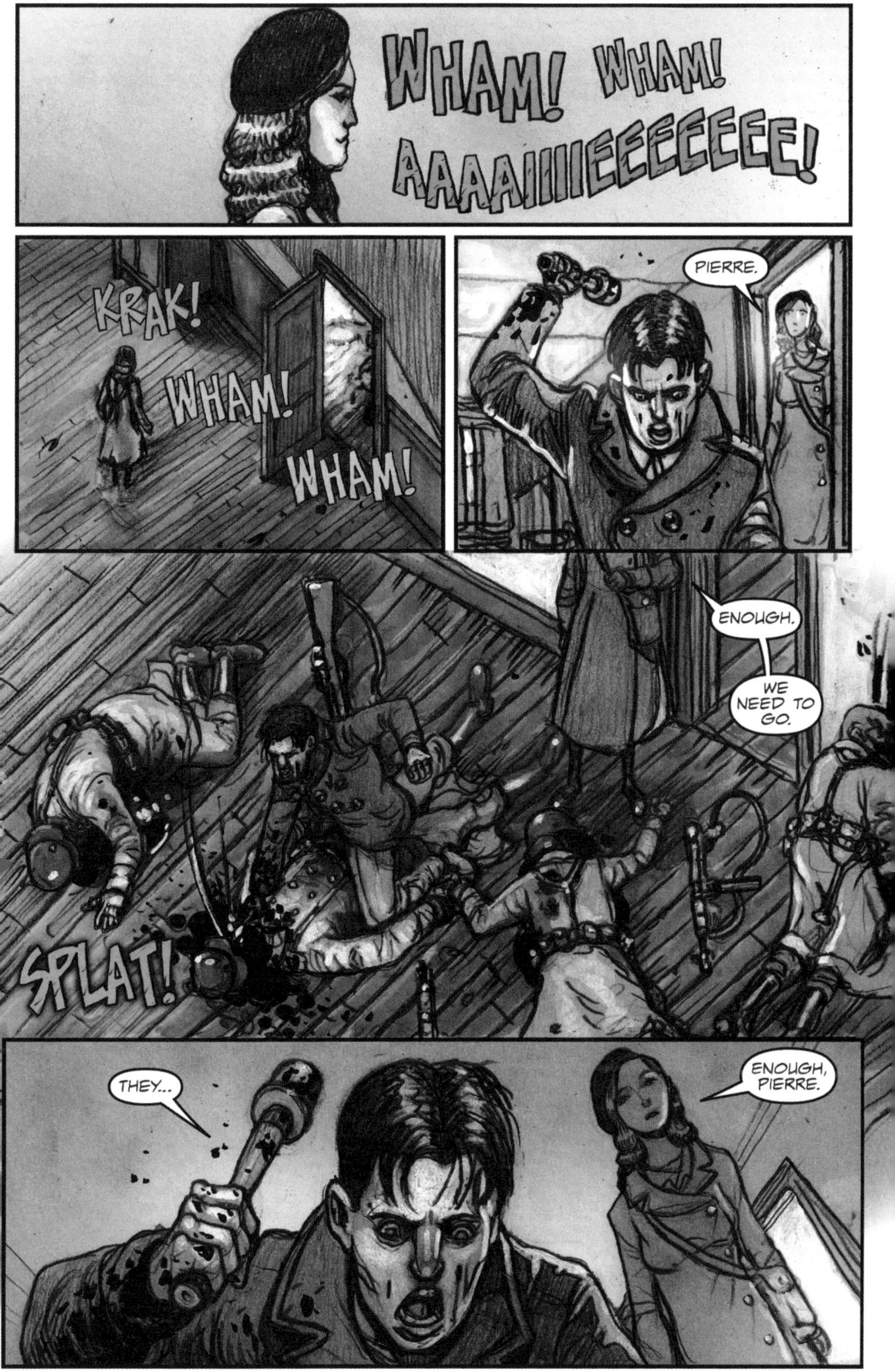
WHAM! WHAM!
AAAAIIIIEEEEEEEE!
KRAK!
WHAM!
WHAM!
PIERRE.
ENOUGH.
WE NEED TO GO.
SPLAT!
THEY...
ENOUGH, PIERRE.

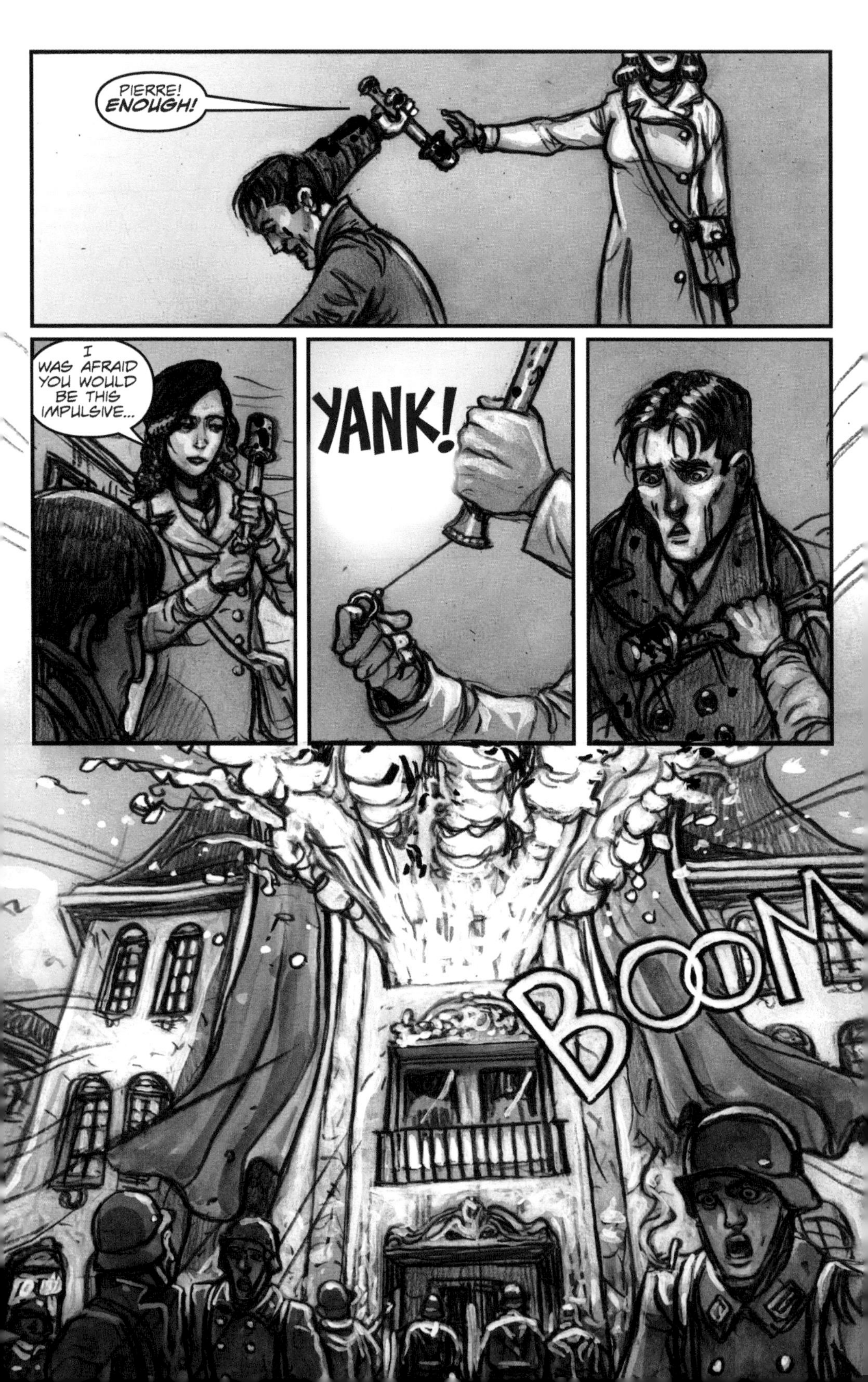
PIERRE! ENOUGH!
I WAS AFRAID YOU WOULD BE THIS IMPULSIVE...
YANK!
BOOM

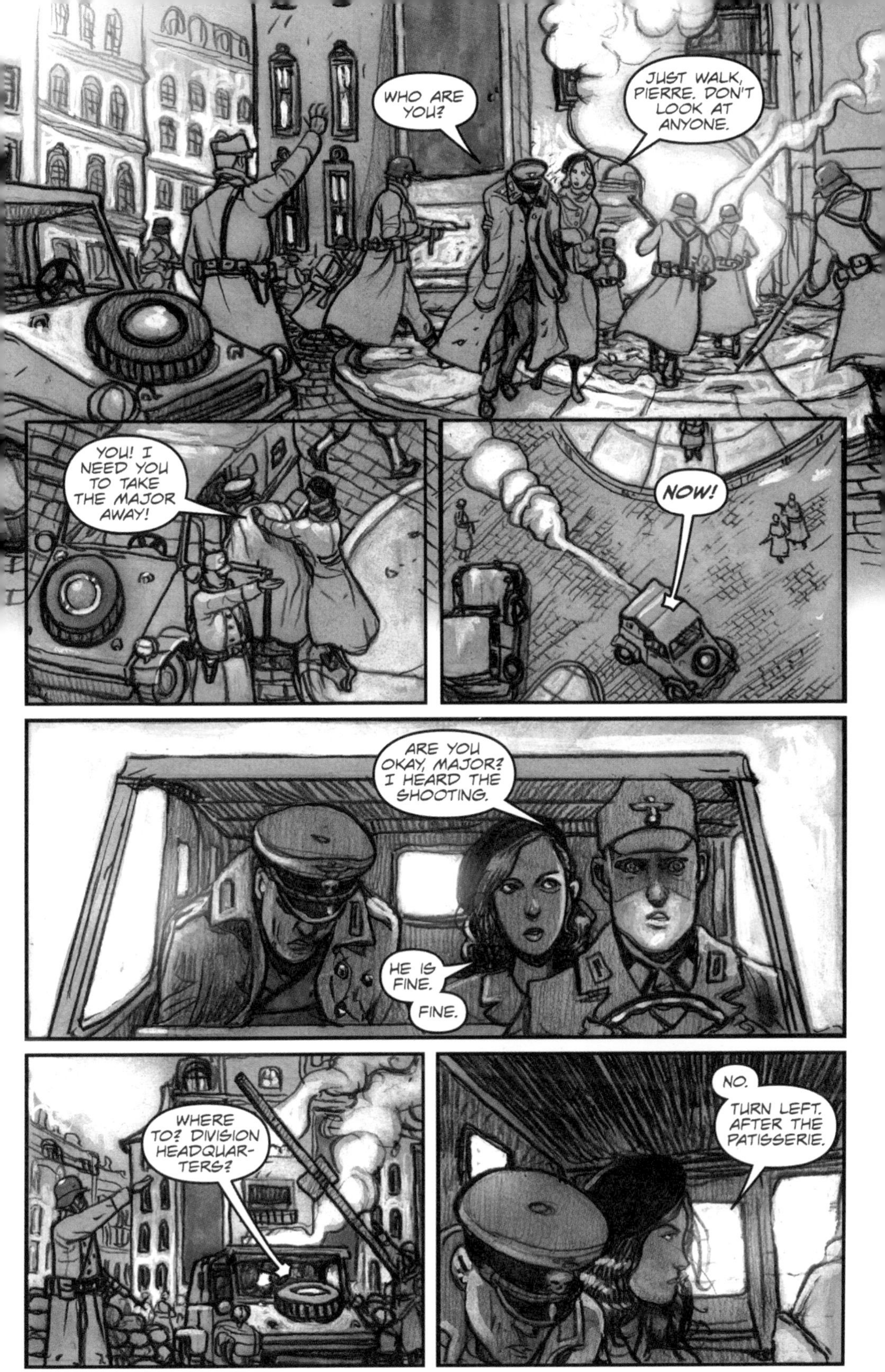
WHO ARE YOU?
JUST WALK, PIERRE. DON'T LOOK AT ANYONE.
YOU! I NEED YOU TO TAKE THE MAJOR AWAY!
NOW!
ARE YOU OKAY, MAJOR? I HEARD THE SHOOTING.
HE IS FINE.
FINE.
WHERE TO? DIVISION HEADQUARTERS?
NO.
TURN LEFT. AFTER THE PATISSERIE.

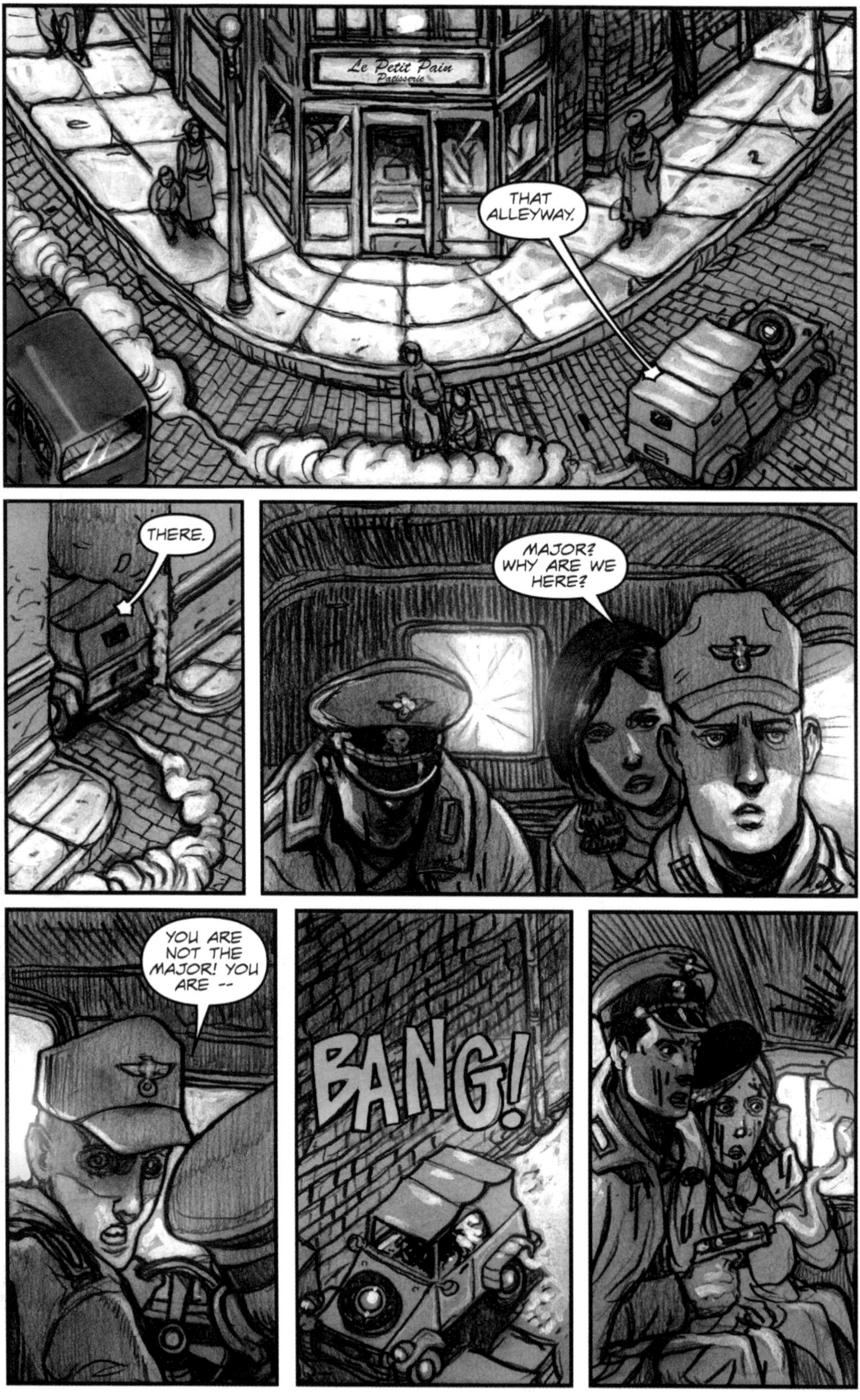
Le Petit Pain
Patisserie
THAT ALLEYWAY.
THERE.
MAJOR? WHY ARE WE HERE?
YOU ARE NOT THE MAJOR! YOU ARE --
BANG!

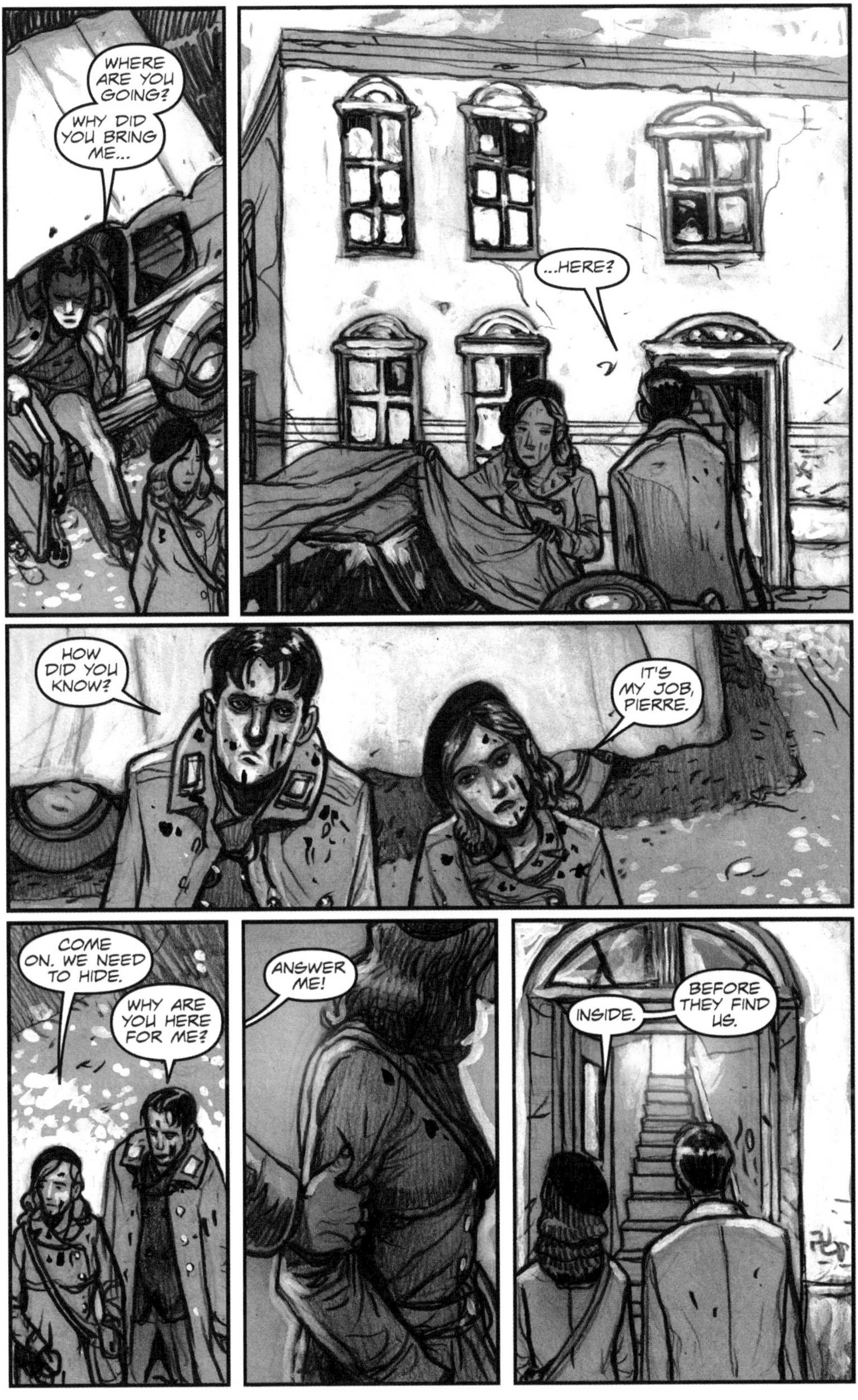
WHERE ARE YOU GOING?
WHY DID YOU BRING ME...
...HERE?
HOW DID YOU KNOW?
IT'S MY JOB, PIERRE.
COME ON. WE NEED TO HIDE.
WHY ARE YOU HERE FOR ME?
ANSWER ME!
INSIDE.
BEFORE THEY FIND US.

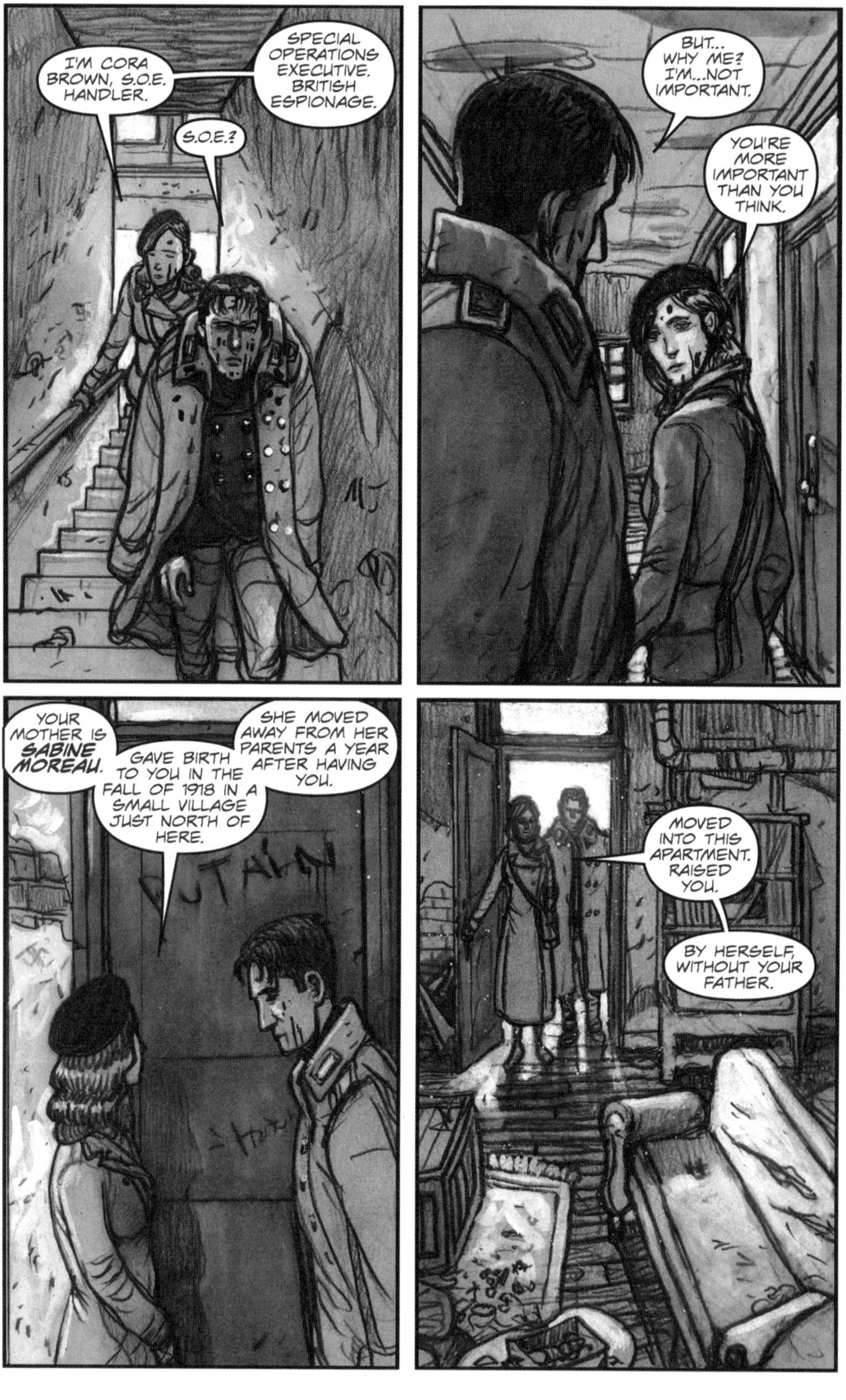
I'M CORA BROWN, S.O.E. HANDLER.
S.O.E.?
SPECIAL OPERATIONS EXECUTIVE. BRITISH ESPIONAGE.
BUT... WHY ME? I'M...NOT IMPORTANT.
YOU'RE MORE IMPORTANT THAN YOU THINK.
YOUR MOTHER IS SABINE MOREAU.
GAVE BIRTH TO YOU IN THE FALL OF 1918 IN A SMALL VILLAGE JUST NORTH OF HERE.
SHE MOVED AWAY FROM HER PARENTS A YEAR AFTER HAVING YOU.
MOVED INTO THIS APARTMENT. RAISED YOU.
BY HERSELF, WITHOUT YOUR FATHER.

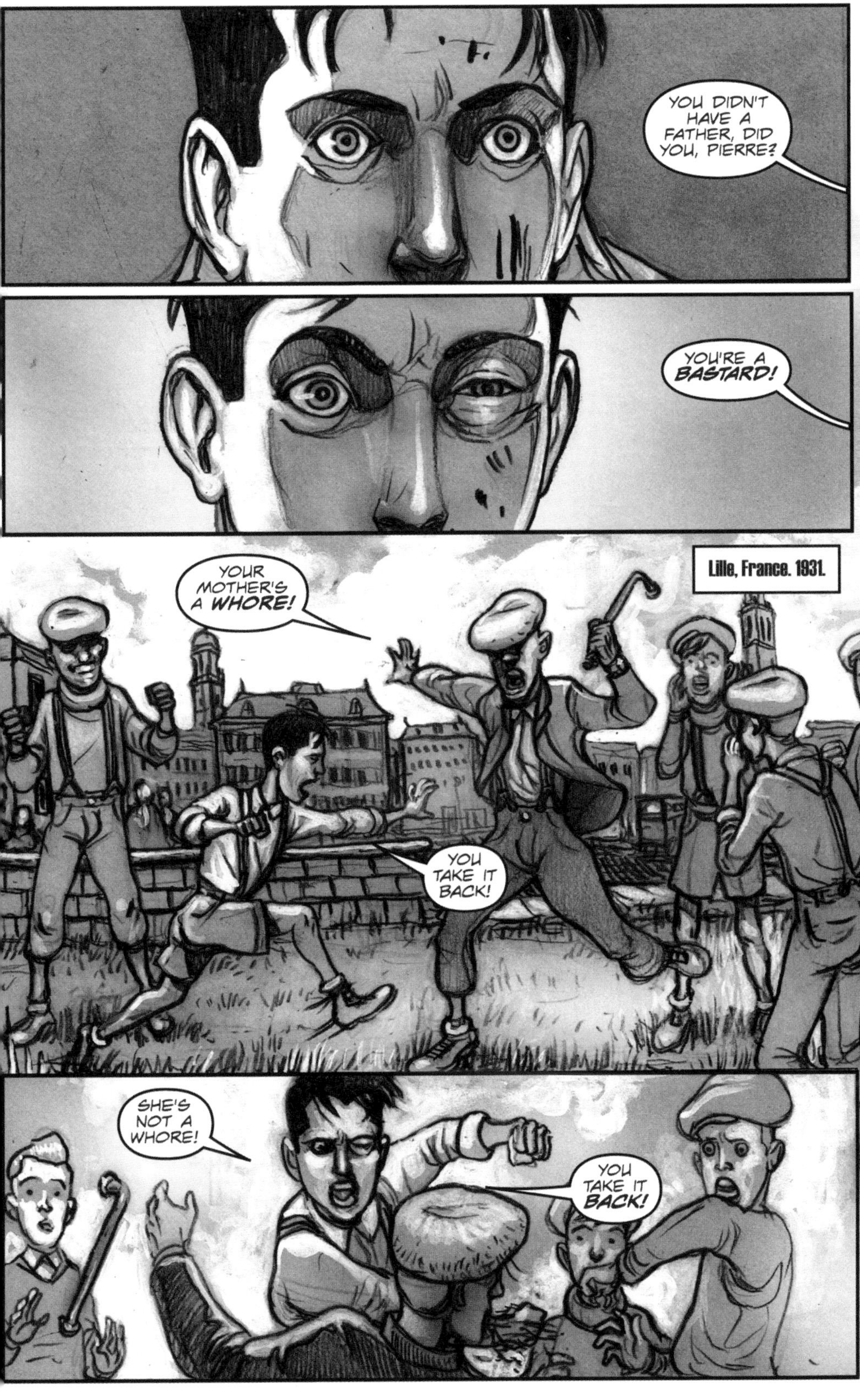
YOU DIDN'T HAVE A FATHER, DID YOU, PIERRE?
YOU'RE A **BASTARD!**
Lille, France. 1931.
YOUR MOTHER'S A **WHORE!**
YOU TAKE IT BACK!
SHE'S NOT A WHORE!
YOU TAKE IT **BACK!**

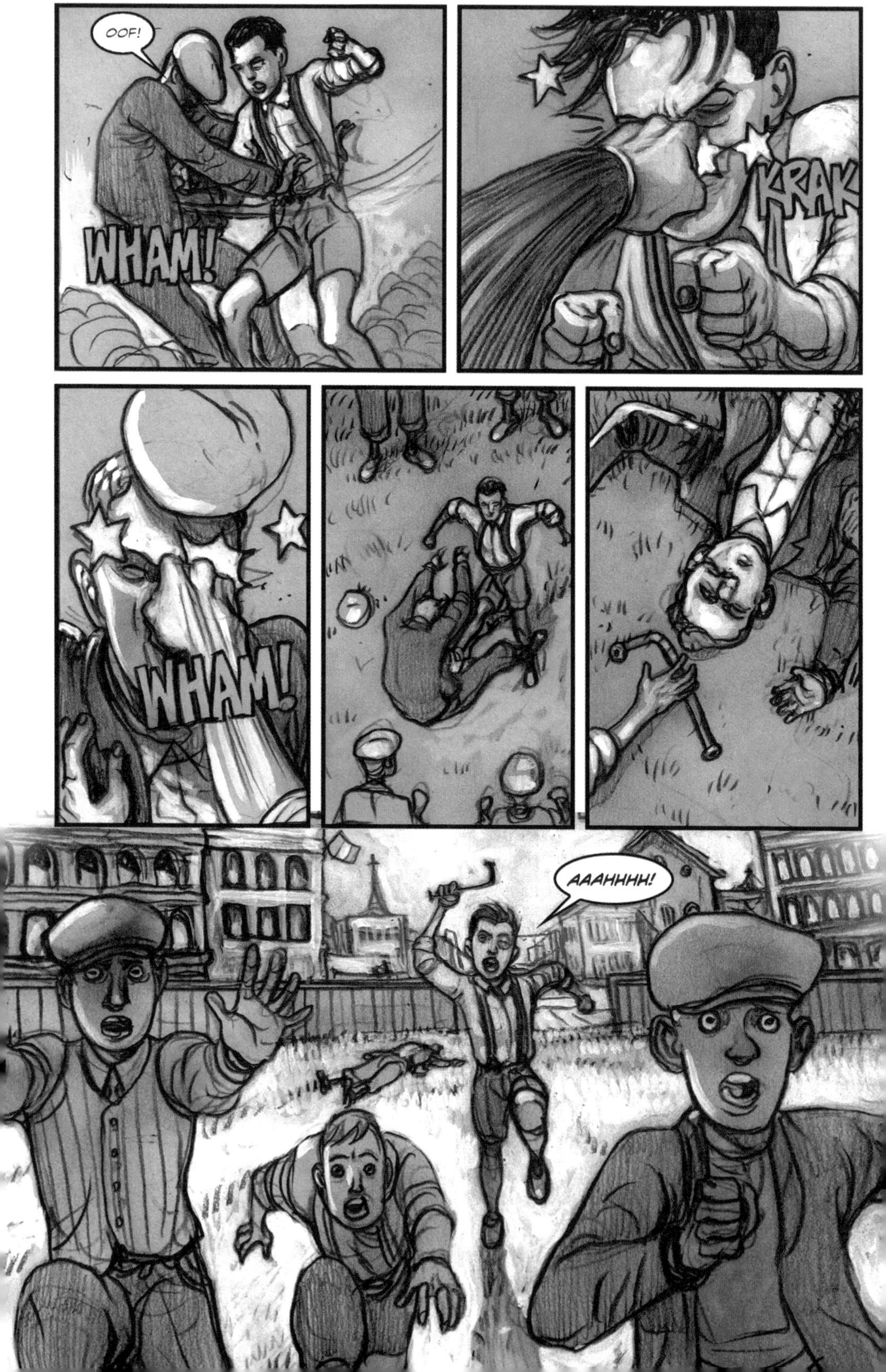
OOF!
WHAM!
KRAK
WHAM!
AAAHHHH!

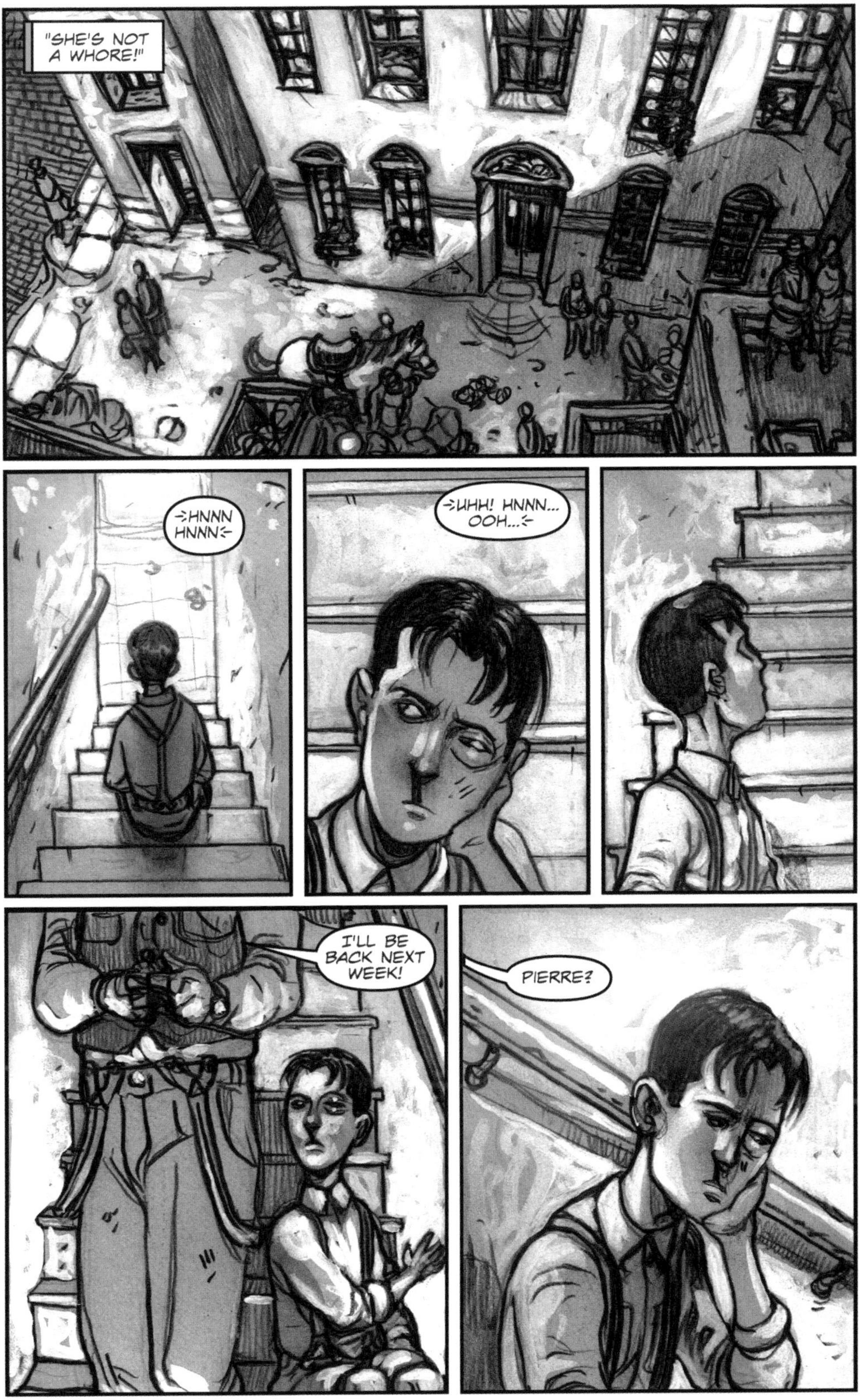
"SHE'S NOT A WHORE!"
HNNN HNNN
UHH! HNNN... OOH...
I'LL BE BACK NEXT WEEK!
PIERRE?

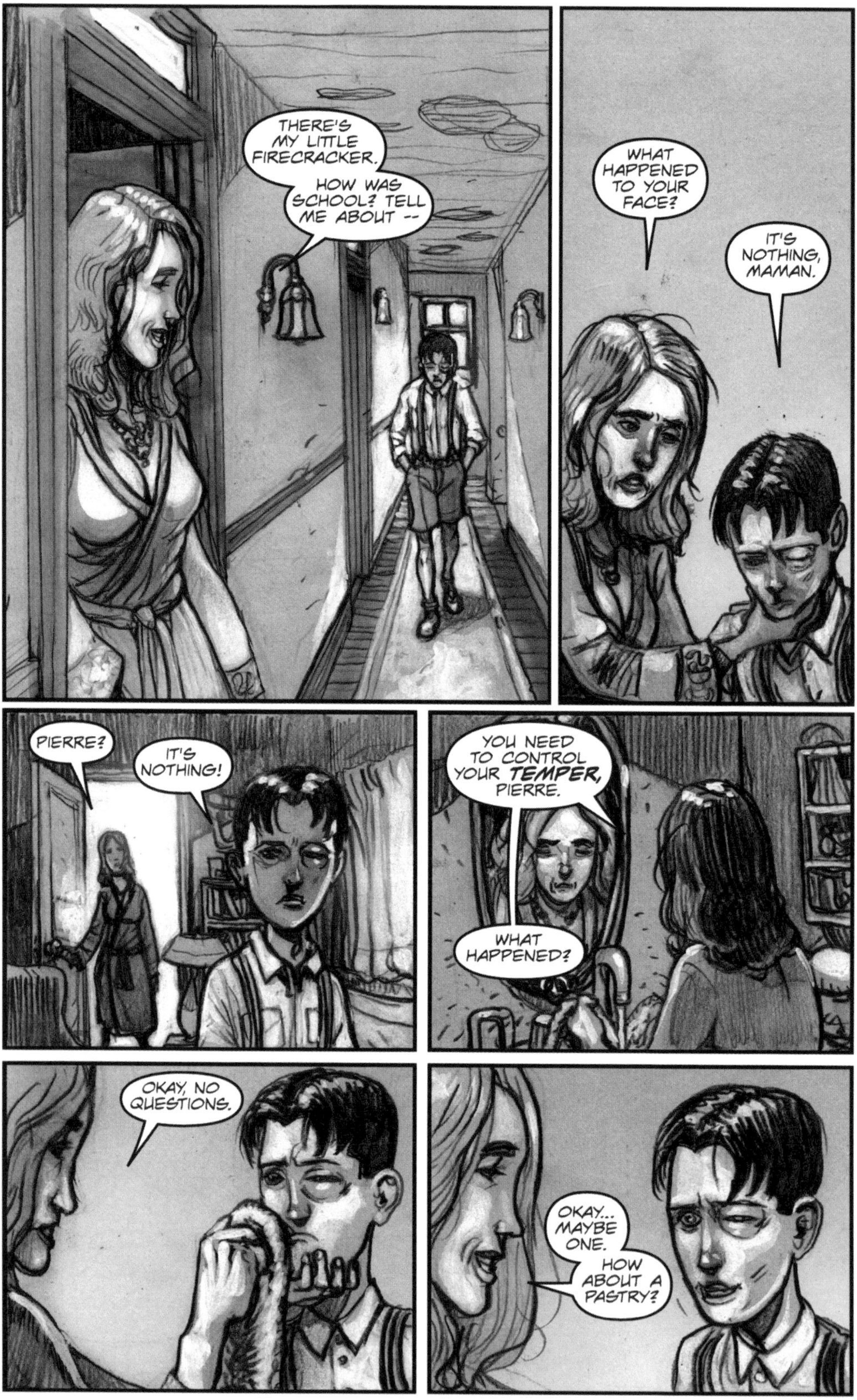
THERE'S MY LITTLE FIRECRACKER.
HOW WAS SCHOOL? TELL ME ABOUT --
WHAT HAPPENED TO YOUR FACE?
IT'S NOTHING, MAMAN.
PIERRE?
IT'S NOTHING!
YOU NEED TO CONTROL YOUR *TEMPER,* PIERRE.
WHAT HAPPENED?
OKAY, NO QUESTIONS.
OKAY... MAYBE ONE.
HOW ABOUT A PASTRY?

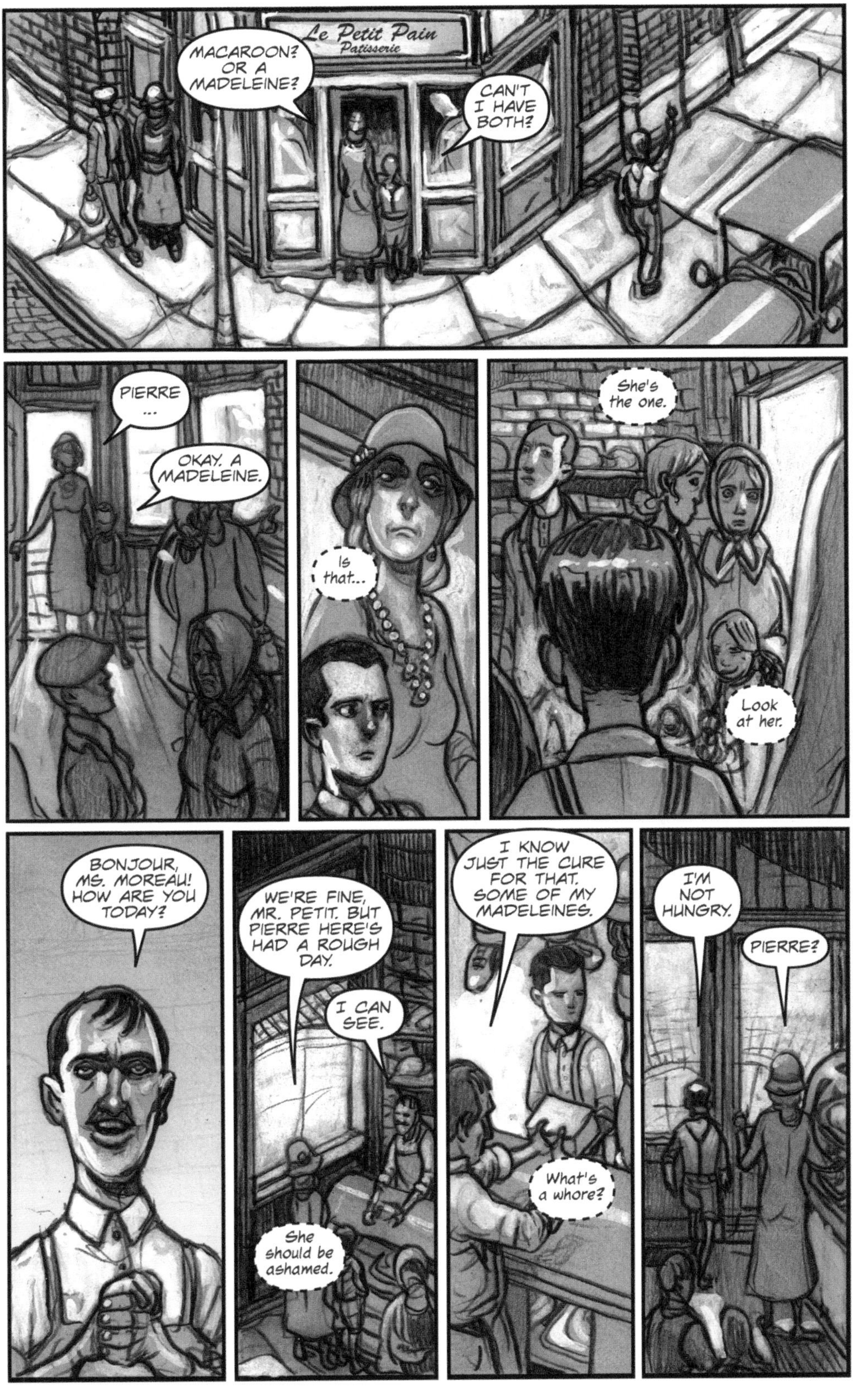
Le Petit Pain
Patisserie
MACAROON? OR A MADELEINE?
CAN'T I HAVE BOTH?
PIERRE ...
OKAY. A MADELEINE.
Is that...
She's the one.
Look at her.
BONJOUR, MS. MOREAU! HOW ARE YOU TODAY?
WE'RE FINE, MR. PETIT. BUT PIERRE HERE'S HAD A ROUGH DAY.
I CAN SEE.
She should be ashamed.
I KNOW JUST THE CURE FOR THAT. SOME OF MY MADELEINES.
What's a whore?
I'M NOT HUNGRY.
PIERRE?

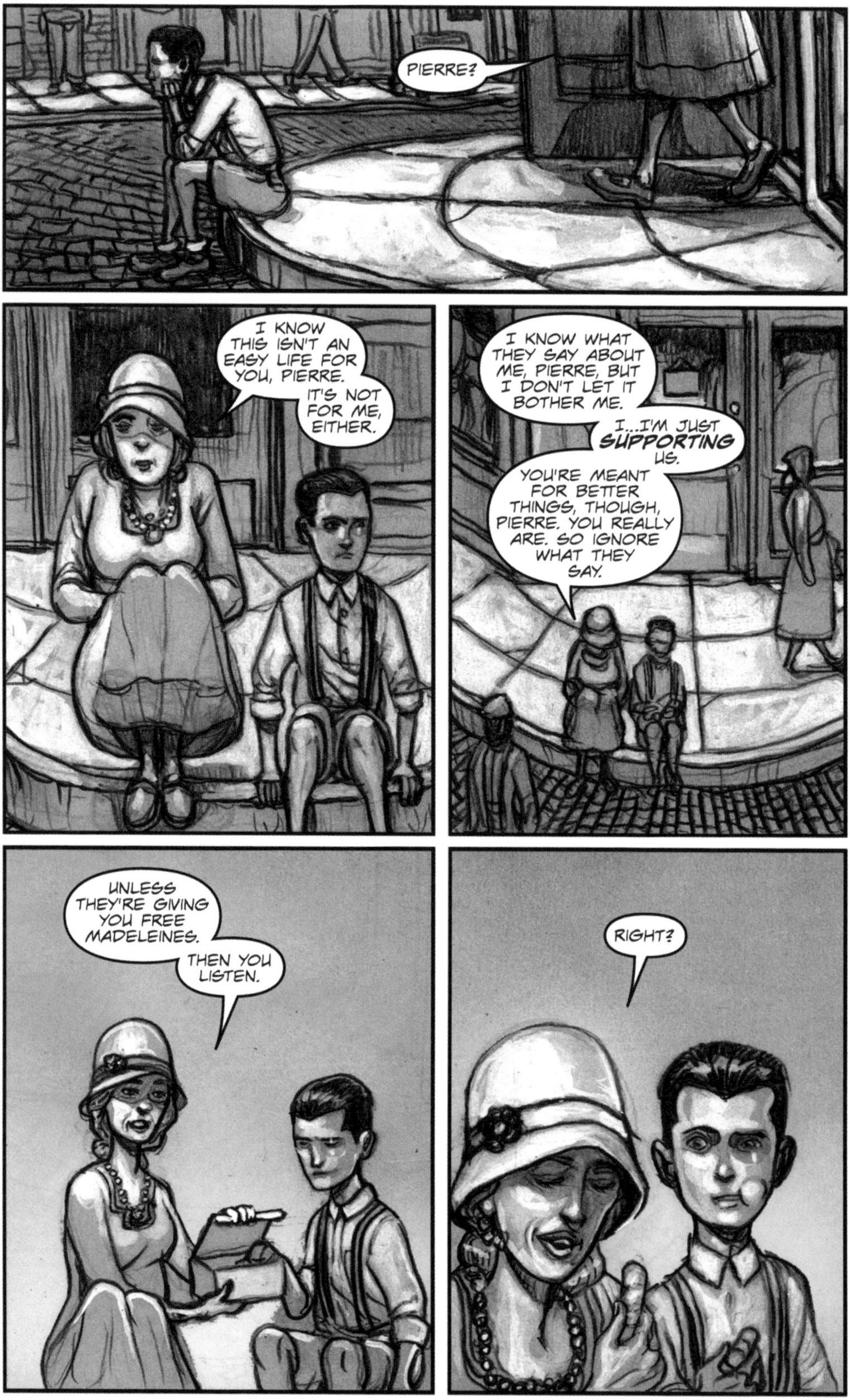
PIERRE?
I KNOW THIS ISN'T AN EASY LIFE FOR YOU, PIERRE.
IT'S NOT FOR ME, EITHER.
I KNOW WHAT THEY SAY ABOUT ME, PIERRE, BUT I DON'T LET IT BOTHER ME.
I...I'M JUST SUPPORTING US.
YOU'RE MEANT FOR BETTER THINGS, THOUGH, PIERRE. YOU REALLY ARE. SO IGNORE WHAT THEY SAY.
UNLESS THEY'RE GIVING YOU FREE MADELEINES.
THEN YOU LISTEN.
RIGHT?

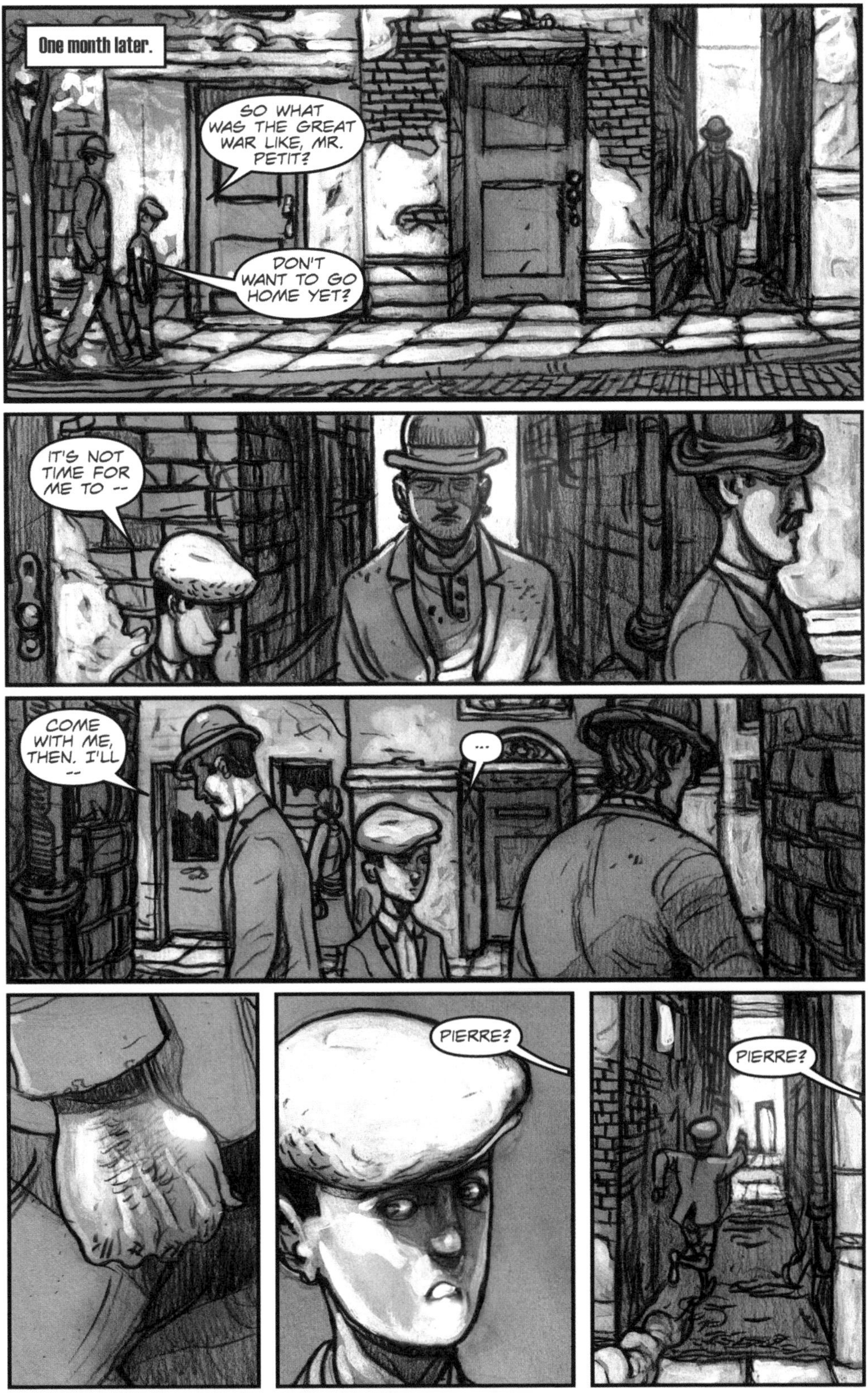
One month later.
SO WHAT WAS THE GREAT WAR LIKE, MR. PETIT?
DON'T WANT TO GO HOME YET?
IT'S NOT TIME FOR ME TO --
COME WITH ME, THEN. I'LL --
...
PIERRE?
PIERRE?

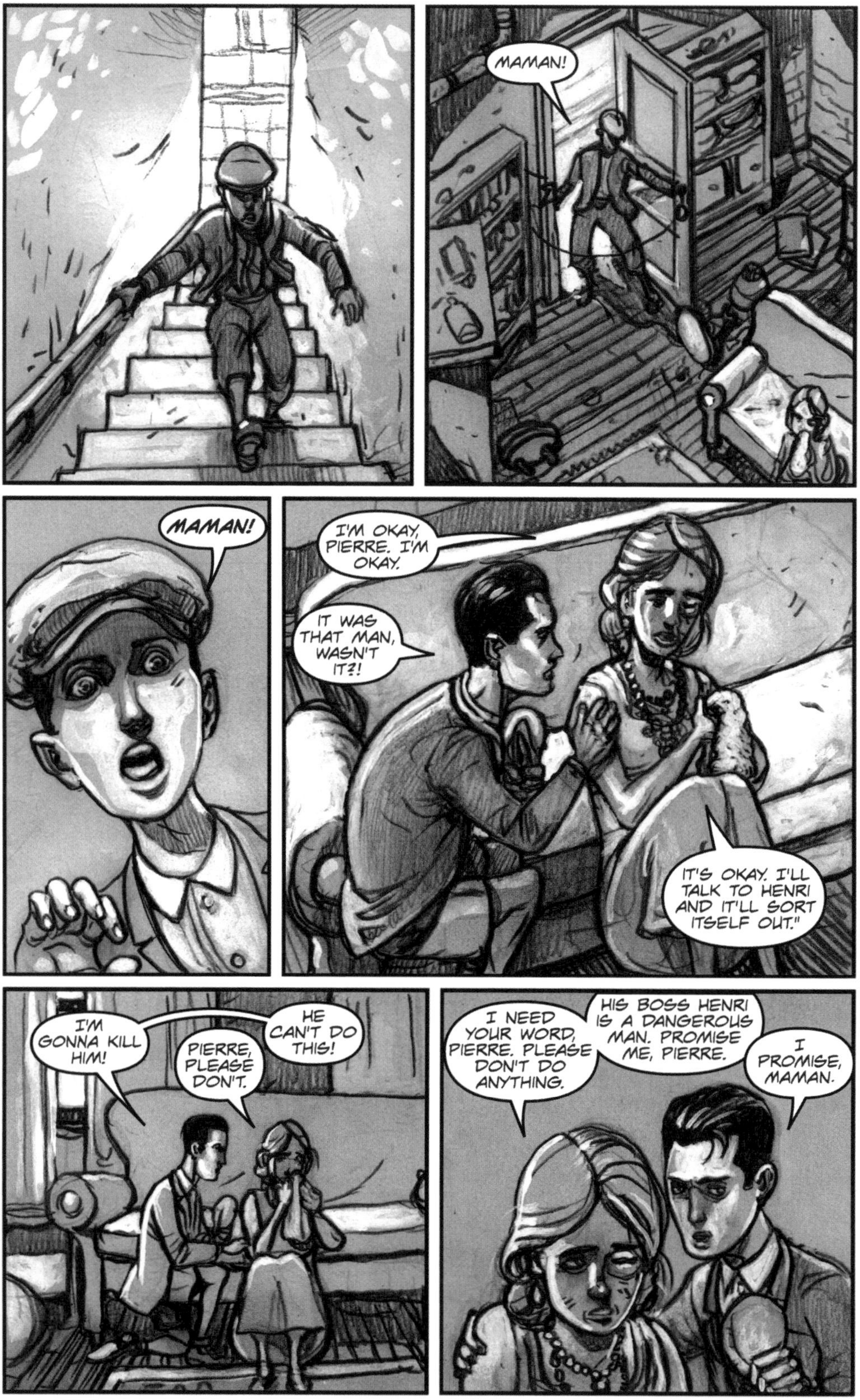
MAMAN!
MAMAN!
I'M OKAY, PIERRE. I'M OKAY.
IT WAS THAT MAN, WASN'T IT?!
IT'S OKAY. I'LL TALK TO HENRI AND IT'LL SORT ITSELF OUT."
I'M GONNA KILL HIM!
HE CAN'T DO THIS!
PIERRE, PLEASE DON'T.
I NEED YOUR WORD, PIERRE. PLEASE DON'T DO ANYTHING.
HIS BOSS HENRI IS A DANGEROUS MAN. PROMISE ME, PIERRE.
I PROMISE, MAMAN.

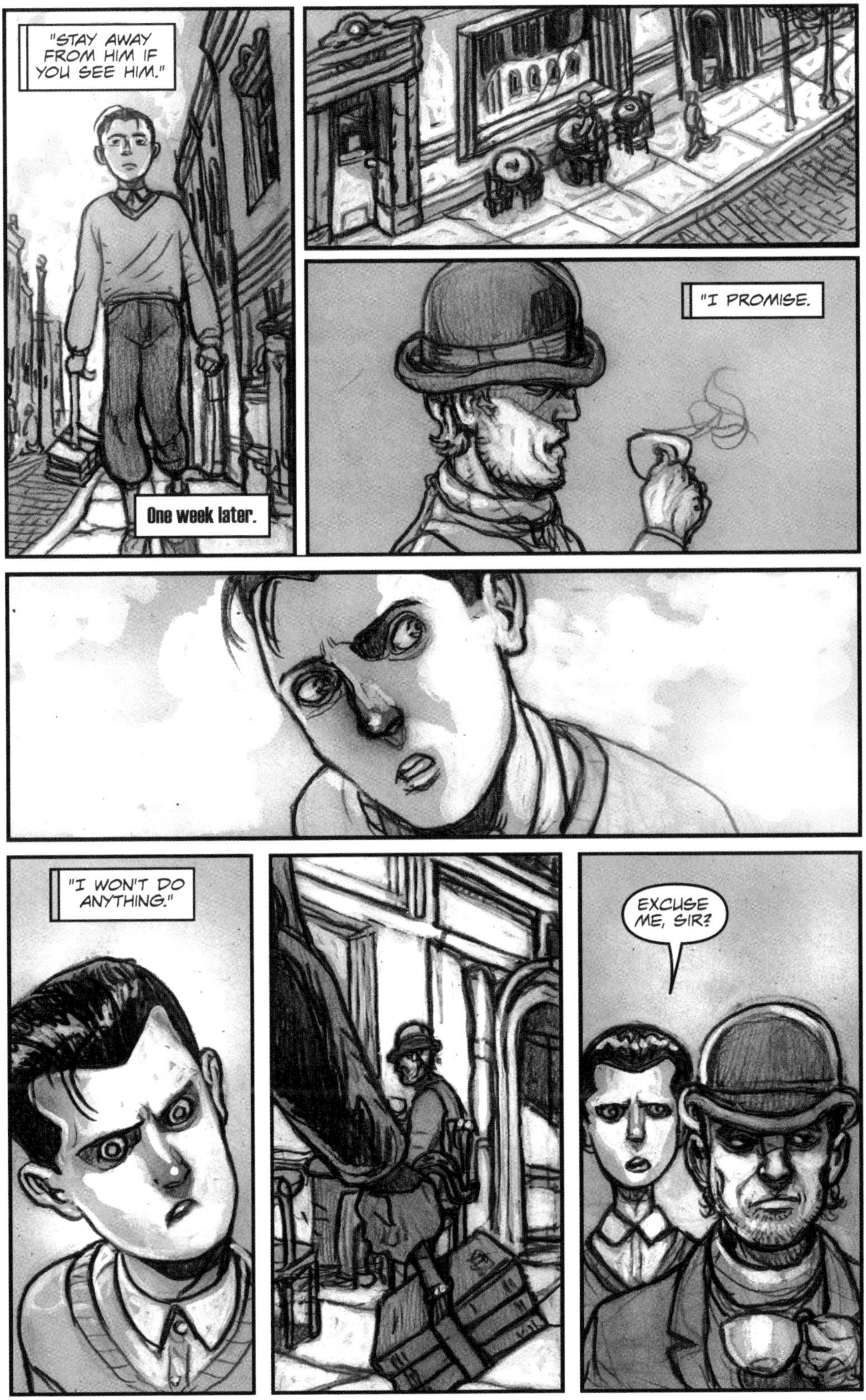
"STAY AWAY FROM HIM IF YOU SEE HIM."
One week later.
"I PROMISE.
"I WON'T DO ANYTHING."
EXCUSE ME, SIR?

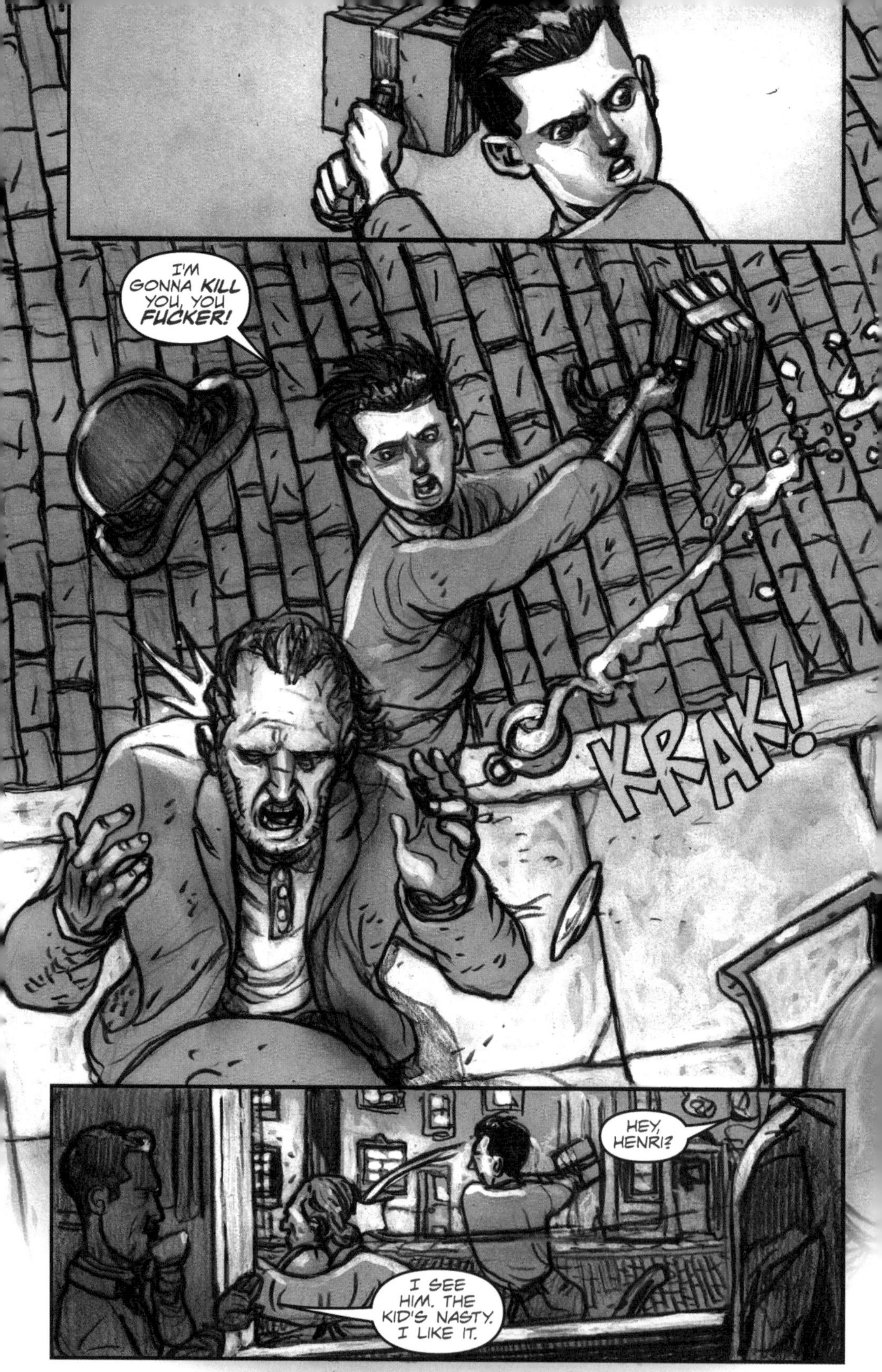
I'M GONNA KILL YOU, YOU FUCKER!
KRAK!
HEY, HENRI?
I SEE HIM. THE KID'S NASTY. I LIKE IT.

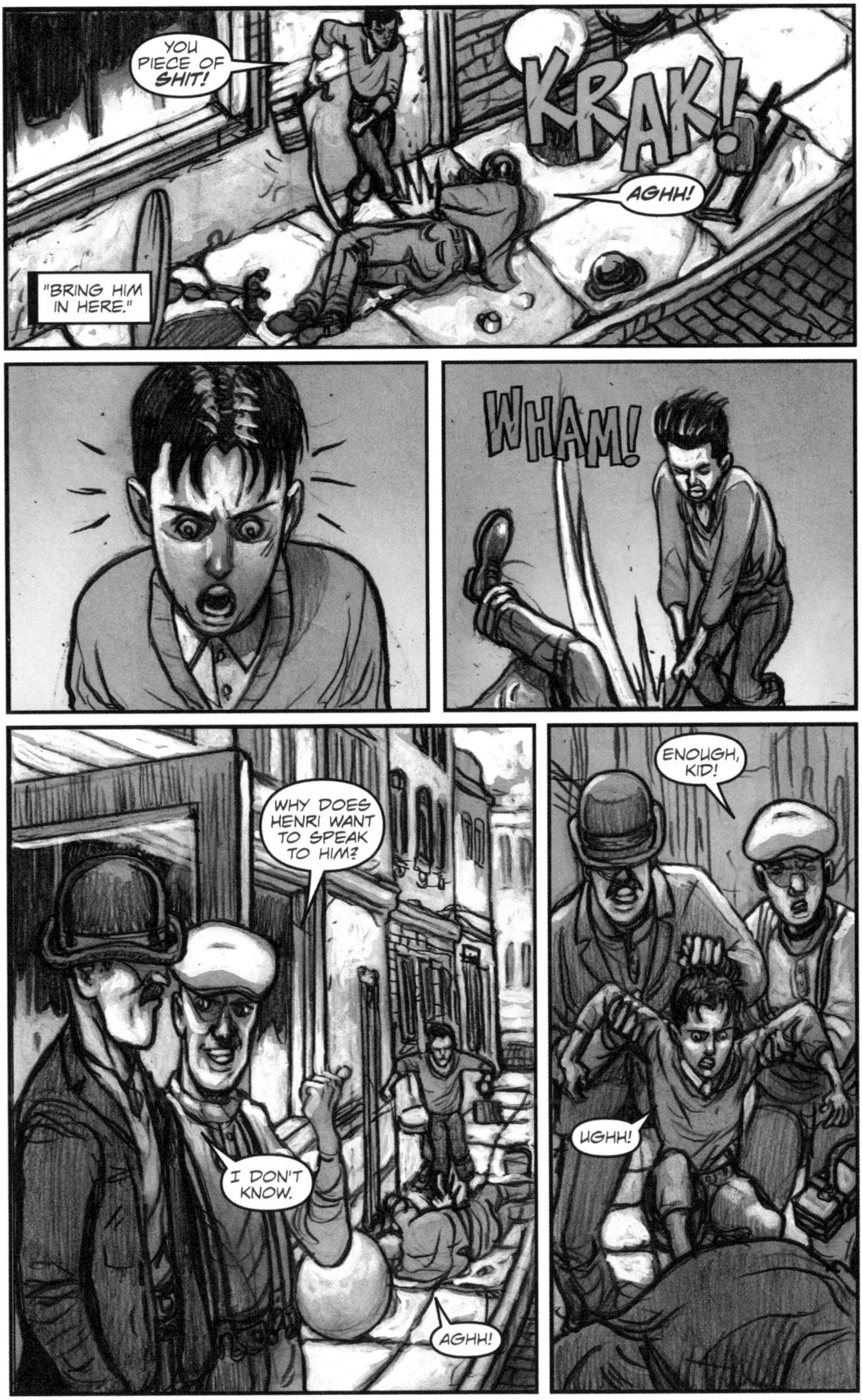
YOU PIECE OF SHIT!
KRAK!
AGHH!
"BRING HIM IN HERE."
WHAM!
WHY DOES HENRI WANT TO SPEAK TO HIM?
I DON'T KNOW.
AGHH!
ENOUGH, KID!
UGHH!

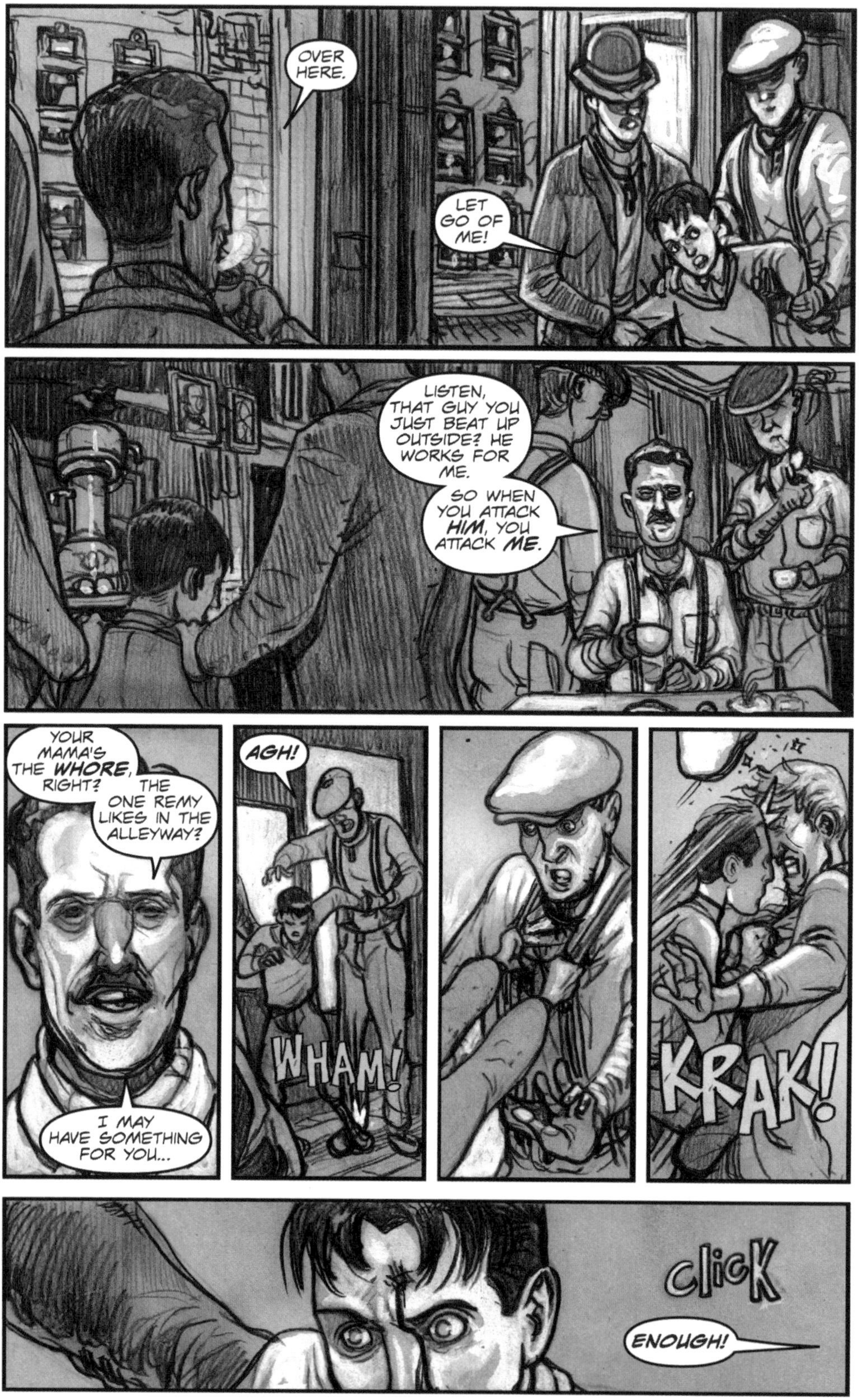
OVER HERE.
LET GO OF ME!
LISTEN, THAT GUY YOU JUST BEAT UP OUTSIDE? HE WORKS FOR ME.
SO WHEN YOU ATTACK **HIM**, YOU ATTACK **ME**.
YOUR MAMA'S THE **WHORE**, RIGHT?
THE ONE REMY LIKES IN THE ALLEYWAY?
I MAY HAVE SOMETHING FOR YOU...
AGH!
WHAM!
KRAK!
CLICK
ENOUGH!

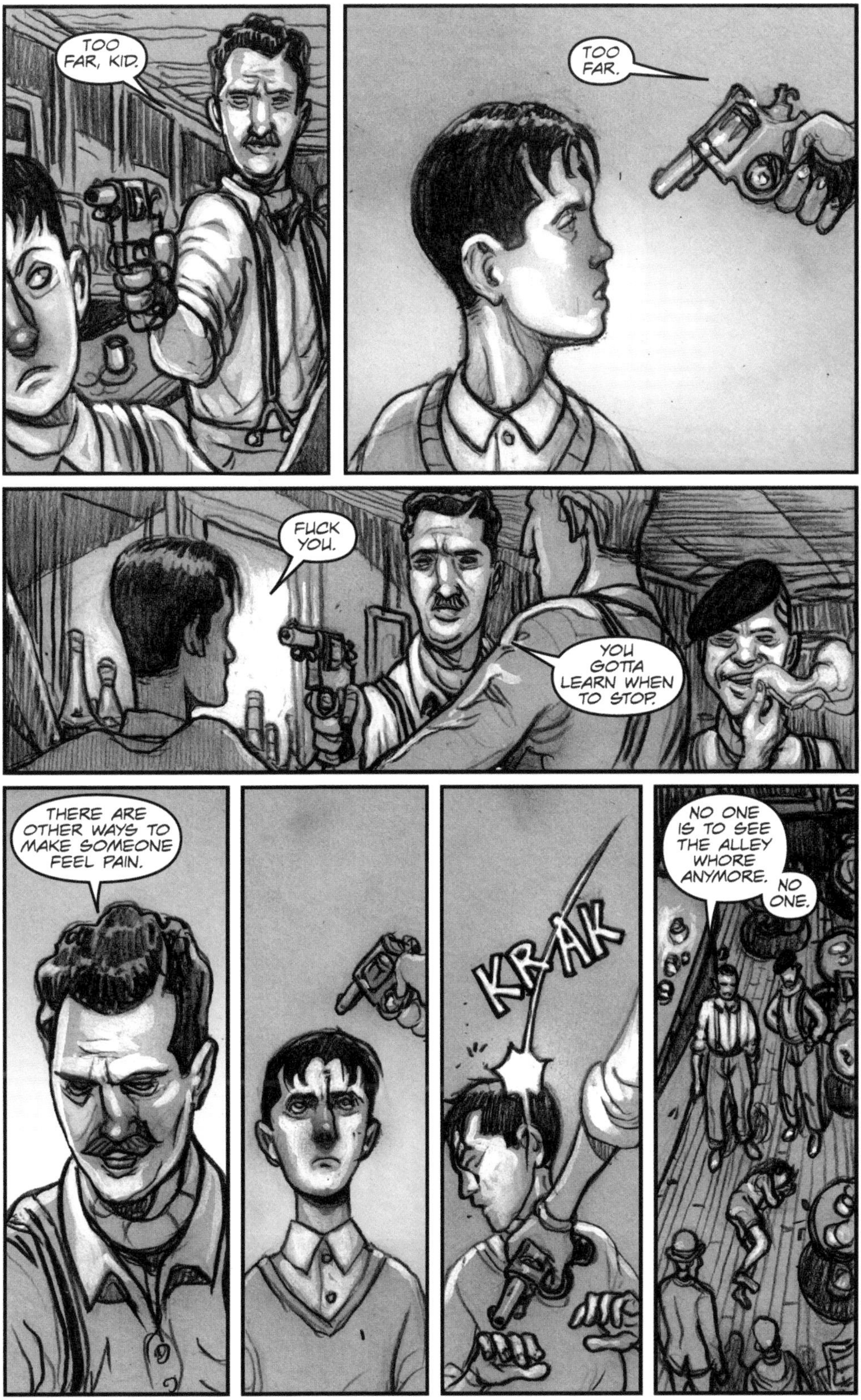
TOO FAR, KID.
TOO FAR.
FUCK YOU.
YOU GOTTA LEARN WHEN TO STOP.
THERE ARE OTHER WAYS TO MAKE SOMEONE FEEL PAIN.
KRAK
NO ONE IS TO SEE THE ALLEY WHORE ANYMORE.
NO ONE.

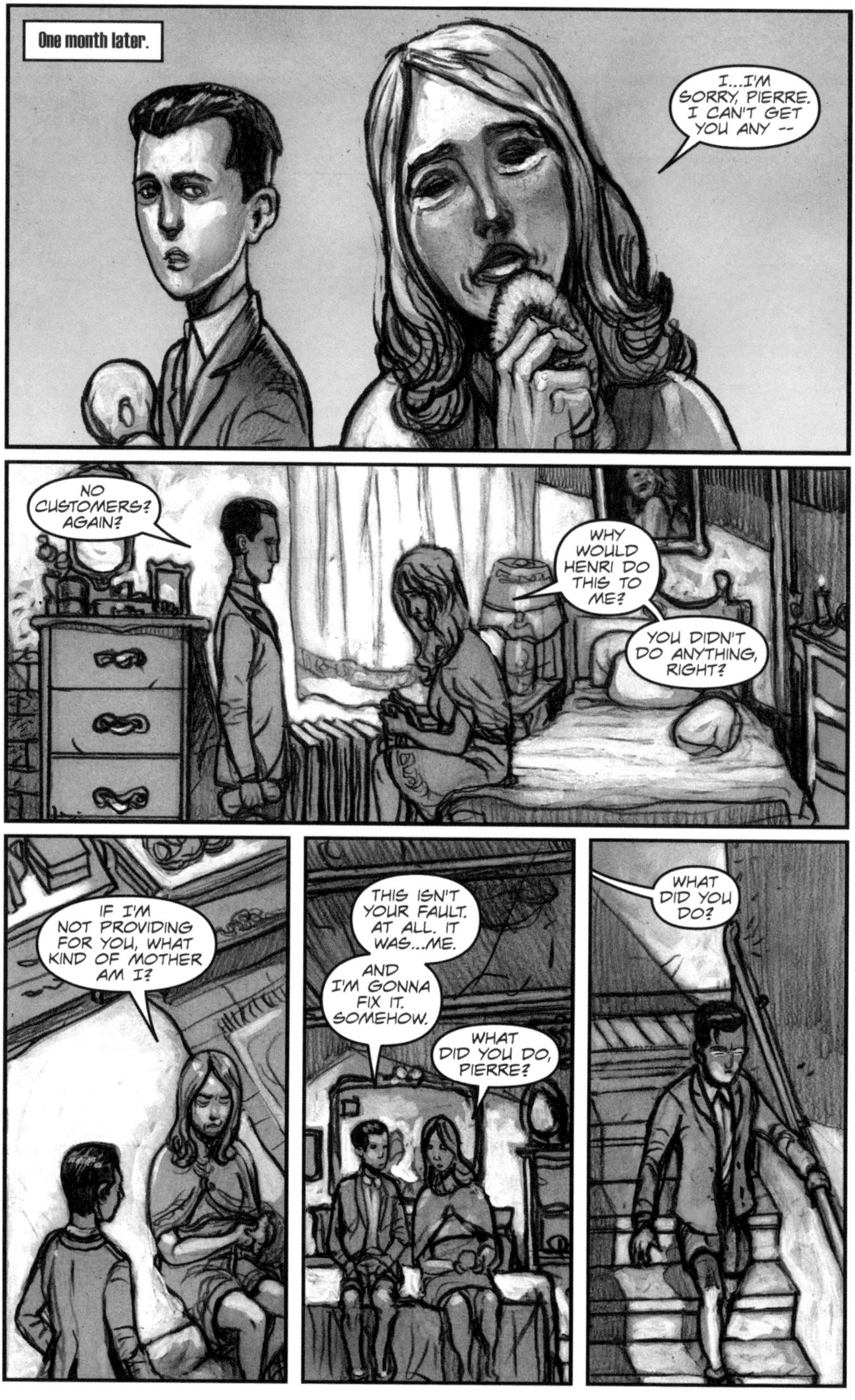
One month later.
I...I'M SORRY, PIERRE. I CAN'T GET YOU ANY --
NO CUSTOMERS? AGAIN?
WHY WOULD HENRI DO THIS TO ME?
YOU DIDN'T DO ANYTHING, RIGHT?
IF I'M NOT PROVIDING FOR YOU, WHAT KIND OF MOTHER AM I?
THIS ISN'T YOUR FAULT. AT ALL. IT WAS...ME.
AND I'M GONNA FIX IT. SOMEHOW.
WHAT DID YOU DO, PIERRE?
WHAT DID YOU DO?

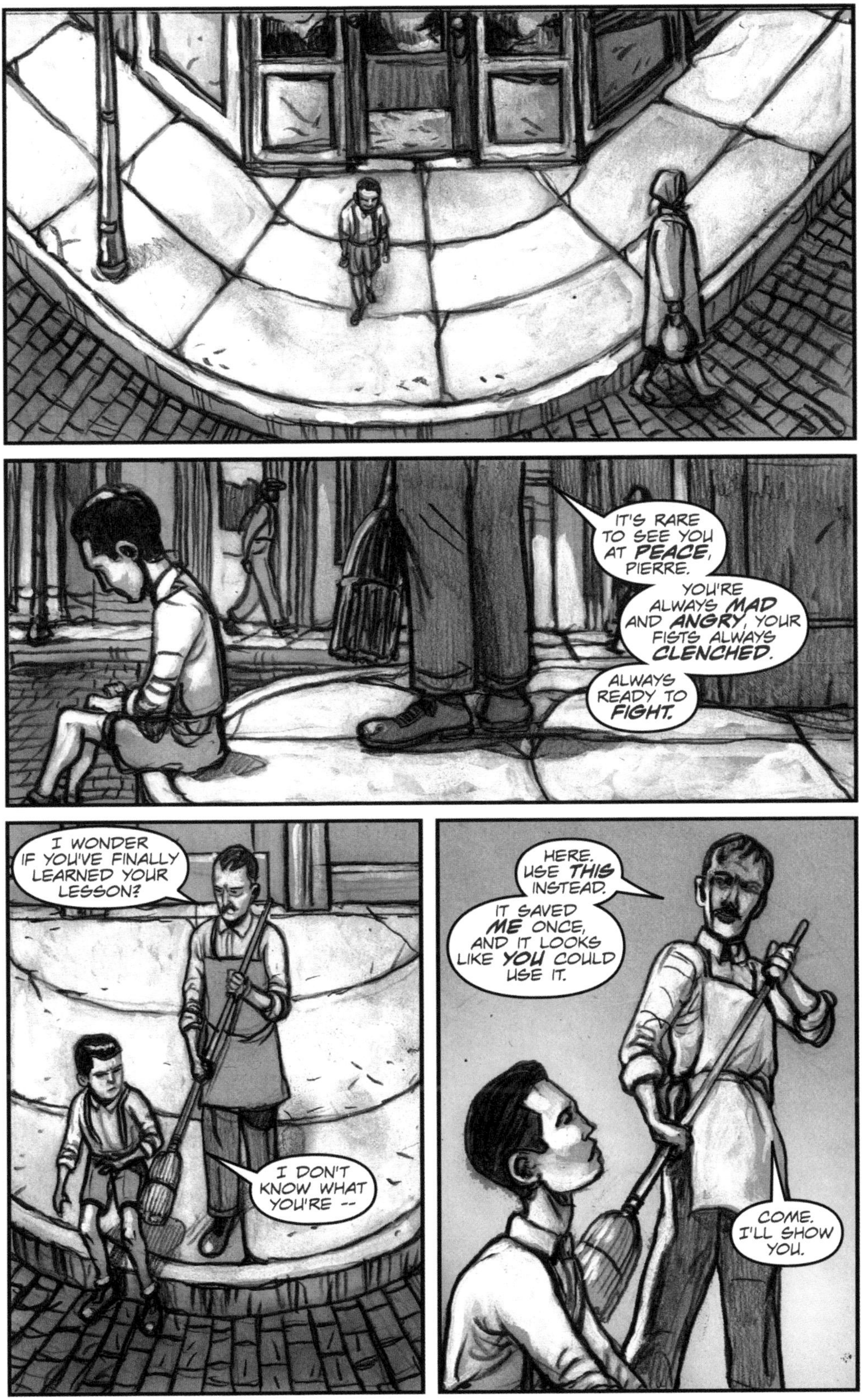
IT'S RARE TO SEE YOU AT PEACE, PIERRE.
YOU'RE ALWAYS MAD AND ANGRY, YOUR FISTS ALWAYS CLENCHED.
ALWAYS READY TO FIGHT.
I WONDER IF YOU'VE FINALLY LEARNED YOUR LESSON?
I DON'T KNOW WHAT YOU'RE --
HERE. USE THIS INSTEAD.
IT SAVED ME ONCE, AND IT LOOKS LIKE YOU COULD USE IT.
COME. I'LL SHOW YOU.

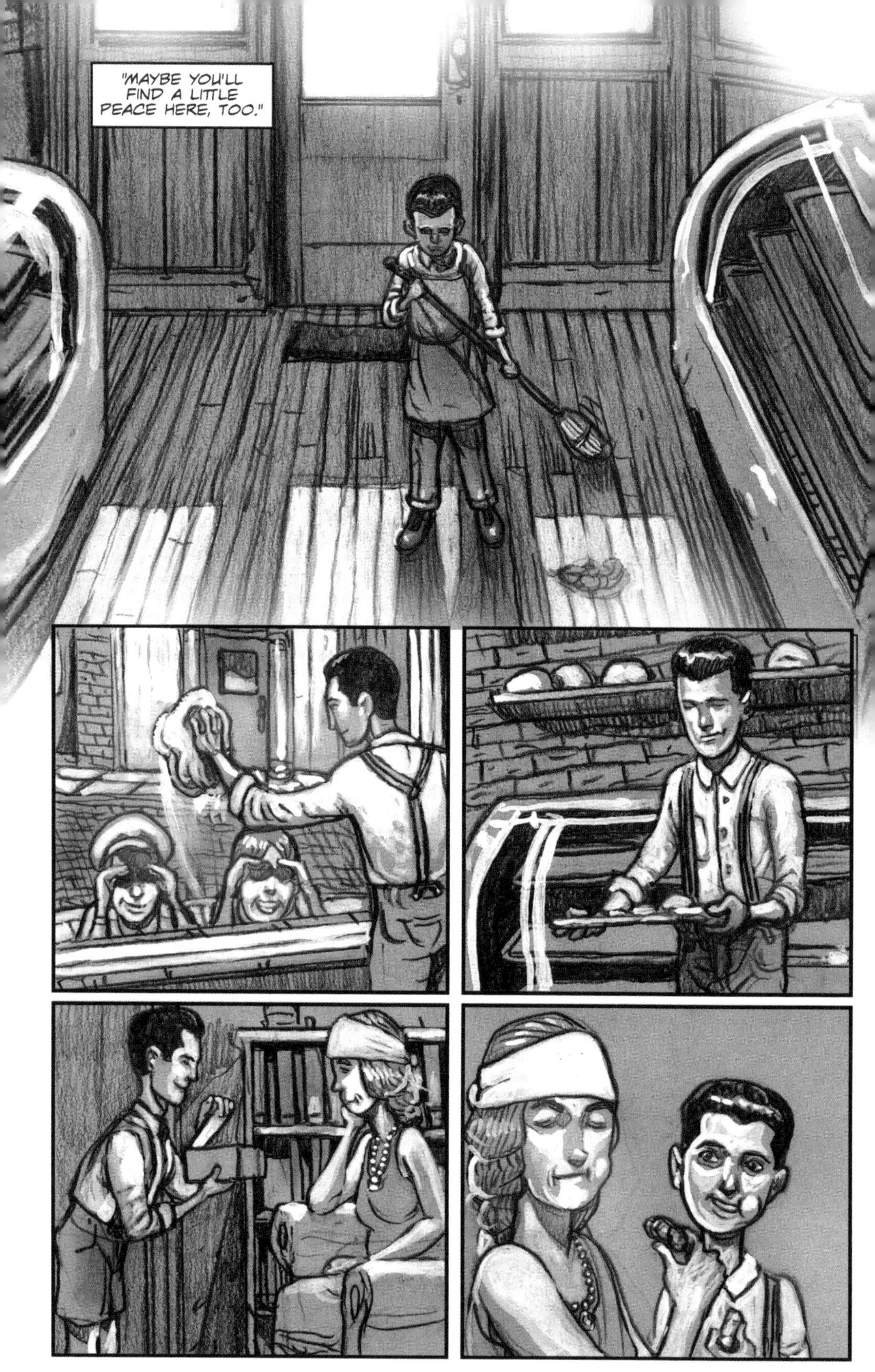
"MAYBE YOU'LL FIND A LITTLE PEACE HERE, TOO."

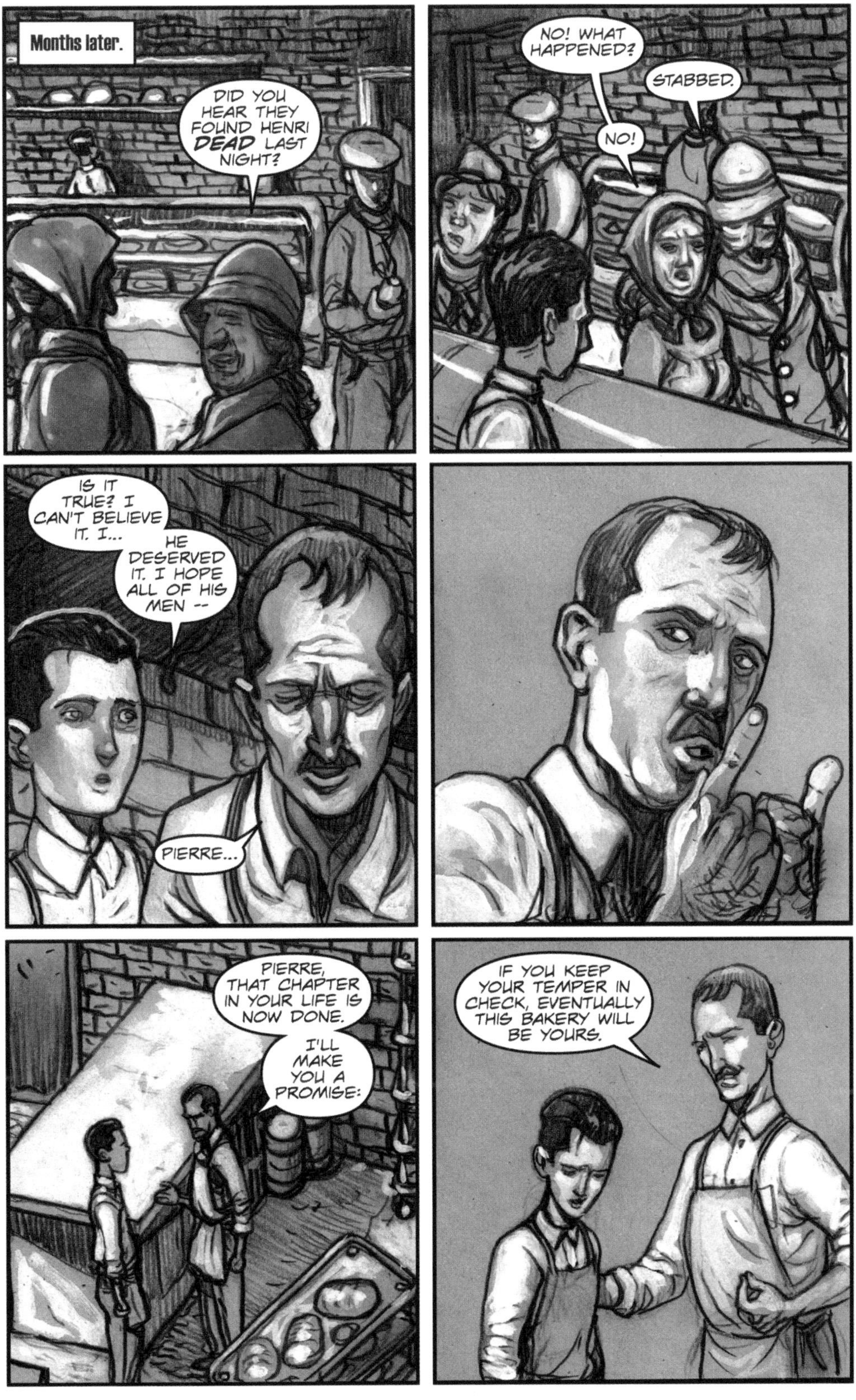
Months later.
DID YOU HEAR THEY FOUND HENRI DEAD LAST NIGHT?
NO! WHAT HAPPENED?
STABBED.
NO!
IS IT TRUE? I CAN'T BELIEVE IT. I...
HE DESERVED IT. I HOPE ALL OF HIS MEN --
PIERRE...
PIERRE, THAT CHAPTER IN YOUR LIFE IS NOW DONE.
I'LL MAKE YOU A PROMISE:
IF YOU KEEP YOUR TEMPER IN CHECK, EVENTUALLY THIS BAKERY WILL BE YOURS.

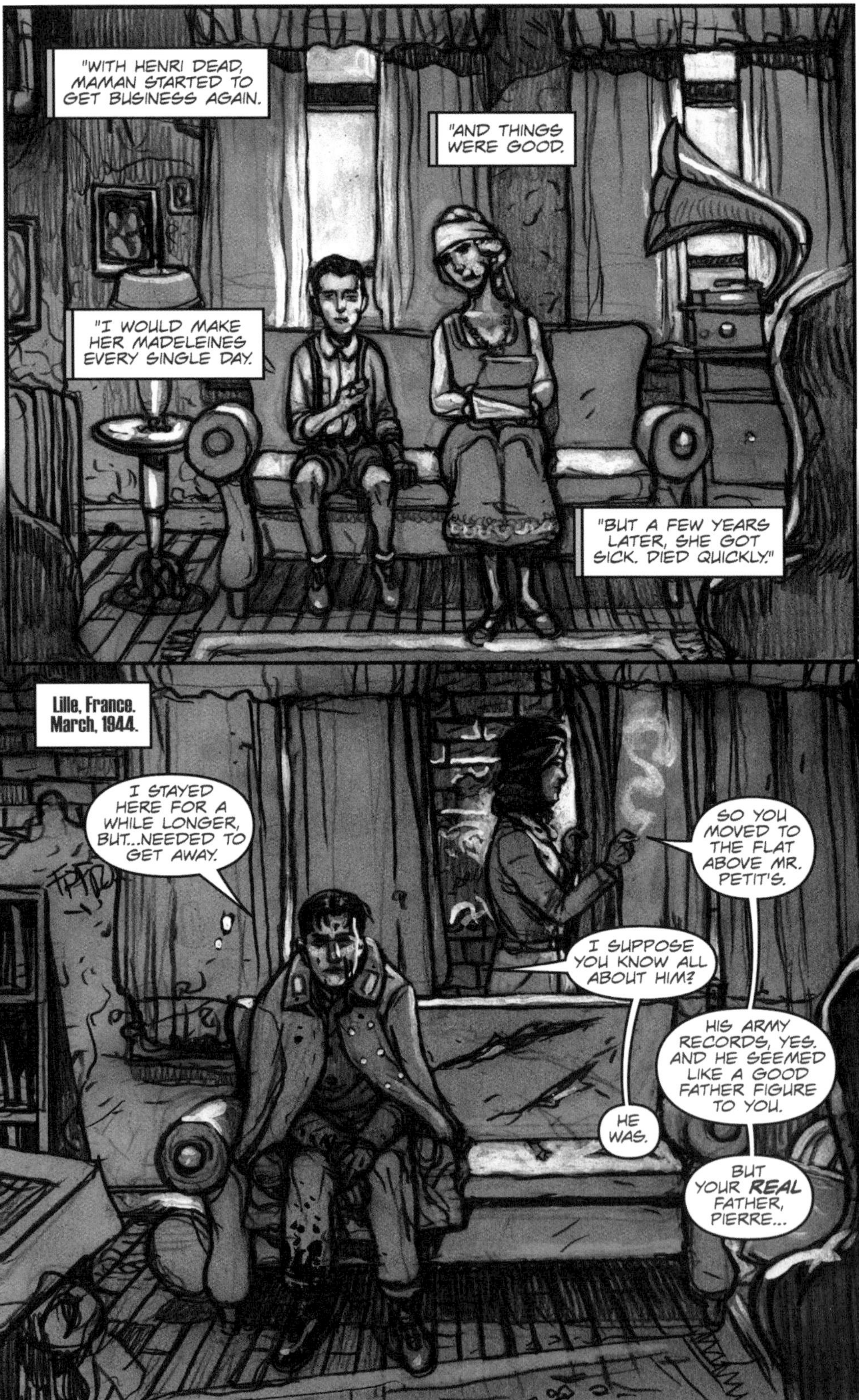
"WITH HENRI DEAD, MAMAN STARTED TO GET BUSINESS AGAIN.
"AND THINGS WERE GOOD.
"I WOULD MAKE HER MADELEINES EVERY SINGLE DAY.
"BUT A FEW YEARS LATER, SHE GOT SICK. DIED QUICKLY."
Lille, France. March, 1944.
I STAYED HERE FOR A WHILE LONGER, BUT...NEEDED TO GET AWAY.
SO YOU MOVED TO THE FLAT ABOVE MR. PETIT'S.
I SUPPOSE YOU KNOW ALL ABOUT HIM?
HIS ARMY RECORDS, YES. AND HE SEEMED LIKE A GOOD FATHER FIGURE TO YOU.
HE WAS.
BUT YOUR **REAL** FATHER, PIERRE...

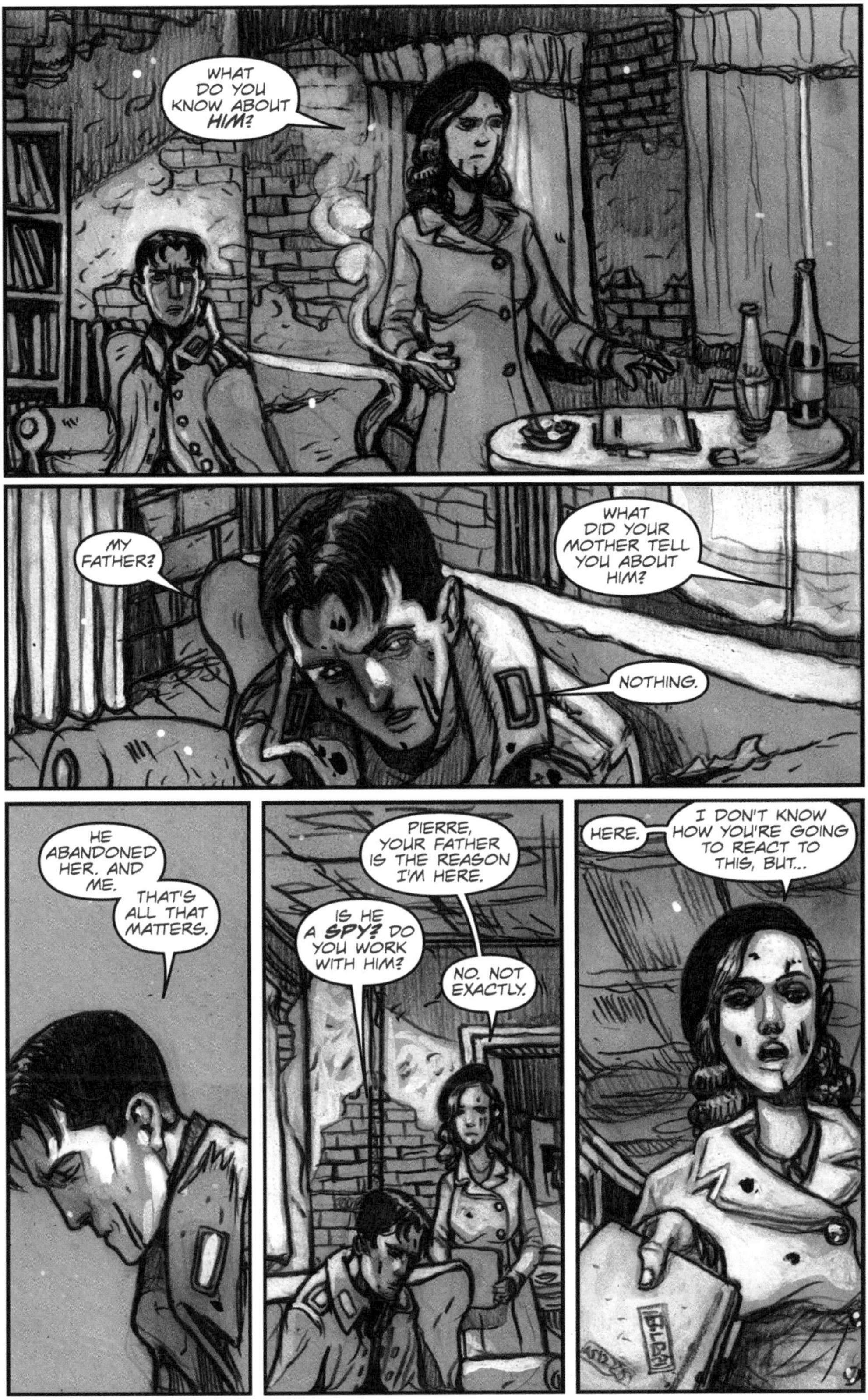
WHAT DO YOU KNOW ABOUT HIM?
MY FATHER?
WHAT DID YOUR MOTHER TELL YOU ABOUT HIM?
NOTHING.
HE ABANDONED HER. AND ME.
THAT'S ALL THAT MATTERS.
PIERRE, YOUR FATHER IS THE REASON I'M HERE.
IS HE A SPY? DO YOU WORK WITH HIM?
NO. NOT EXACTLY.
HERE.
I DON'T KNOW HOW YOU'RE GOING TO REACT TO THIS, BUT...

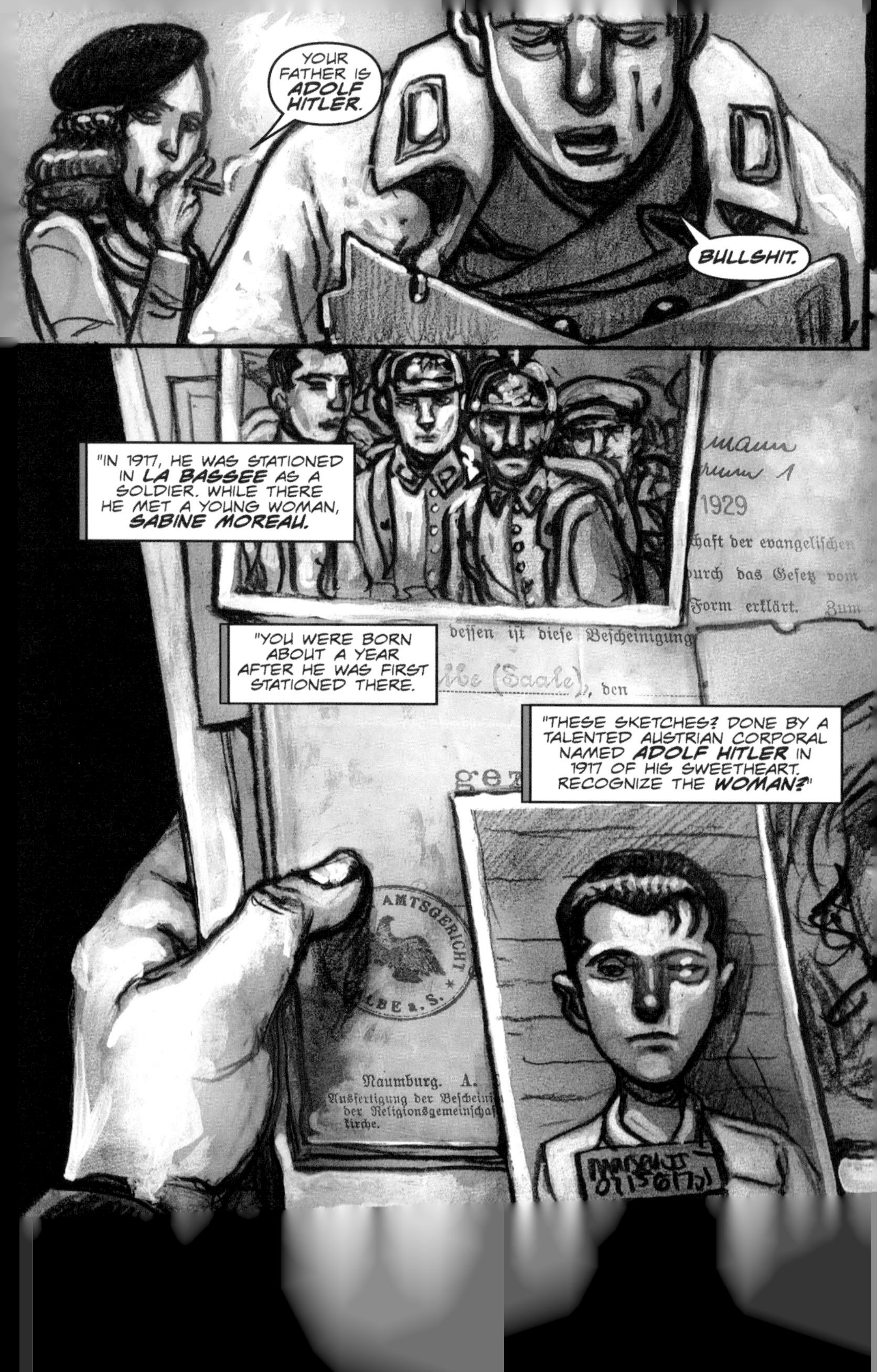
YOUR FATHER IS ADOLF HITLER.
BULLSHIT.
"IN 1917, HE WAS STATIONED IN LA BASSEE AS A SOLDIER. WHILE THERE HE MET A YOUNG WOMAN, SABINE MOREAU.
"YOU WERE BORN ABOUT A YEAR AFTER HE WAS FIRST STATIONED THERE.
"THESE SKETCHES? DONE BY A TALENTED AUSTRIAN CORPORAL NAMED ADOLF HITLER IN 1917 OF HIS SWEETHEART. RECOGNIZE THE WOMAN?"

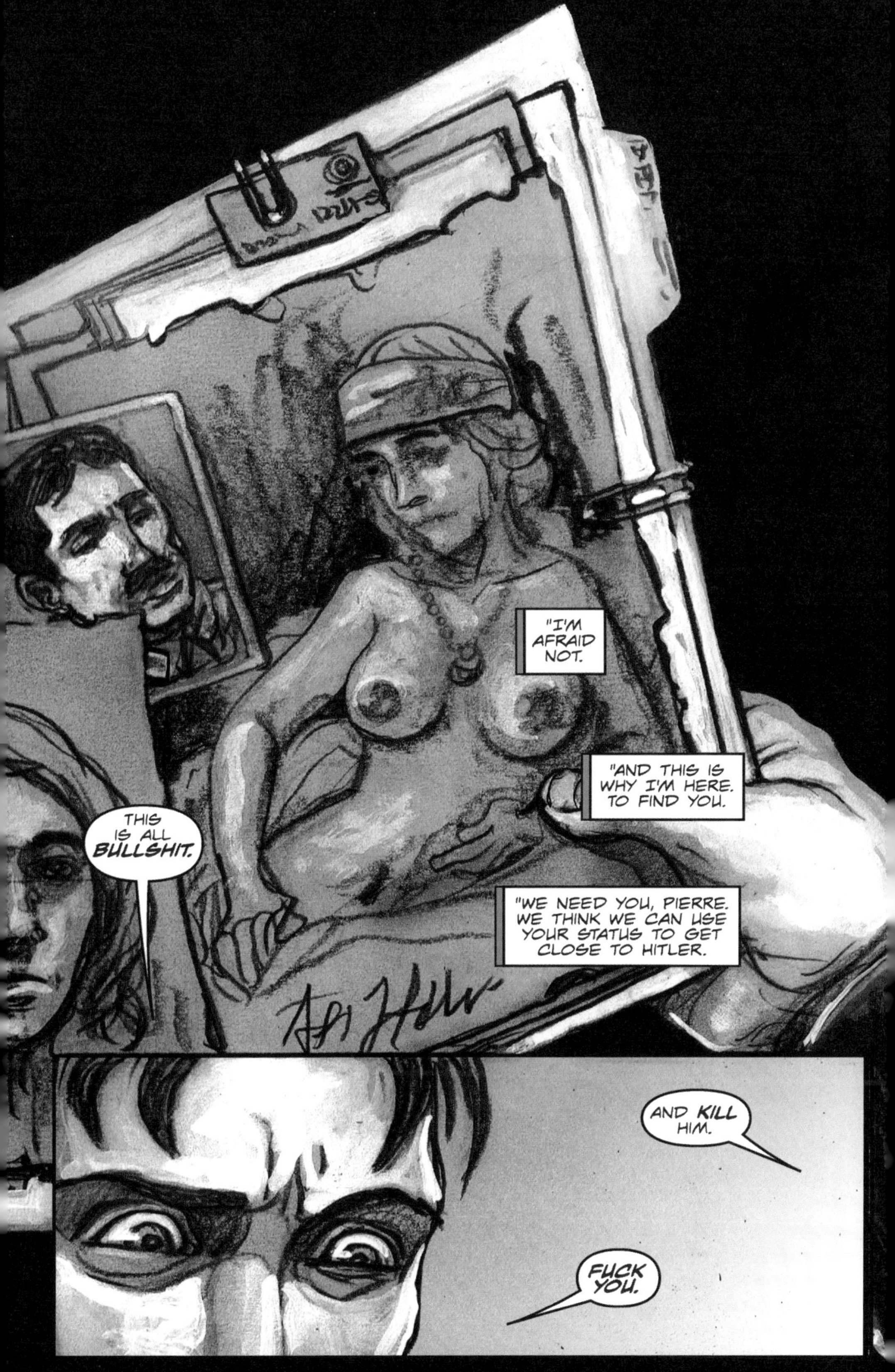
"I'M AFRAID NOT.
THIS IS ALL BULLSHIT.
"AND THIS IS WHY I'M HERE. TO FIND YOU.
"WE NEED YOU, PIERRE. WE THINK WE CAN USE YOUR STATUS TO GET CLOSE TO HITLER.
AND KILL HIM.
FUCK YOU.

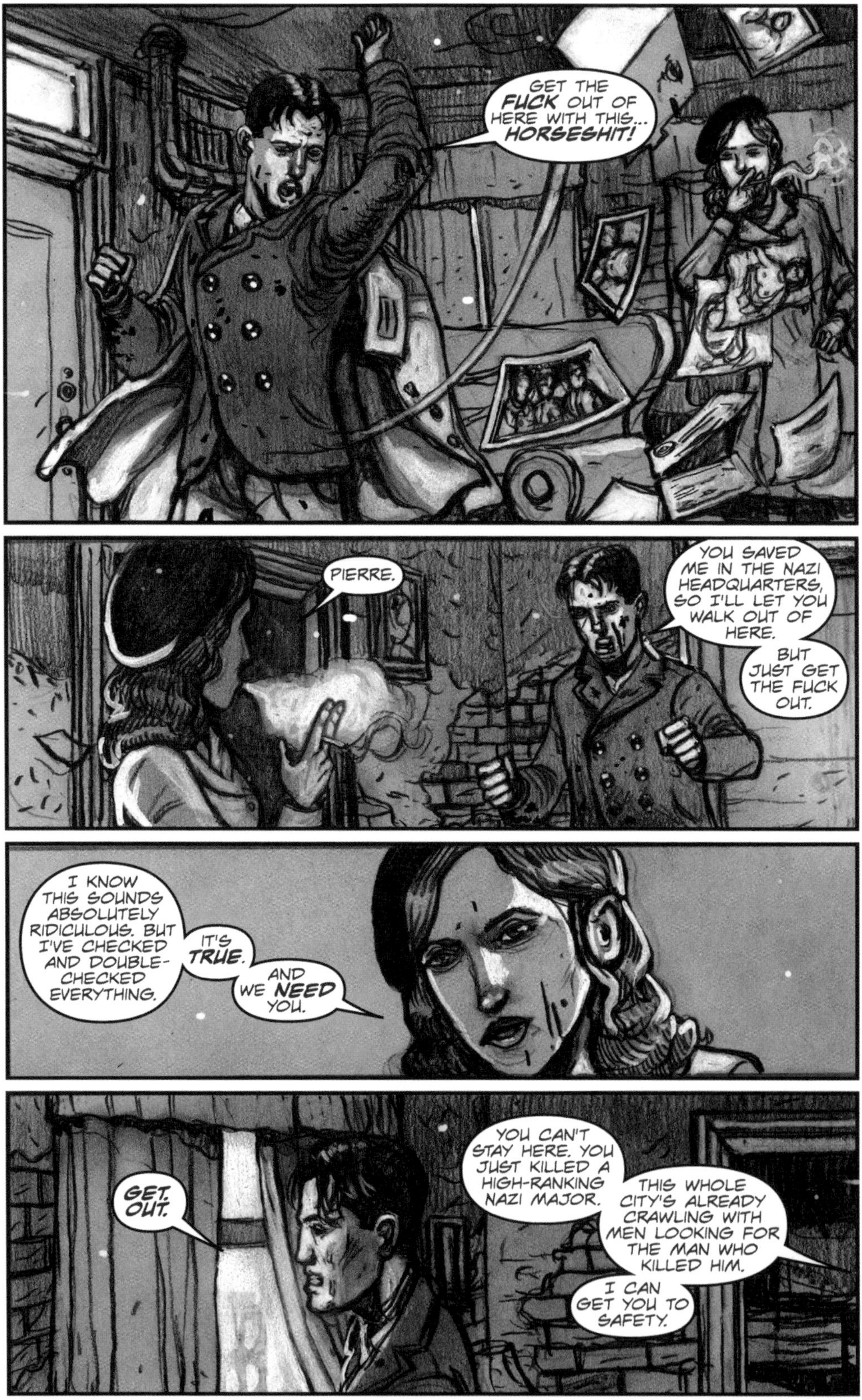
GET THE FUCK OUT OF HERE WITH THIS... HORSESHIT!
PIERRE.
YOU SAVED ME IN THE NAZI HEADQUARTERS, SO I'LL LET YOU WALK OUT OF HERE.
BUT JUST GET THE FUCK OUT.
I KNOW THIS SOUNDS ABSOLUTELY RIDICULOUS. BUT I'VE CHECKED AND DOUBLE-CHECKED EVERYTHING.
IT'S TRUE.
AND WE NEED YOU.
GET. OUT.
YOU CAN'T STAY HERE. YOU JUST KILLED A HIGH-RANKING NAZI MAJOR.
THIS WHOLE CITY'S ALREADY CRAWLING WITH MEN LOOKING FOR THE MAN WHO KILLED HIM.
I CAN GET YOU TO SAFETY.

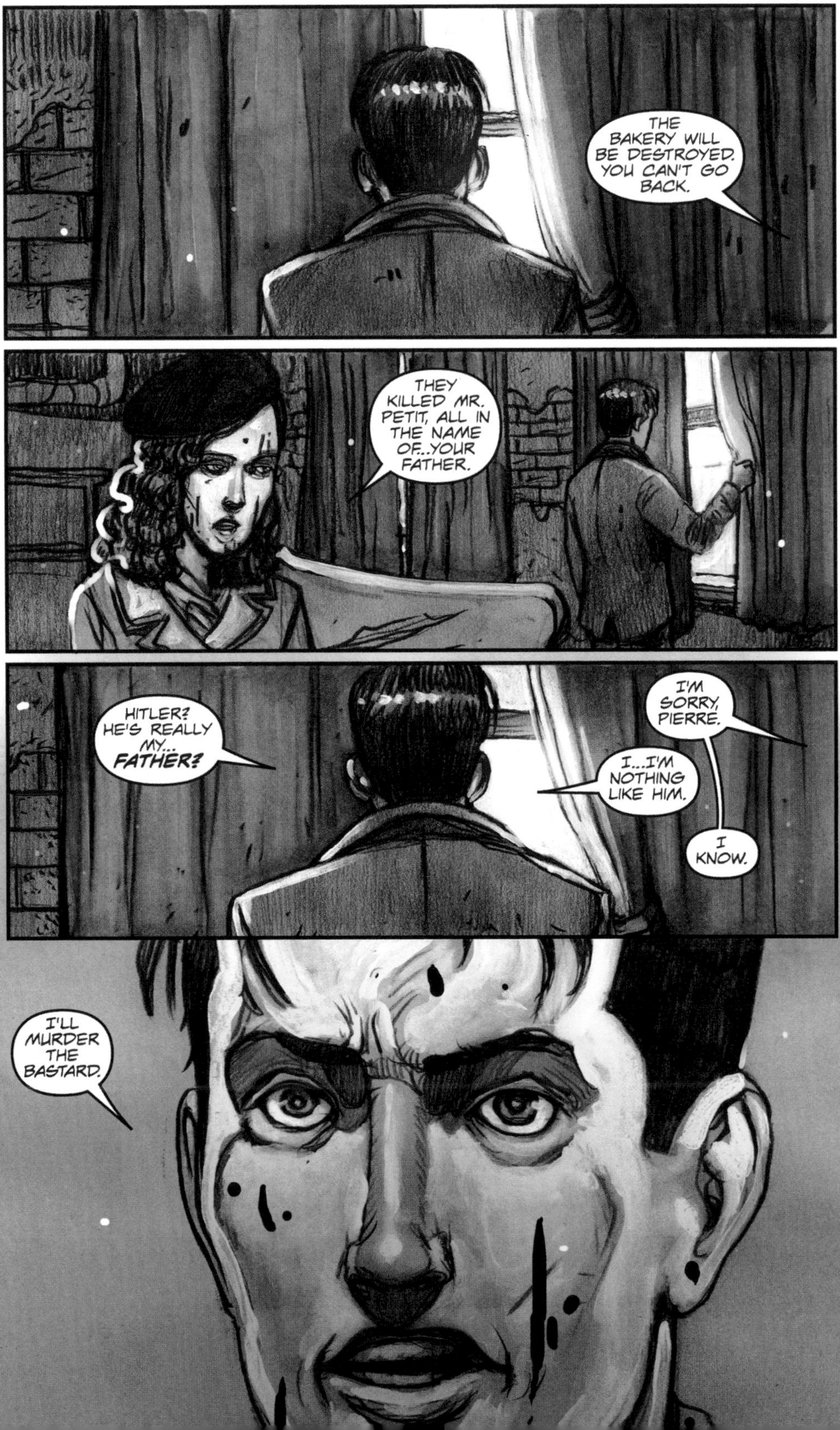
THE BAKERY WILL BE DESTROYED. YOU CAN'T GO BACK.
THEY KILLED MR. PETIT, ALL IN THE NAME OF...YOUR FATHER.
HITLER? HE'S REALLY MY... **FATHER?**
I'M SORRY, PIERRE.
I...I'M NOTHING LIKE HIM.
I KNOW.
I'LL MURDER THE BASTARD.

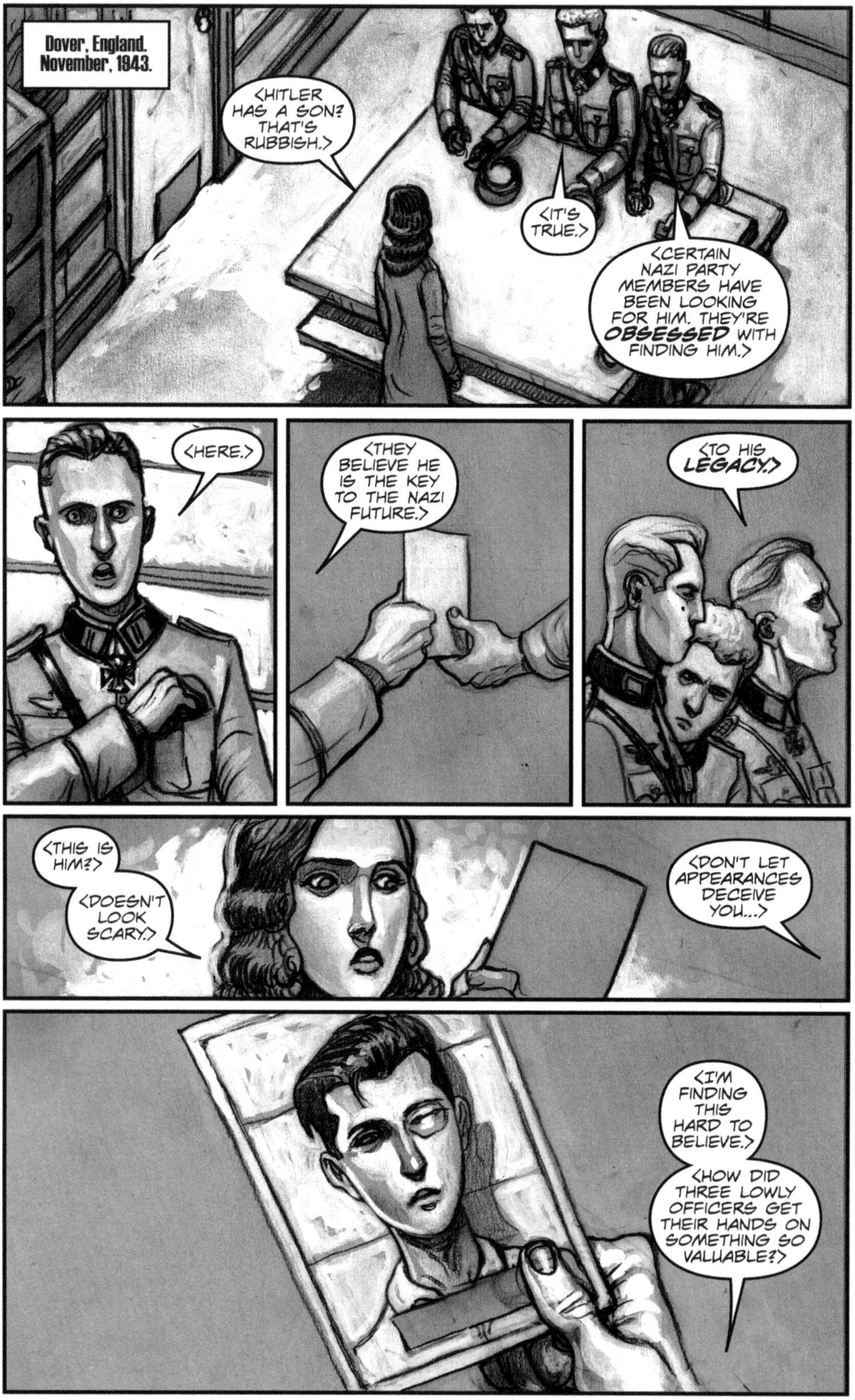
Dover, England. November, 1943.
<HITLER HAS A SON? THAT'S RUBBISH.>
<IT'S TRUE.>
<CERTAIN NAZI PARTY MEMBERS HAVE BEEN LOOKING FOR HIM. THEY'RE OBSESSED WITH FINDING HIM.>
<HERE.>
<THEY BELIEVE HE IS THE KEY TO THE NAZI FUTURE.>
<TO HIS LEGACY.>
<THIS IS HIM?>
<DOESN'T LOOK SCARY.>
<DON'T LET APPEARANCES DECEIVE YOU...>
<I'M FINDING THIS HARD TO BELIEVE.>
<HOW DID THREE LOWLY OFFICERS GET THEIR HANDS ON SOMETHING SO VALUABLE?>

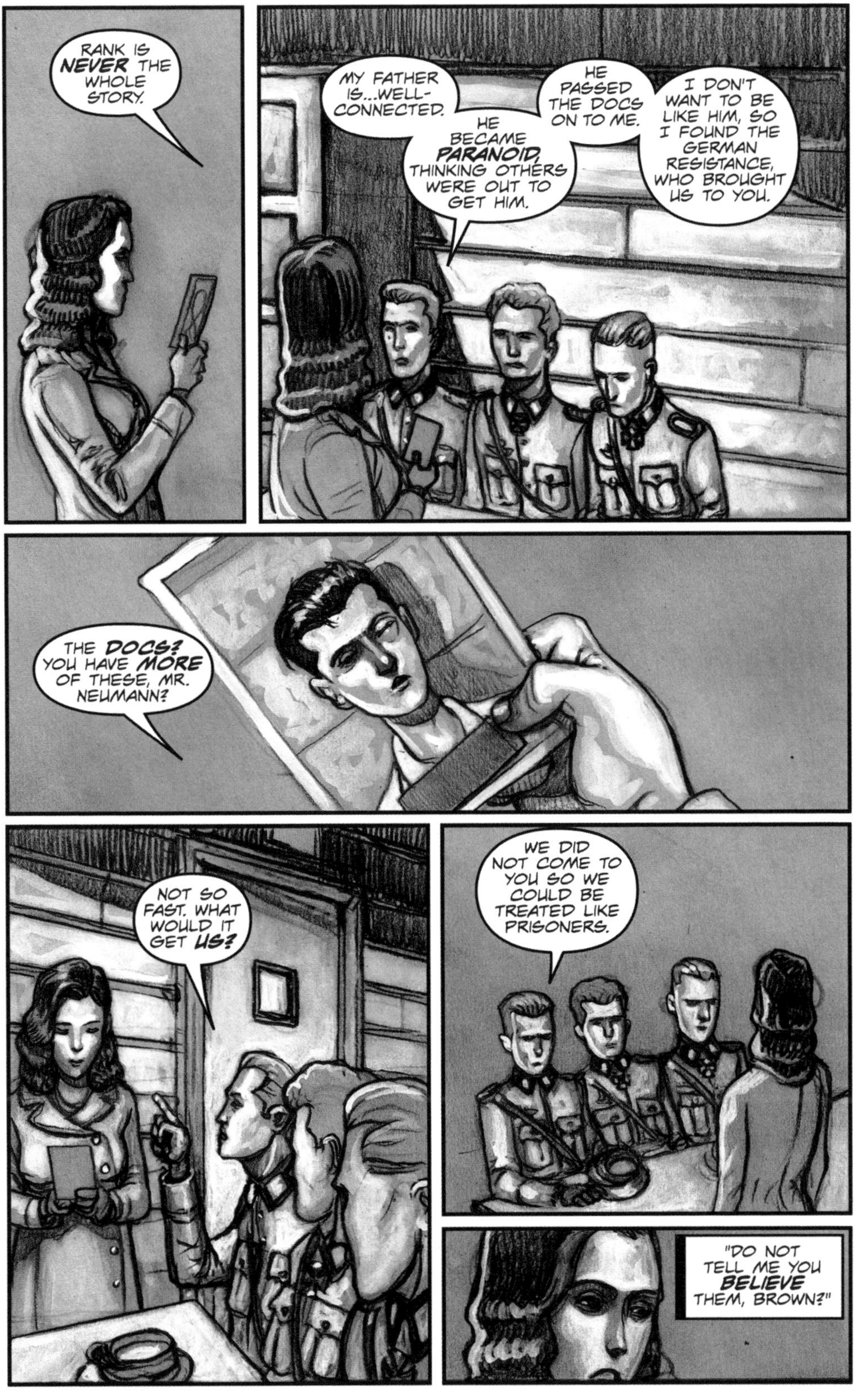
RANK IS NEVER THE WHOLE STORY.
MY FATHER IS...WELL-CONNECTED.
HE BECAME PARANOID, THINKING OTHERS WERE OUT TO GET HIM.
HE PASSED THE DOCS ON TO ME.
I DON'T WANT TO BE LIKE HIM, SO I FOUND THE GERMAN RESISTANCE, WHO BROUGHT US TO YOU.
THE DOCS? YOU HAVE MORE OF THESE, MR. NEUMANN?
NOT SO FAST. WHAT WOULD IT GET US?
WE DID NOT COME TO YOU SO WE COULD BE TREATED LIKE PRISONERS.
"DO NOT TELL ME YOU BELIEVE THEM, BROWN?"

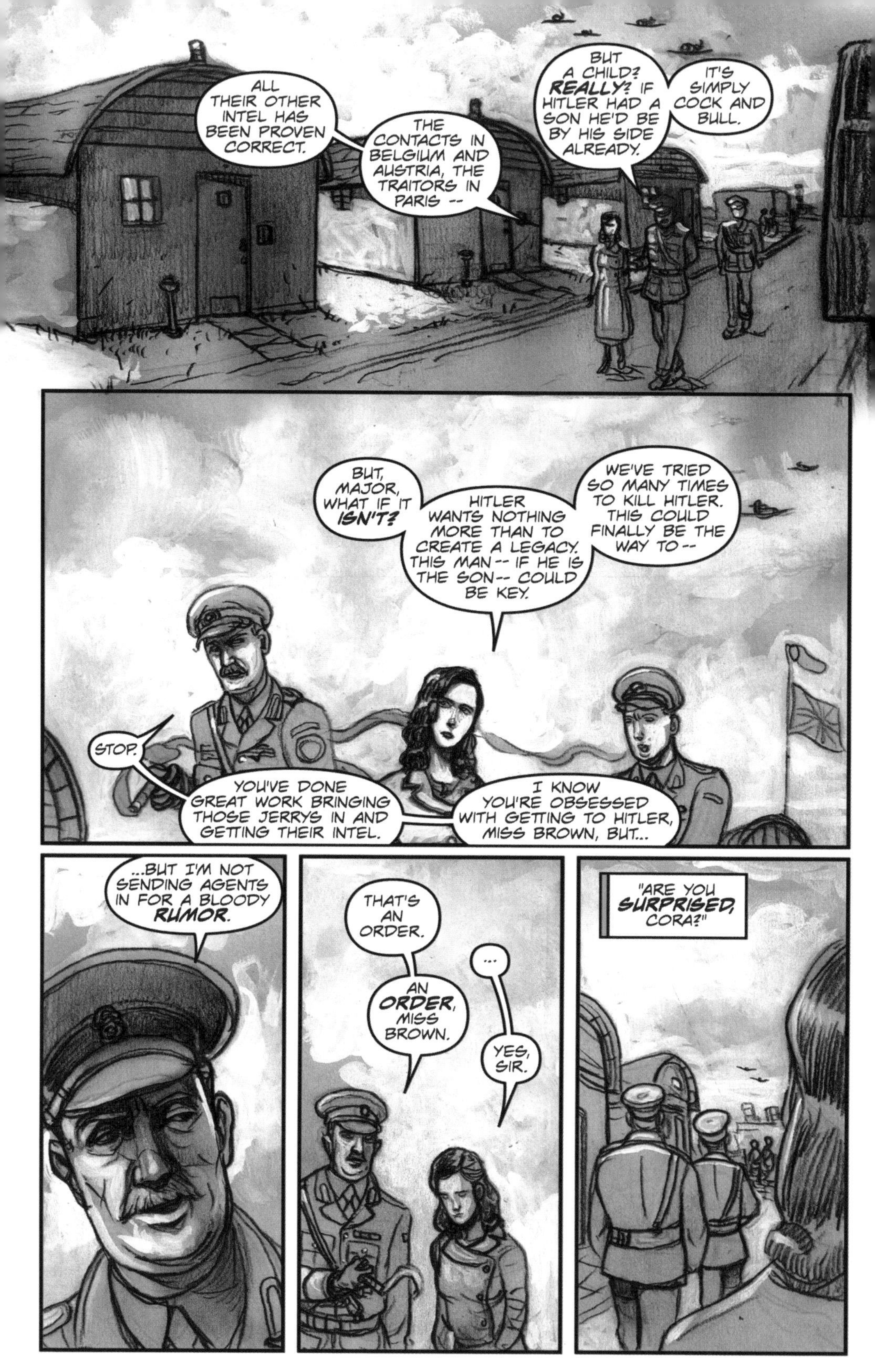
ALL THEIR OTHER INTEL HAS BEEN PROVEN CORRECT.
THE CONTACTS IN BELGIUM AND AUSTRIA, THE TRAITORS IN PARIS --
BUT A CHILD? REALLY? IF HITLER HAD A SON HE'D BE BY HIS SIDE ALREADY.
IT'S SIMPLY COCK AND BULL.
BUT, MAJOR, WHAT IF IT ISN'T?
HITLER WANTS NOTHING MORE THAN TO CREATE A LEGACY. THIS MAN -- IF HE IS THE SON -- COULD BE KEY.
WE'VE TRIED SO MANY TIMES TO KILL HITLER. THIS COULD FINALLY BE THE WAY TO --
STOP.
YOU'VE DONE GREAT WORK BRINGING THOSE JERRYS IN AND GETTING THEIR INTEL.
I KNOW YOU'RE OBSESSED WITH GETTING TO HITLER, MISS BROWN, BUT...
...BUT I'M NOT SENDING AGENTS IN FOR A BLOODY RUMOR.
THAT'S AN ORDER.
...
AN ORDER, MISS BROWN.
YES, SIR.
"ARE YOU SURPRISED, CORA?"

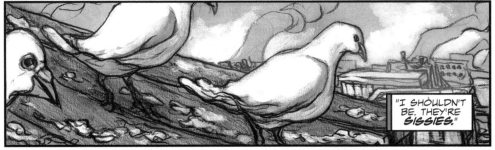

"I SHOULDN'T BE. THEY'RE *SISSIES*."

THOSE SISSIES HAVE KEPT *HERR HITLER* AT BAY SO FAR.

AS LONG AS HE'S ALIVE, HE'S STILL DANGEROUS.

WHAT SHOULD WE *DO*, RUFUS?

WE? THIS IS *YOU*, CORA. *I'M* NOT INTERESTED.

OSS DOESN'T MEDDLE IN BRITISH OPERATIONS.

AND I HAPPEN TO AGREE WITH YOUR OFFICE. IT'S...TOO TALL A TALE.

DIDN'T YOU ONCE TELL ME THAT EVERY BIG LIE HAS SOME TRUTH TO IT?

WELL, THIS IS A BIG ONE. THE *BIGGEST* OF ONES.

AND IF IT'S *TRUE*, WE CAN USE HIM.

AS A TROJAN HORSE, RIGHT?

WELL...I'VE HEARD YOUR SIDE IS PUTTING TOGETHER AN OPERATION UNDER THE NAME OF *FOXLEY*.

HE COULD BE ROLLED INTO IT.

THAT'S PERFECT. BUT BE CAREFUL, RUFUS...

...YOU SOUND *INTERESTED*.

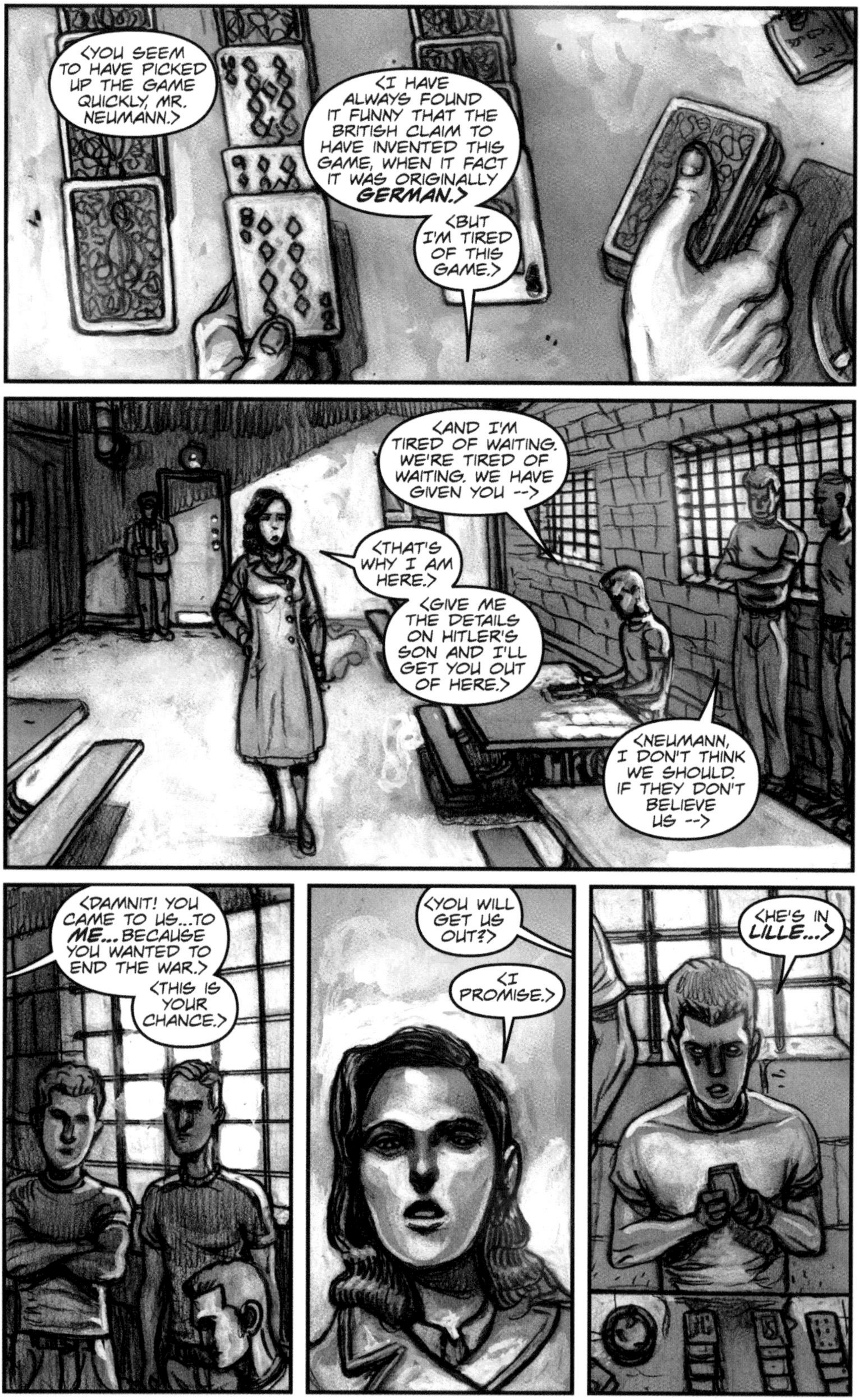
<YOU SEEM TO HAVE PICKED UP THE GAME QUICKLY, MR. NEUMANN.>
<I HAVE ALWAYS FOUND IT FUNNY THAT THE BRITISH CLAIM TO HAVE INVENTED THIS GAME, WHEN IT FACT IT WAS ORIGINALLY **GERMAN.**>
<BUT I'M TIRED OF THIS GAME.>
<AND I'M TIRED OF WAITING. WE'RE TIRED OF WAITING. WE HAVE GIVEN YOU -->
<THAT'S WHY I AM HERE.>
<GIVE ME THE DETAILS ON HITLER'S SON AND I'LL GET YOU OUT OF HERE.>
<NEUMANN, I DON'T THINK WE SHOULD. IF THEY DON'T BELIEVE US -->
<DAMNIT! YOU CAME TO US...TO **ME...** BECAUSE YOU WANTED TO END THE WAR.>
<THIS IS YOUR CHANCE.>
<YOU WILL GET US OUT?>
<I PROMISE.>
<HE'S IN **LILLE...**>

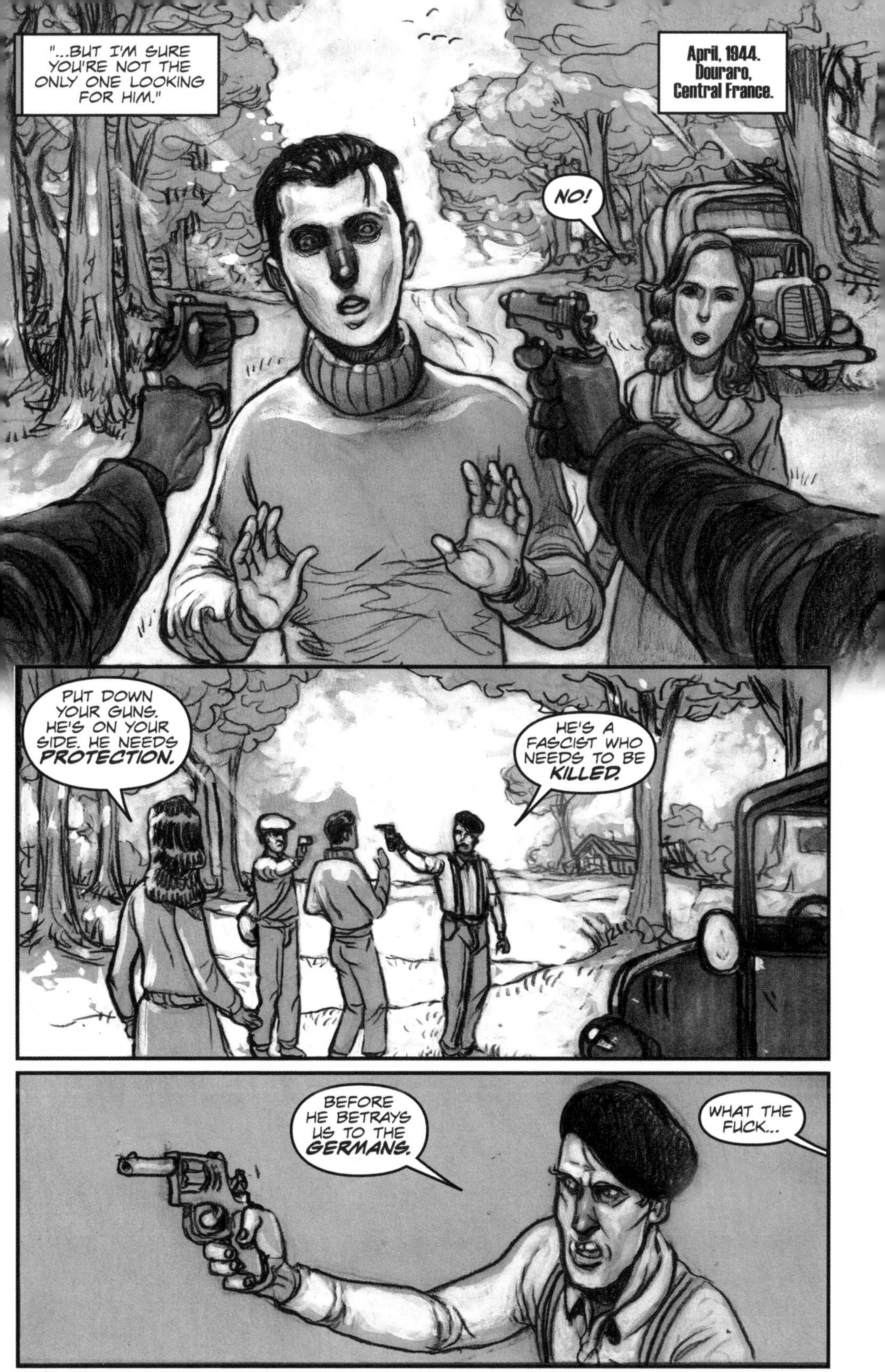
"...BUT I'M SURE YOU'RE NOT THE ONLY ONE LOOKING FOR HIM."
April, 1944. Douraro, Central France.
NO!
PUT DOWN YOUR GUNS. HE'S ON YOUR SIDE. HE NEEDS PROTECTION.
HE'S A FASCIST WHO NEEDS TO BE KILLED.
BEFORE HE BETRAYS US TO THE GERMANS.
WHAT THE FUCK...

...IS GOING ON HERE?

THIS *COWARD* IS HIDING BEHIND HIS GUN.

FUCK YOU, NAZI.

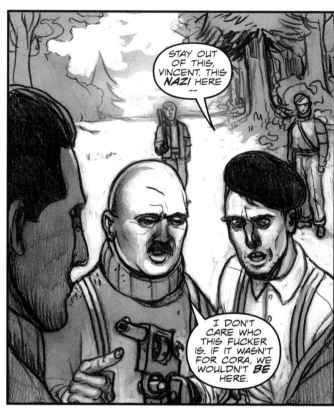

STAY OUT OF THIS, VINCENT. THIS *NAZI* HERE --

I DON'T CARE WHO THIS FUCKER IS. IF IT WASN'T FOR CORA, WE WOULDN'T *BE* HERE.

WE'D HAVE NO WEAPONS, LIKE THE ONE IN YOUR HAND.

SO, NO, I'M *NOT* STAYING THE FUCK OUT OF THIS.

NOW DON'T YOU HAVE A RUN TO MAKE?

YES, SIR.

THEN GO.

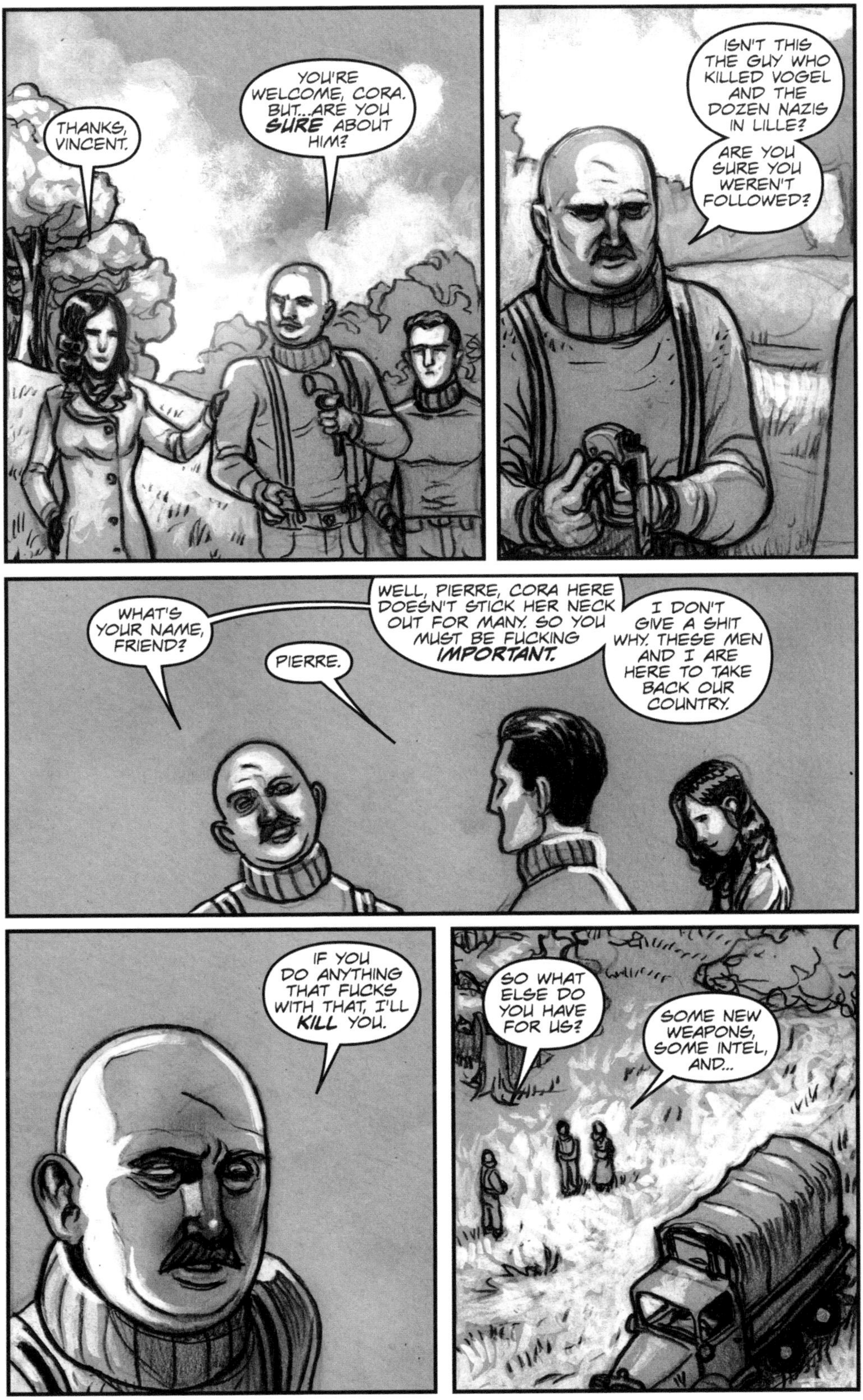
THANKS, VINCENT.
YOU'RE WELCOME, CORA. BUT...ARE YOU SURE ABOUT HIM?
ISN'T THIS THE GUY WHO KILLED VOGEL AND THE DOZEN NAZIS IN LILLE?
ARE YOU SURE YOU WEREN'T FOLLOWED?
WHAT'S YOUR NAME, FRIEND?
PIERRE.
WELL, PIERRE, CORA HERE DOESN'T STICK HER NECK OUT FOR MANY. SO YOU MUST BE FUCKING IMPORTANT.
I DON'T GIVE A SHIT WHY. THESE MEN AND I ARE HERE TO TAKE BACK OUR COUNTRY.
IF YOU DO ANYTHING THAT FUCKS WITH THAT, I'LL KILL YOU.
SO WHAT ELSE DO YOU HAVE FOR US?
SOME NEW WEAPONS, SOME INTEL, AND...

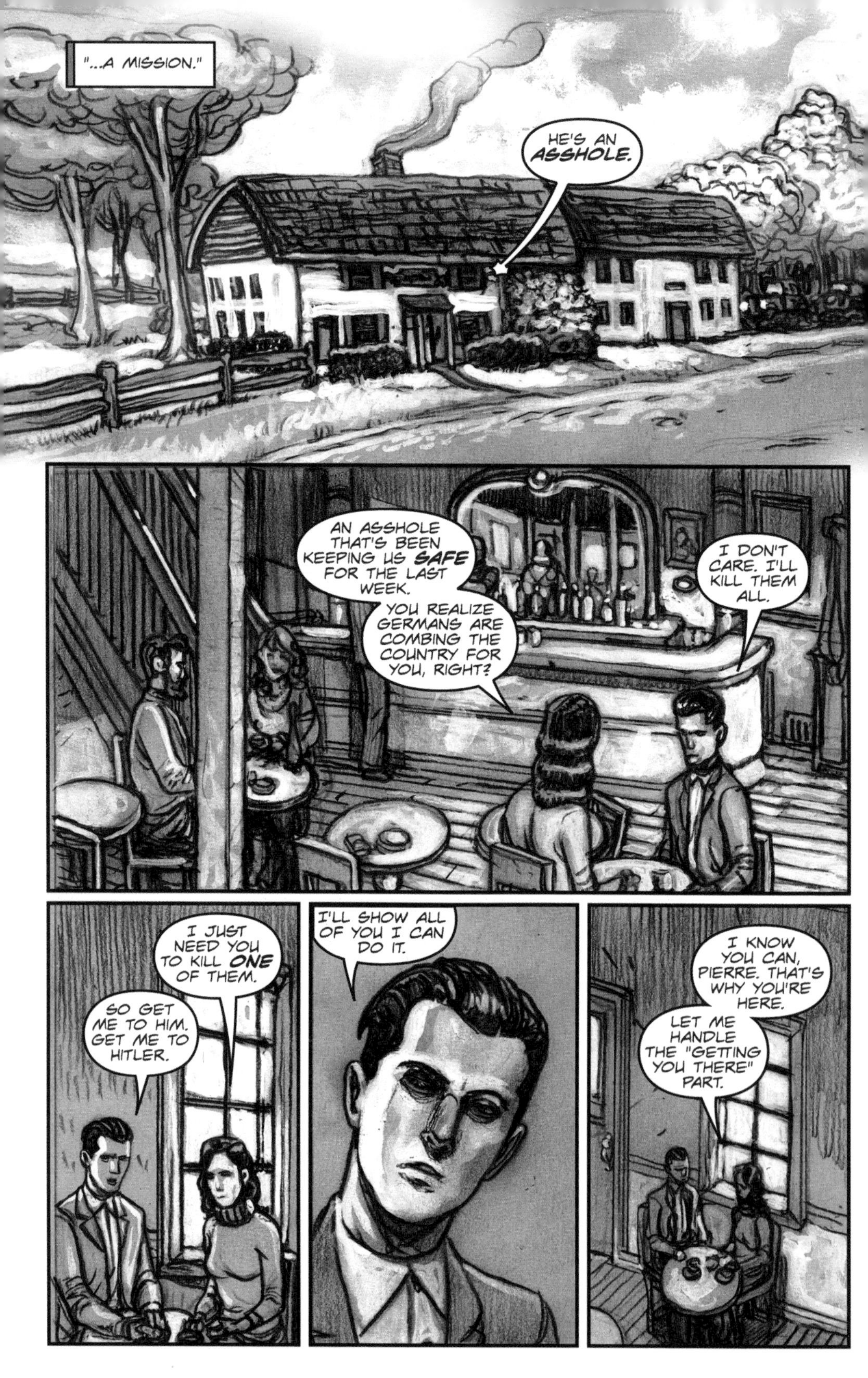
"...A MISSION."
HE'S AN ASSHOLE.
AN ASSHOLE THAT'S BEEN KEEPING US SAFE FOR THE LAST WEEK.
YOU REALIZE GERMANS ARE COMBING THE COUNTRY FOR YOU, RIGHT?
I DON'T CARE. I'LL KILL THEM ALL.
I JUST NEED YOU TO KILL ONE OF THEM.
SO GET ME TO HIM. GET ME TO HITLER.
I'LL SHOW ALL OF YOU I CAN DO IT.
I KNOW YOU CAN, PIERRE. THAT'S WHY YOU'RE HERE.
LET ME HANDLE THE "GETTING YOU THERE" PART.

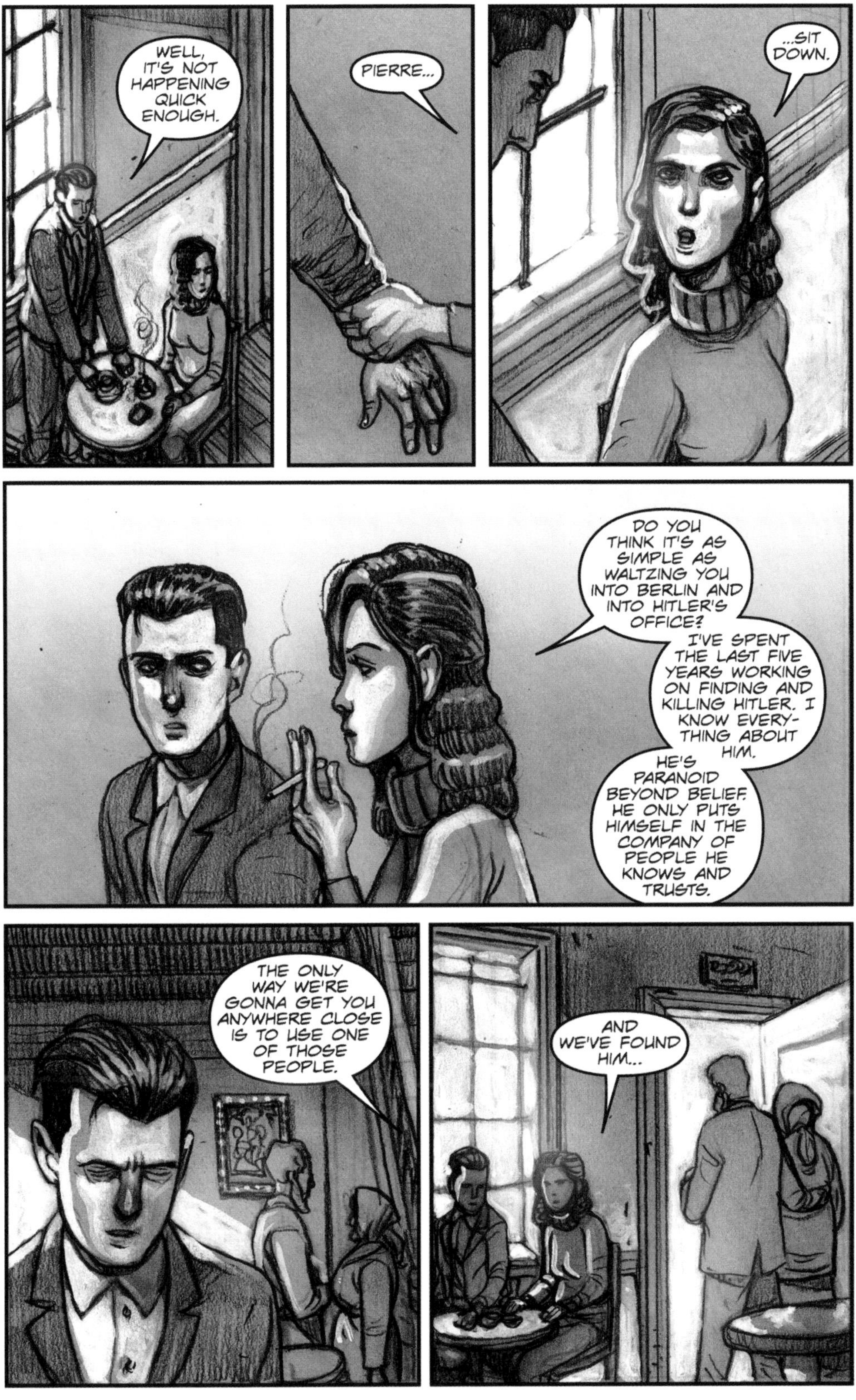
WELL, IT'S NOT HAPPENING QUICK ENOUGH.
PIERRE...
...SIT DOWN.
DO YOU THINK IT'S AS SIMPLE AS WALTZING YOU INTO BERLIN AND INTO HITLER'S OFFICE?
I'VE SPENT THE LAST FIVE YEARS WORKING ON FINDING AND KILLING HITLER. I KNOW EVERY-THING ABOUT HIM.
HE'S PARANOID BEYOND BELIEF. HE ONLY PUTS HIMSELF IN THE COMPANY OF PEOPLE HE KNOWS AND TRUSTS.
THE ONLY WAY WE'RE GONNA GET YOU ANYWHERE CLOSE IS TO USE ONE OF THOSE PEOPLE.
AND WE'VE FOUND HIM...

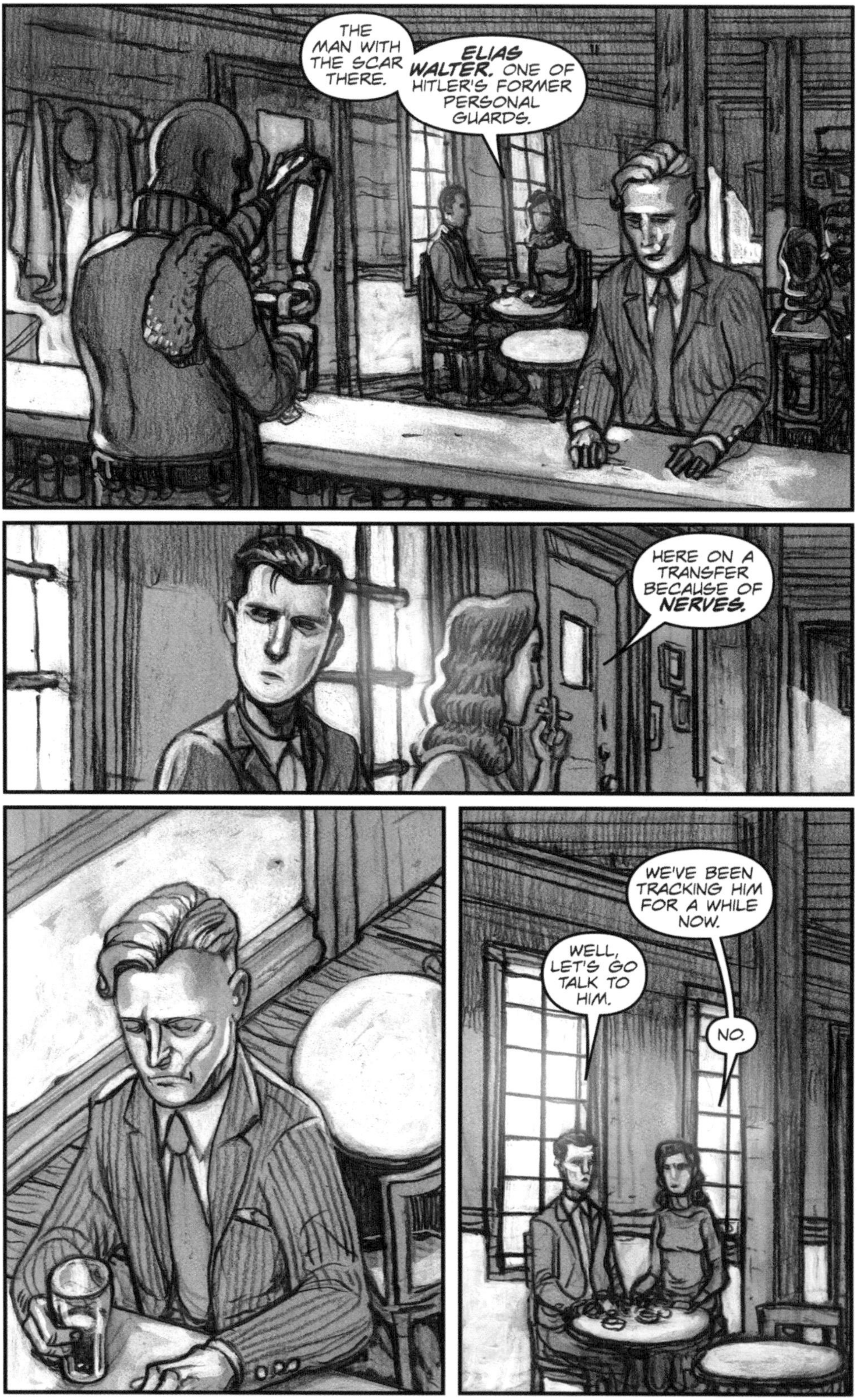
THE MAN WITH THE SCAR THERE.
ELIAS WALTER. ONE OF HITLER'S FORMER PERSONAL GUARDS.
HERE ON A TRANSFER BECAUSE OF NERVES.
WE'VE BEEN TRACKING HIM FOR A WHILE NOW.
WELL, LET'S GO TALK TO HIM.
NO.

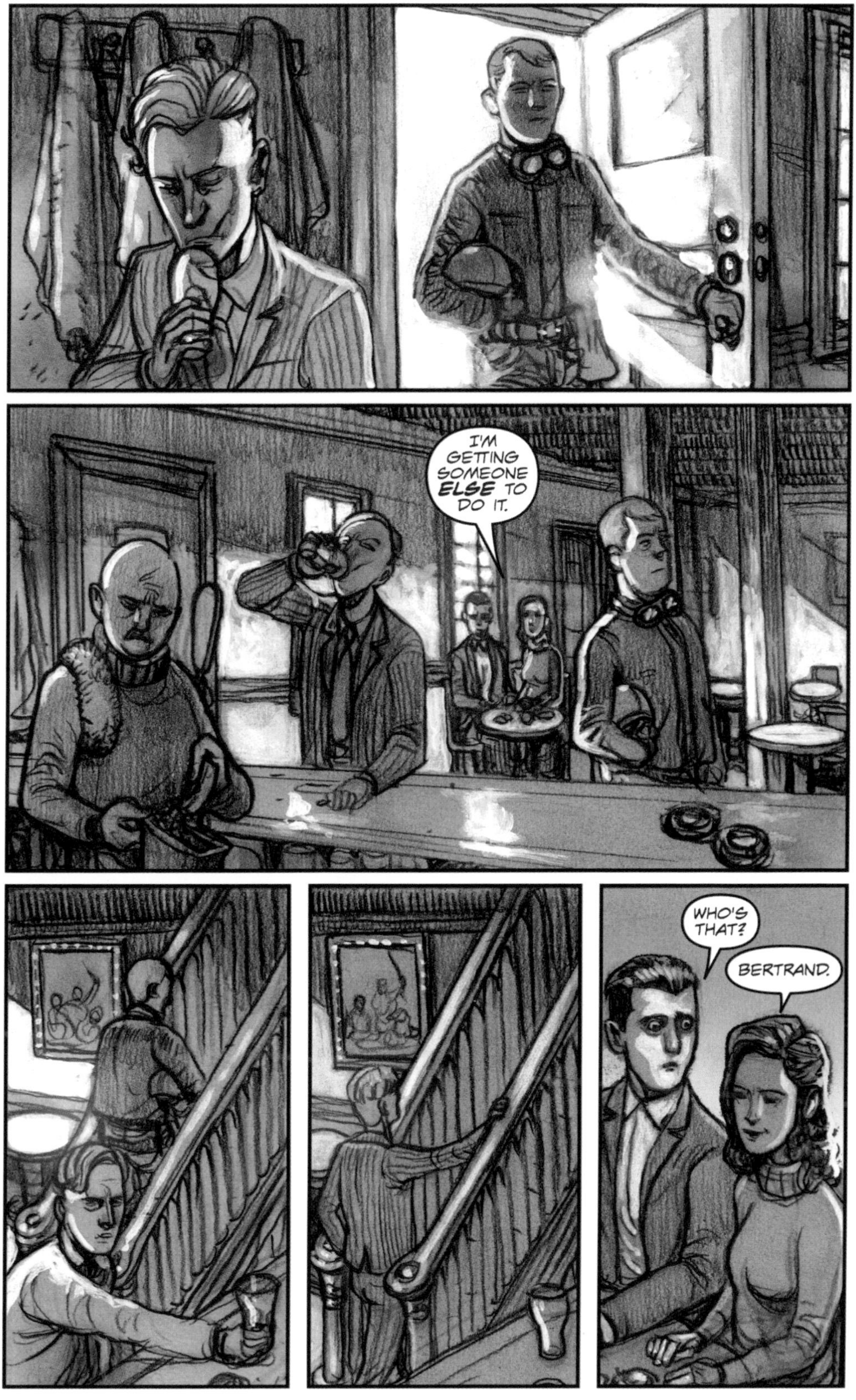
I'M GETTING SOMEONE ELSE TO DO IT.
WHO'S THAT?
BERTRAND.

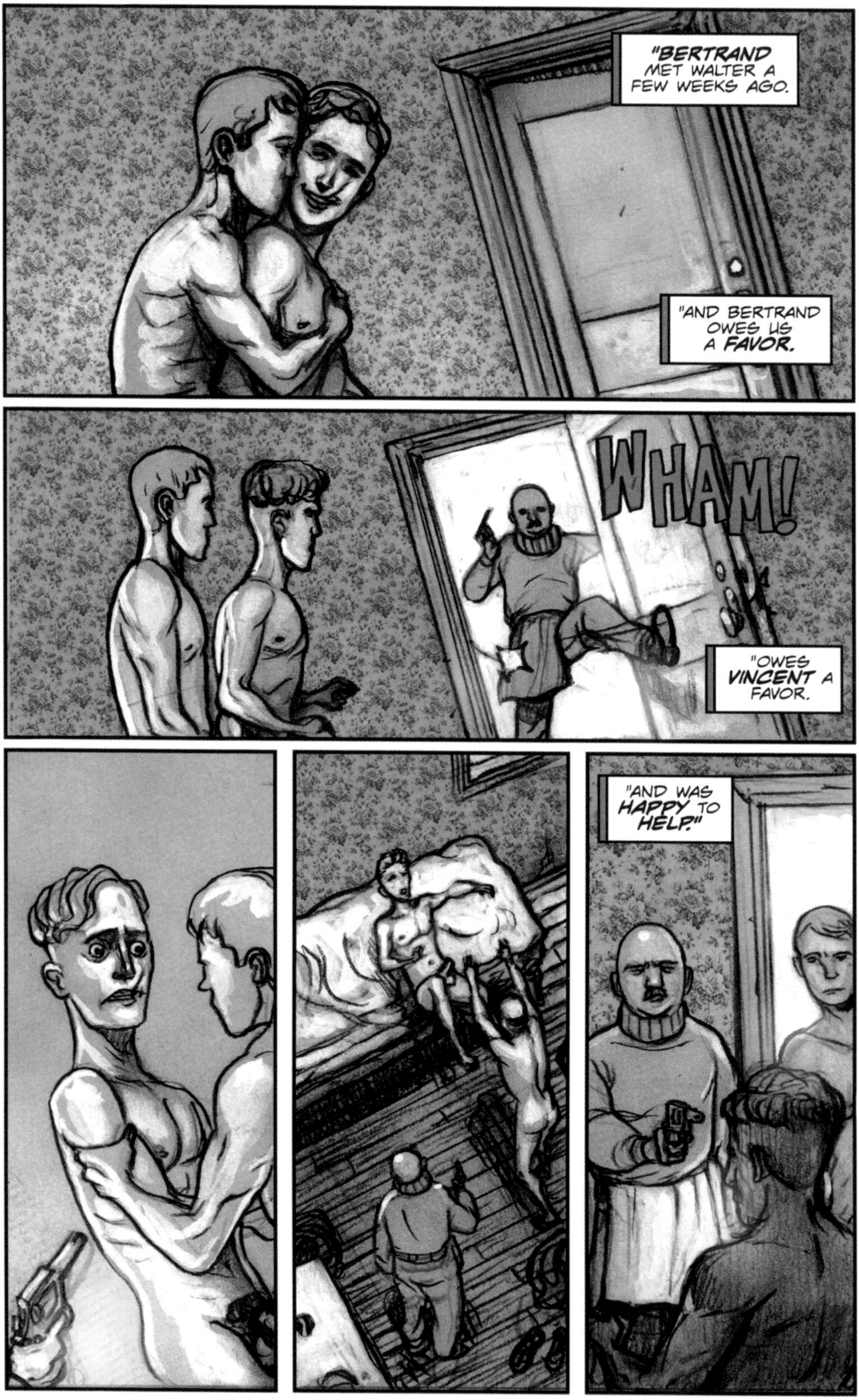
"BERTRAND MET WALTER A FEW WEEKS AGO.
"AND BERTRAND OWES US A FAVOR.
WHAM!
"OWES VINCENT A FAVOR.
"AND WAS HAPPY TO HELP."

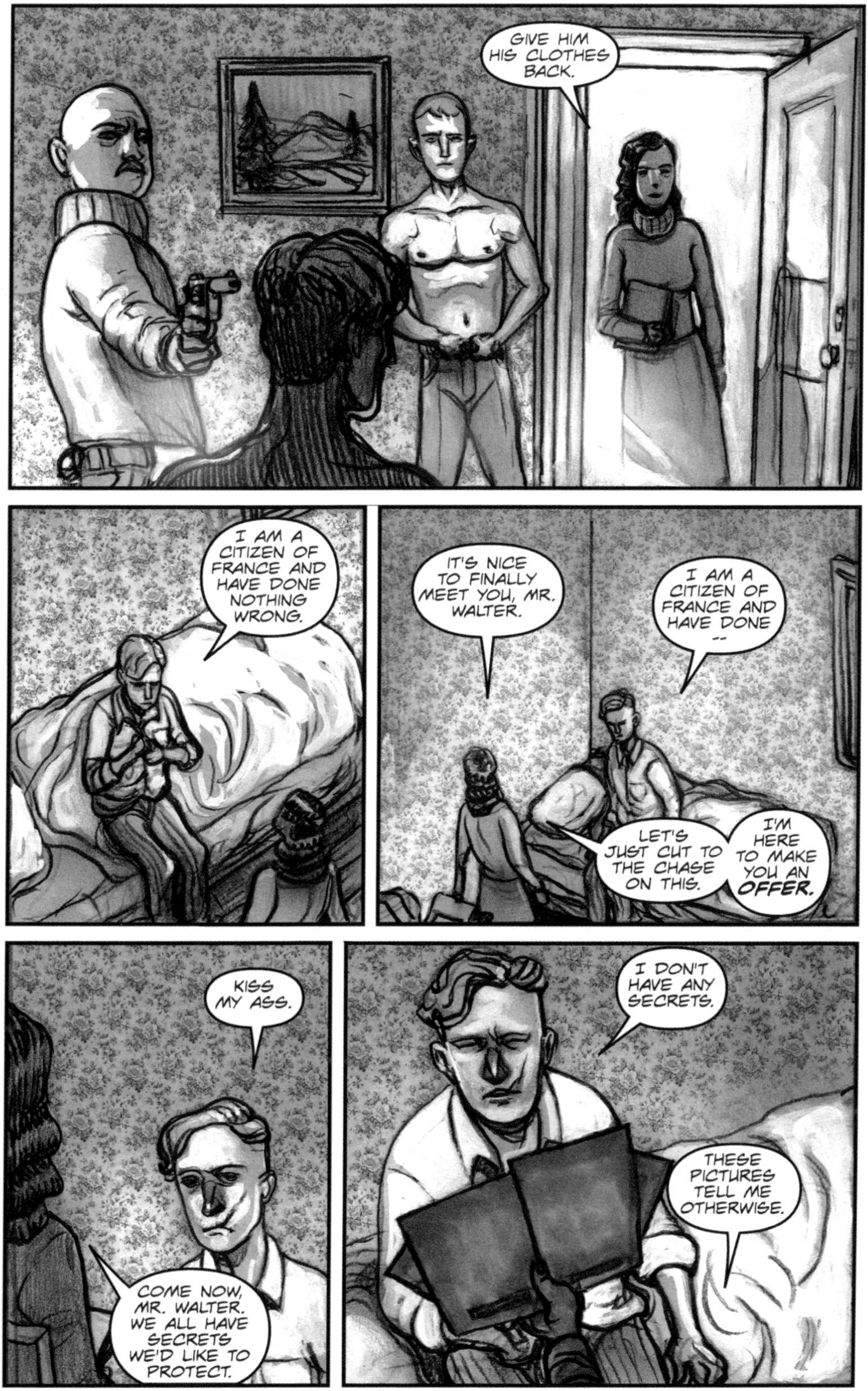
GIVE HIM HIS CLOTHES BACK.
I AM A CITIZEN OF FRANCE AND HAVE DONE NOTHING WRONG.
IT'S NICE TO FINALLY MEET YOU, MR. WALTER.
I AM A CITIZEN OF FRANCE AND HAVE DONE --
LET'S JUST CUT TO THE CHASE ON THIS.
I'M HERE TO MAKE YOU AN OFFER.
KISS MY ASS.
COME NOW, MR. WALTER. WE ALL HAVE SECRETS WE'D LIKE TO PROTECT.
I DON'T HAVE ANY SECRETS.
THESE PICTURES TELL ME OTHERWISE.

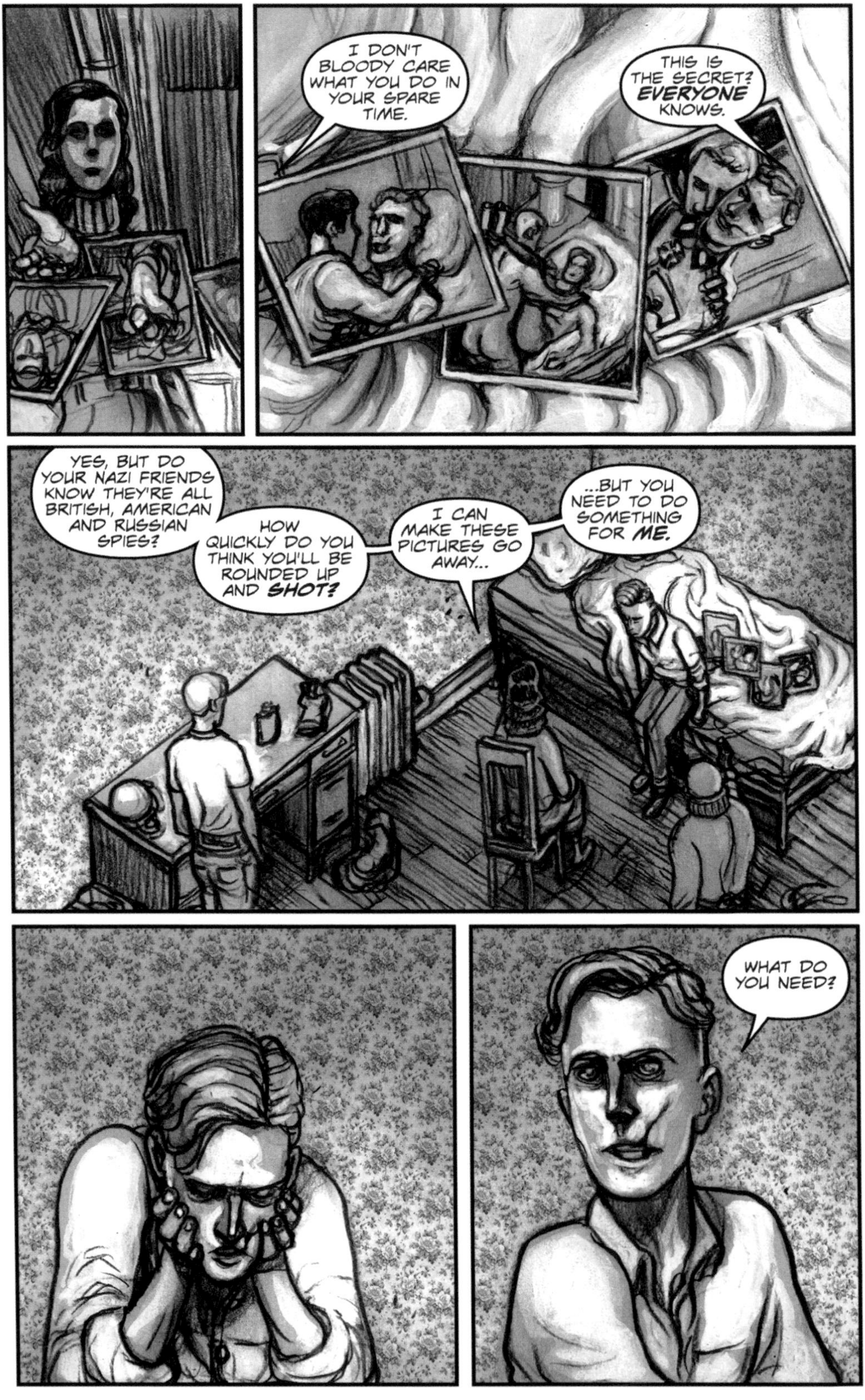
I DON'T BLOODY CARE WHAT YOU DO IN YOUR SPARE TIME.
THIS IS THE SECRET? EVERYONE KNOWS.
YES, BUT DO YOUR NAZI FRIENDS KNOW THEY'RE ALL BRITISH, AMERICAN AND RUSSIAN SPIES?
HOW QUICKLY DO YOU THINK YOU'LL BE ROUNDED UP AND SHOT?
I CAN MAKE THESE PICTURES GO AWAY...
...BUT YOU NEED TO DO SOMETHING FOR ME.
WHAT DO YOU NEED?

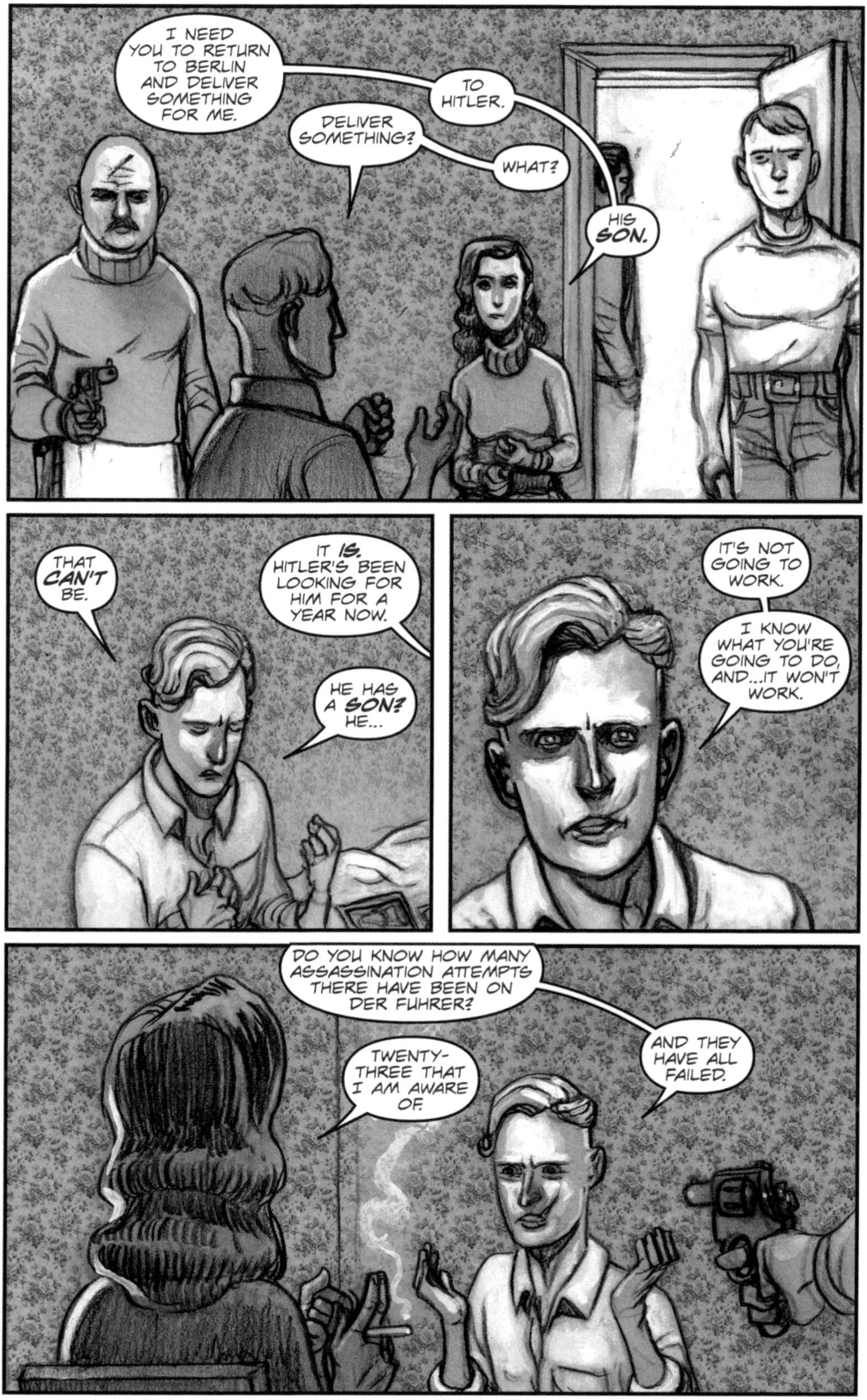

I NEED YOU TO RETURN TO BERLIN AND DELIVER SOMETHING FOR ME.
DELIVER SOMETHING?
WHAT?
TO HITLER.
HIS **SON.**
THAT **CAN'T** BE.
IT **IS.** HITLER'S BEEN LOOKING FOR HIM FOR A YEAR NOW.
HE HAS A **SON?** HE...
IT'S NOT GOING TO WORK.
I KNOW WHAT YOU'RE GOING TO DO, AND...IT WON'T WORK.
DO YOU KNOW HOW MANY ASSASSINATION ATTEMPTS THERE HAVE BEEN ON DER FUHRER?
TWENTY-THREE THAT I AM AWARE OF.
AND THEY HAVE ALL FAILED.

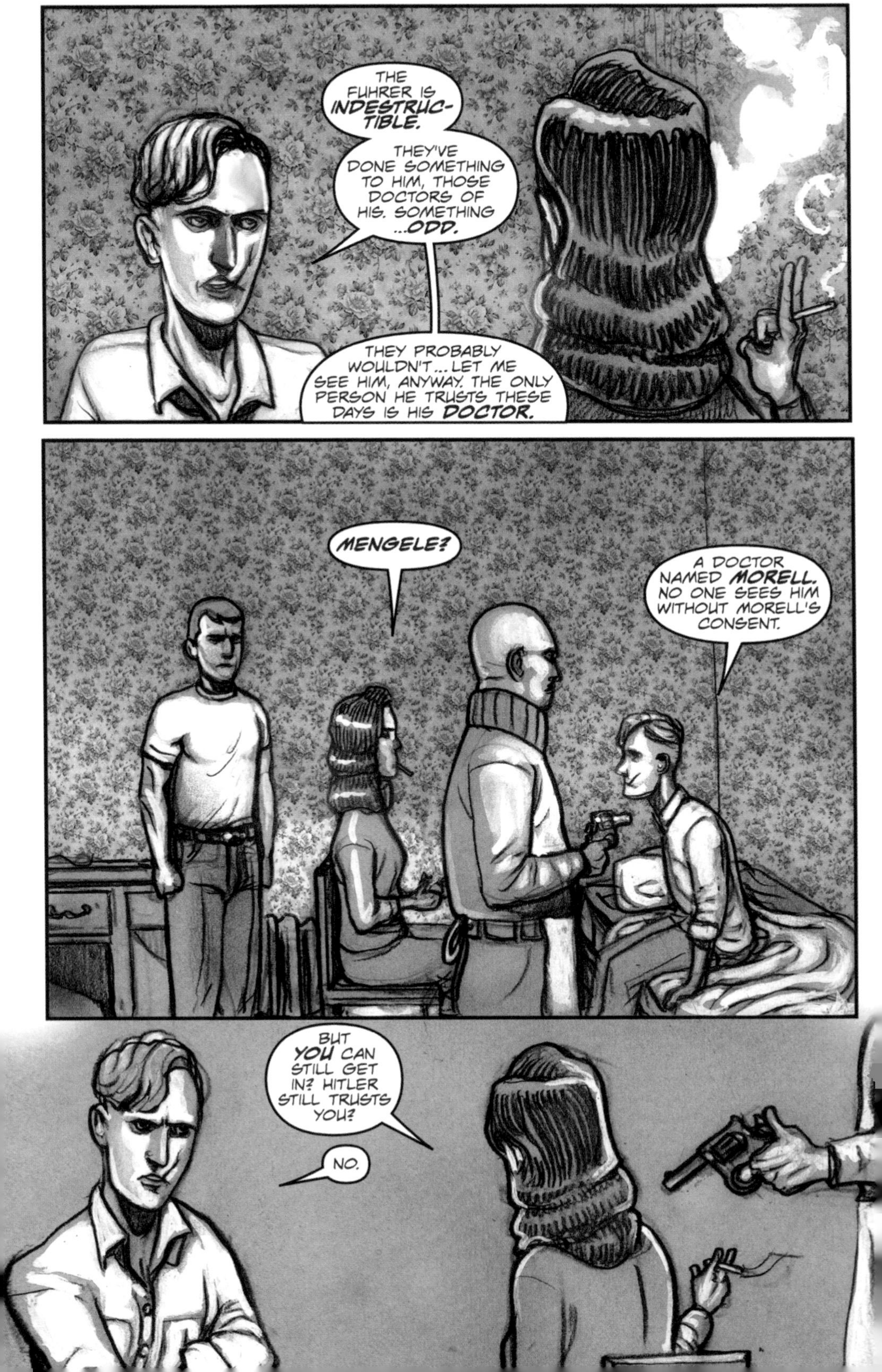
THE FUHRER IS INDESTRUCTIBLE.
THEY'VE DONE SOMETHING TO HIM, THOSE DOCTORS OF HIS. SOMETHING ...ODD.
THEY PROBABLY WOULDN'T... LET ME SEE HIM, ANYWAY. THE ONLY PERSON HE TRUSTS THESE DAYS IS HIS DOCTOR.
MENGELE?
A DOCTOR NAMED MORELL. NO ONE SEES HIM WITHOUT MORELL'S CONSENT.
BUT YOU CAN STILL GET IN? HITLER STILL TRUSTS YOU?
NO.

THIS IS THE MAN? HITLER'S *SON?*

LOOK AT HIM.

HITLER WOULDN'T WANT TO RECOGNIZE A FRENCH BASTARD SON.

LET ME GUESS: YOUR MOTHER WAS SOME FRENCH *WHORE?*

FUCK YOU, NAZI!

KRAK!

YOU BETTER FUCKIN' TAKE ME TO HIM!

WHAT THE FUCK?!

I'VE HAD ENOUGH OF HIS BULLSHIT ABOUT DOCTORS.

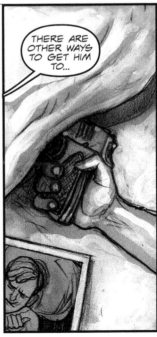

THERE ARE OTHER WAYS TO GET HIM TO...

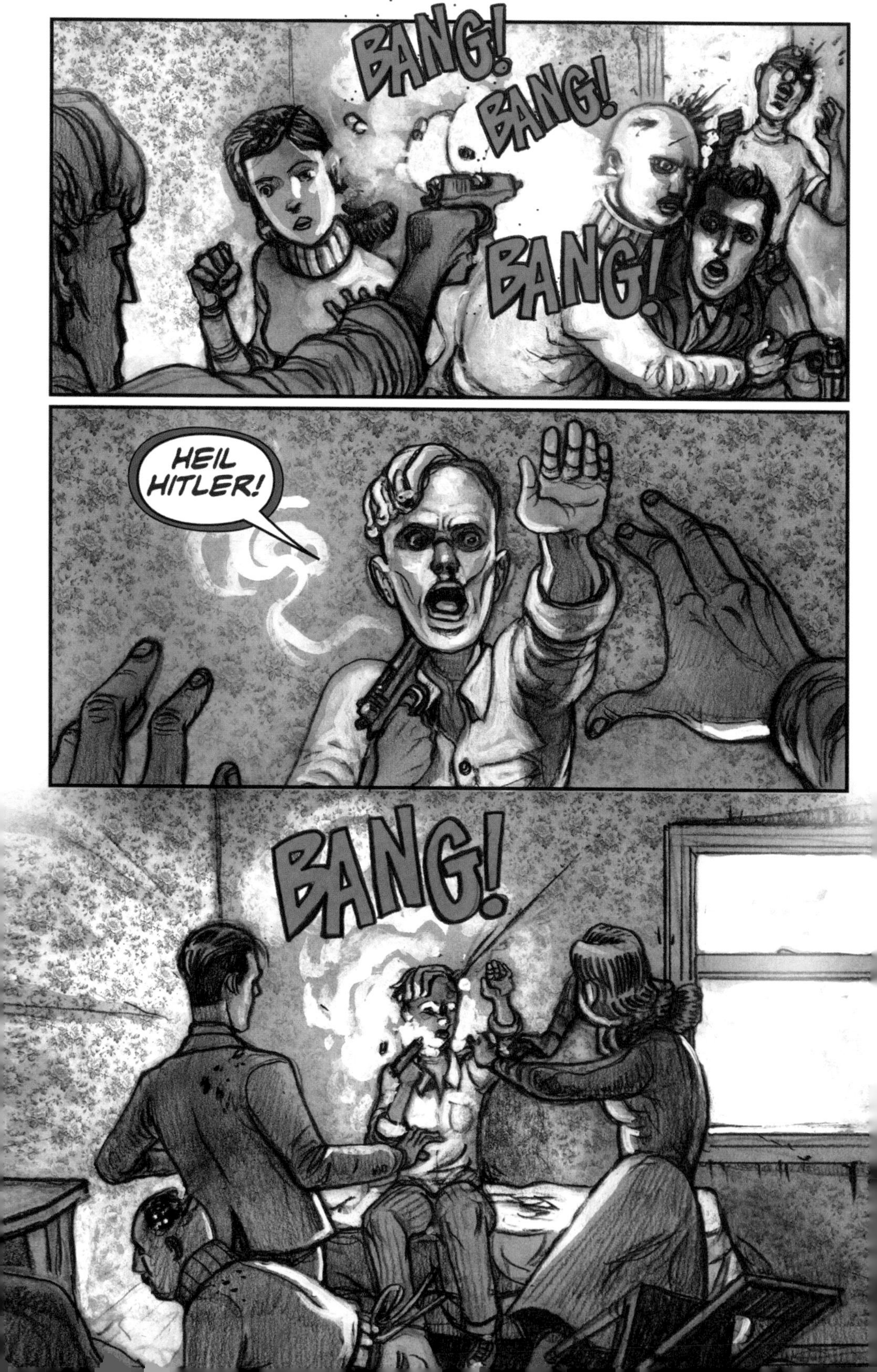
BANG!
BANG!
BANG!
HEIL HITLER!
BANG!

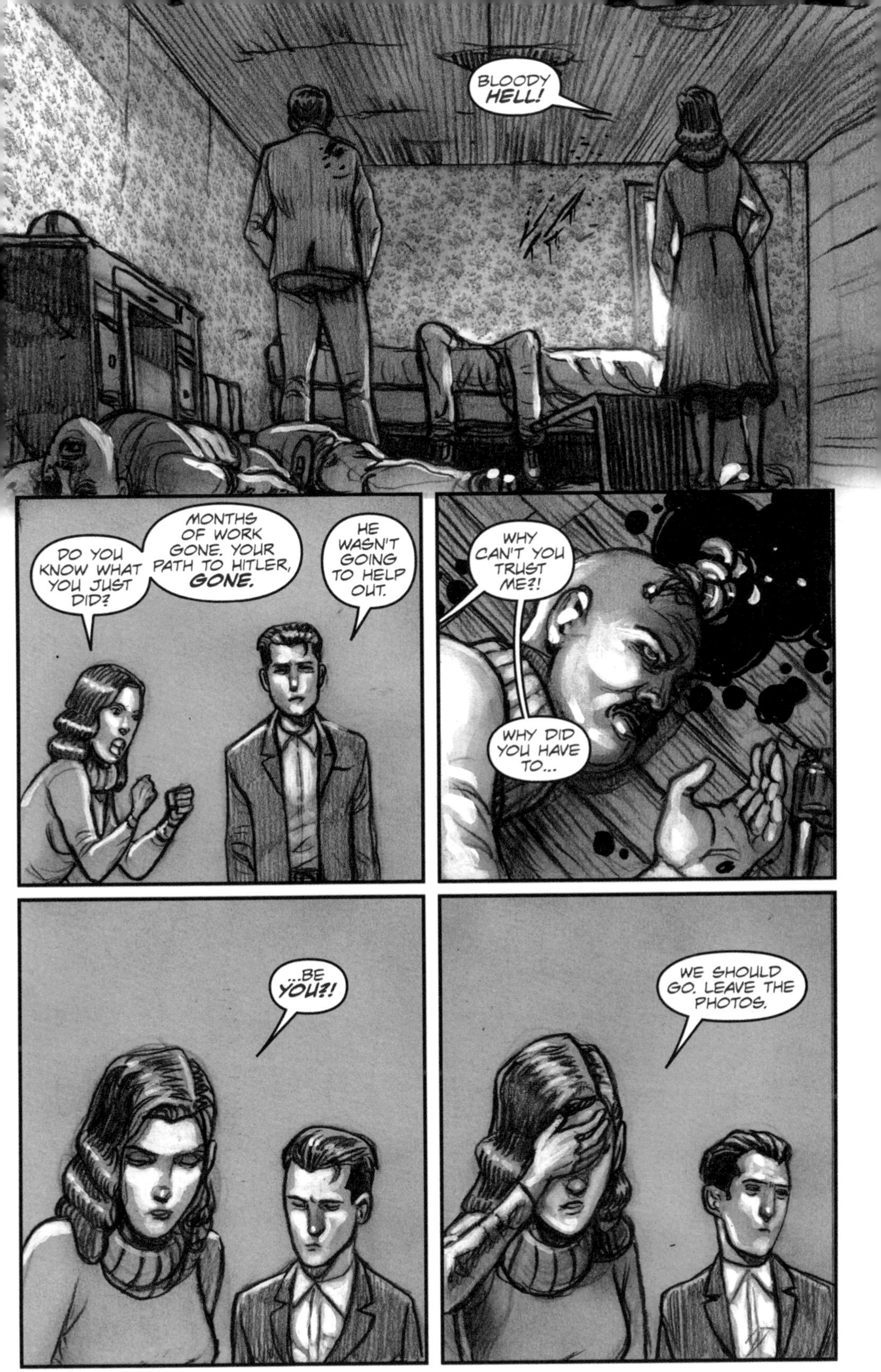
BLOODY HELL!
DO YOU KNOW WHAT YOU JUST DID?
MONTHS OF WORK GONE. YOUR PATH TO HITLER, GONE.
HE WASN'T GOING TO HELP OUT.
WHY CAN'T YOU TRUST ME?!
WHY DID YOU HAVE TO...
...BE YOU?!
WE SHOULD GO. LEAVE THE PHOTOS.

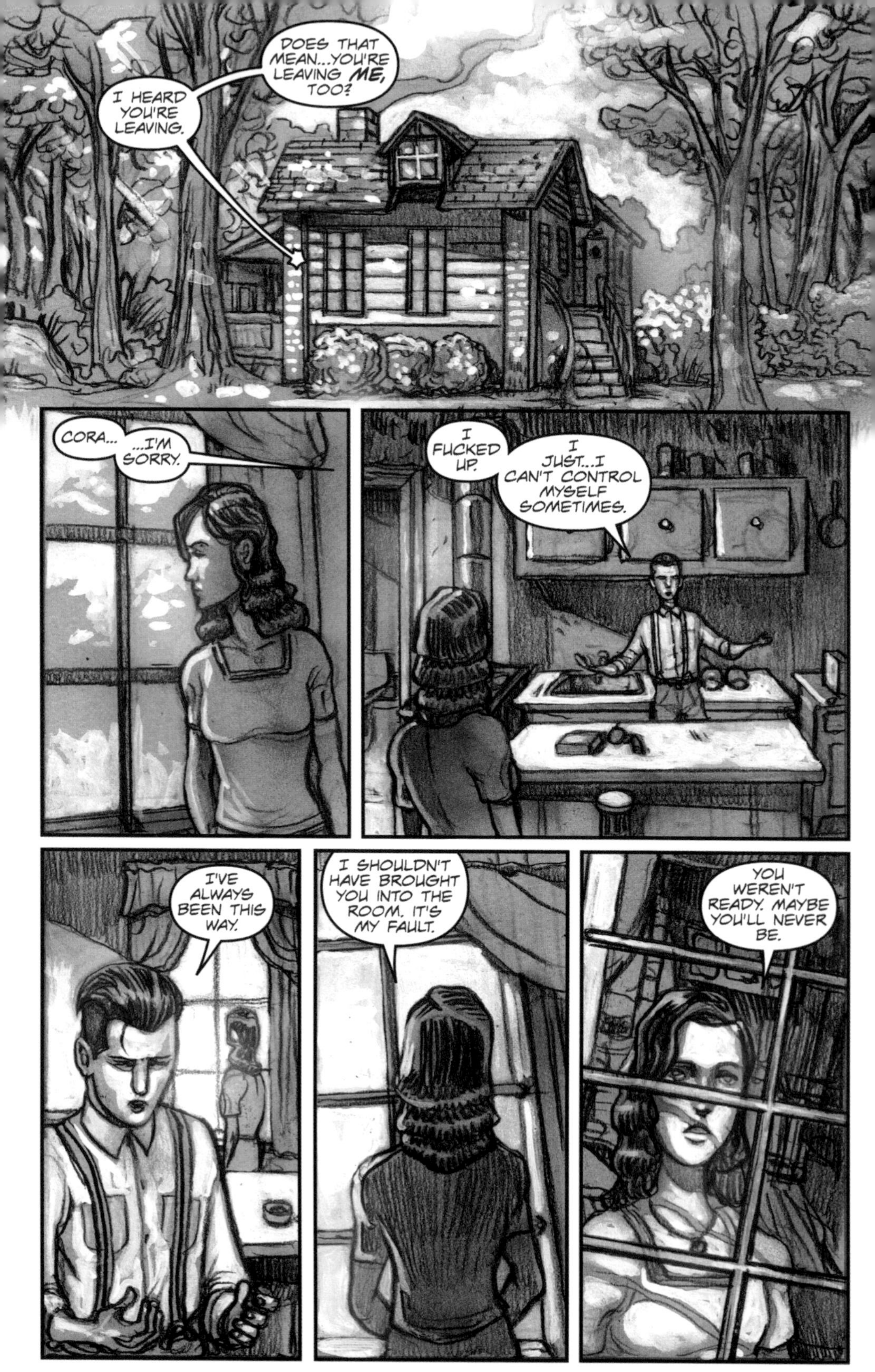
I HEARD YOU'RE LEAVING.
DOES THAT MEAN...YOU'RE LEAVING **ME,** TOO?
CORA...
...I'M SORRY.
I FUCKED UP.
I JUST...I CAN'T CONTROL MYSELF SOMETIMES.
I'VE ALWAYS BEEN THIS WAY.
I SHOULDN'T HAVE BROUGHT YOU INTO THE ROOM. IT'S MY FAULT.
YOU WEREN'T READY. MAYBE YOU'LL NEVER BE.

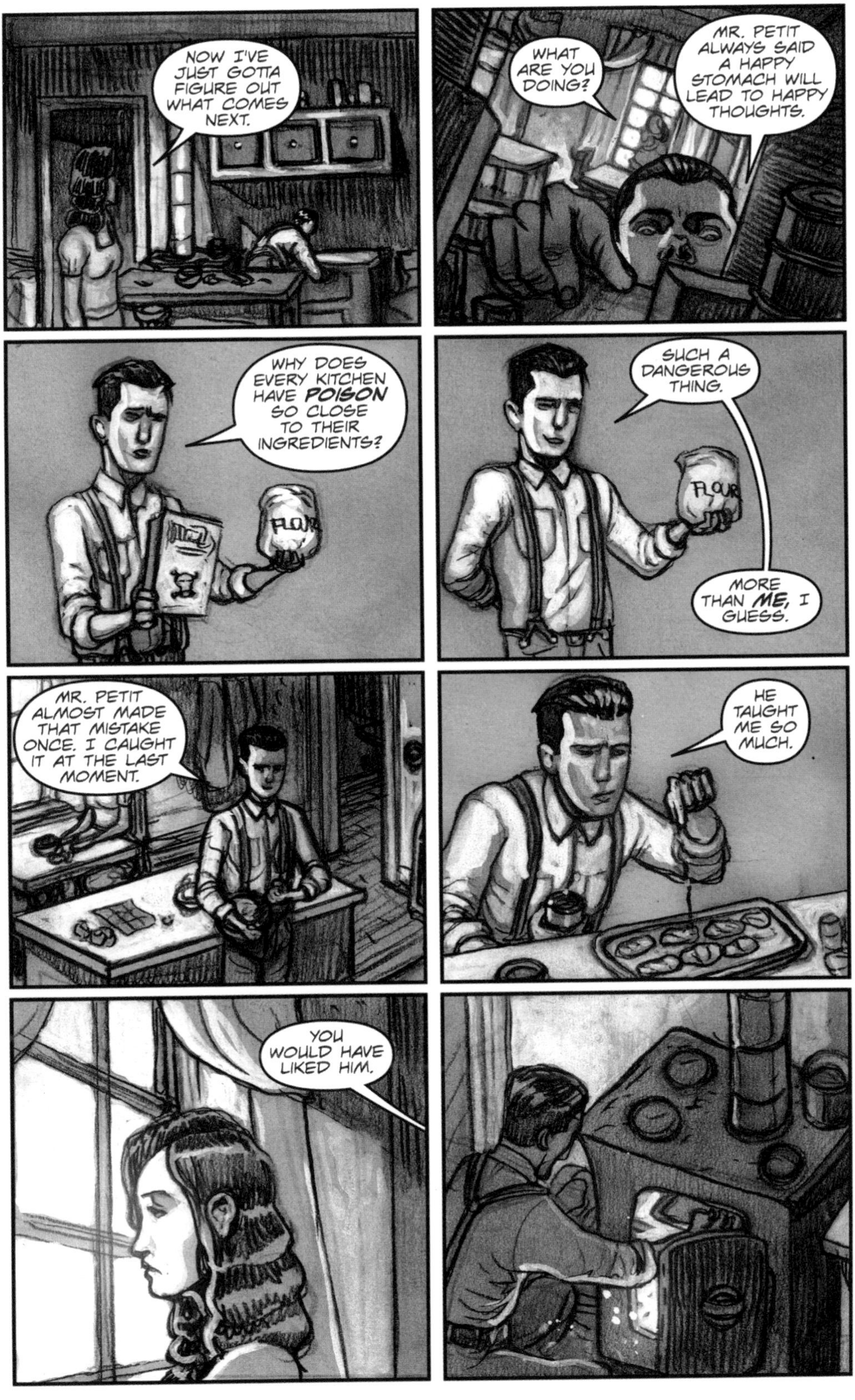
NOW I'VE JUST GOTTA FIGURE OUT WHAT COMES NEXT.
WHAT ARE YOU DOING?
MR. PETIT ALWAYS SAID A HAPPY STOMACH WILL LEAD TO HAPPY THOUGHTS.
WHY DOES EVERY KITCHEN HAVE POISON SO CLOSE TO THEIR INGREDIENTS?
FLOUR
SUCH A DANGEROUS THING.
FLOUR
MORE THAN ME, I GUESS.
MR. PETIT ALMOST MADE THAT MISTAKE ONCE. I CAUGHT IT AT THE LAST MOMENT.
HE TAUGHT ME SO MUCH.
YOU WOULD HAVE LIKED HIM.

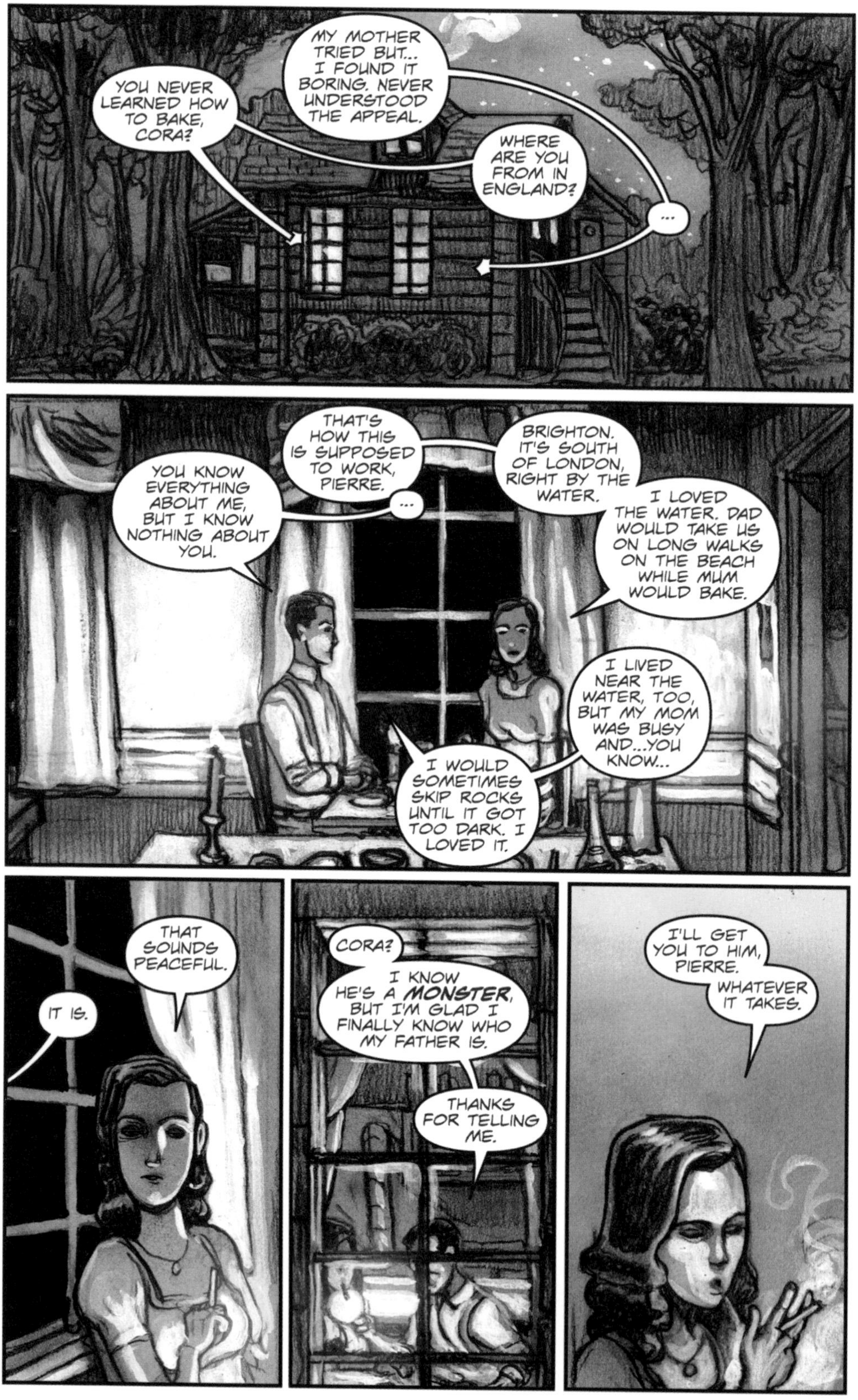
YOU NEVER LEARNED HOW TO BAKE, CORA?
MY MOTHER TRIED BUT... I FOUND IT BORING. NEVER UNDERSTOOD THE APPEAL.
WHERE ARE YOU FROM IN ENGLAND?
...
YOU KNOW EVERYTHING ABOUT ME, BUT I KNOW NOTHING ABOUT YOU.
...
THAT'S HOW THIS IS SUPPOSED TO WORK, PIERRE.
BRIGHTON. IT'S SOUTH OF LONDON, RIGHT BY THE WATER.
I LOVED THE WATER. DAD WOULD TAKE US ON LONG WALKS ON THE BEACH WHILE MUM WOULD BAKE.
I LIVED NEAR THE WATER, TOO, BUT MY MOM WAS BUSY AND...YOU KNOW...
I WOULD SOMETIMES SKIP ROCKS UNTIL IT GOT TOO DARK. I LOVED IT.
THAT SOUNDS PEACEFUL.
IT IS.
CORA?
I KNOW HE'S A MONSTER, BUT I'M GLAD I FINALLY KNOW WHO MY FATHER IS.
THANKS FOR TELLING ME.
I'LL GET YOU TO HIM, PIERRE.
WHATEVER IT TAKES.

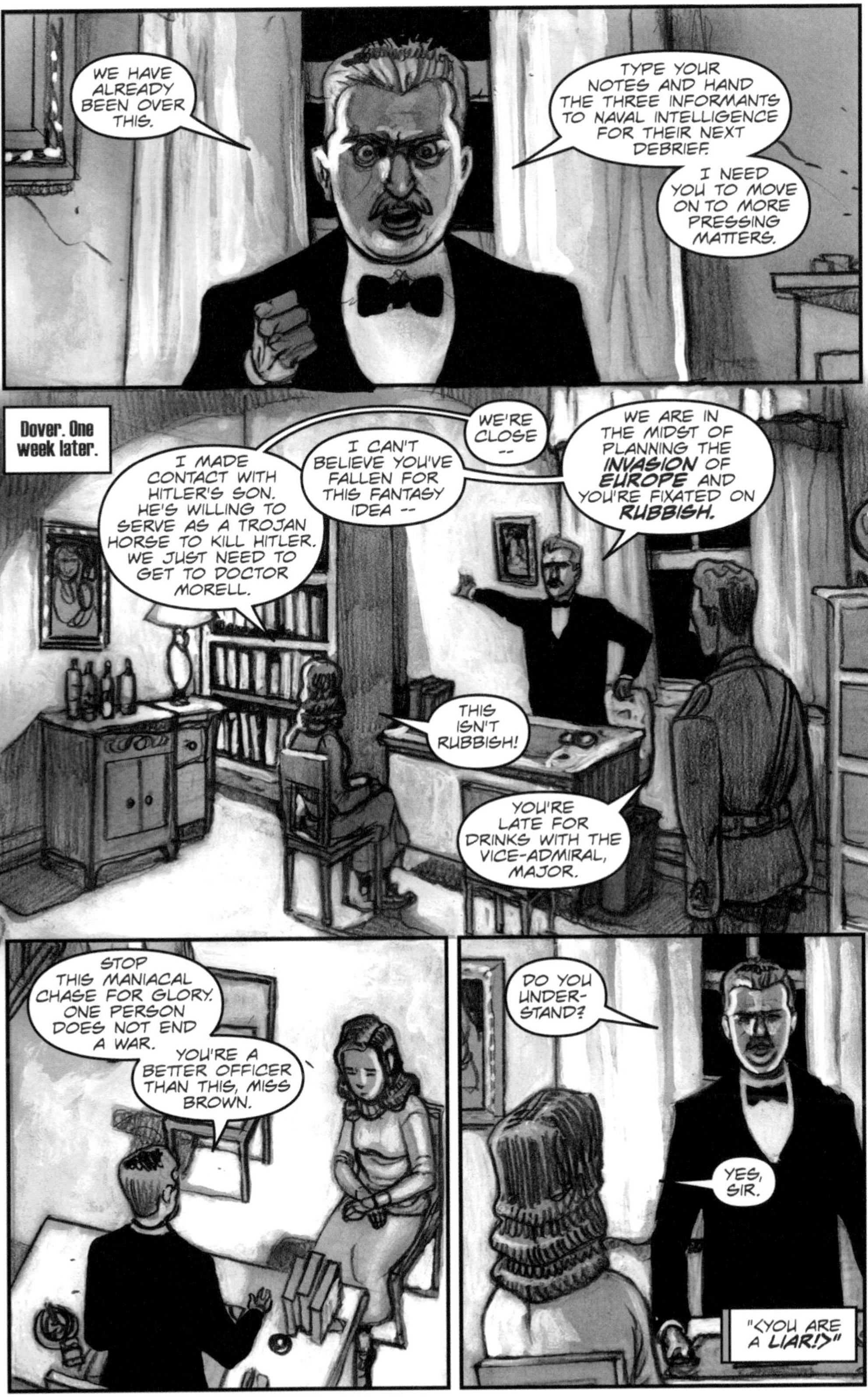
WE HAVE ALREADY BEEN OVER THIS.
TYPE YOUR NOTES AND HAND THE THREE INFORMANTS TO NAVAL INTELLIGENCE FOR THEIR NEXT DEBRIEF.
I NEED YOU TO MOVE ON TO MORE PRESSING MATTERS.
Dover. One week later.
I MADE CONTACT WITH HITLER'S SON. HE'S WILLING TO SERVE AS A TROJAN HORSE TO KILL HITLER. WE JUST NEED TO GET TO DOCTOR MORELL.
WE'RE CLOSE --
I CAN'T BELIEVE YOU'VE FALLEN FOR THIS FANTASY IDEA --
WE ARE IN THE MIDST OF PLANNING THE INVASION OF EUROPE AND YOU'RE FIXATED ON RUBBISH.
THIS ISN'T RUBBISH!
YOU'RE LATE FOR DRINKS WITH THE VICE-ADMIRAL, MAJOR.
STOP THIS MANIACAL CHASE FOR GLORY. ONE PERSON DOES NOT END A WAR.
YOU'RE A BETTER OFFICER THAN THIS, MISS BROWN.
DO YOU UNDER-STAND?
YES, SIR.
"<YOU ARE A LIAR!>"

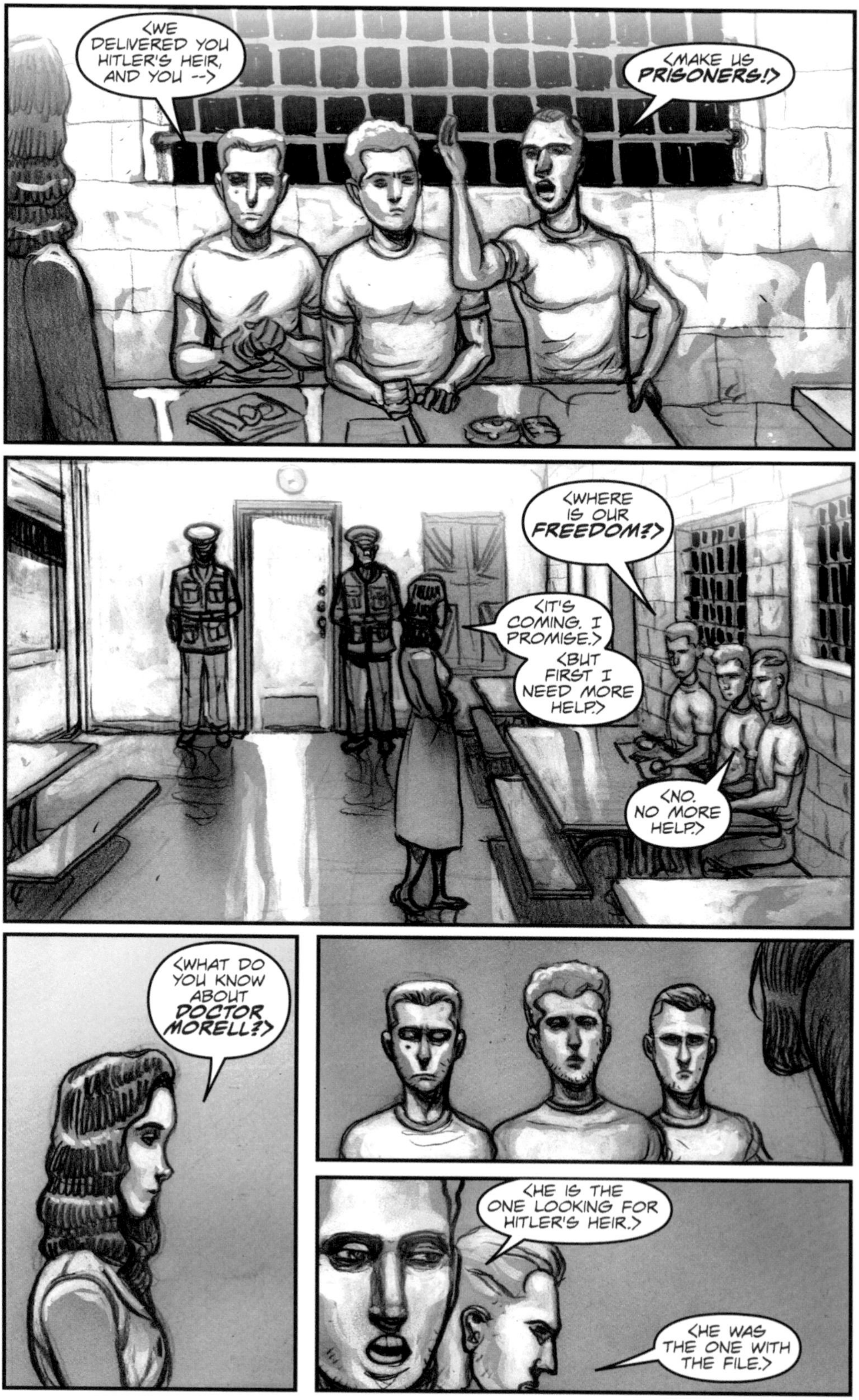
<WE DELIVERED YOU HITLER'S HEIR, AND YOU -->
<MAKE US PRISONERS!>
<WHERE IS OUR FREEDOM?>
<IT'S COMING. I PROMISE.>
<BUT FIRST I NEED MORE HELP.>
<NO. NO MORE HELP.>
<WHAT DO YOU KNOW ABOUT DOCTOR MORELL?>
<HE IS THE ONE LOOKING FOR HITLER'S HEIR.>
<HE WAS THE ONE WITH THE FILE.>

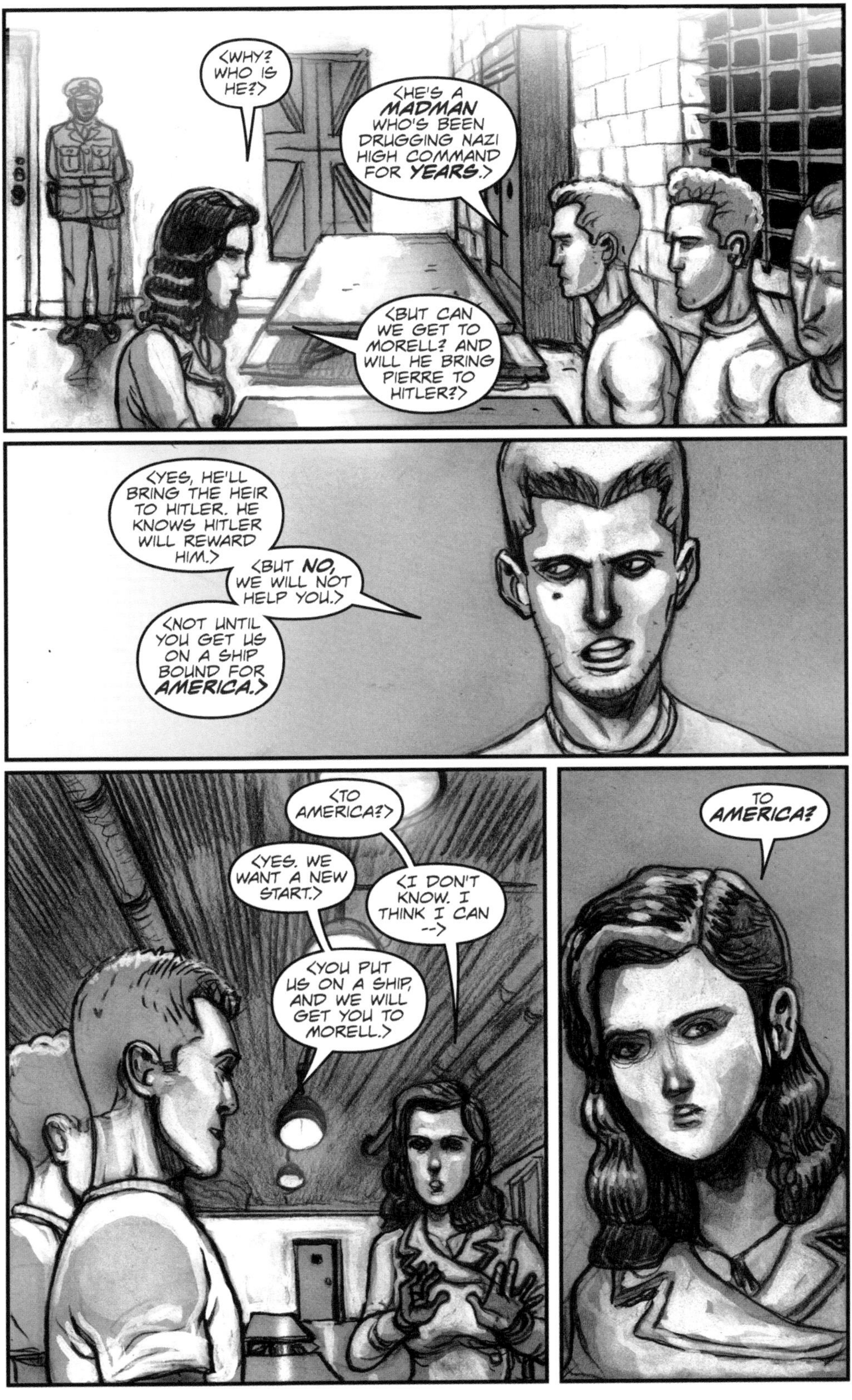
<WHY? WHO IS HE?>
<HE'S A MADMAN WHO'S BEEN DRUGGING NAZI HIGH COMMAND FOR YEARS.>
<BUT CAN WE GET TO MORELL? AND WILL HE BRING PIERRE TO HITLER?>
<YES, HE'LL BRING THE HEIR TO HITLER. HE KNOWS HITLER WILL REWARD HIM.>
<BUT NO, WE WILL NOT HELP YOU.>
<NOT UNTIL YOU GET US ON A SHIP BOUND FOR AMERICA.>
<TO AMERICA?>
<YES. WE WANT A NEW START.>
<I DON'T KNOW. I THINK I CAN -->
<YOU PUT US ON A SHIP, AND WE WILL GET YOU TO MORELL.>
TO AMERICA?

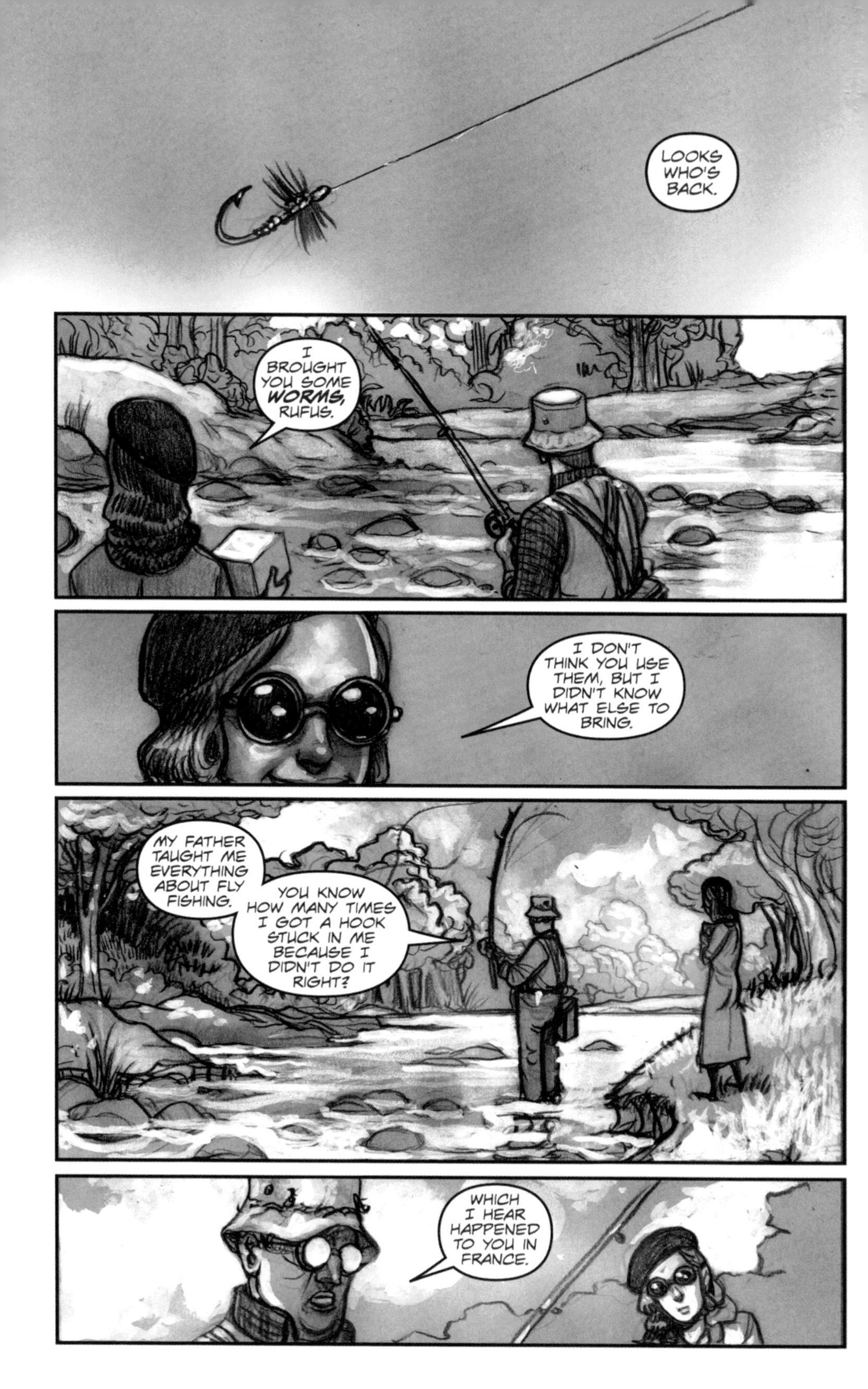

LOOKS WHO'S BACK.
I BROUGHT YOU SOME WORMS, RUFUS.
I DON'T THINK YOU USE THEM, BUT I DIDN'T KNOW WHAT ELSE TO BRING.
MY FATHER TAUGHT ME EVERYTHING ABOUT FLY FISHING.
YOU KNOW HOW MANY TIMES I GOT A HOOK STUCK IN ME BECAUSE I DIDN'T DO IT RIGHT?
WHICH I HEAR HAPPENED TO YOU IN FRANCE.

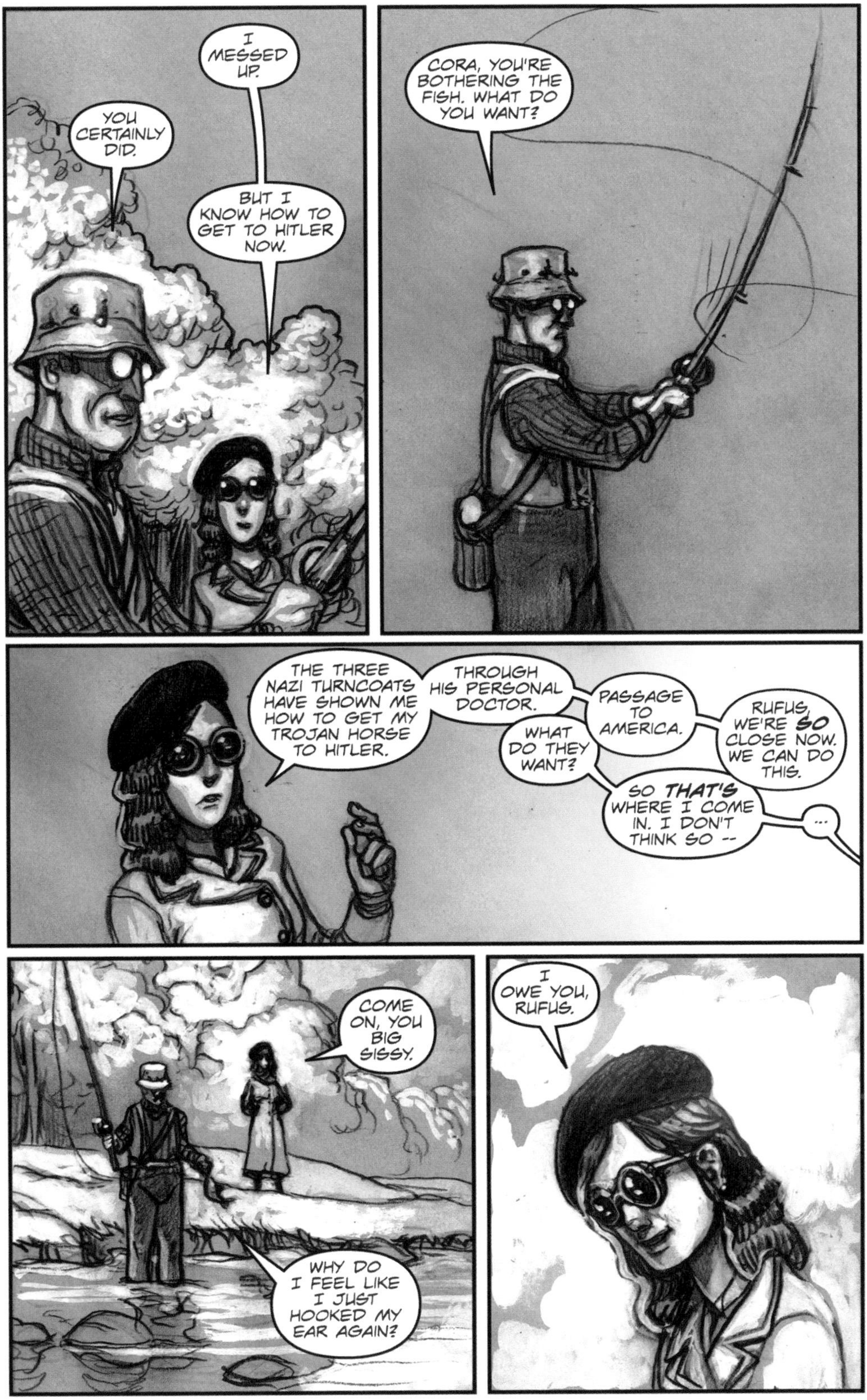
I MESSED UP.
YOU CERTAINLY DID.
BUT I KNOW HOW TO GET TO HITLER NOW.
CORA, YOU'RE BOTHERING THE FISH. WHAT DO YOU WANT?
THE THREE NAZI TURNCOATS HAVE SHOWN ME HOW TO GET MY TROJAN HORSE TO HITLER.
THROUGH HIS PERSONAL DOCTOR.
WHAT DO THEY WANT?
PASSAGE TO AMERICA.
SO **THAT'S** WHERE I COME IN. I DON'T THINK SO --
RUFUS, WE'RE **SO** CLOSE NOW. WE CAN DO THIS.
...
COME ON, YOU BIG SISSY.
WHY DO I FEEL LIKE I JUST HOOKED MY EAR AGAIN?
I OWE YOU, RUFUS.

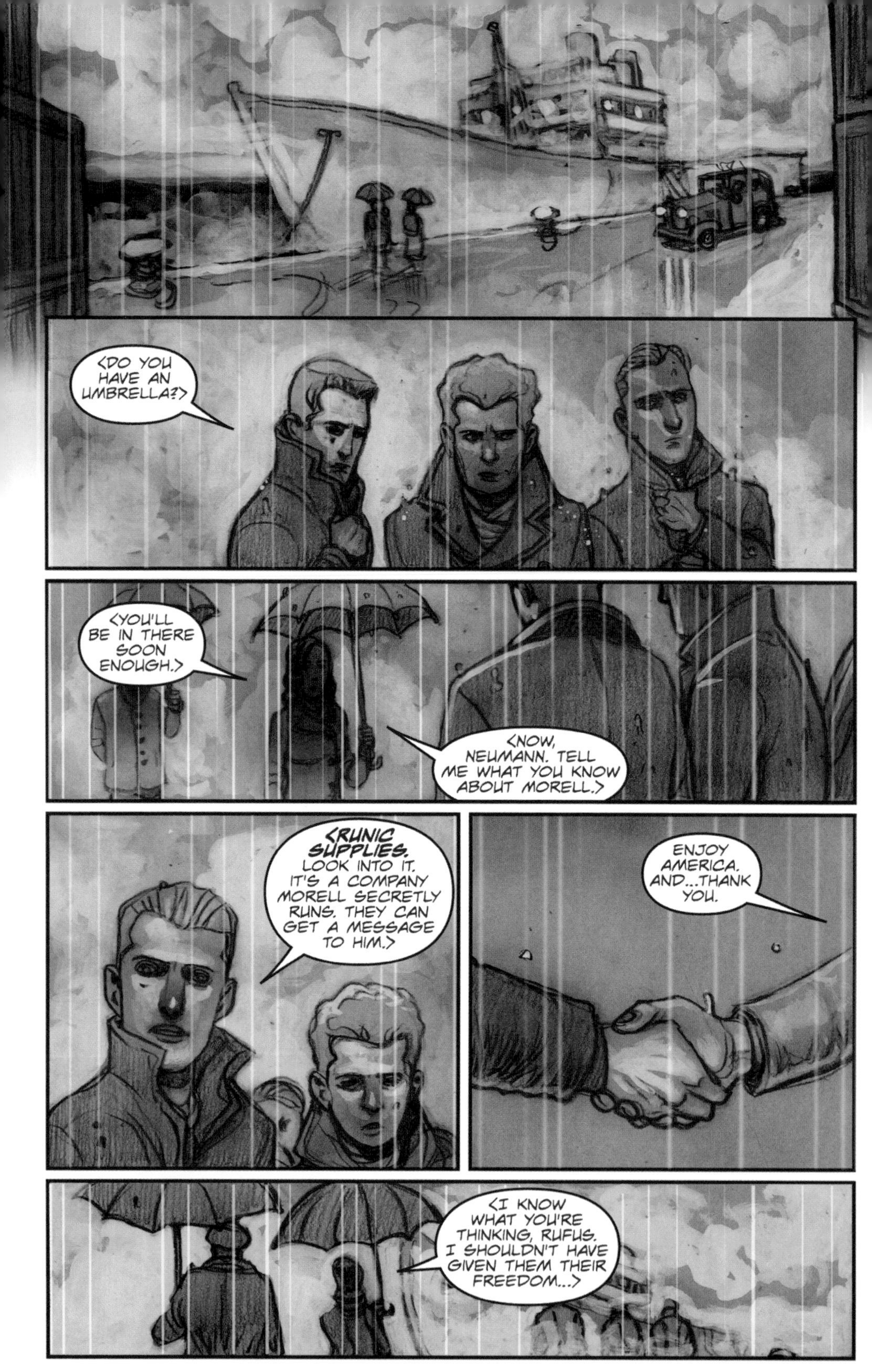
<DO YOU HAVE AN UMBRELLA?>
<YOU'LL BE IN THERE SOON ENOUGH.>
<NOW, NEUMANN. TELL ME WHAT YOU KNOW ABOUT MORELL.>
<RUNIC SUPPLIES. LOOK INTO IT. IT'S A COMPANY MORELL SECRETLY RUNS. THEY CAN GET A MESSAGE TO HIM.>
ENJOY AMERICA. AND...THANK YOU.
<I KNOW WHAT YOU'RE THINKING, RUFUS. I SHOULDN'T HAVE GIVEN THEM THEIR FREEDOM...>

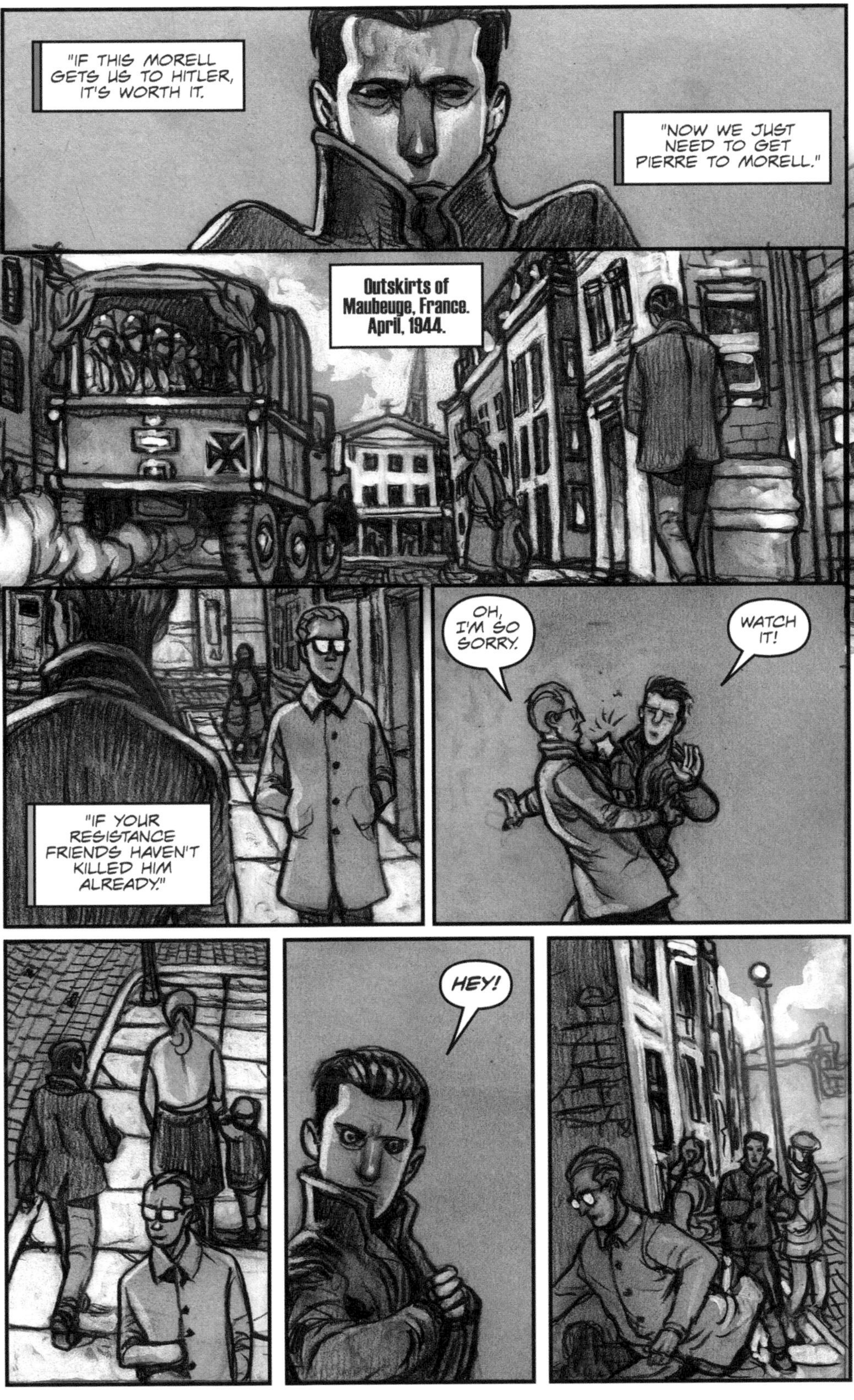
"IF THIS MORELL GETS US TO HITLER, IT'S WORTH IT.
"NOW WE JUST NEED TO GET PIERRE TO MORELL."
Outskirts of Maubeuge, France. April, 1944.
"IF YOUR RESISTANCE FRIENDS HAVEN'T KILLED HIM ALREADY."
OH, I'M SO SORRY.
WATCH IT!
HEY!

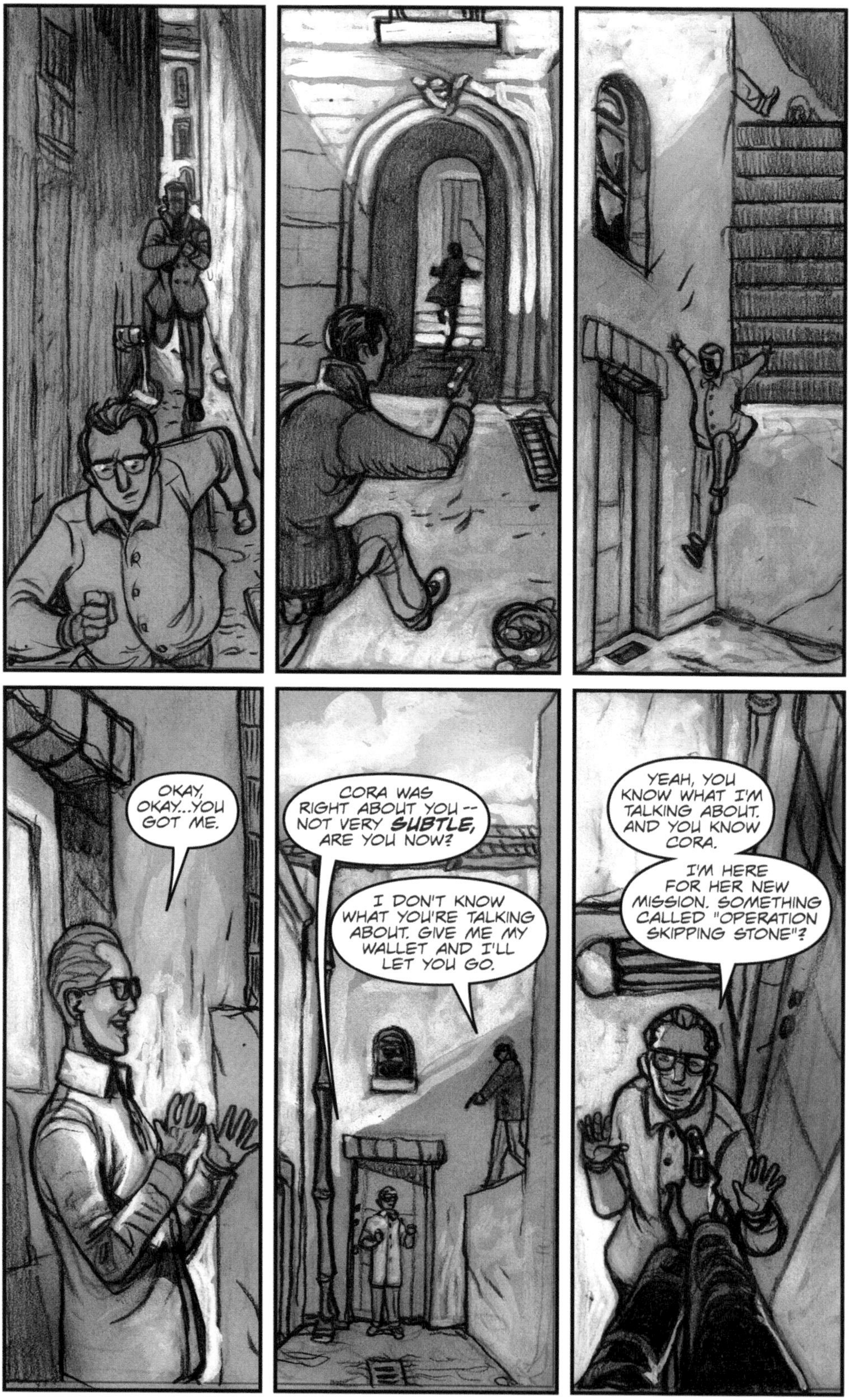
OKAY, OKAY...YOU GOT ME.
CORA WAS RIGHT ABOUT YOU -- NOT VERY SUBTLE, ARE YOU NOW?
I DON'T KNOW WHAT YOU'RE TALKING ABOUT. GIVE ME MY WALLET AND I'LL LET YOU GO.
YEAH, YOU KNOW WHAT I'M TALKING ABOUT. AND YOU KNOW CORA.
I'M HERE FOR HER NEW MISSION. SOMETHING CALLED "OPERATION SKIPPING STONE"?

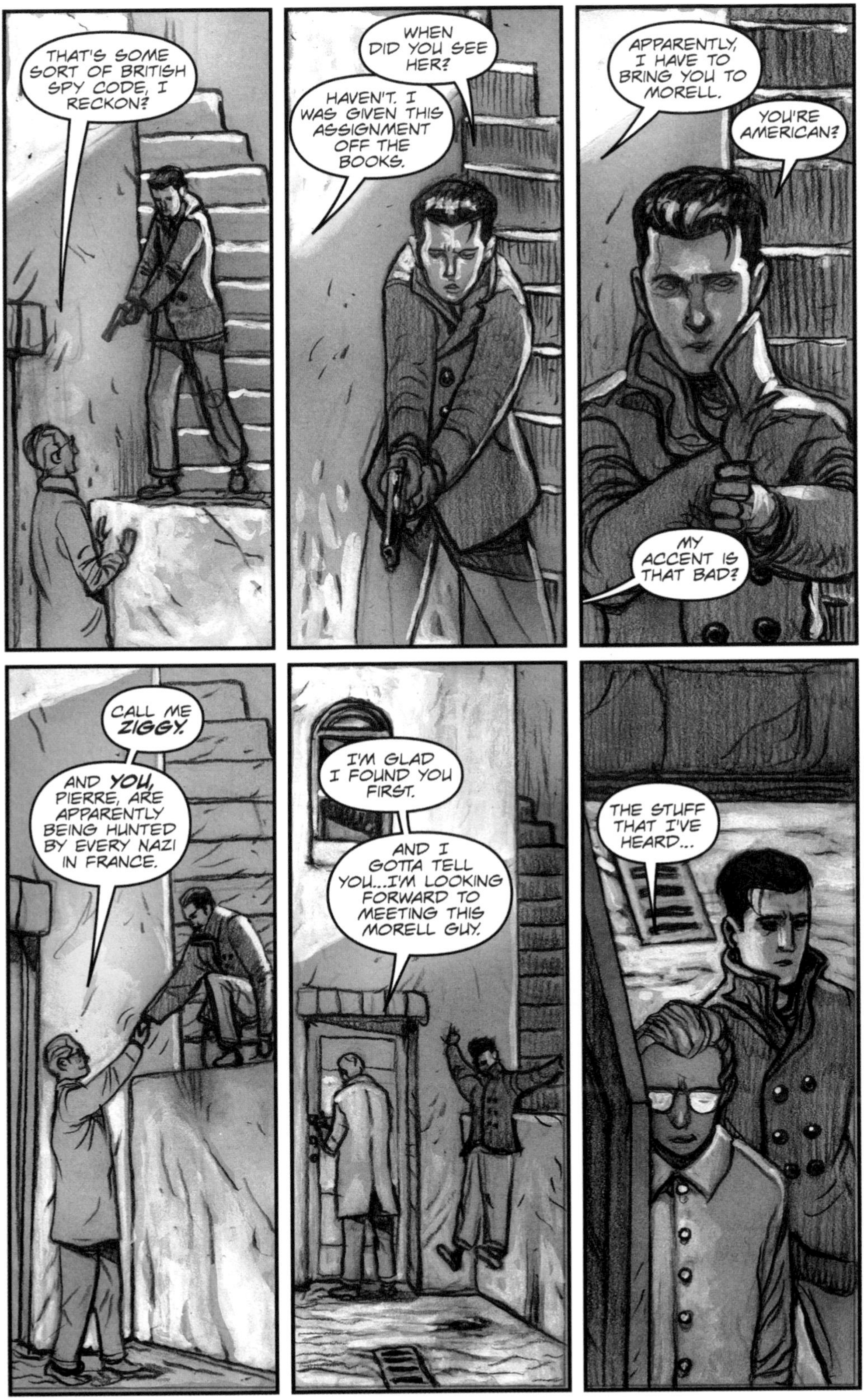
THAT'S SOME SORT OF BRITISH SPY CODE, I RECKON?
WHEN DID YOU SEE HER?
HAVEN'T. I WAS GIVEN THIS ASSIGNMENT OFF THE BOOKS.
APPARENTLY, I HAVE TO BRING YOU TO MORELL.
YOU'RE AMERICAN?
MY ACCENT IS THAT BAD?
CALL ME ZIGGY.
AND YOU, PIERRE, ARE APPARENTLY BEING HUNTED BY EVERY NAZI IN FRANCE.
I'M GLAD I FOUND YOU FIRST.
AND I GOTTA TELL YOU...I'M LOOKING FORWARD TO MEETING THIS MORELL GUY.
THE STUFF THAT I'VE HEARD...

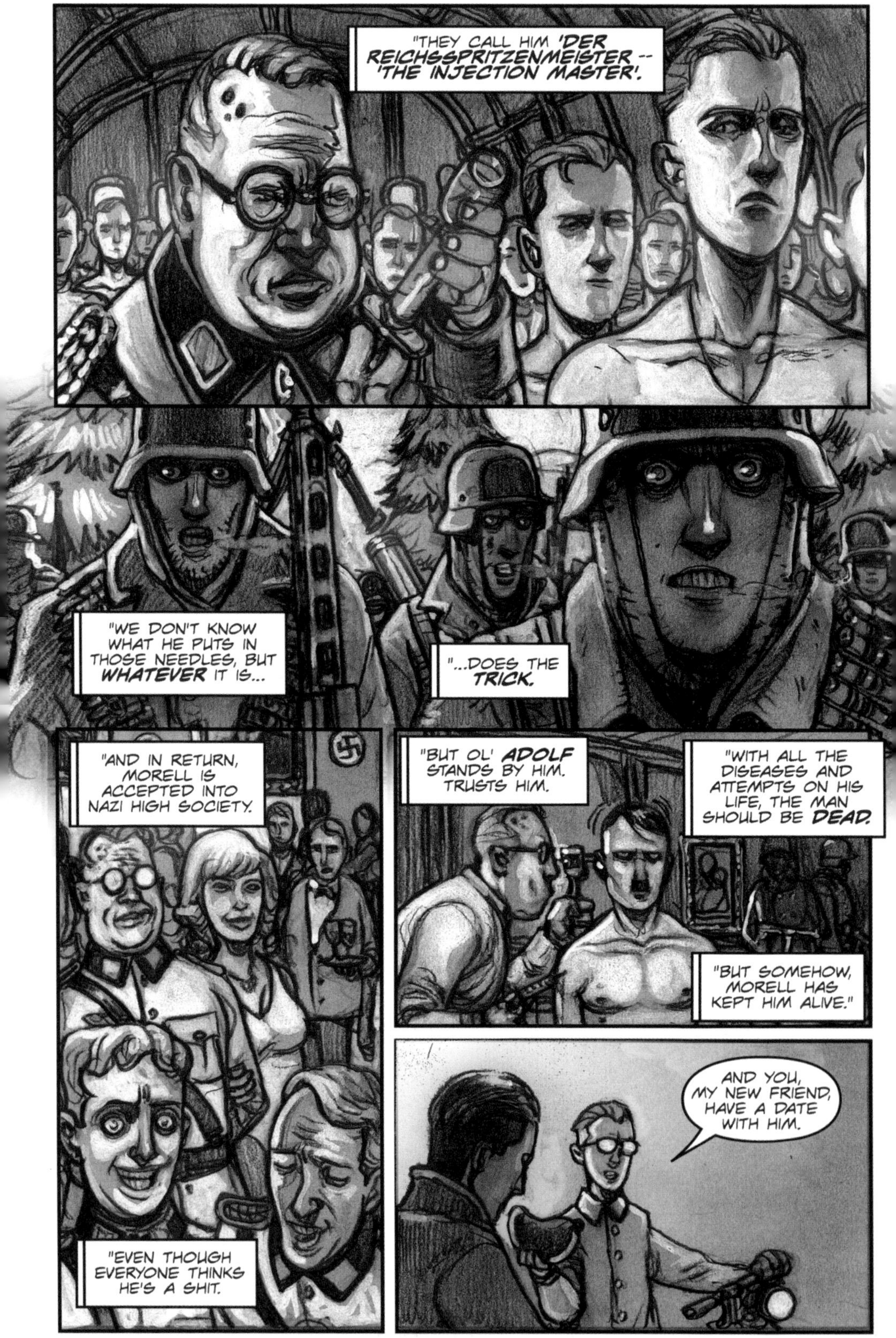
"THEY CALL HIM 'DER REICHSSPRITZENMEISTER -- 'THE INJECTION MASTER'.
"WE DON'T KNOW WHAT HE PUTS IN THOSE NEEDLES, BUT WHATEVER IT IS...
"...DOES THE TRICK.
"AND IN RETURN, MORELL IS ACCEPTED INTO NAZI HIGH SOCIETY.
"EVEN THOUGH EVERYONE THINKS HE'S A SHIT.
"BUT OL' ADOLF STANDS BY HIM. TRUSTS HIM.
"WITH ALL THE DISEASES AND ATTEMPTS ON HIS LIFE, THE MAN SHOULD BE DEAD.
"BUT SOMEHOW, MORELL HAS KEPT HIM ALIVE."
AND YOU, MY NEW FRIEND, HAVE A DATE WITH HIM.

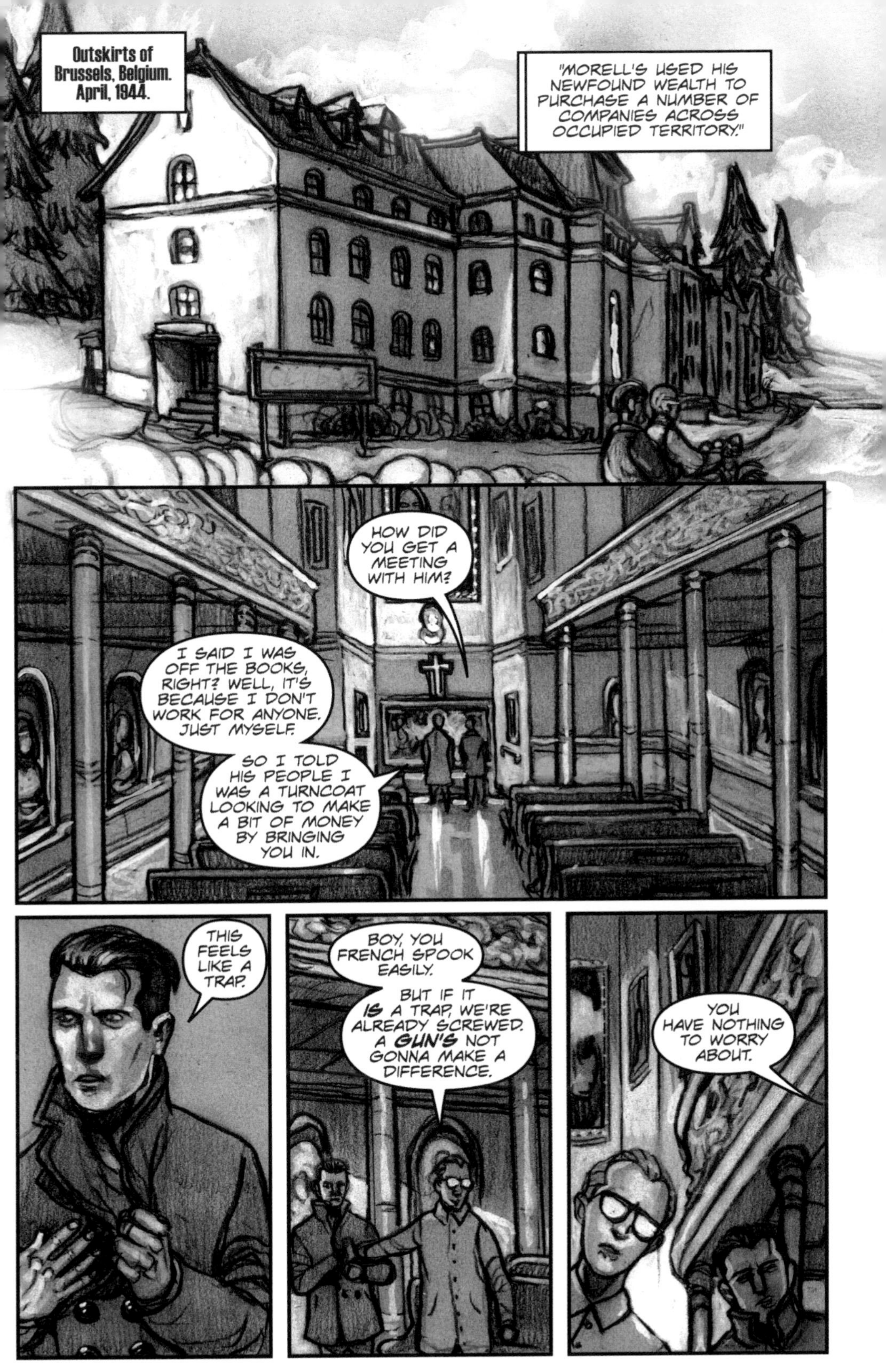
Outskirts of Brussels, Belgium. April, 1944.
"MORELL'S USED HIS NEWFOUND WEALTH TO PURCHASE A NUMBER OF COMPANIES ACROSS OCCUPIED TERRITORY."
HOW DID YOU GET A MEETING WITH HIM?
I SAID I WAS OFF THE BOOKS, RIGHT? WELL, IT'S BECAUSE I DON'T WORK FOR ANYONE. JUST MYSELF.
SO I TOLD HIS PEOPLE I WAS A TURNCOAT LOOKING TO MAKE A BIT OF MONEY BY BRINGING YOU IN.
THIS FEELS LIKE A TRAP.
BOY, YOU FRENCH SPOOK EASILY.
BUT IF IT IS A TRAP, WE'RE ALREADY SCREWED. A GUN'S NOT GONNA MAKE A DIFFERENCE.
YOU HAVE NOTHING TO WORRY ABOUT.

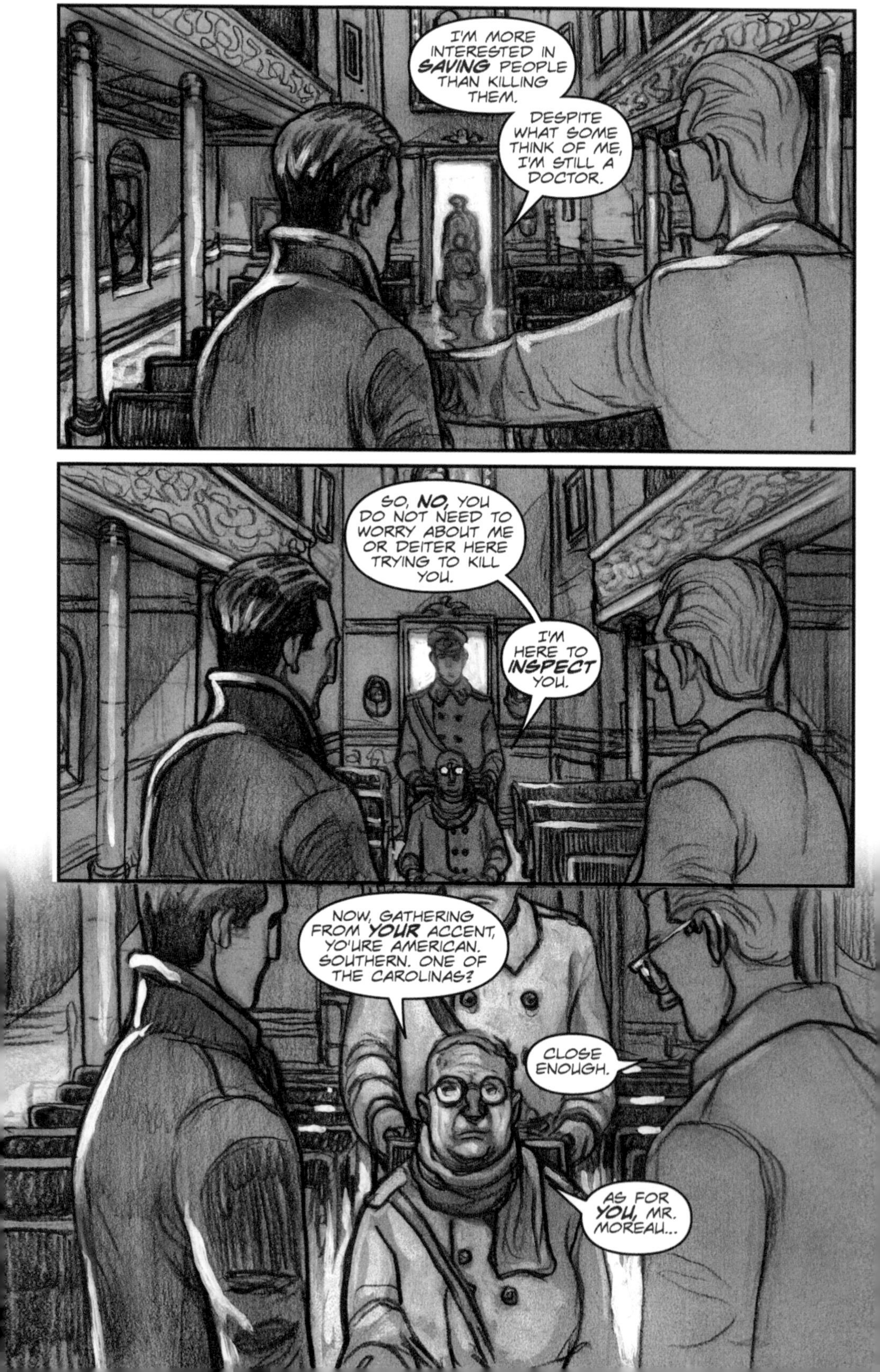
I'M MORE INTERESTED IN SAVING PEOPLE THAN KILLING THEM.
DESPITE WHAT SOME THINK OF ME, I'M STILL A DOCTOR.
SO, NO, YOU DO NOT NEED TO WORRY ABOUT ME OR DEITER HERE TRYING TO KILL YOU.
I'M HERE TO INSPECT YOU.
NOW, GATHERING FROM YOUR ACCENT, YOU'RE AMERICAN. SOUTHERN. ONE OF THE CAROLINAS?
CLOSE ENOUGH.
AS FOR YOU, MR. MOREAU...

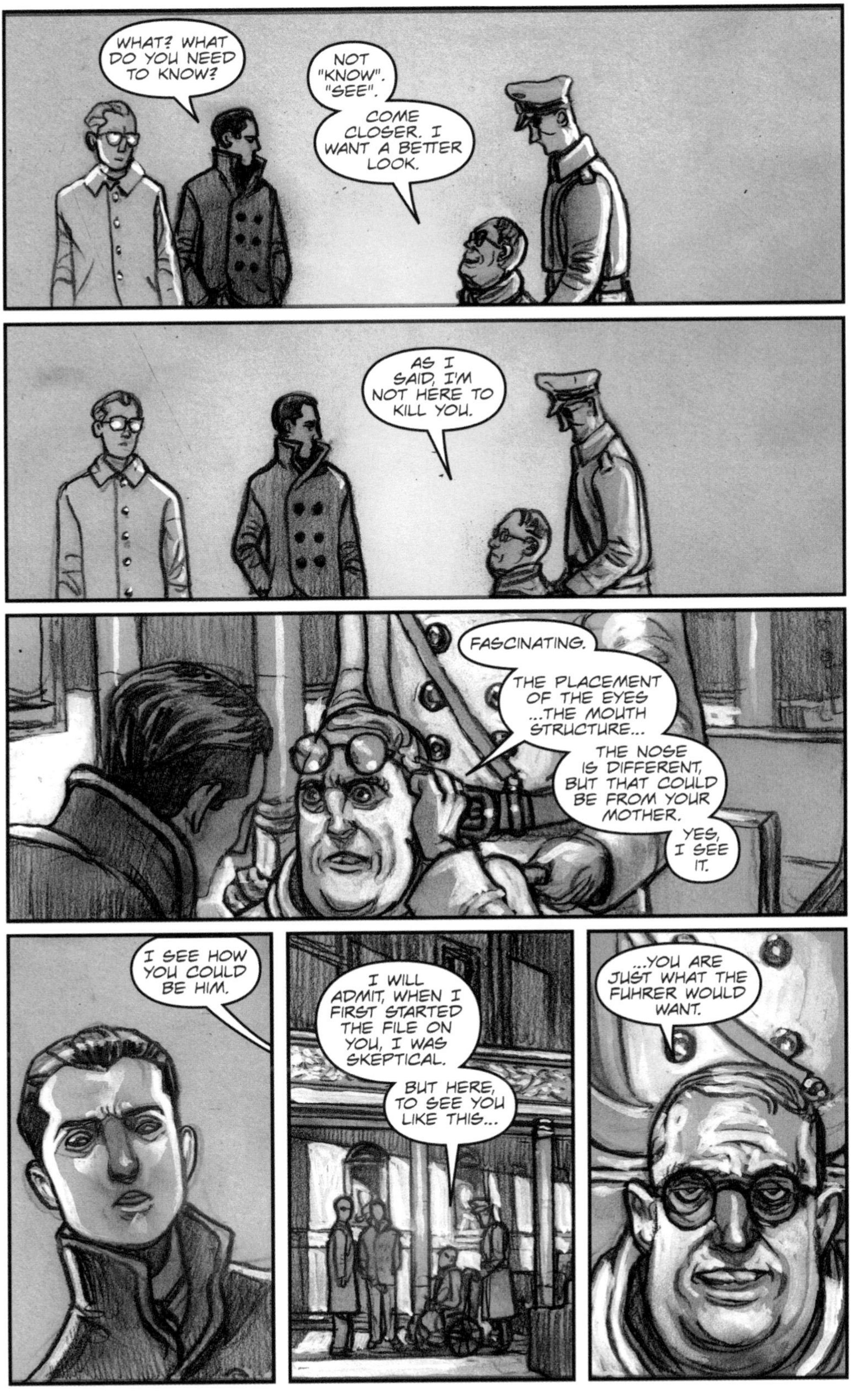
WHAT? WHAT DO YOU NEED TO KNOW?
NOT "KNOW". "SEE".
COME CLOSER. I WANT A BETTER LOOK.
AS I SAID, I'M NOT HERE TO KILL YOU.
FASCINATING.
THE PLACEMENT OF THE EYES ...THE MOUTH STRUCTURE...
THE NOSE IS DIFFERENT, BUT THAT COULD BE FROM YOUR MOTHER.
YES, I SEE IT.
I SEE HOW YOU COULD BE HIM.
I WILL ADMIT, WHEN I FIRST STARTED THE FILE ON YOU, I WAS SKEPTICAL.
BUT HERE, TO SEE YOU LIKE THIS...
...YOU ARE JUST WHAT THE FUHRER WOULD WANT.

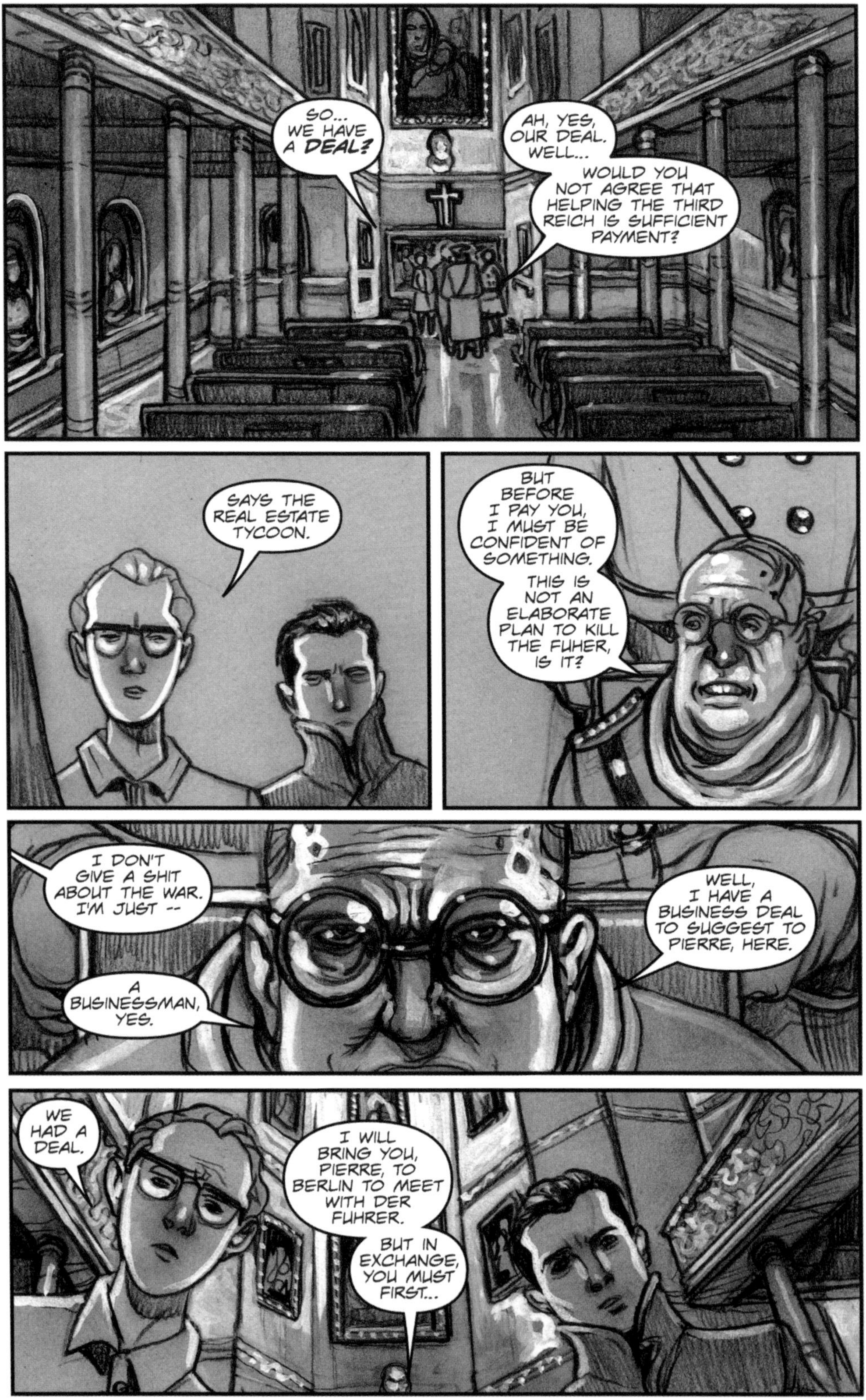
SO... WE HAVE A DEAL?
AH, YES, OUR DEAL. WELL...
WOULD YOU NOT AGREE THAT HELPING THE THIRD REICH IS SUFFICIENT PAYMENT?
SAYS THE REAL ESTATE TYCOON.
BUT BEFORE I PAY YOU, I MUST BE CONFIDENT OF SOMETHING.
THIS IS NOT AN ELABORATE PLAN TO KILL THE FUHER, IS IT?
I DON'T GIVE A SHIT ABOUT THE WAR. I'M JUST --
A BUSINESSMAN, YES.
WELL, I HAVE A BUSINESS DEAL TO SUGGEST TO PIERRE, HERE.
WE HAD A DEAL.
I WILL BRING YOU, PIERRE, TO BERLIN TO MEET WITH DER FUHRER.
BUT IN EXCHANGE, YOU MUST FIRST...

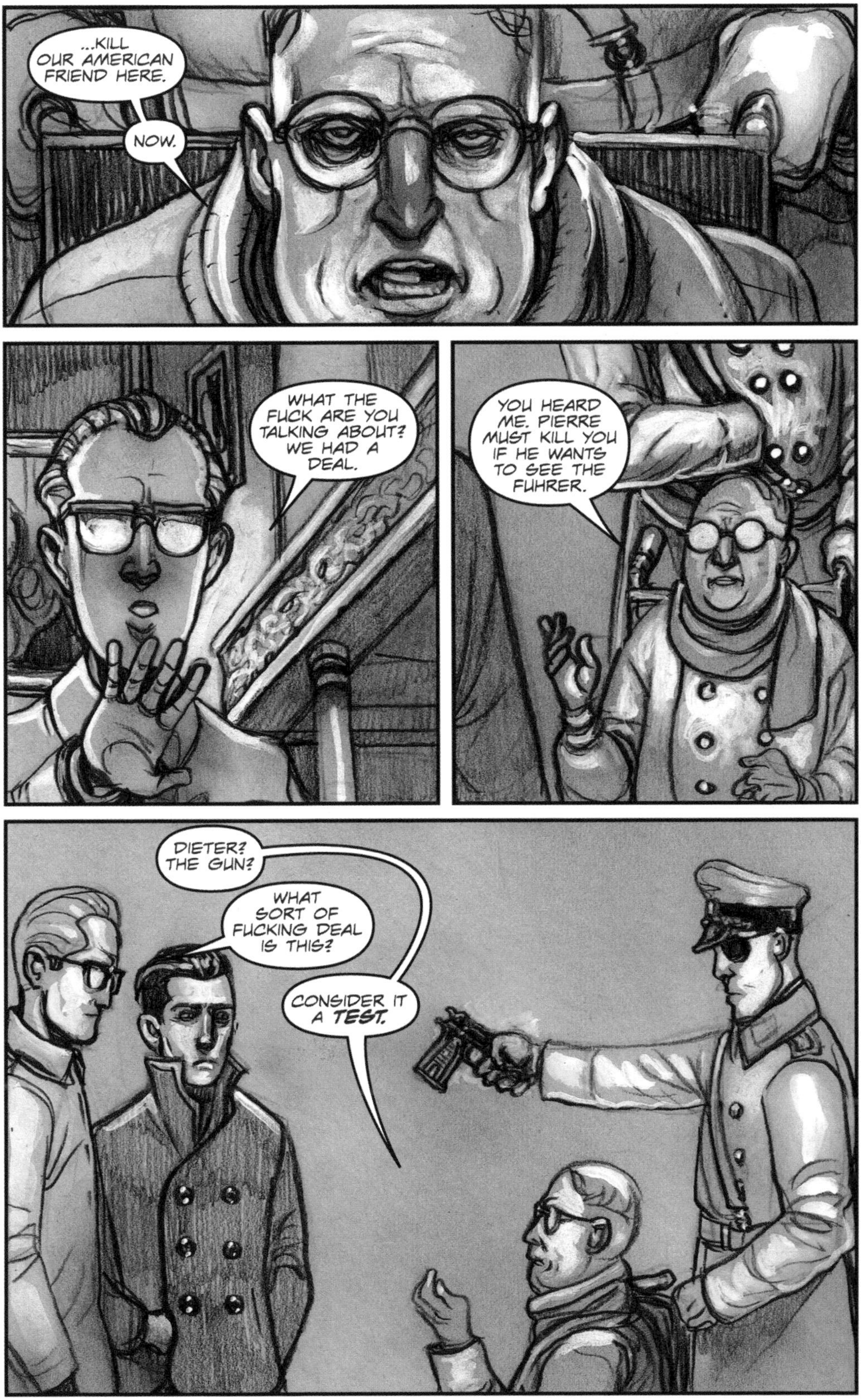
...KILL OUR AMERICAN FRIEND HERE.
NOW.
WHAT THE FUCK ARE YOU TALKING ABOUT? WE HAD A DEAL.
YOU HEARD ME. PIERRE MUST KILL YOU IF HE WANTS TO SEE THE FUHRER.
DIETER? THE GUN?
WHAT SORT OF FUCKING DEAL IS THIS?
CONSIDER IT A TEST.

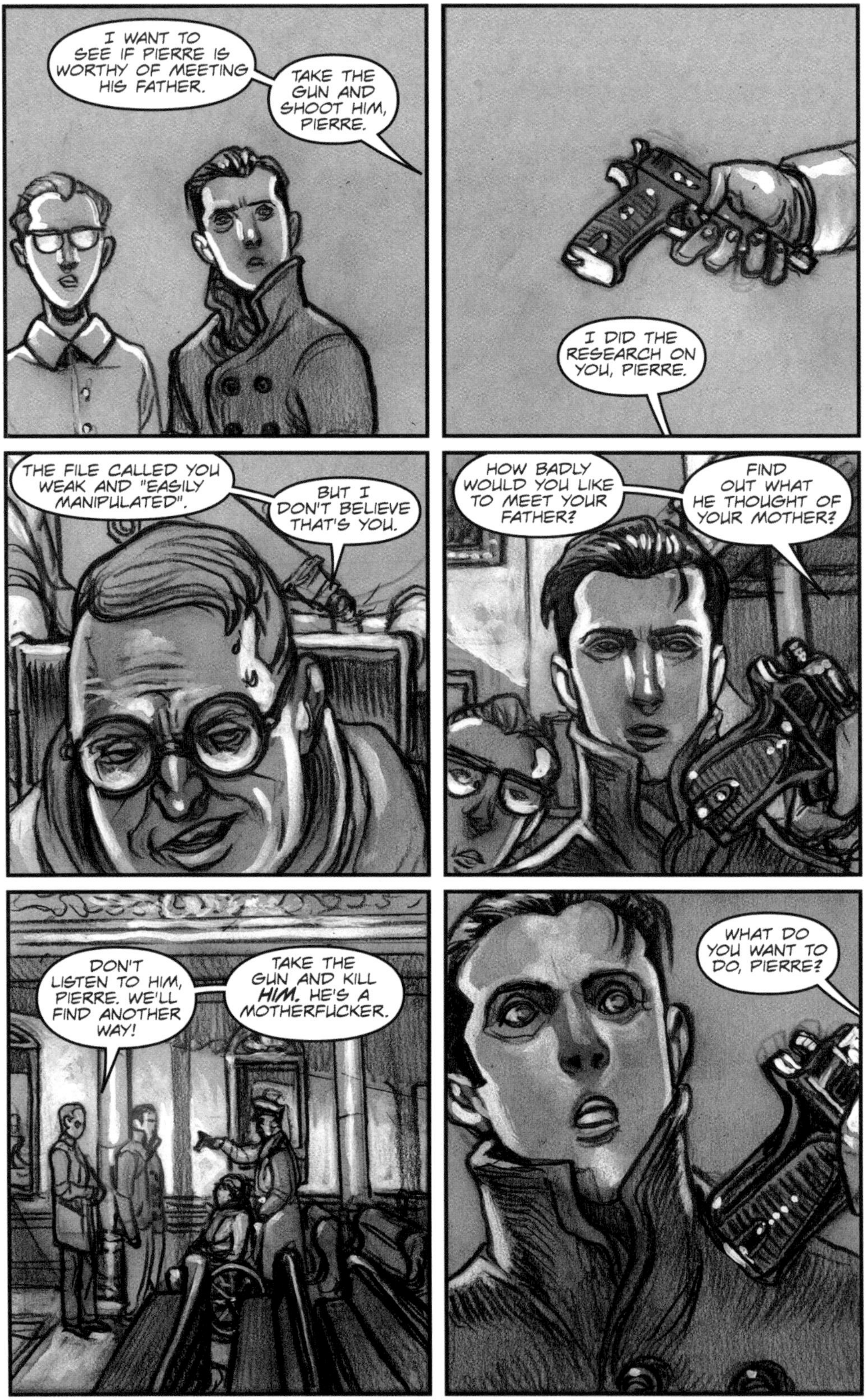
I WANT TO SEE IF PIERRE IS WORTHY OF MEETING HIS FATHER.
TAKE THE GUN AND SHOOT HIM, PIERRE.
I DID THE RESEARCH ON YOU, PIERRE.
THE FILE CALLED YOU WEAK AND "EASILY MANIPULATED".
BUT I DON'T BELIEVE THAT'S YOU.
HOW BADLY WOULD YOU LIKE TO MEET YOUR FATHER?
FIND OUT WHAT HE THOUGHT OF YOUR MOTHER?
DON'T LISTEN TO HIM, PIERRE. WE'LL FIND ANOTHER WAY!
TAKE THE GUN AND KILL HIM. HE'S A MOTHERFUCKER.
WHAT DO YOU WANT TO DO, PIERRE?

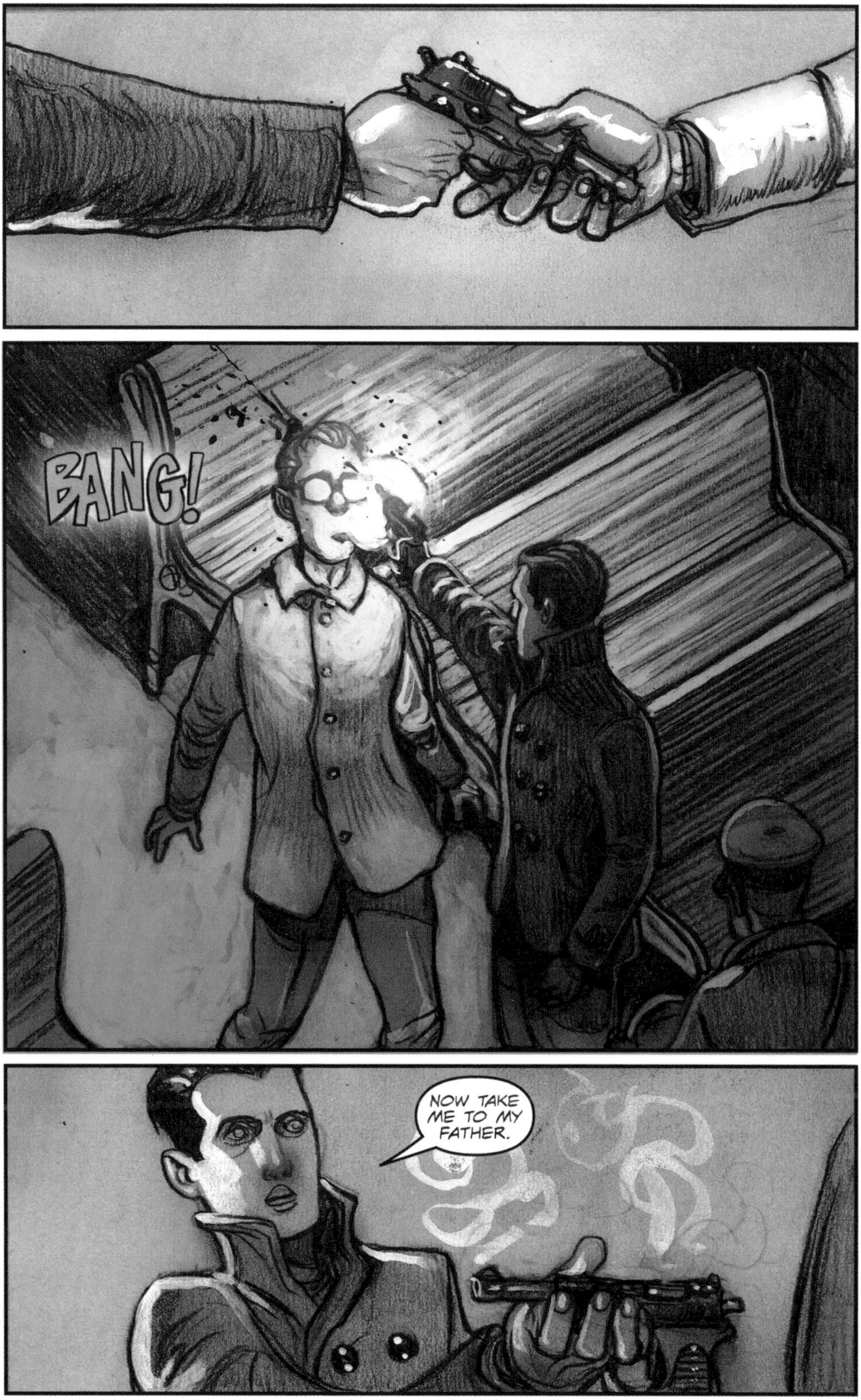
BANG!
NOW TAKE ME TO MY FATHER.

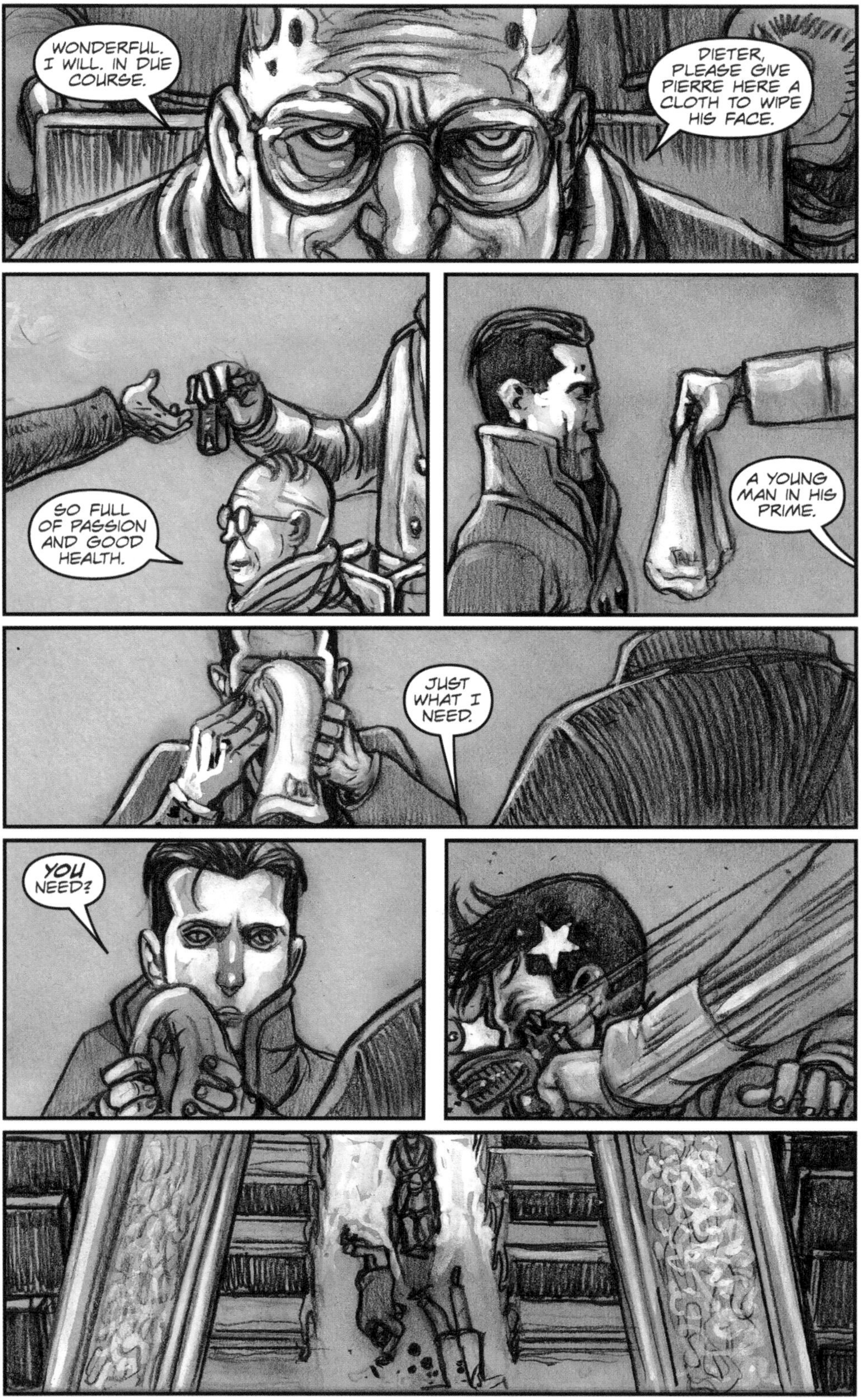
WONDERFUL. I WILL. IN DUE COURSE.
DIETER, PLEASE GIVE PIERRE HERE A CLOTH TO WIPE HIS FACE.
SO FULL OF PASSION AND GOOD HEALTH.
A YOUNG MAN IN HIS PRIME.
JUST WHAT I NEED.
YOU NEED?

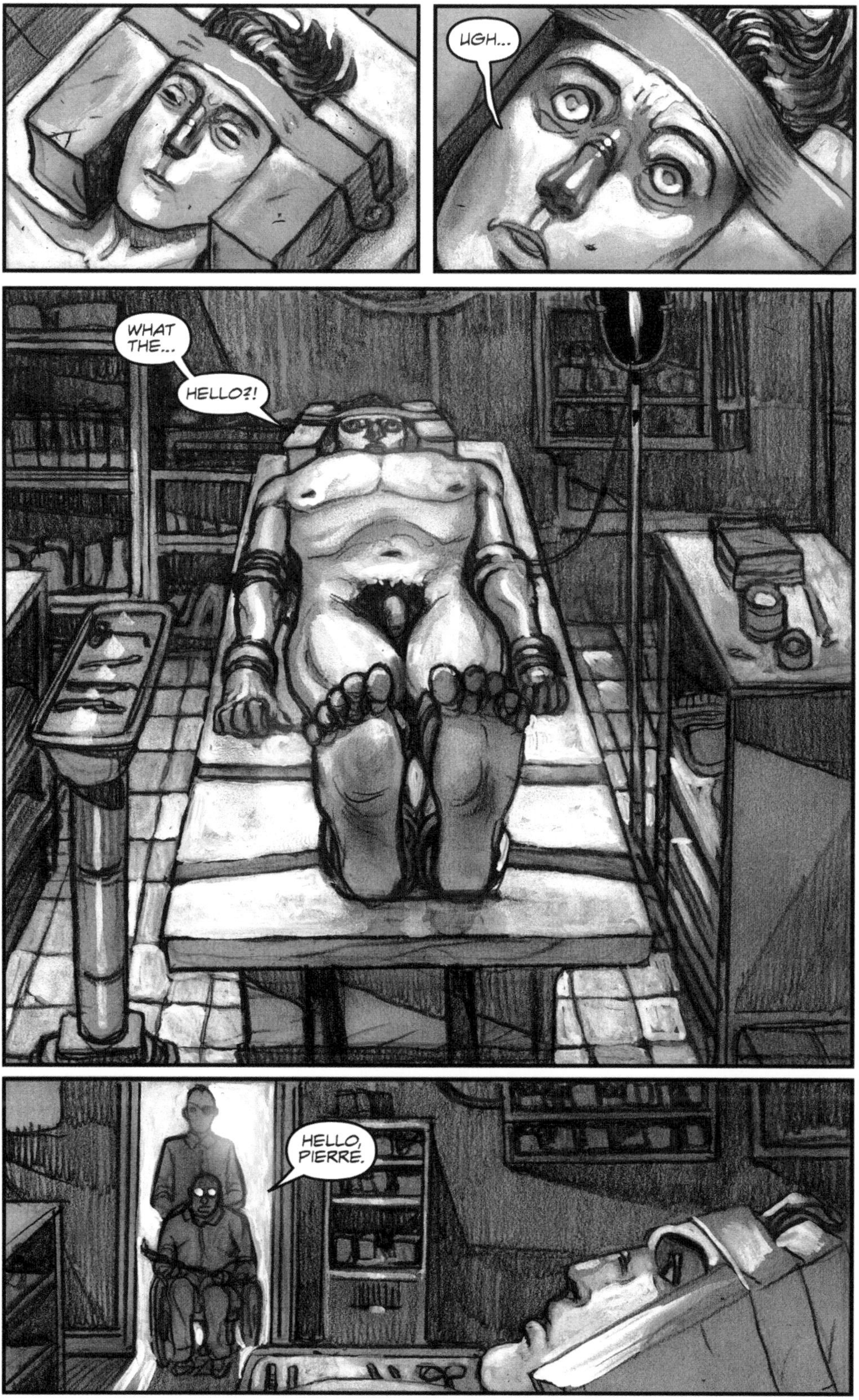
UGH...
WHAT THE...
HELLO?!
HELLO, PIERRE.

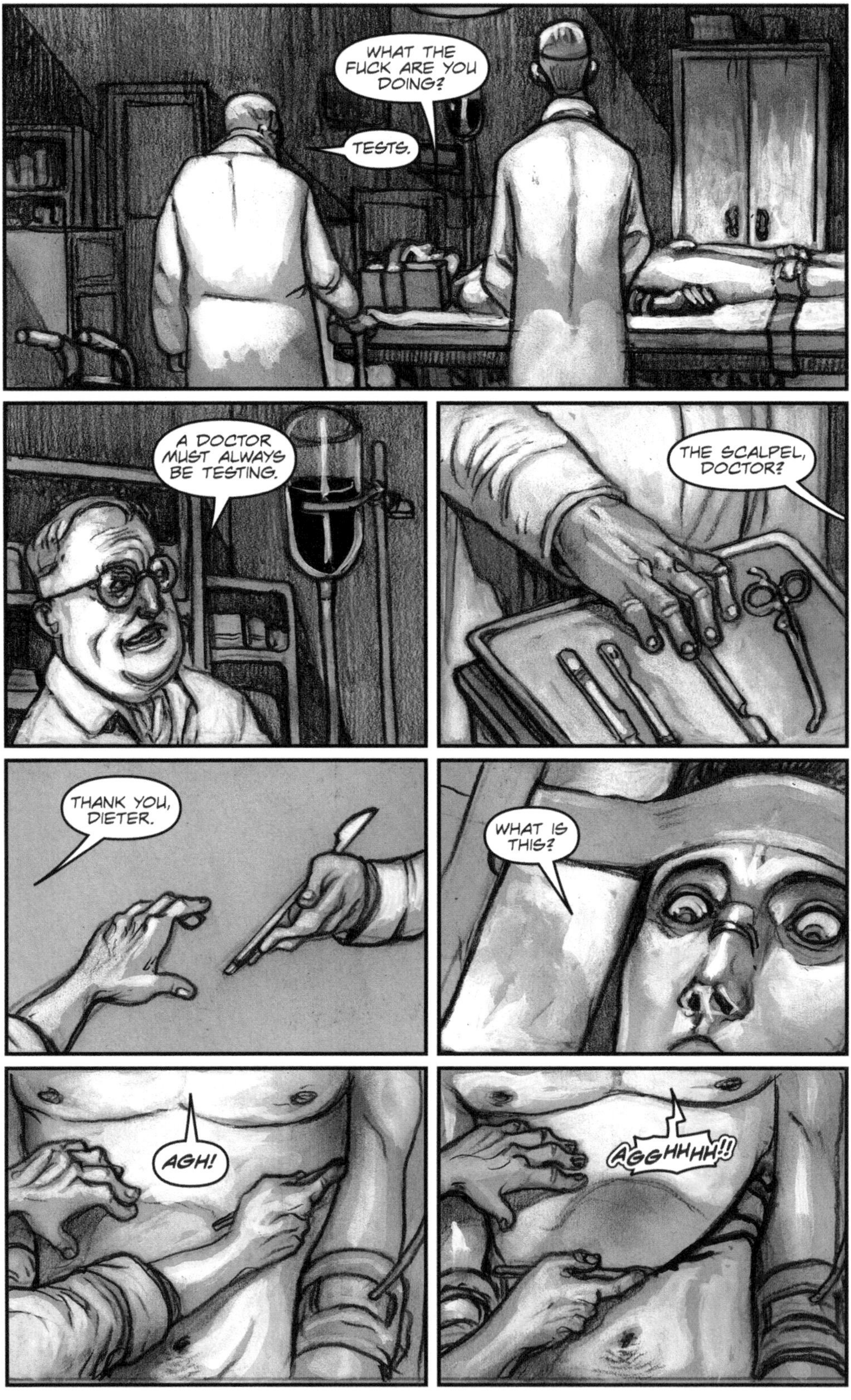
WHAT THE FUCK ARE YOU DOING?
TESTS.
A DOCTOR MUST ALWAYS BE TESTING.
THE SCALPEL, DOCTOR?
THANK YOU, DIETER.
WHAT IS THIS?
AGH!
AGGHHHH!!

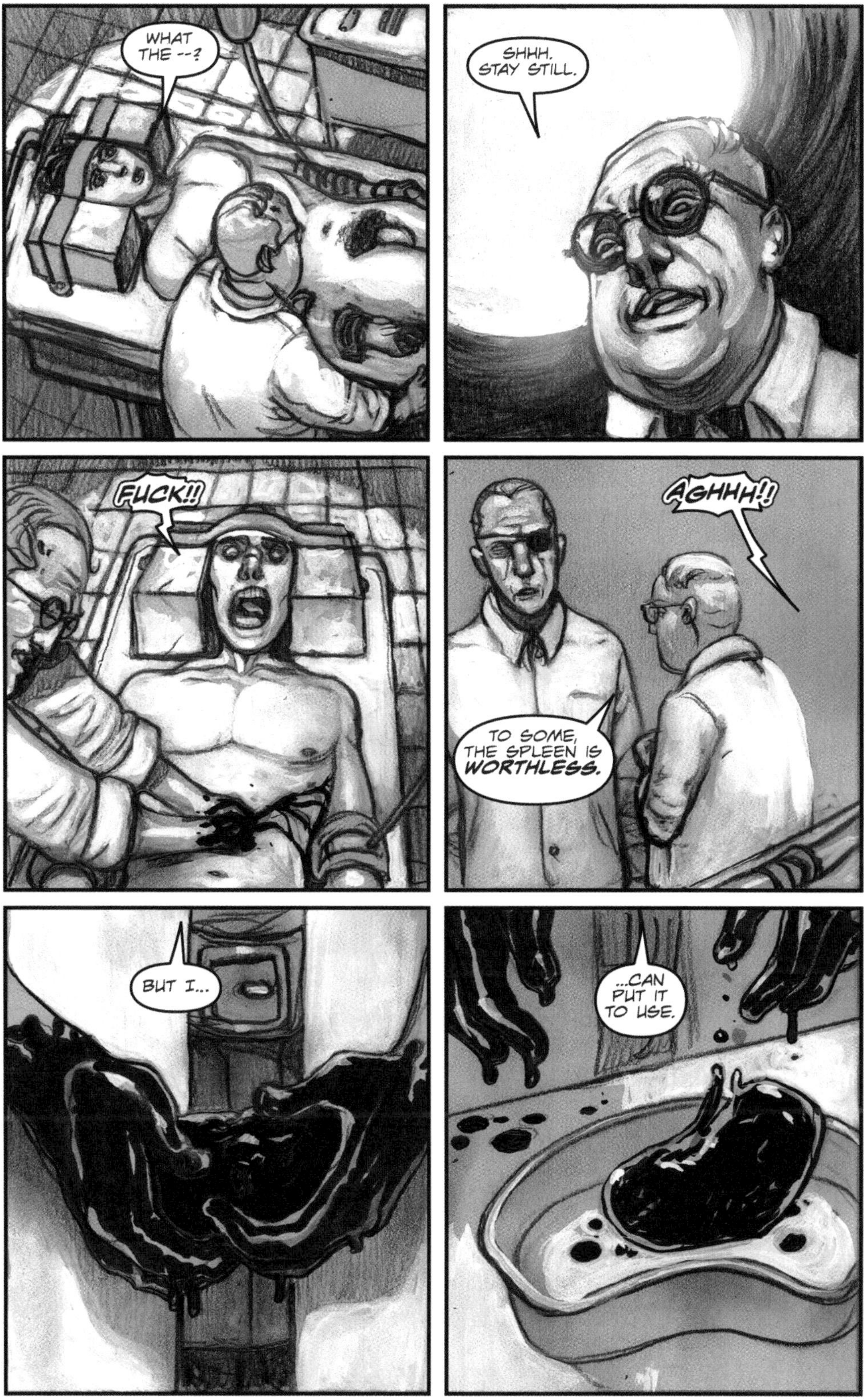
WHAT THE --?
SHHH. STAY STILL.
FUCK!!
AGHHH!!
TO SOME, THE SPLEEN IS **WORTHLESS.**
BUT I...
...CAN PUT IT TO USE.

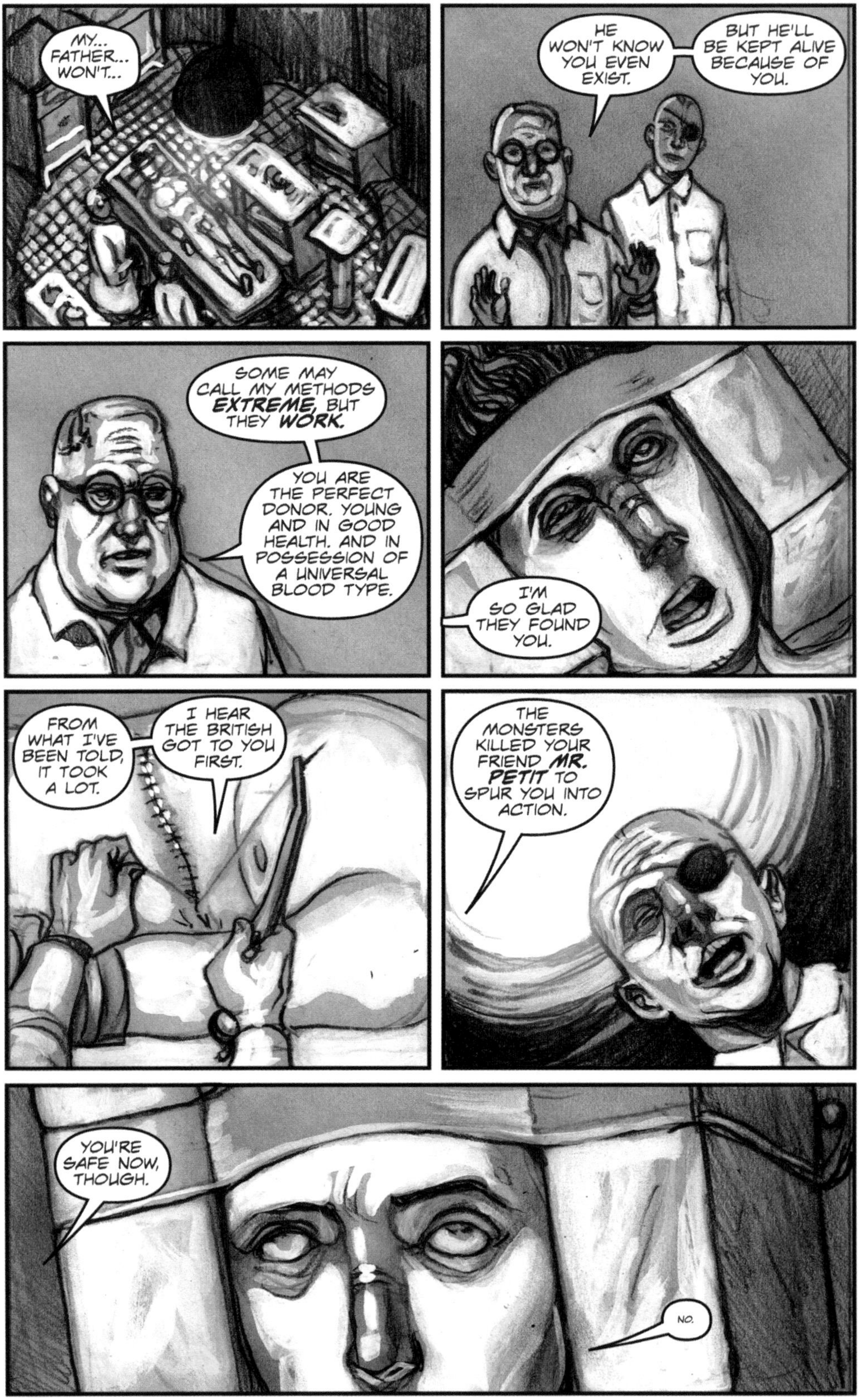
MY... FATHER... WON'T...
HE WON'T KNOW YOU EVEN EXIST.
BUT HE'LL BE KEPT ALIVE BECAUSE OF YOU.
SOME MAY CALL MY METHODS EXTREME, BUT THEY WORK.
YOU ARE THE PERFECT DONOR. YOUNG AND IN GOOD HEALTH. AND IN POSSESSION OF A UNIVERSAL BLOOD TYPE.
I'M SO GLAD THEY FOUND YOU.
FROM WHAT I'VE BEEN TOLD, IT TOOK A LOT.
I HEAR THE BRITISH GOT TO YOU FIRST.
THE MONSTERS KILLED YOUR FRIEND MR. PETIT TO SPUR YOU INTO ACTION.
YOU'RE SAFE NOW, THOUGH.
NO.

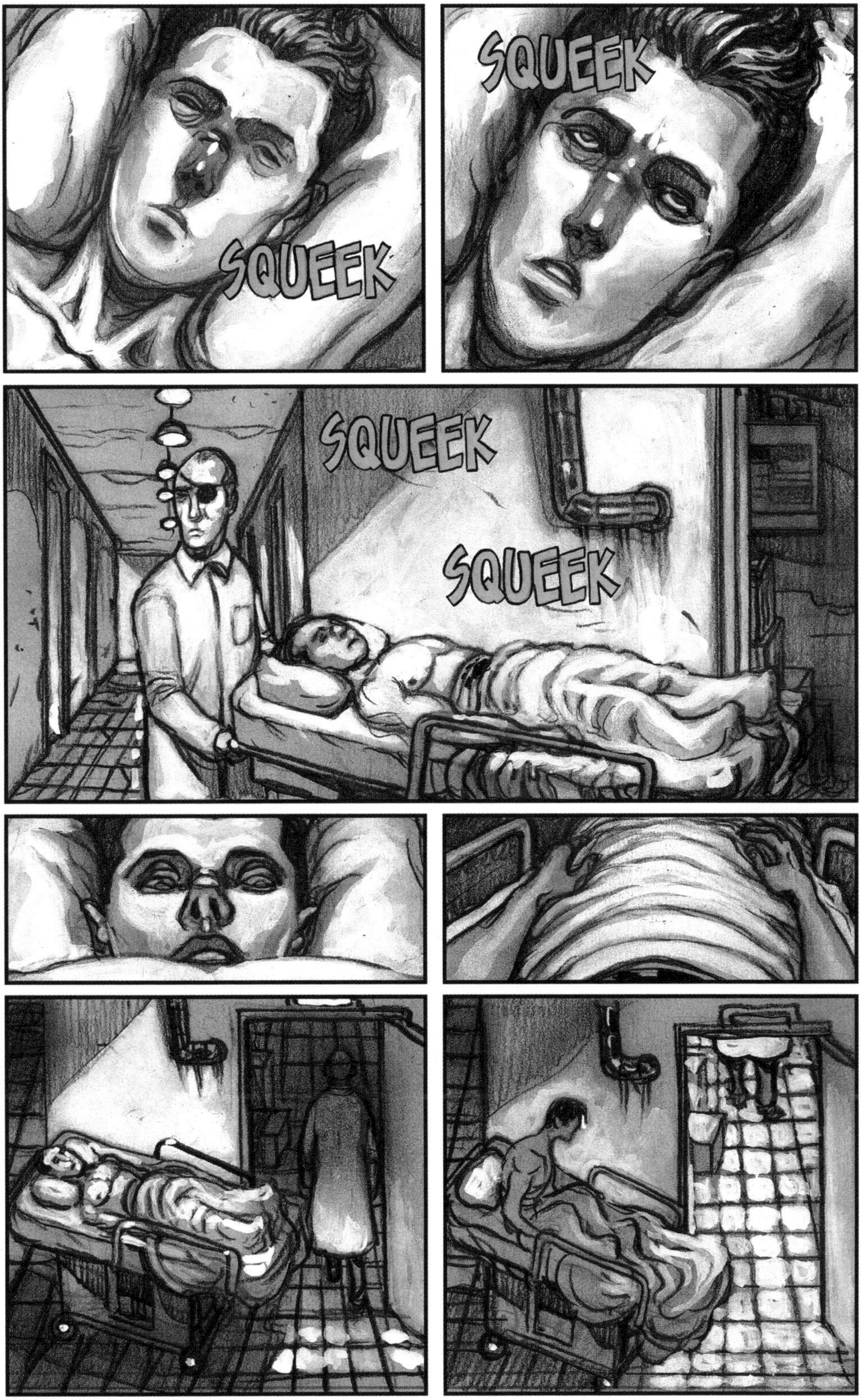
SQUEEK
SQUEEK
SQUEEK
SQUEEK

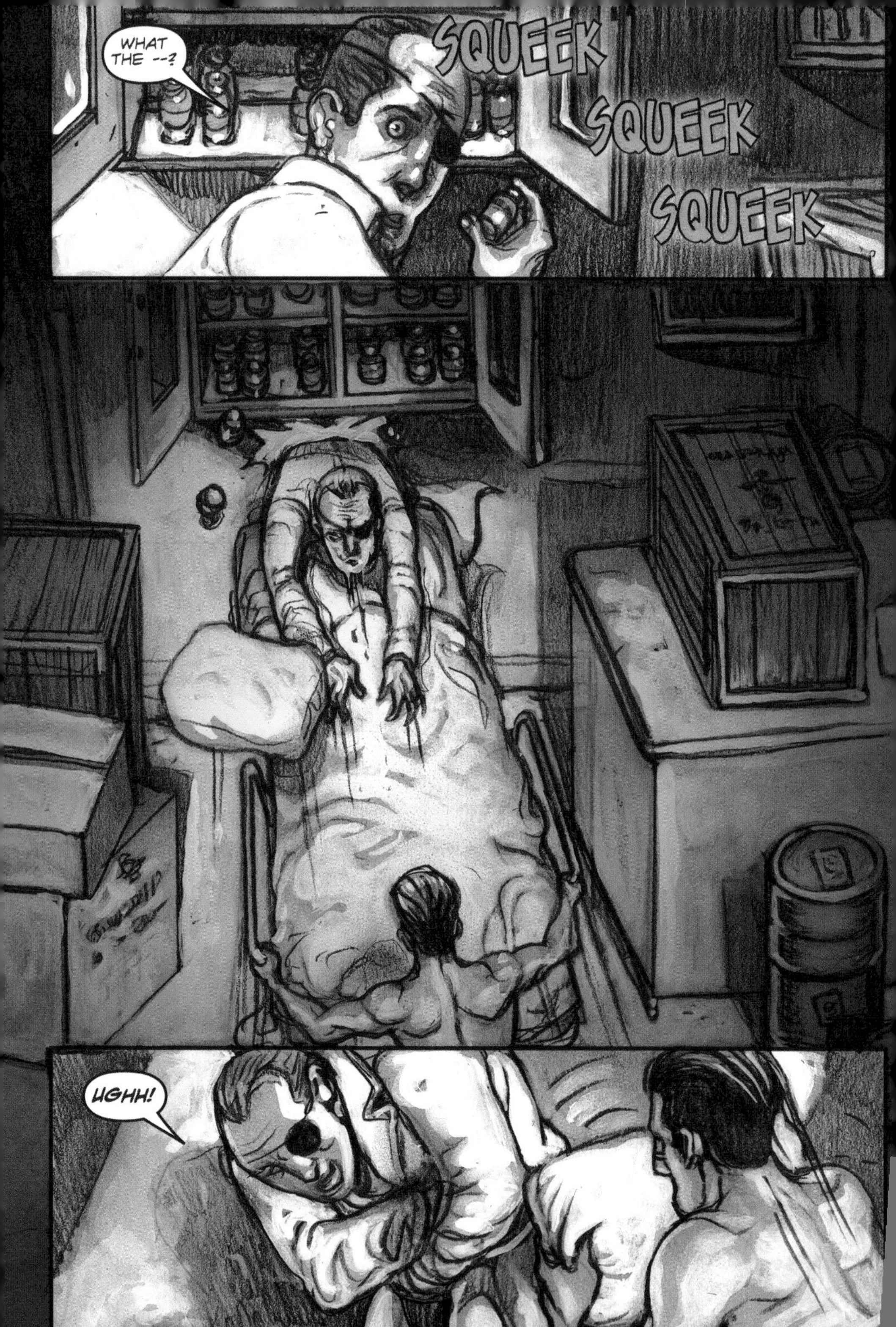
WHAT THE --?
SQUEEK
SQUEEK
SQUEEK
UGHH!

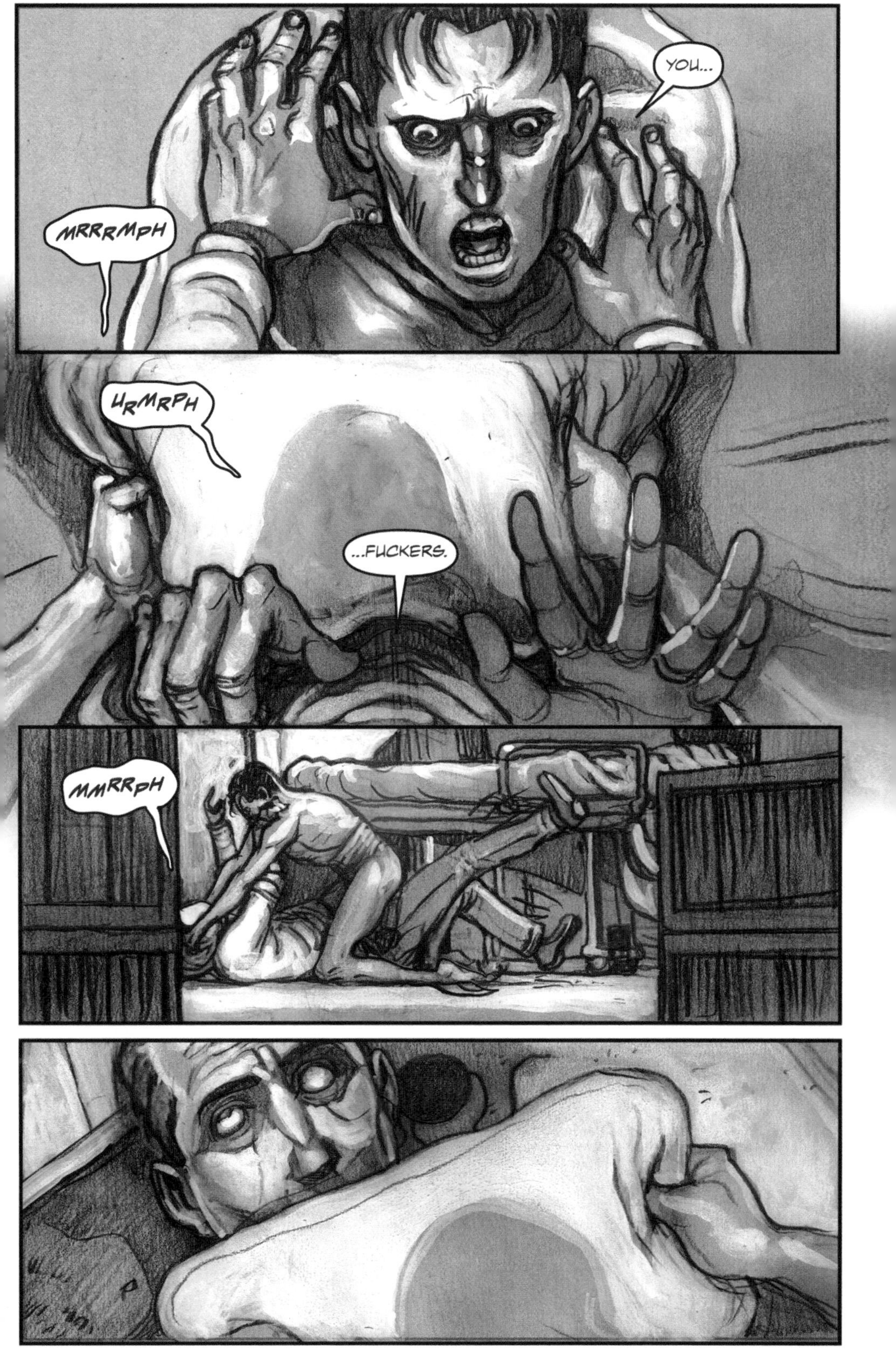
YOU...
MRRRMPH
URMRPH
...FUCKERS.
MMRRPH

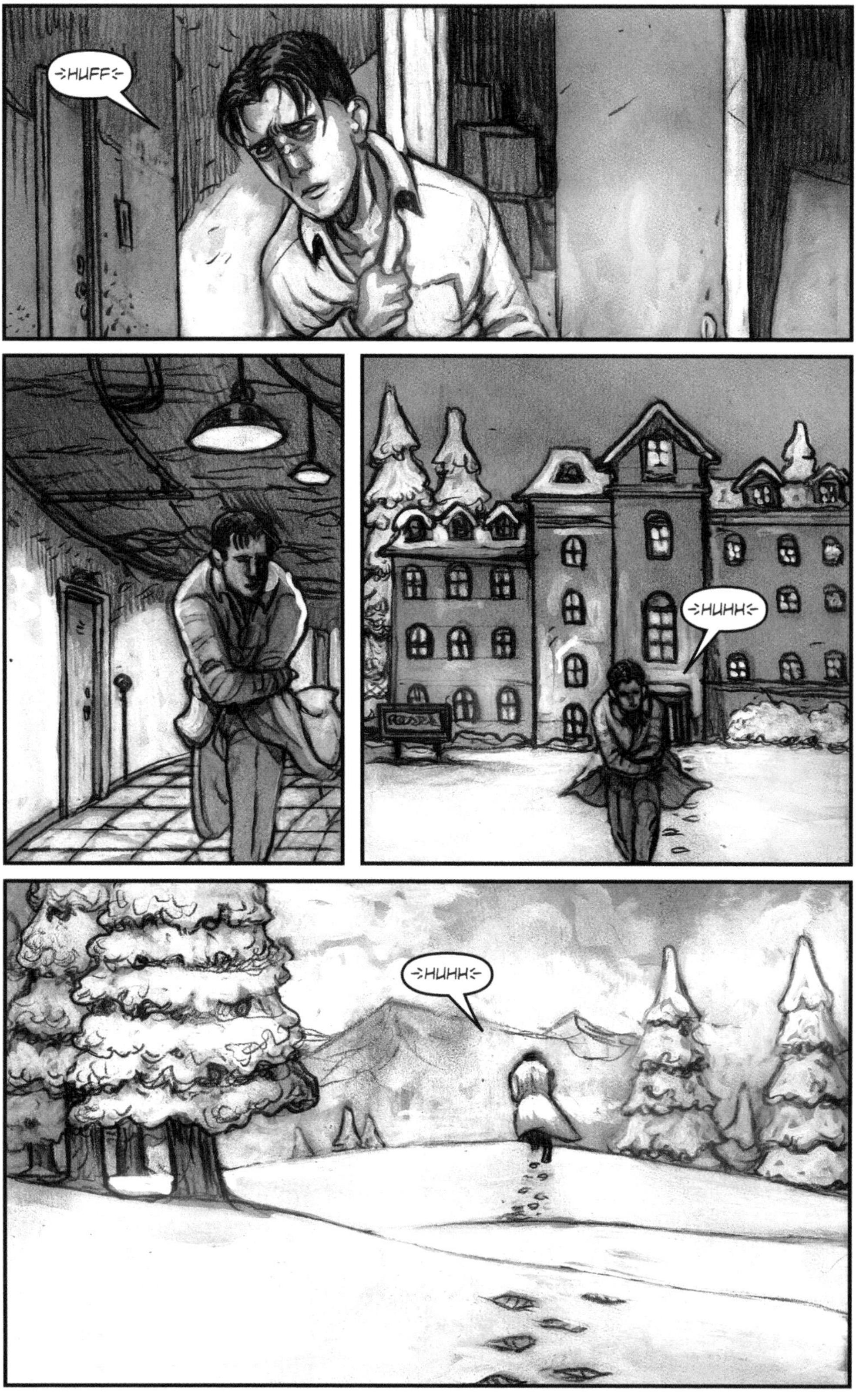
HUFF
HUHH
HUHH

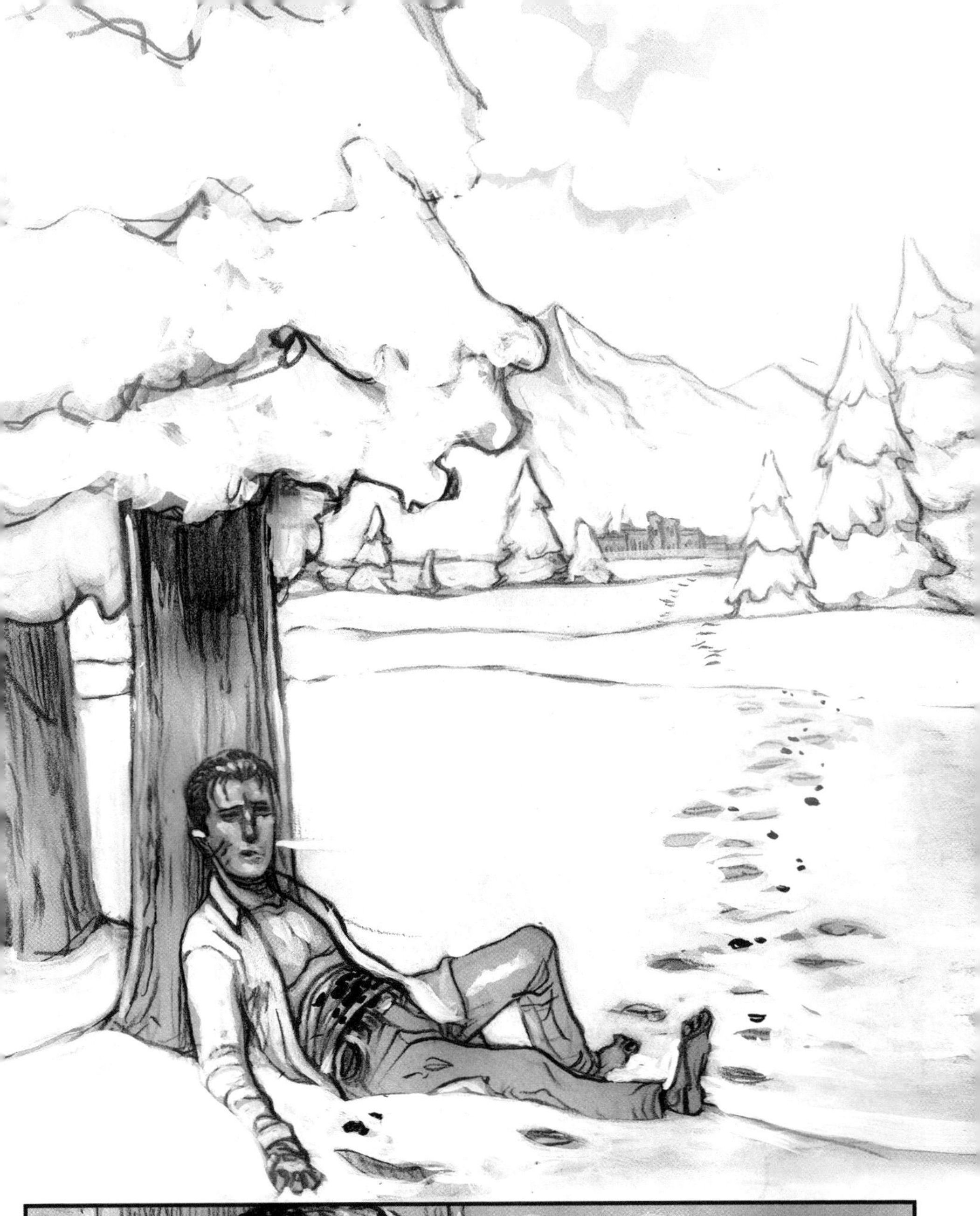
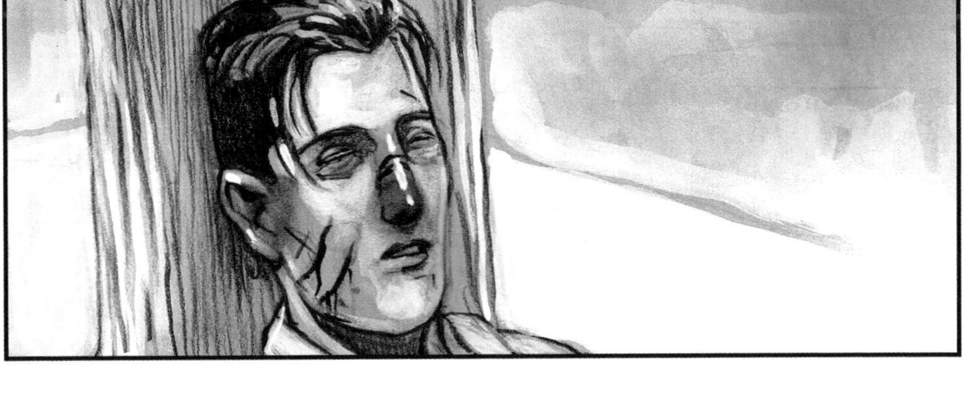

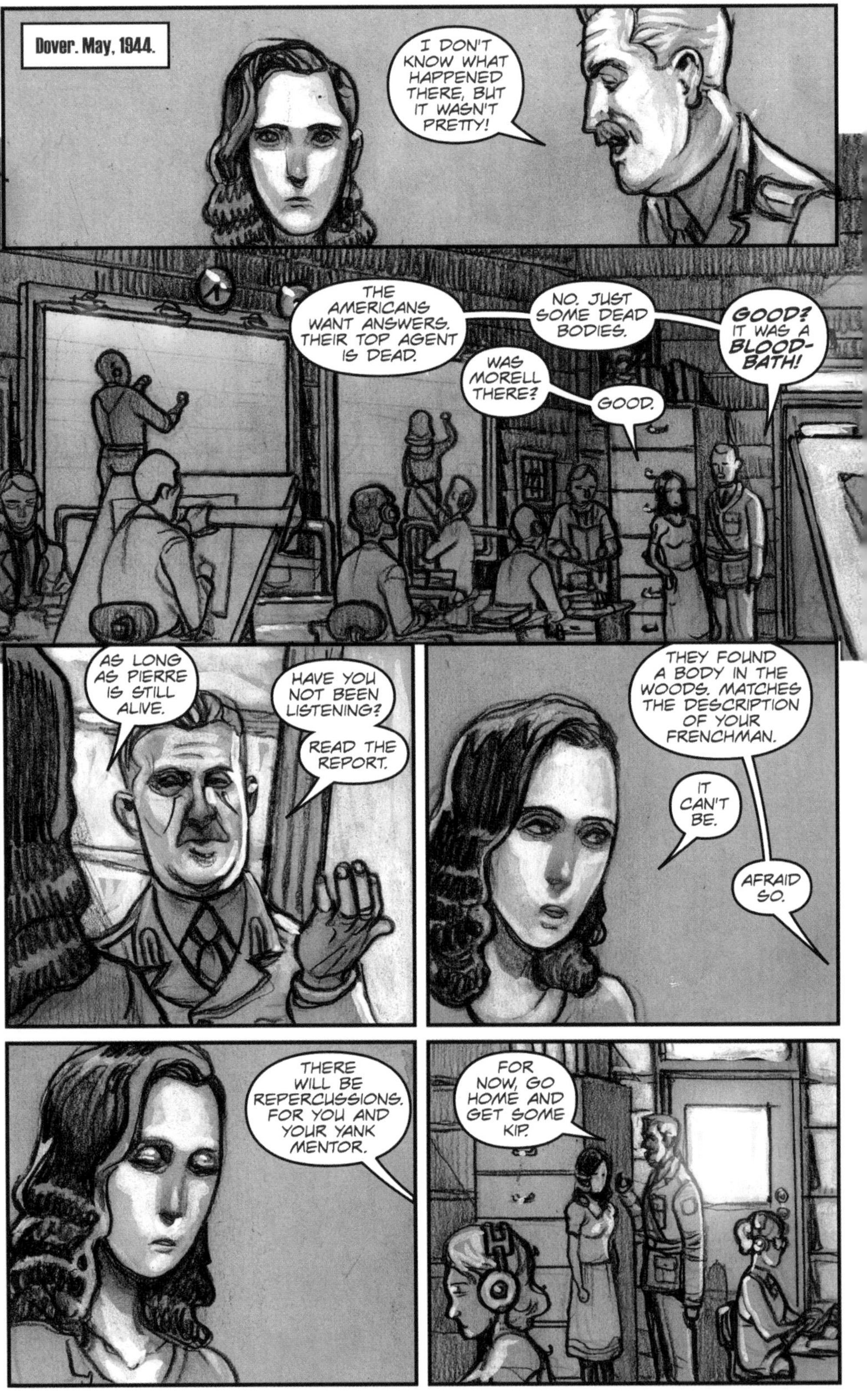
Dover. May, 1944.
I DON'T KNOW WHAT HAPPENED THERE, BUT IT WASN'T PRETTY!
THE AMERICANS WANT ANSWERS. THEIR TOP AGENT IS DEAD.
WAS MORELL THERE?
NO. JUST SOME DEAD BODIES.
GOOD.
GOOD? IT WAS A BLOOD-BATH!
AS LONG AS PIERRE IS STILL ALIVE.
HAVE YOU NOT BEEN LISTENING?
READ THE REPORT.
THEY FOUND A BODY IN THE WOODS. MATCHES THE DESCRIPTION OF YOUR FRENCHMAN.
IT CAN'T BE.
AFRAID SO.
THERE WILL BE REPERCUSSIONS. FOR YOU AND YOUR YANK MENTOR.
FOR NOW, GO HOME AND GET SOME KIP.

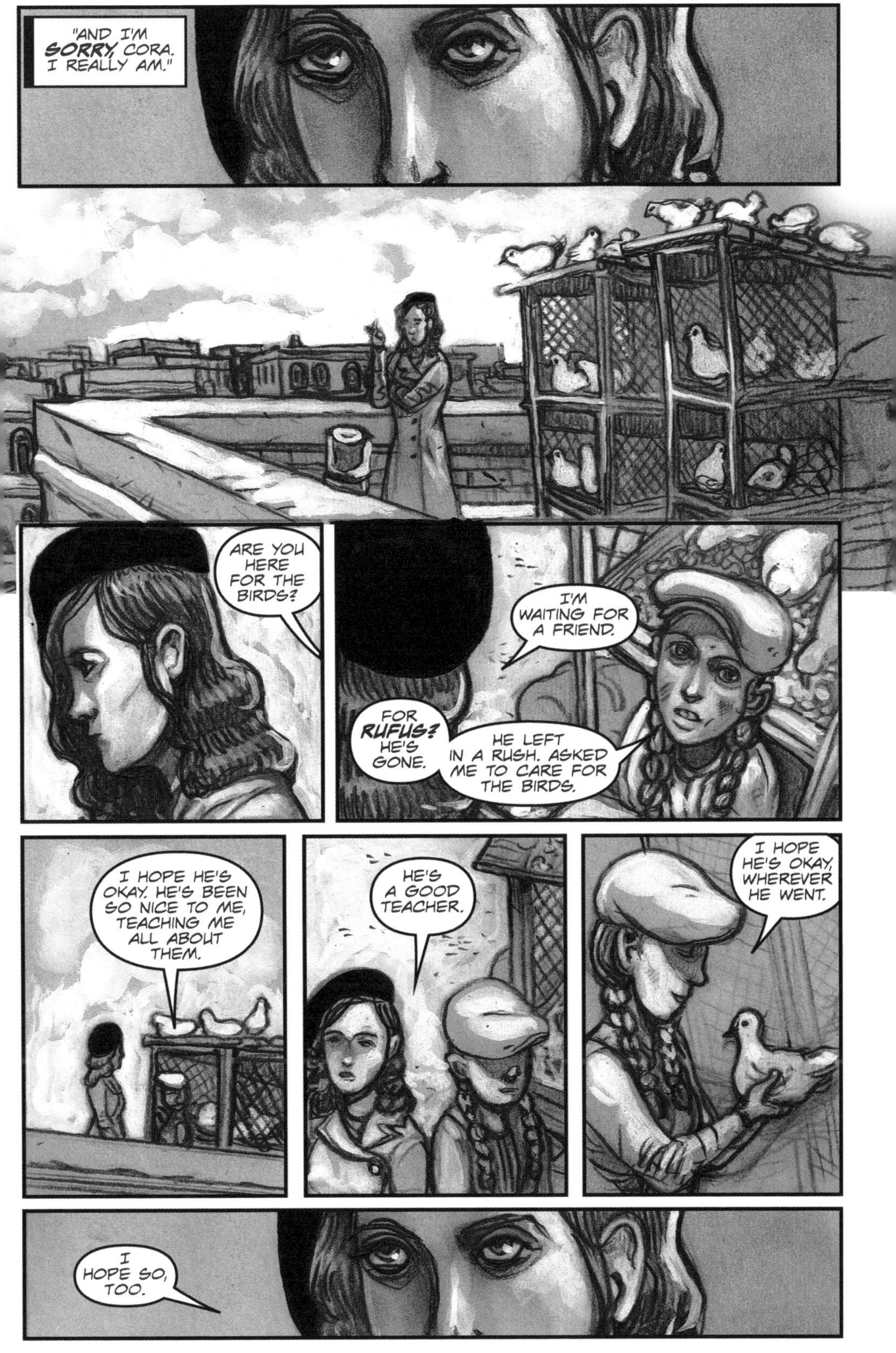
"AND I'M SORRY, CORA. I REALLY AM."
ARE YOU HERE FOR THE BIRDS?
I'M WAITING FOR A FRIEND.
FOR RUFUS? HE'S GONE.
HE LEFT IN A RUSH. ASKED ME TO CARE FOR THE BIRDS.
I HOPE HE'S OKAY. HE'S BEEN SO NICE TO ME, TEACHING ME ALL ABOUT THEM.
HE'S A GOOD TEACHER.
I HOPE HE'S OKAY, WHEREVER HE WENT.
I HOPE SO, TOO.

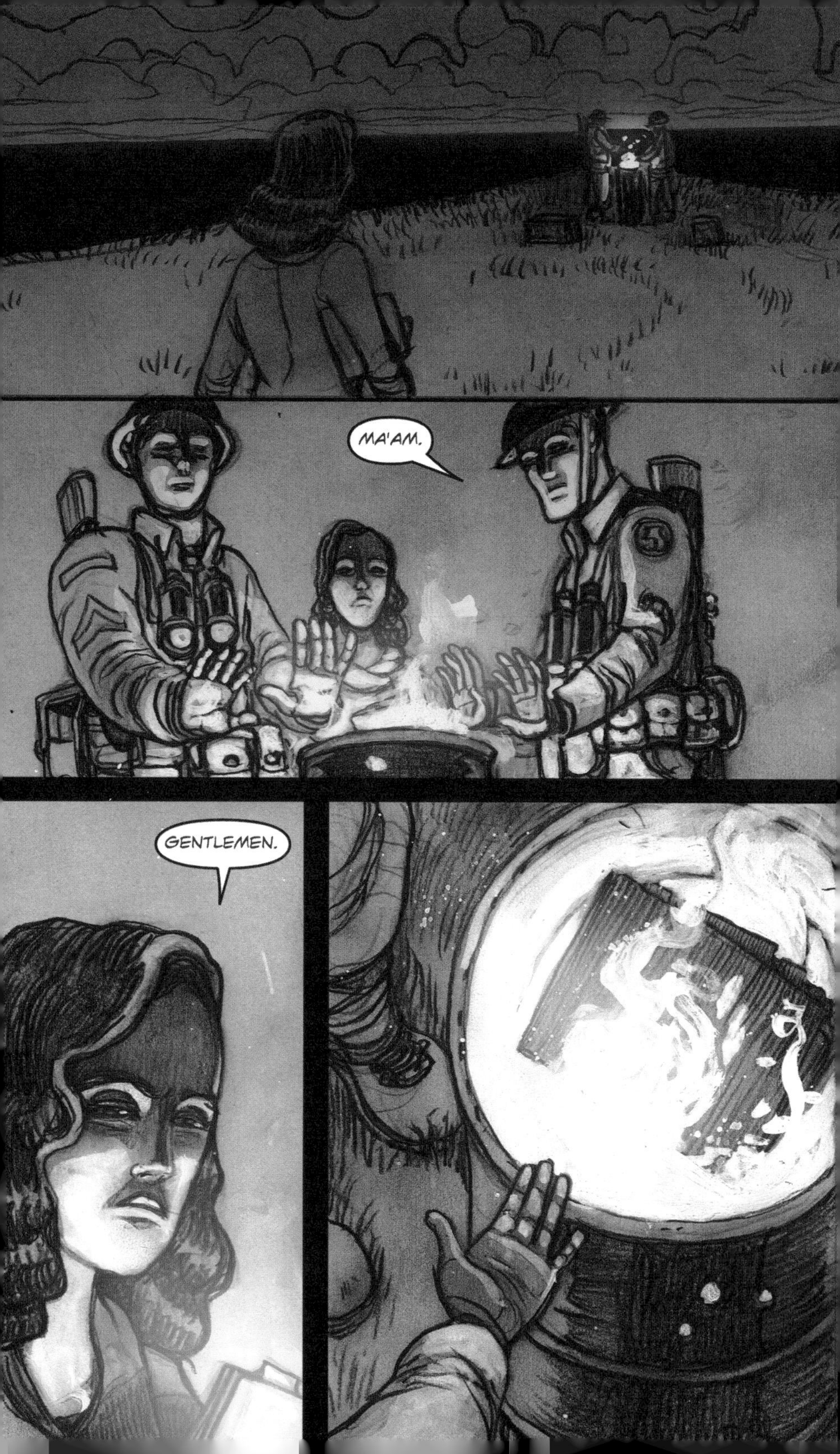
MA'AM.
GENTLEMEN.

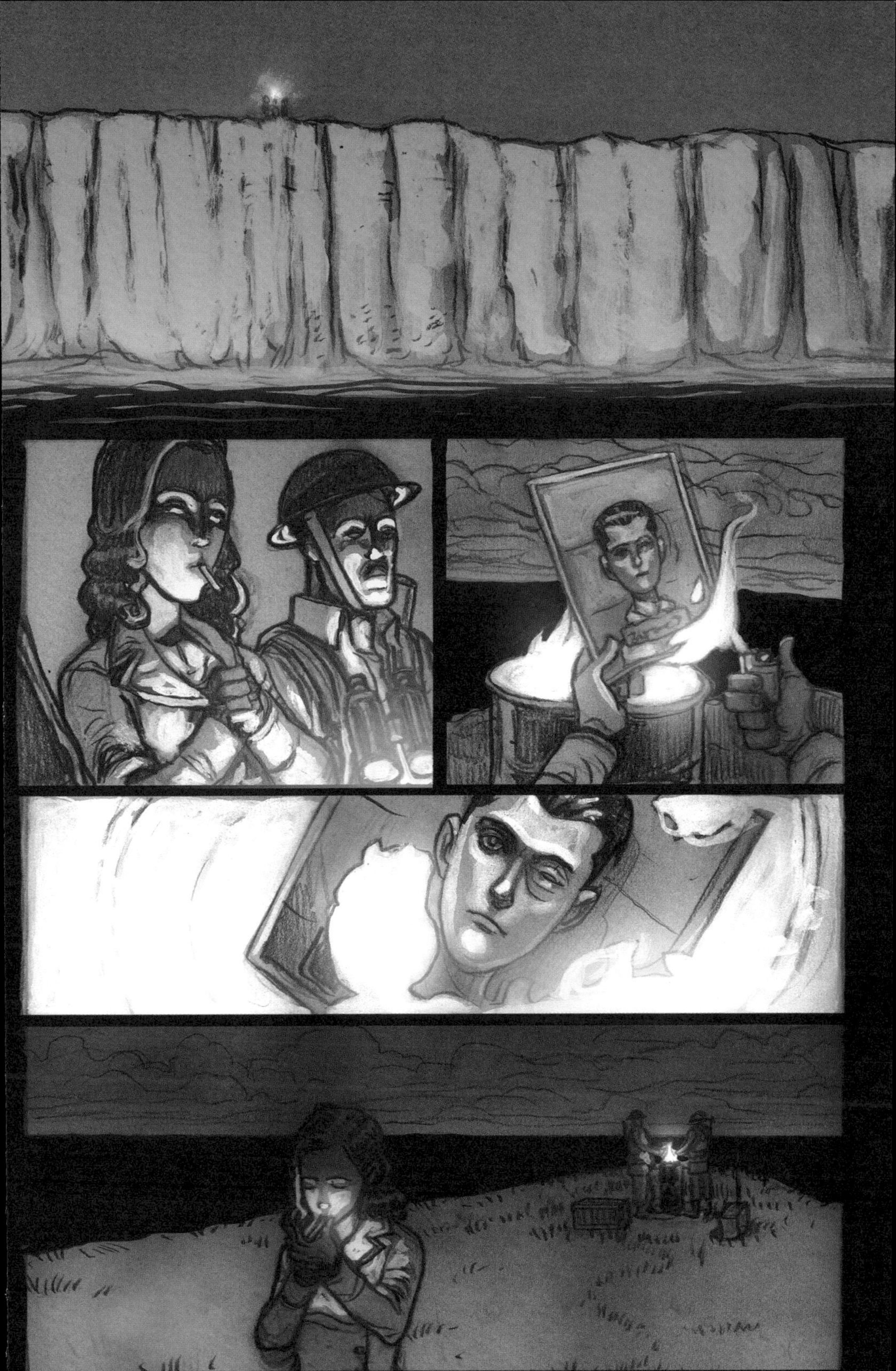

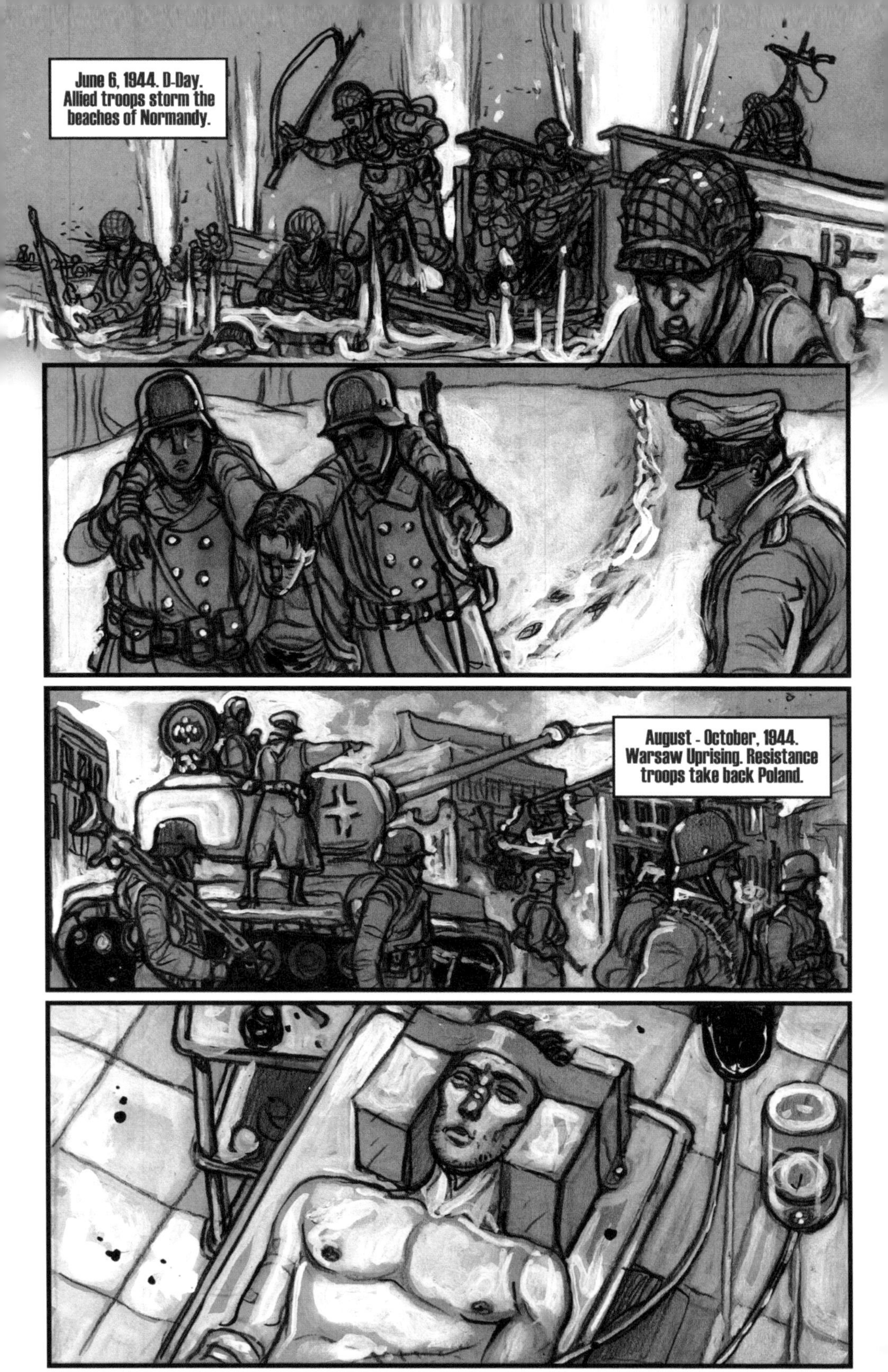
June 6, 1944. D-Day. Allied troops storm the beaches of Normandy.
August - October, 1944. Warsaw Uprising. Resistance troops take back Poland.

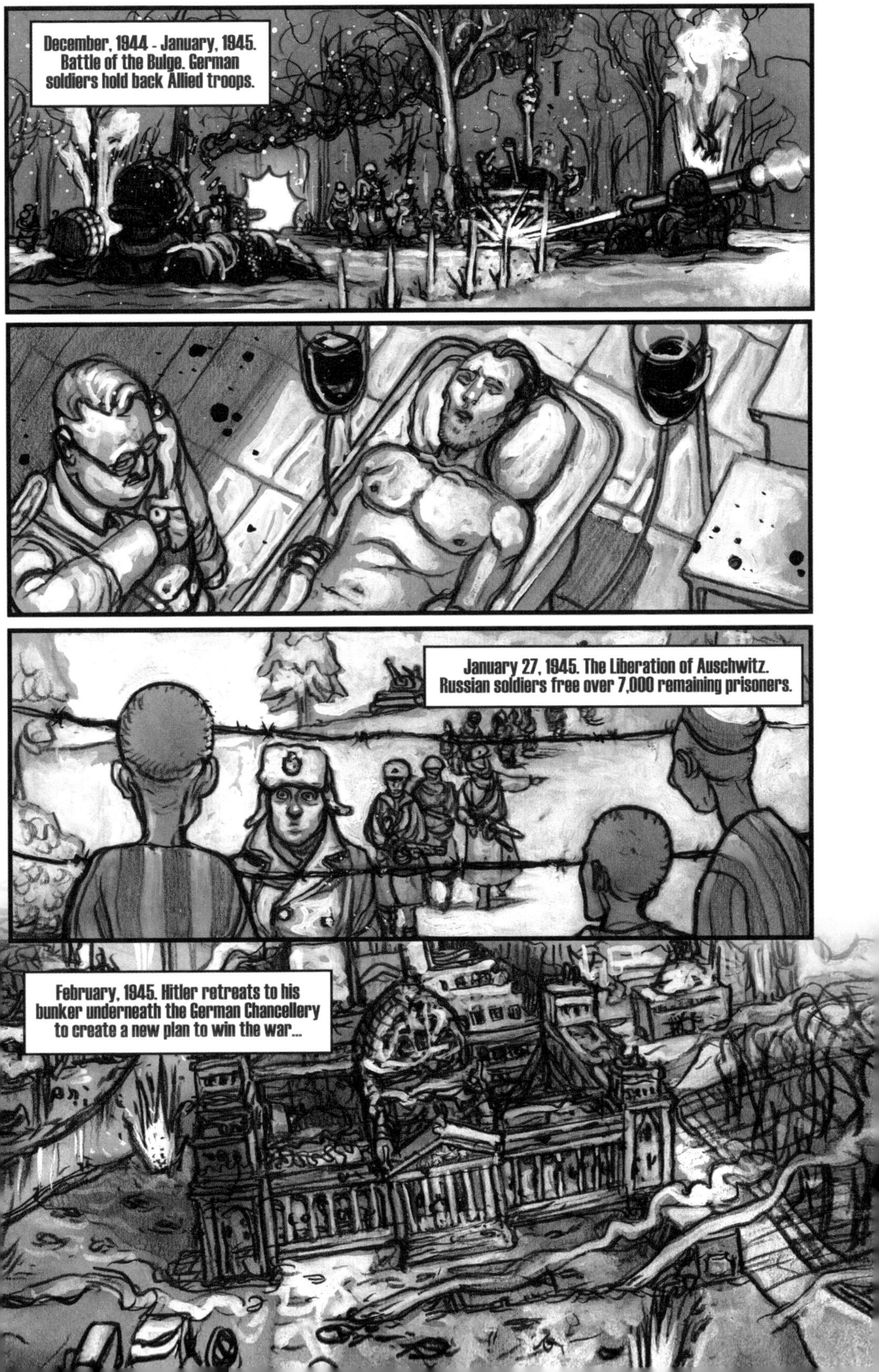
December, 1944 - January, 1945. Battle of the Bulge. German soldiers hold back Allied troops.
January 27, 1945. The Liberation of Auschwitz. Russian soldiers free over 7,000 remaining prisoners.
February, 1945. Hitler retreats to his bunker underneath the German Chancellery to create a new plan to win the war...

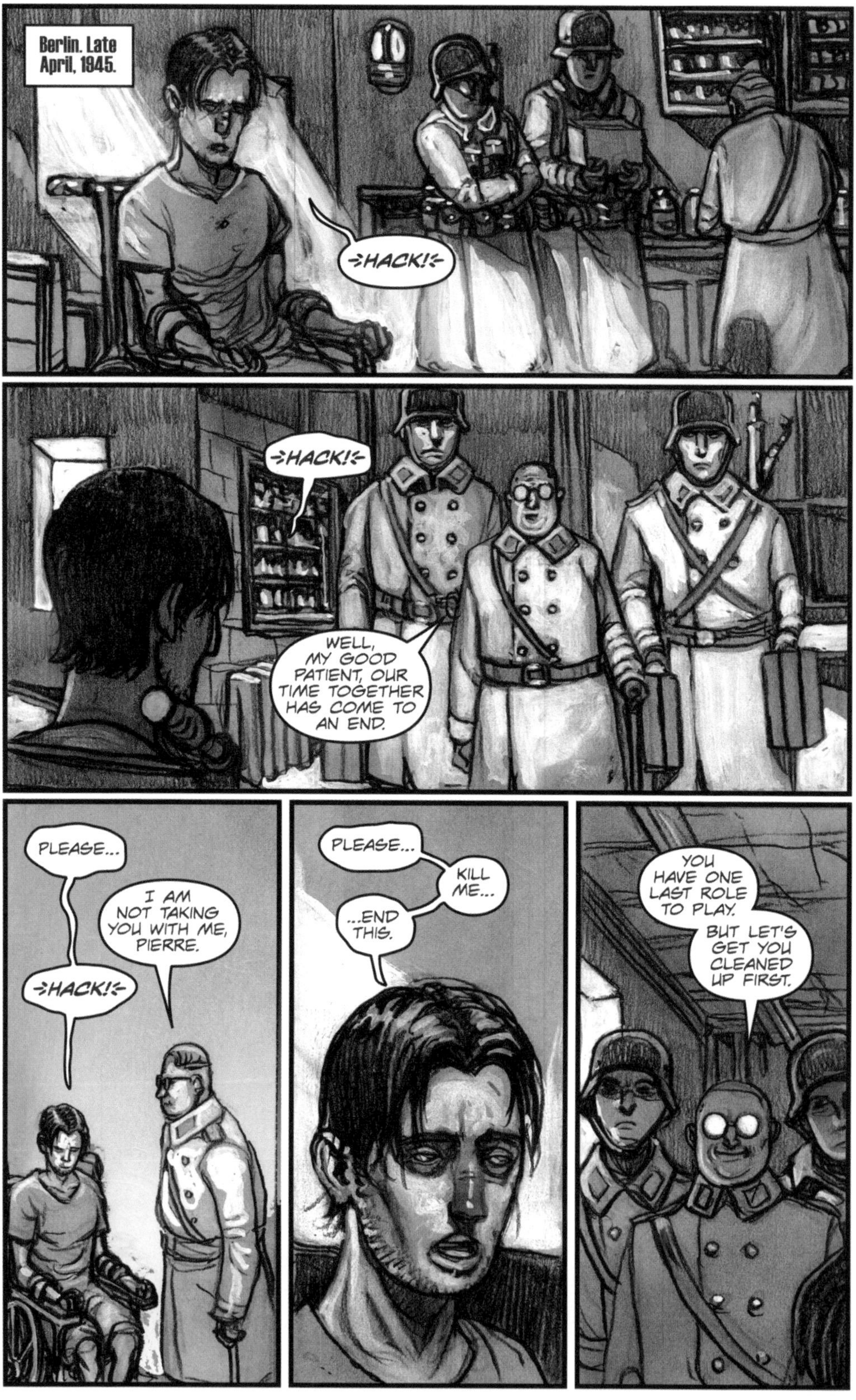
Berlin. Late April, 1945.
HACK!
HACK!
WELL, MY GOOD PATIENT, OUR TIME TOGETHER HAS COME TO AN END.
PLEASE...
I AM NOT TAKING YOU WITH ME, PIERRE.
HACK!
PLEASE...
KILL ME...
...END THIS.
YOU HAVE ONE LAST ROLE TO PLAY.
BUT LET'S GET YOU CLEANED UP FIRST.

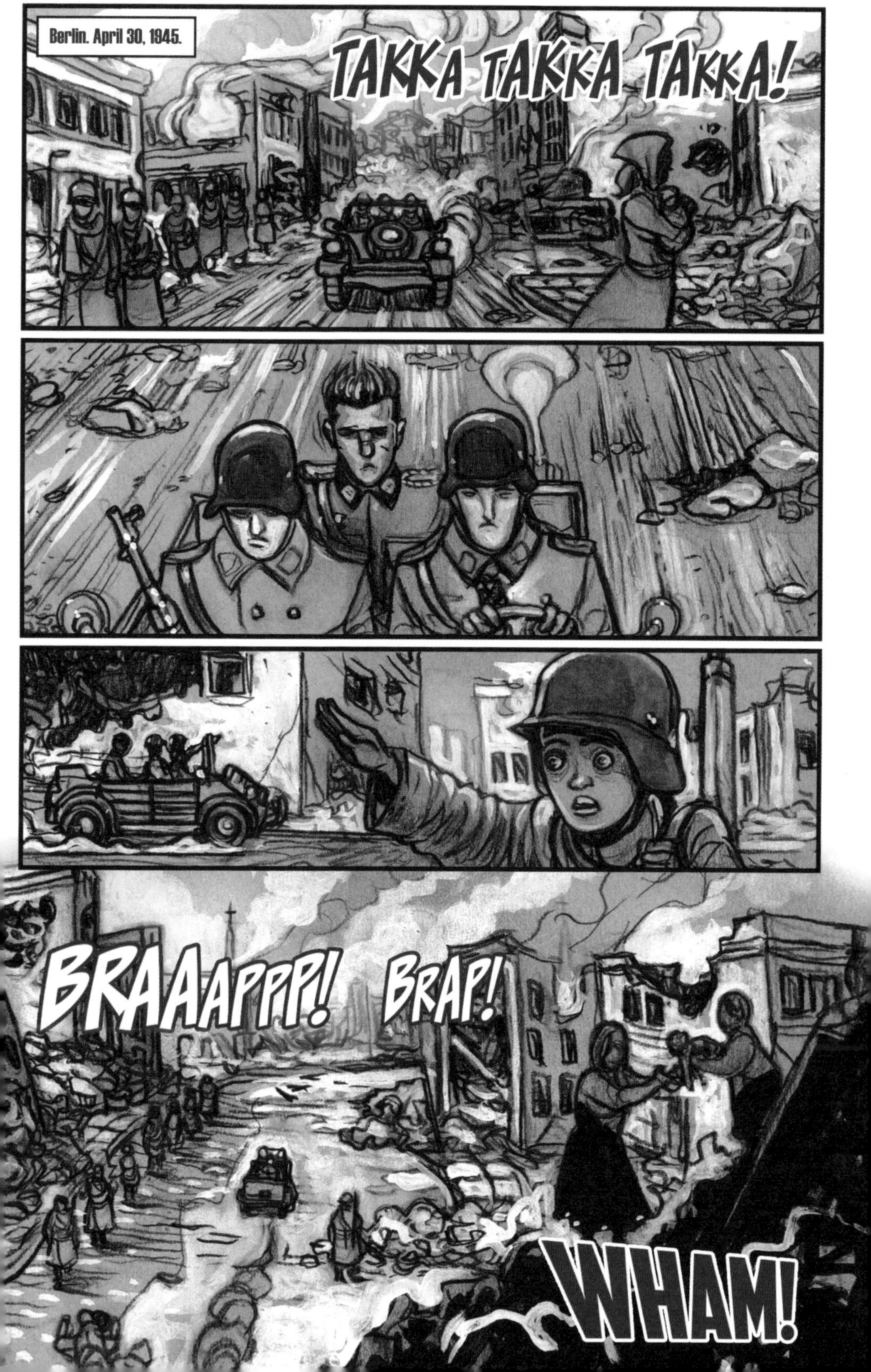
Berlin. April 30, 1945.
TAKKA TAKKA TAKKA!
BRAAAPPP! BRAP!
WHAM!

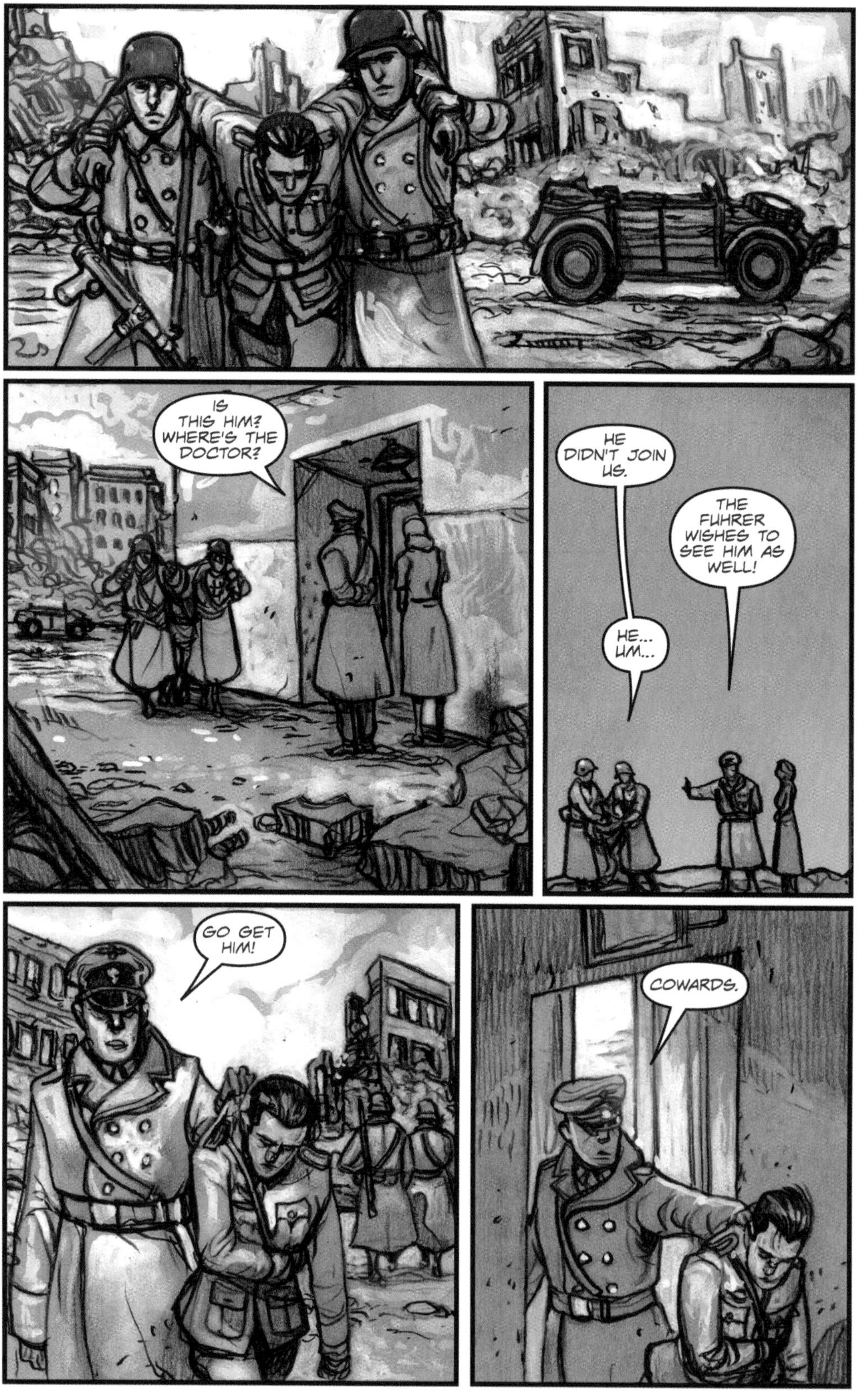
IS THIS HIM? WHERE'S THE DOCTOR?
HE DIDN'T JOIN US.
HE... UM...
THE FUHRER WISHES TO SEE HIM AS WELL!
GO GET HIM!
COWARDS.

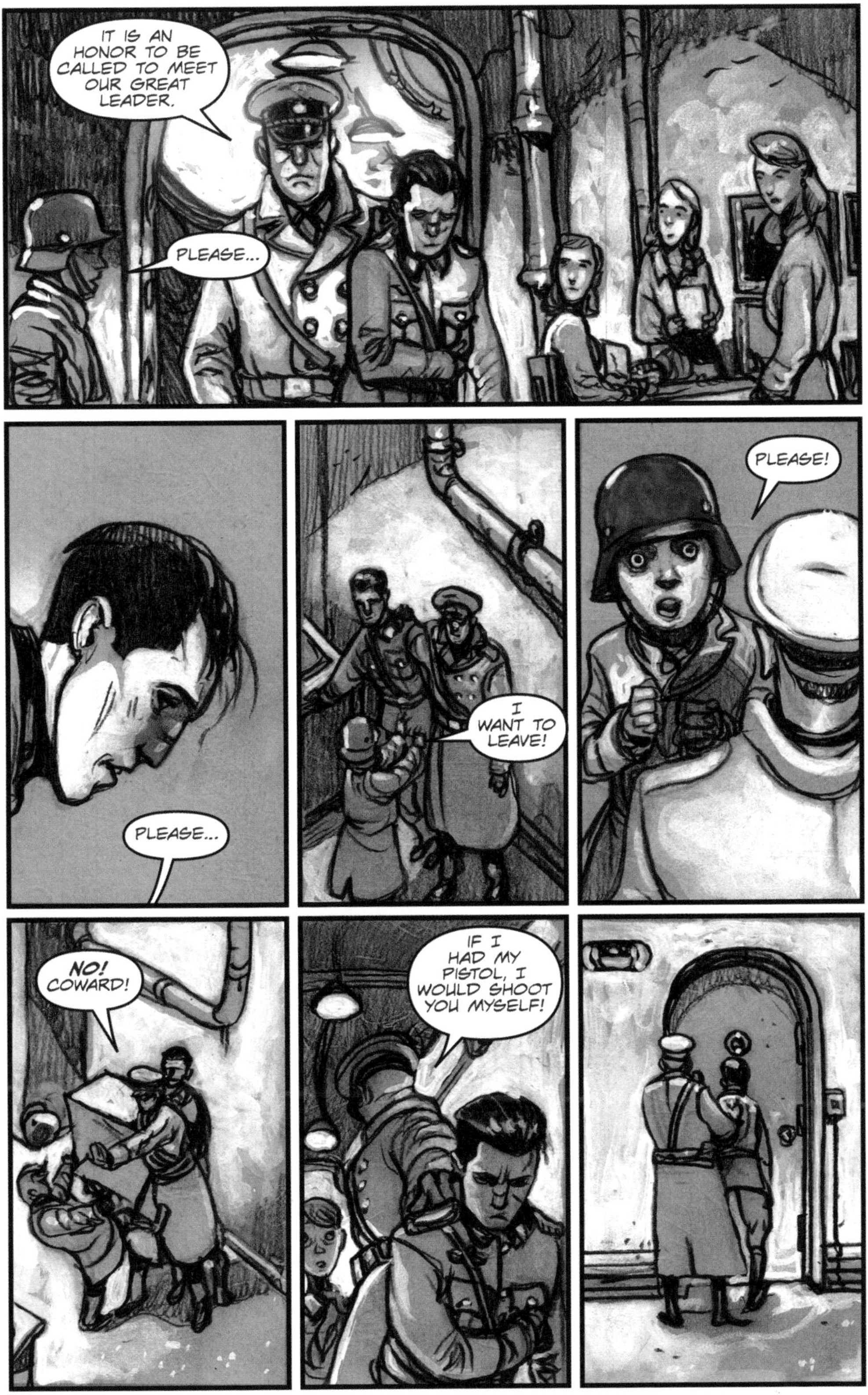
IT IS AN HONOR TO BE CALLED TO MEET OUR GREAT LEADER.
PLEASE...
PLEASE...
I WANT TO LEAVE!
PLEASE!
NO! COWARD!
IF I HAD MY PISTOL, I WOULD SHOOT YOU MYSELF!

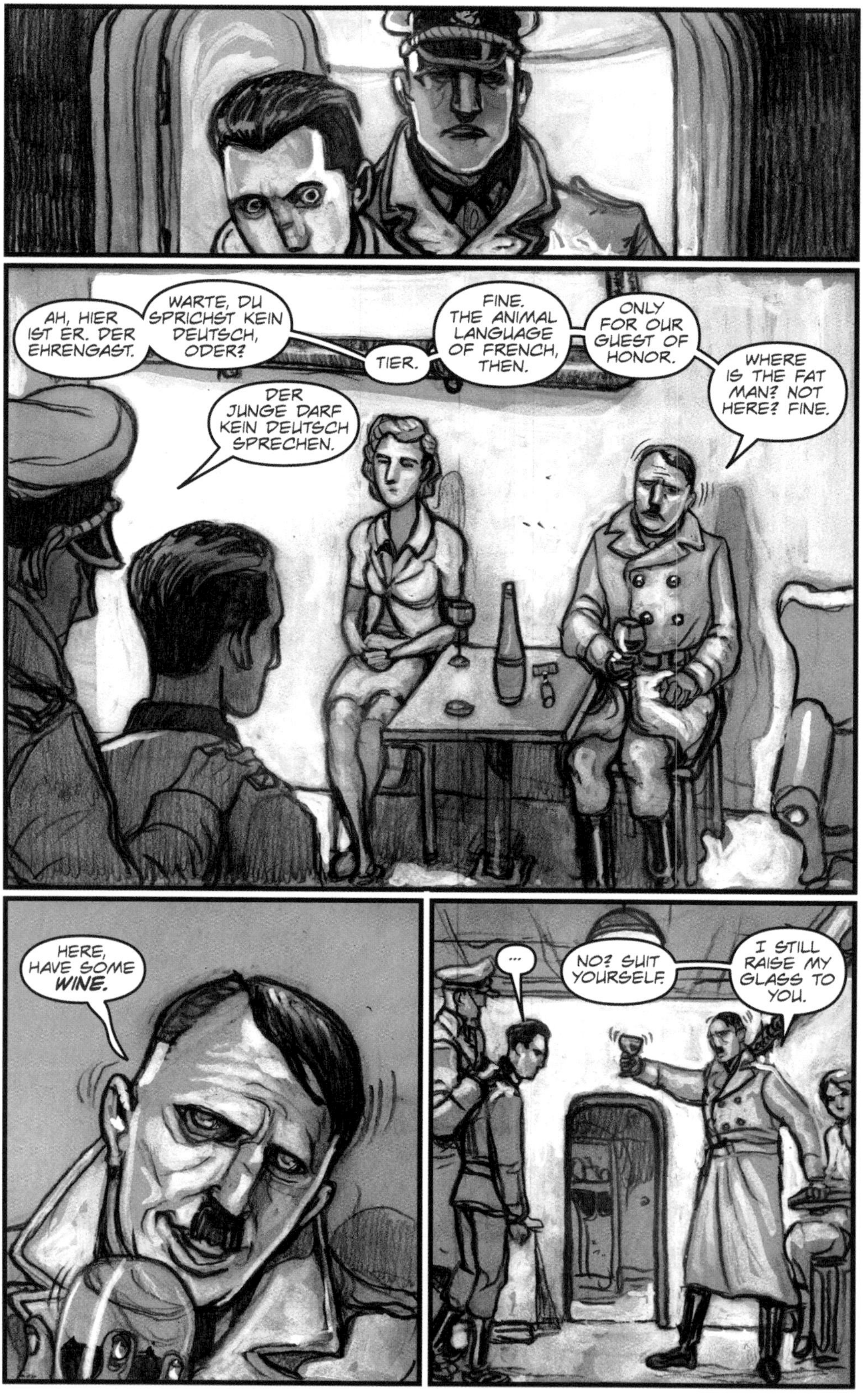
AH, HIER IST ER. DER EHRENGAST.
WARTE, DU SPRICHST KEIN DEUTSCH, ODER?
TIER.
FINE. THE ANIMAL LANGUAGE OF FRENCH, THEN.
ONLY FOR OUR GUEST OF HONOR.
DER JUNGE DARF KEIN DEUTSCH SPRECHEN.
WHERE IS THE FAT MAN? NOT HERE? FINE.
HERE, HAVE SOME **WINE.**
...
NO? SUIT YOURSELF.
I STILL RAISE MY GLASS TO YOU.

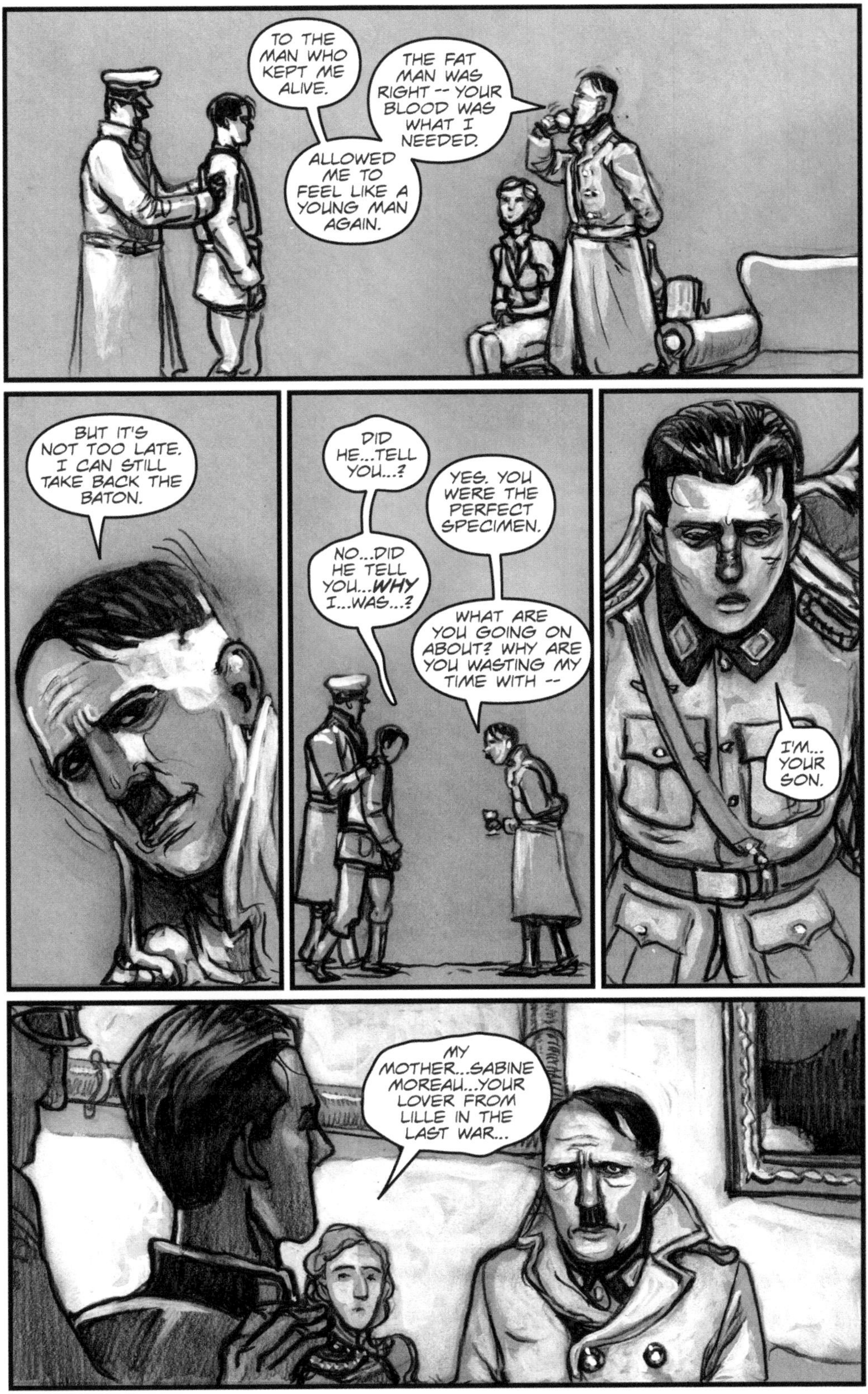
TO THE MAN WHO KEPT ME ALIVE.
ALLOWED ME TO FEEL LIKE A YOUNG MAN AGAIN.
THE FAT MAN WAS RIGHT -- YOUR BLOOD WAS WHAT I NEEDED.
BUT IT'S NOT TOO LATE. I CAN STILL TAKE BACK THE BATON.
DID HE...TELL YOU...?
YES. YOU WERE THE PERFECT SPECIMEN.
NO...DID HE TELL YOU...*WHY* I...WAS...?
WHAT ARE YOU GOING ON ABOUT? WHY ARE YOU WASTING MY TIME WITH --
I'M... YOUR SON.
MY MOTHER...SABINE MOREAU...YOUR LOVER FROM LILLE IN THE LAST WAR...

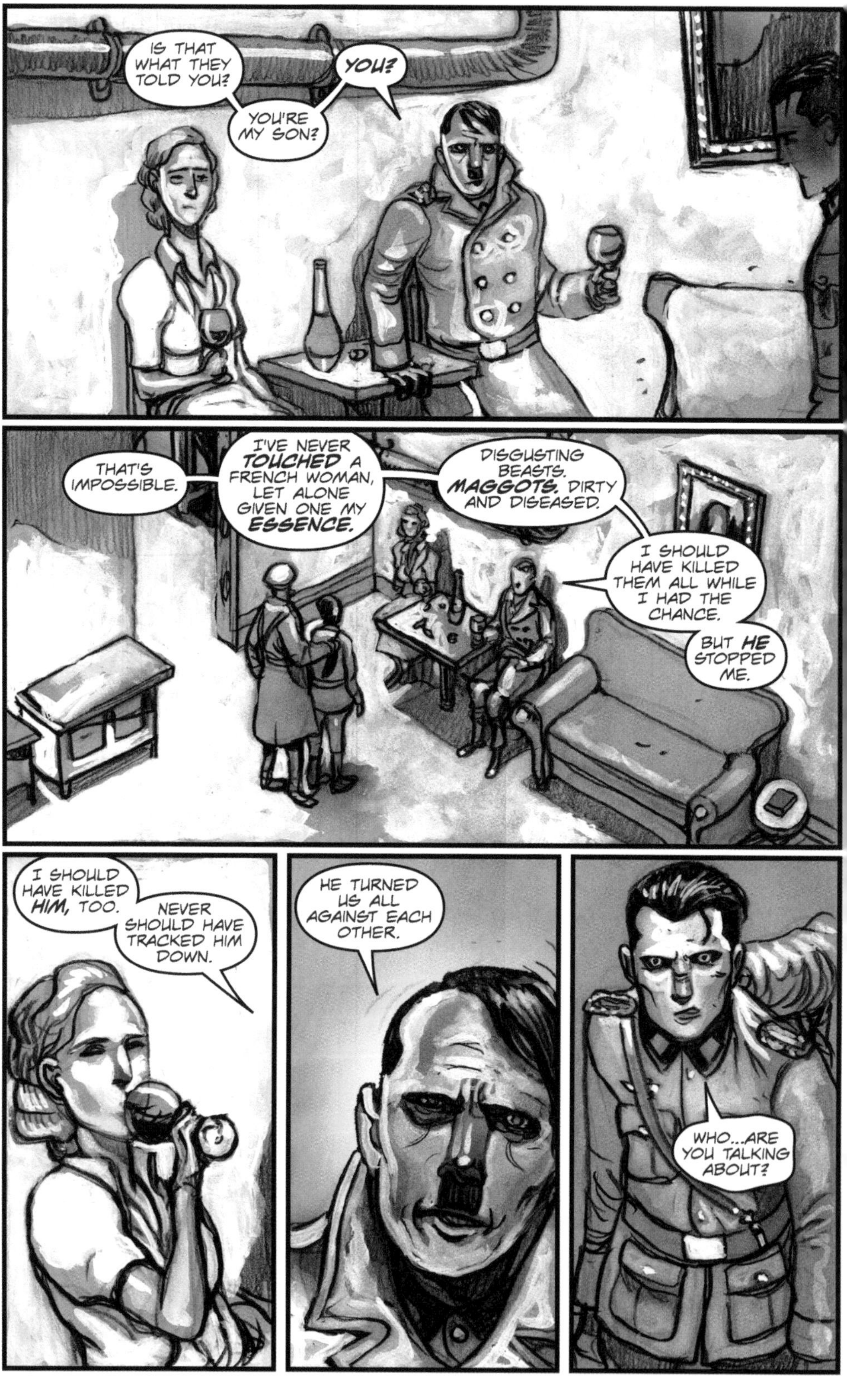
IS THAT WHAT THEY TOLD YOU?
YOU'RE MY SON?
YOU?
THAT'S IMPOSSIBLE.
I'VE NEVER TOUCHED A FRENCH WOMAN, LET ALONE GIVEN ONE MY ESSENCE.
DISGUSTING BEASTS. MAGGOTS. DIRTY AND DISEASED.
I SHOULD HAVE KILLED THEM ALL WHILE I HAD THE CHANCE.
BUT HE STOPPED ME.
I SHOULD HAVE KILLED HIM, TOO.
NEVER SHOULD HAVE TRACKED HIM DOWN.
HE TURNED US ALL AGAINST EACH OTHER.
WHO...ARE YOU TALKING ABOUT?

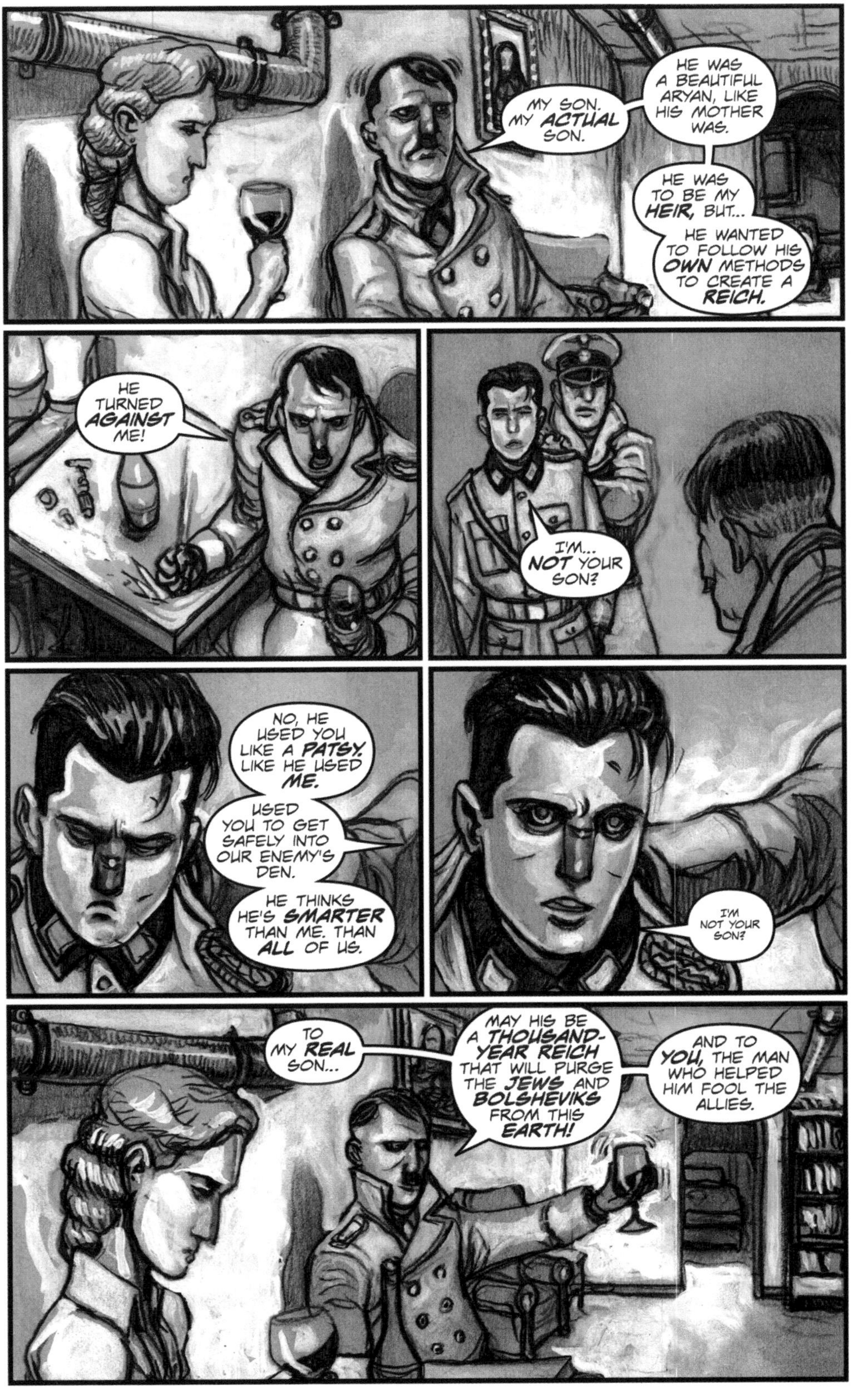
MY SON. MY ACTUAL SON.
HE WAS A BEAUTIFUL ARYAN, LIKE HIS MOTHER WAS.
HE WAS TO BE MY HEIR, BUT...
HE WANTED TO FOLLOW HIS OWN METHODS TO CREATE A REICH.
HE TURNED AGAINST ME!
I'M... NOT YOUR SON?
NO, HE USED YOU LIKE A PATSY. LIKE HE USED ME.
USED YOU TO GET SAFELY INTO OUR ENEMY'S DEN.
HE THINKS HE'S SMARTER THAN ME. THAN ALL OF US.
I'M NOT YOUR SON?
TO MY REAL SON...
MAY HIS BE A THOUSAND-YEAR REICH THAT WILL PURGE THE JEWS AND BOLSHEVIKS FROM THIS EARTH!
AND TO YOU, THE MAN WHO HELPED HIM FOOL THE ALLIES.

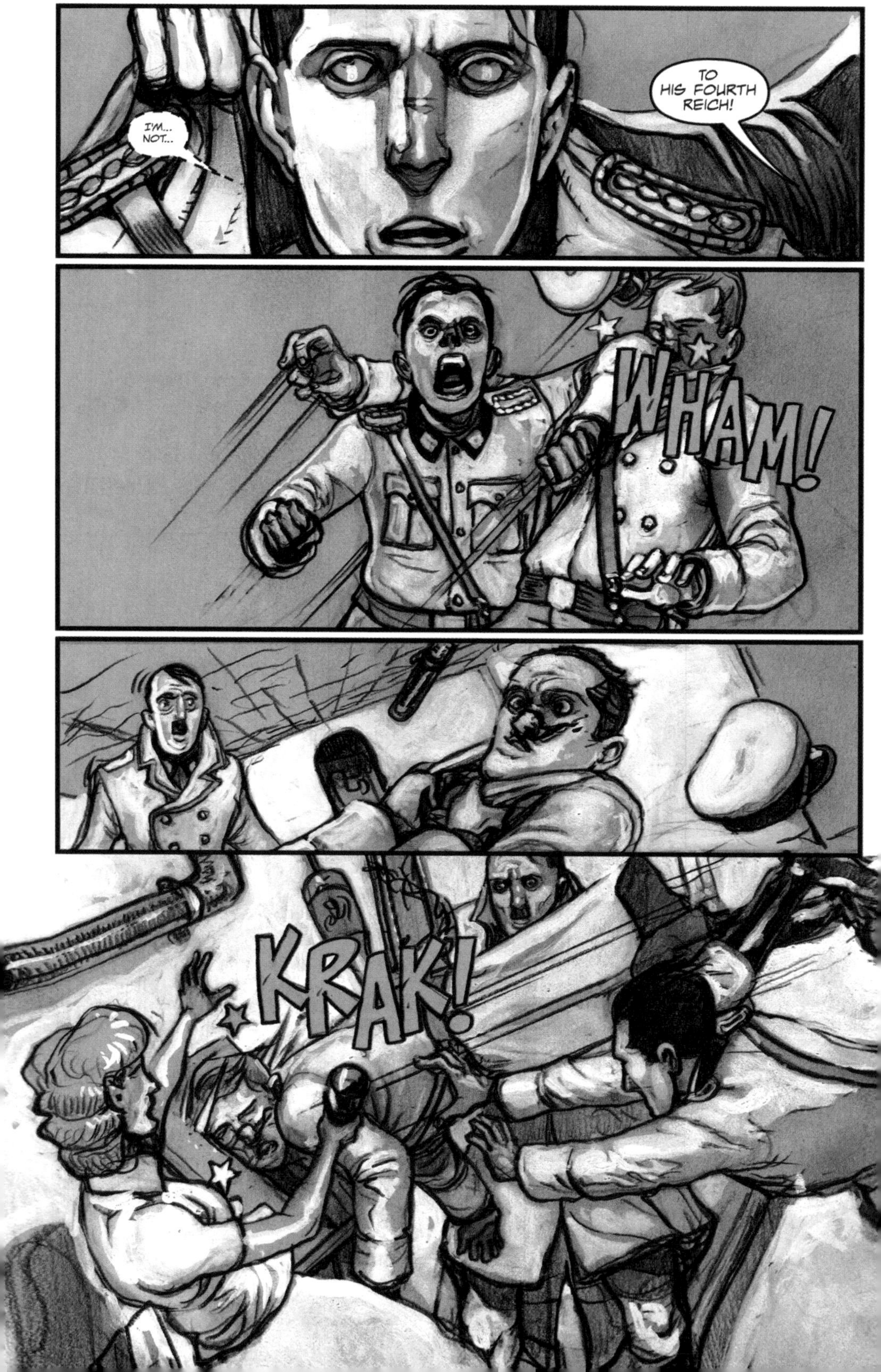
I'M... NOT...
TO HIS FOURTH REICH!
WHAM!
KRAK!

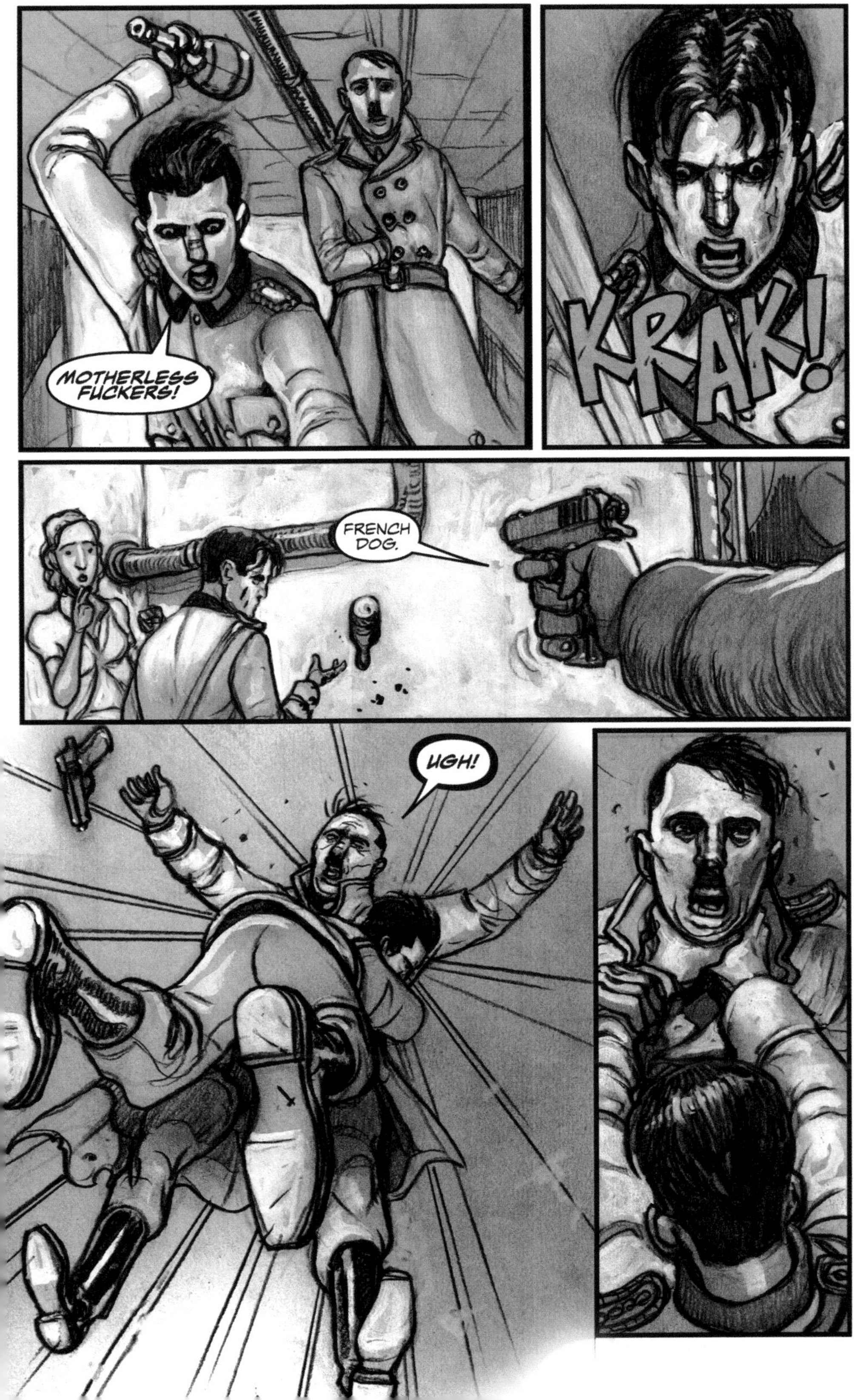
MOTHERLESS FUCKERS!
KRAK!
FRENCH DOG.
UGH!

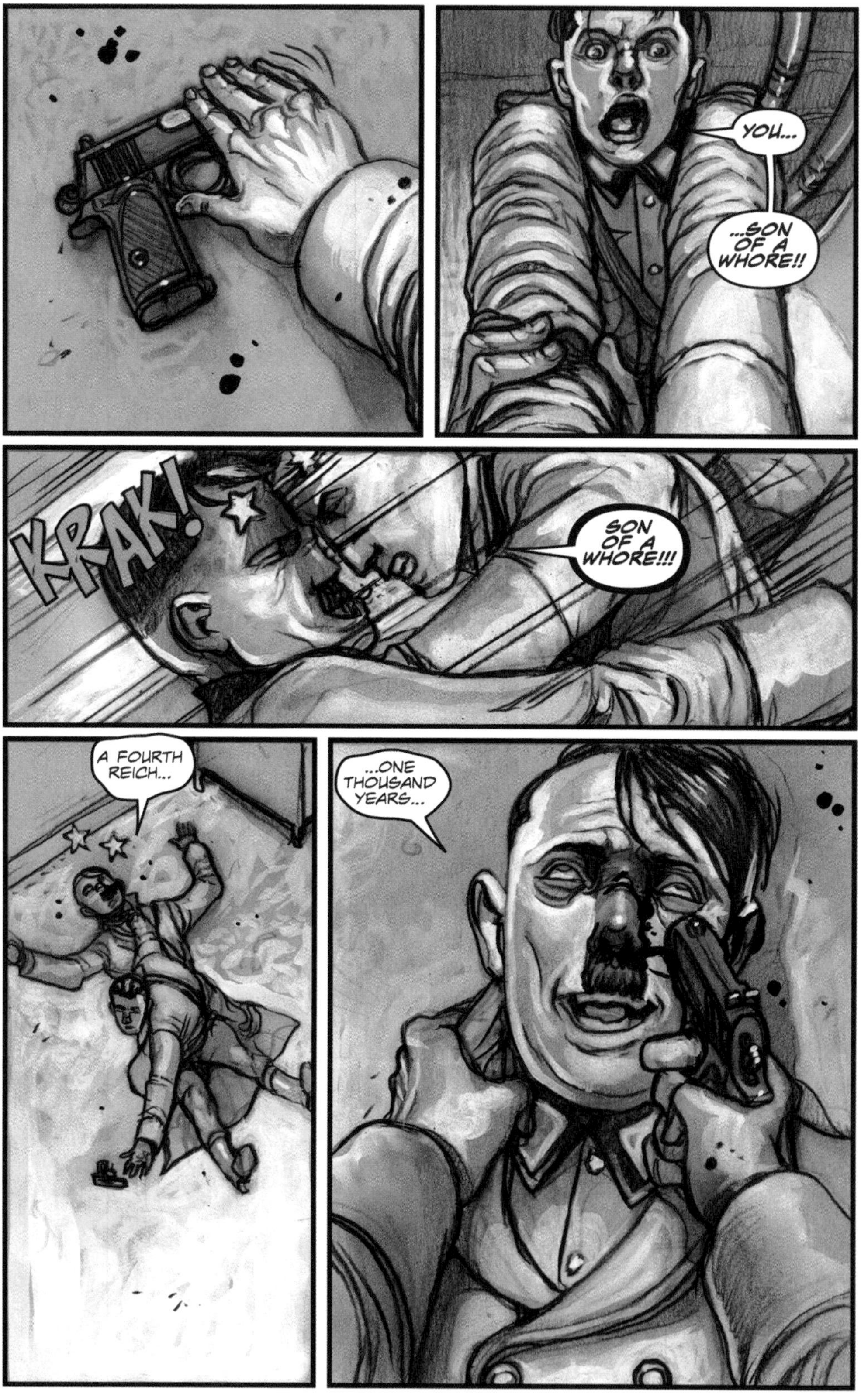
YOU...
...SON OF A WHORE!!
KRAK!
SON OF A WHORE!!!
A FOURTH REICH...
...ONE THOUSAND YEARS...

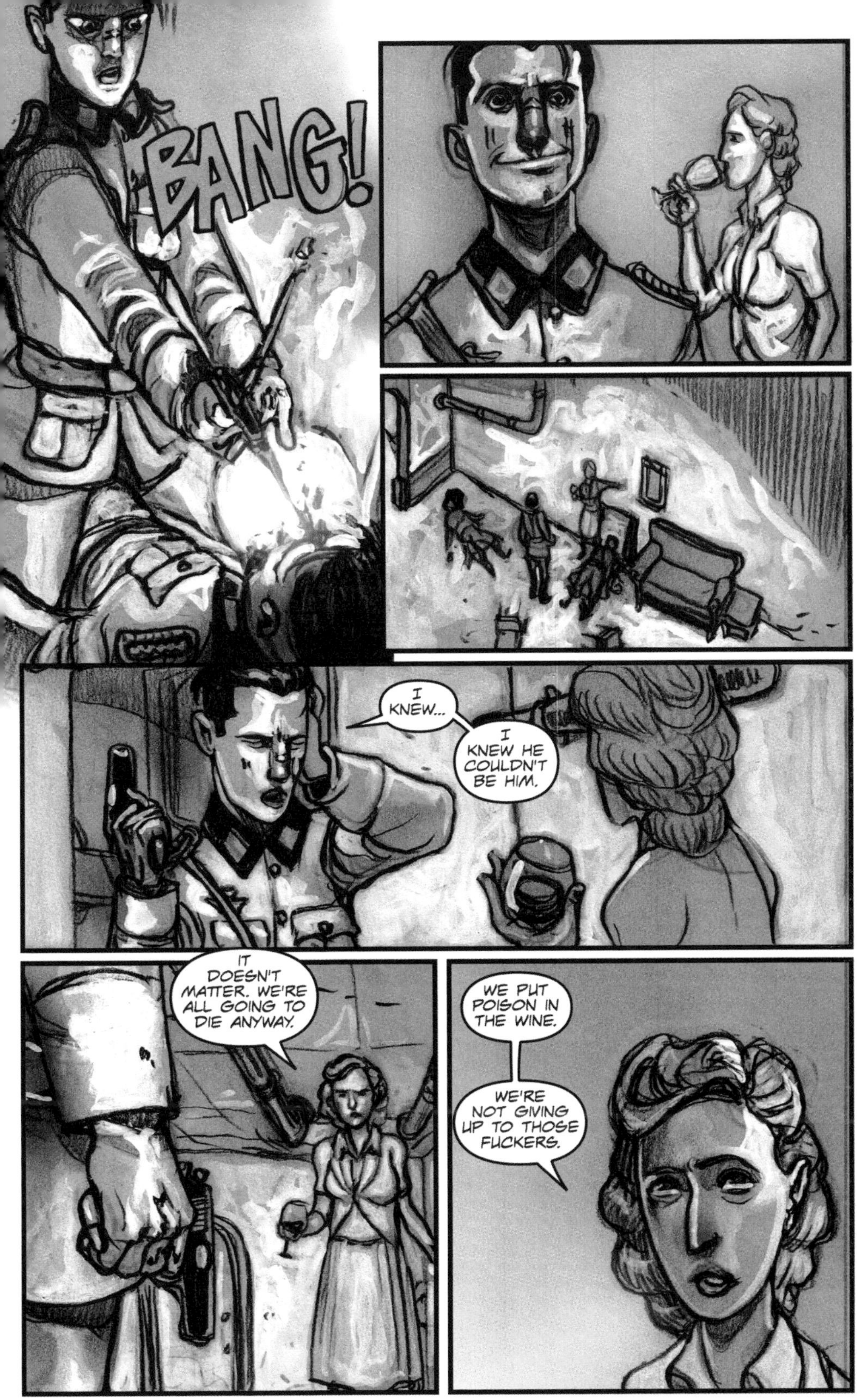
BANG!
I KNEW...
I KNEW HE COULDN'T BE HIM.
IT DOESN'T MATTER. WE'RE ALL GOING TO DIE ANYWAY.
WE PUT POISON IN THE WINE.
WE'RE NOT GIVING UP TO THOSE FUCKERS.

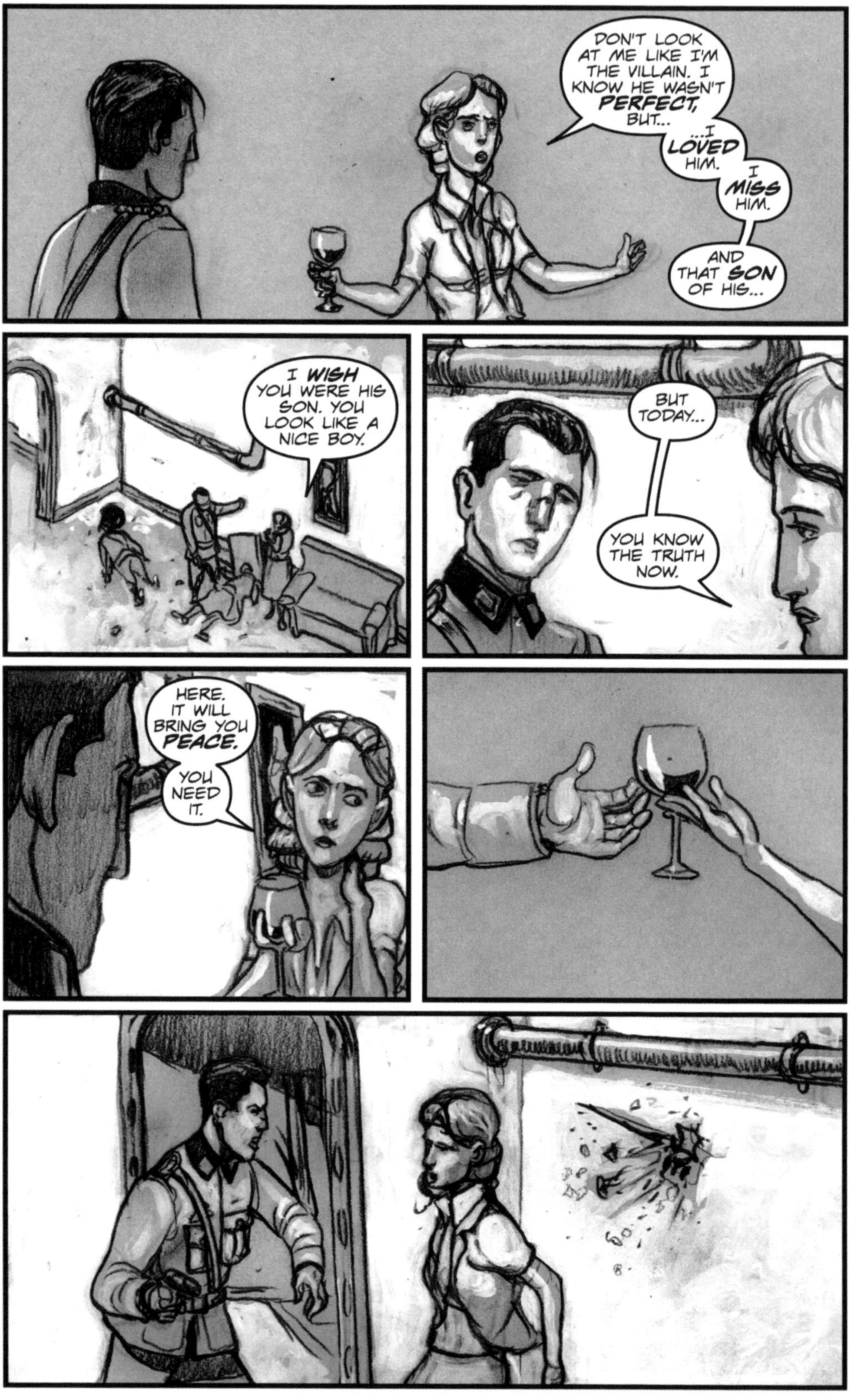
DON'T LOOK AT ME LIKE I'M THE VILLAIN. I KNOW HE WASN'T PERFECT, BUT...
...I LOVED HIM.
I MISS HIM.
AND THAT SON OF HIS...
I WISH YOU WERE HIS SON. YOU LOOK LIKE A NICE BOY.
BUT TODAY...
YOU KNOW THE TRUTH NOW.
HERE. IT WILL BRING YOU PEACE.
YOU NEED IT.

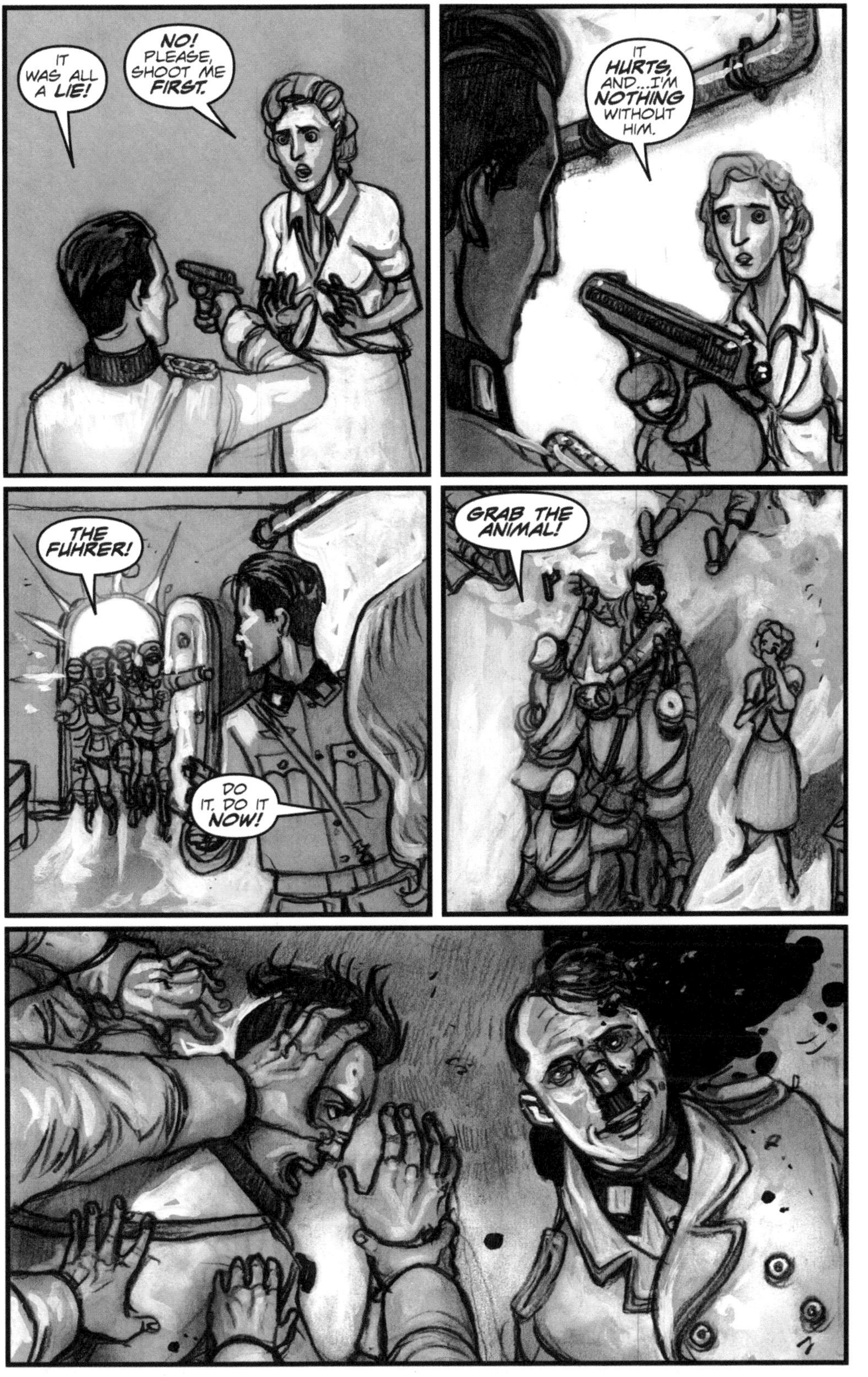
IT WAS ALL A LIE!
NO! PLEASE, SHOOT ME FIRST.
IT HURTS, AND...I'M NOTHING WITHOUT HIM.
THE FUHRER!
DO IT. DO IT NOW!
GRAB THE ANIMAL!

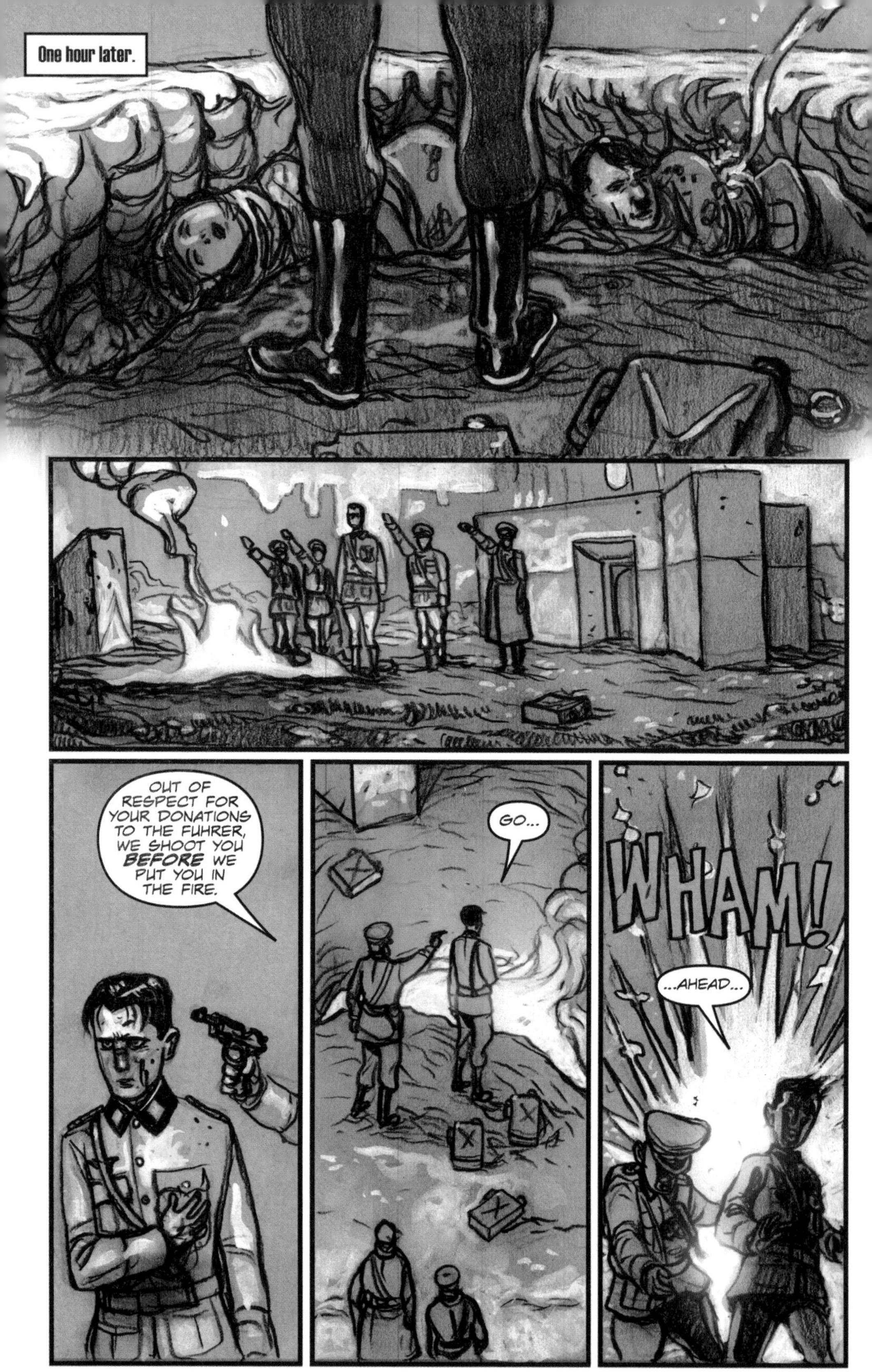
One hour later.
OUT OF RESPECT FOR YOUR DONATIONS TO THE FUHRER, WE SHOOT YOU *BEFORE* WE PUT YOU IN THE FIRE.
GO...
WHAM!
...AHEAD...

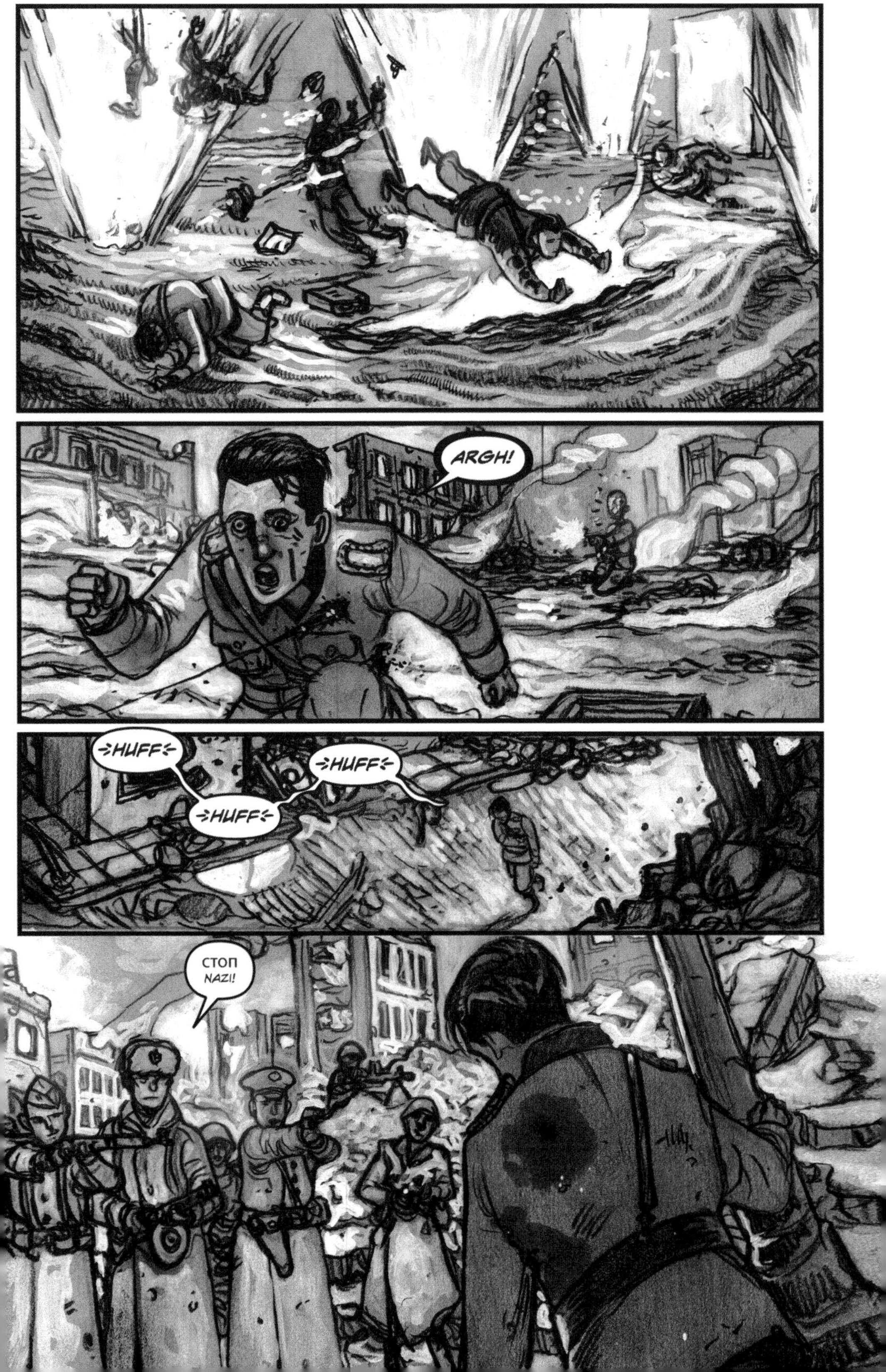
ARGH!
HUFF
HUFF
HUFF
СТОП
NAZI!

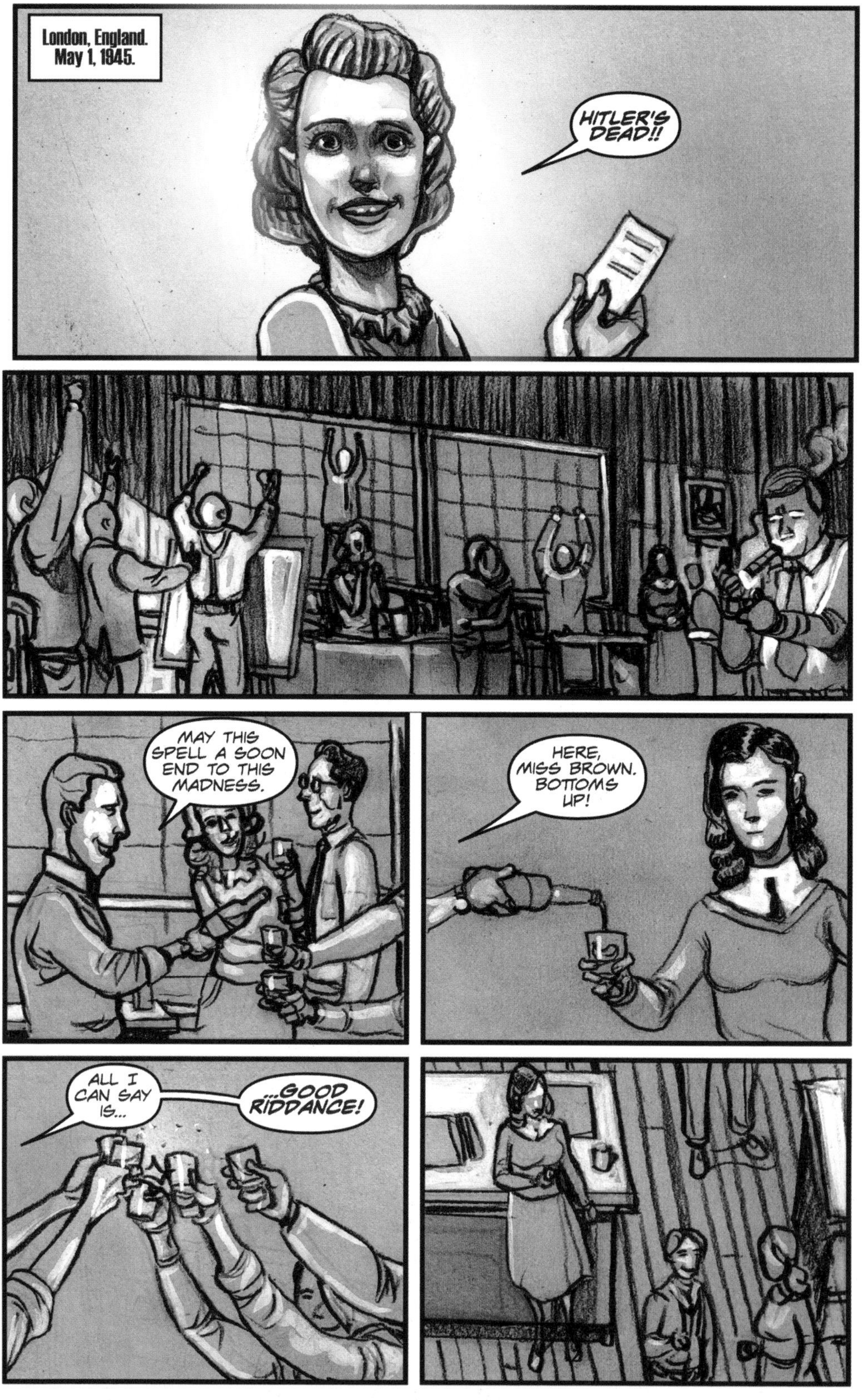
London, England.
May 1, 1945.
HITLER'S DEAD!!
MAY THIS SPELL A SOON END TO THIS MADNESS.
HERE, MISS BROWN. BOTTOMS UP!
ALL I CAN SAY IS...
...GOOD RIDDANCE!

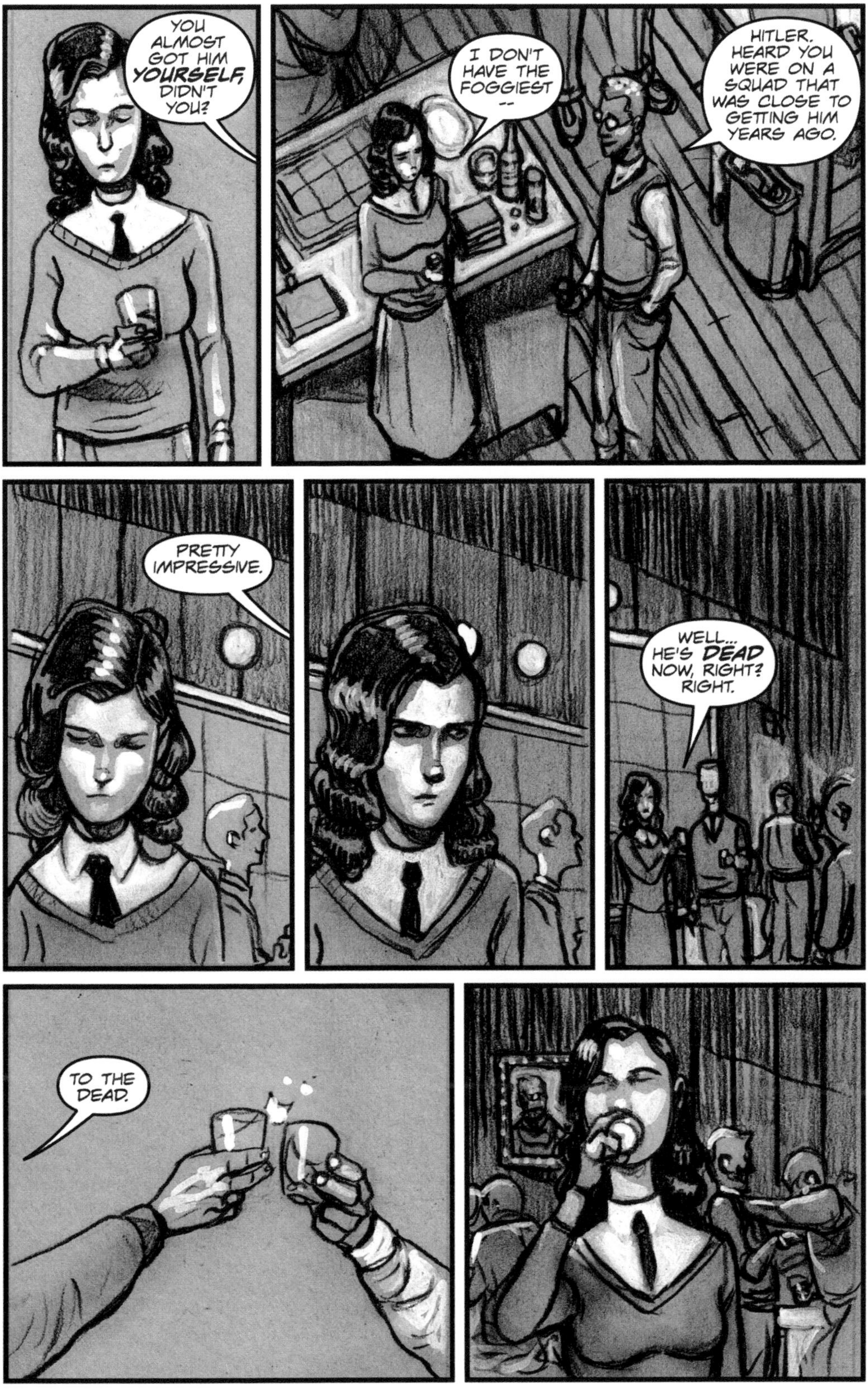
YOU ALMOST GOT HIM YOURSELF, DIDN'T YOU?
I DON'T HAVE THE FOGGIEST --
HITLER. HEARD YOU WERE ON A SQUAD THAT WAS CLOSE TO GETTING HIM YEARS AGO.
PRETTY IMPRESSIVE.
WELL... HE'S DEAD NOW, RIGHT? RIGHT.
TO THE DEAD.

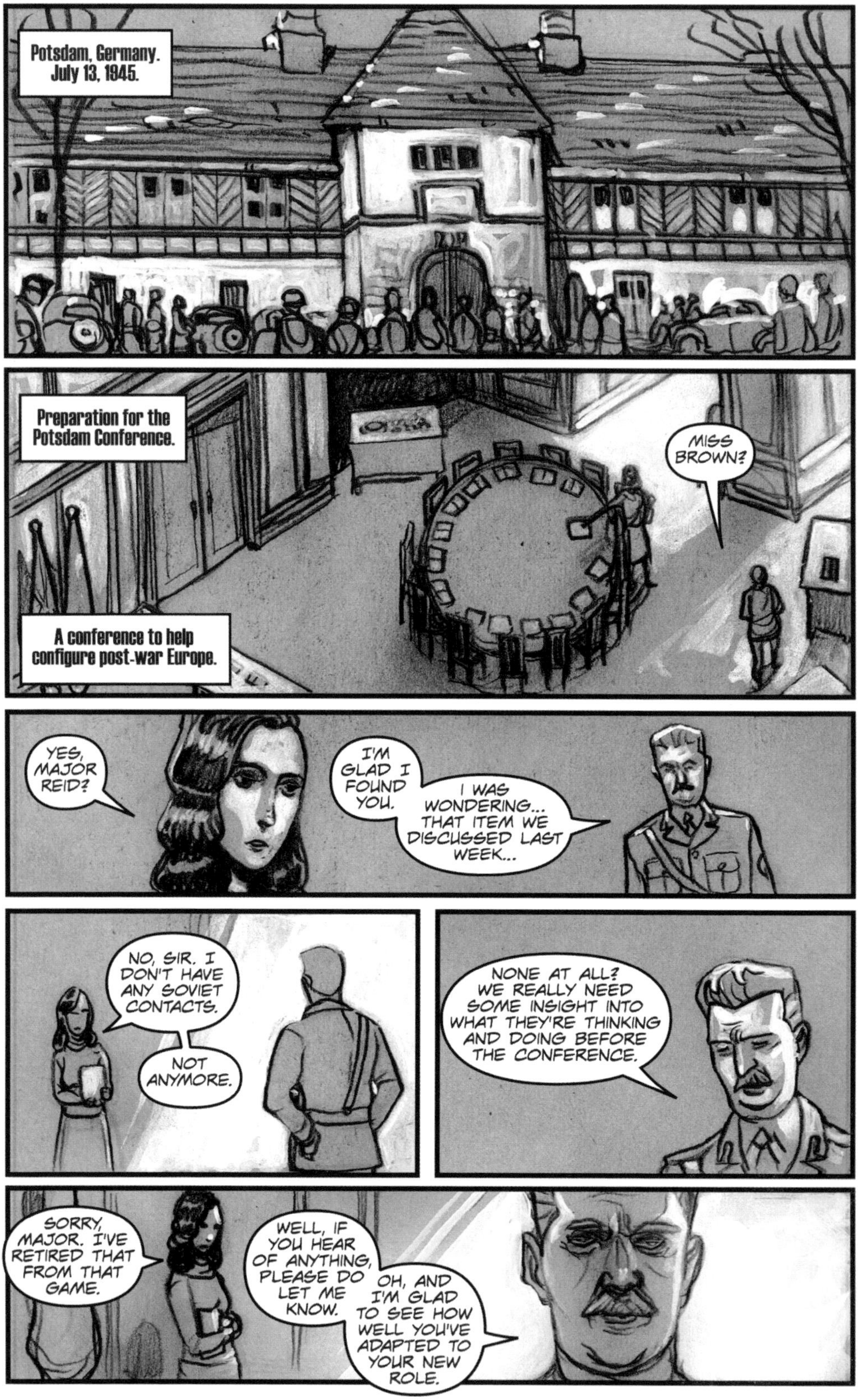
Potsdam, Germany. July 13, 1945.
Preparation for the Potsdam Conference.
A conference to help configure post-war Europe.
MISS BROWN?
YES, MAJOR REID?
I'M GLAD I FOUND YOU.
I WAS WONDERING... THAT ITEM WE DISCUSSED LAST WEEK...
NO, SIR. I DON'T HAVE ANY SOVIET CONTACTS.
NOT ANYMORE.
NONE AT ALL? WE REALLY NEED SOME INSIGHT INTO WHAT THEY'RE THINKING AND DOING BEFORE THE CONFERENCE.
SORRY, MAJOR. I'VE RETIRED THAT FROM THAT GAME.
WELL, IF YOU HEAR OF ANYTHING, PLEASE DO LET ME KNOW.
OH, AND I'M GLAD TO SEE HOW WELL YOU'VE ADAPTED TO YOUR NEW ROLE.

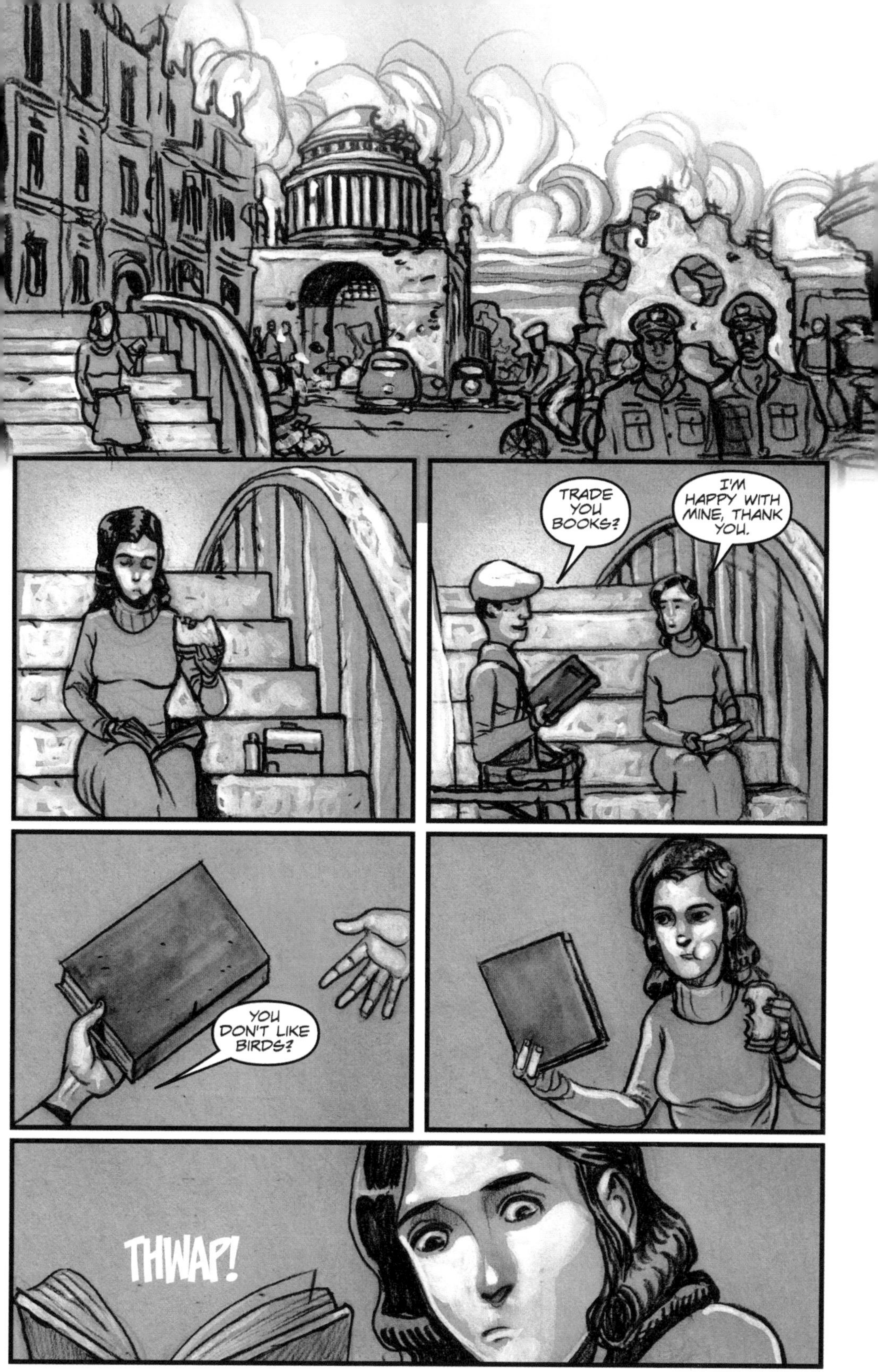
TRADE YOU BOOKS?
I'M HAPPY WITH MINE, THANK YOU.
YOU DON'T LIKE BIRDS?
THWAP!

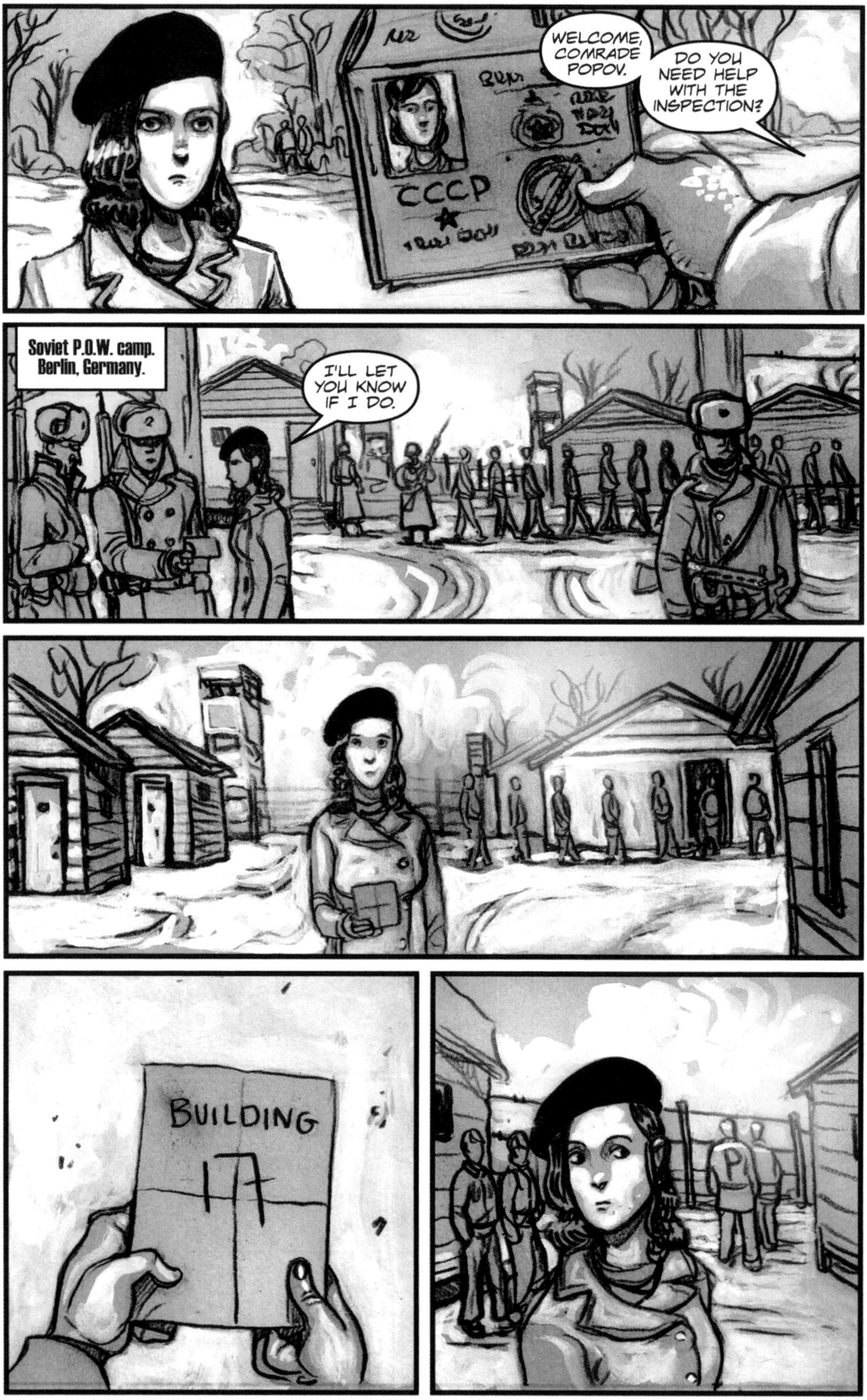

CCCP
WELCOME, COMRADE POPOV.
DO YOU NEED HELP WITH THE INSPECTION?
Soviet P.O.W. camp. Berlin, Germany.
I'LL LET YOU KNOW IF I DO.
BUILDING 17

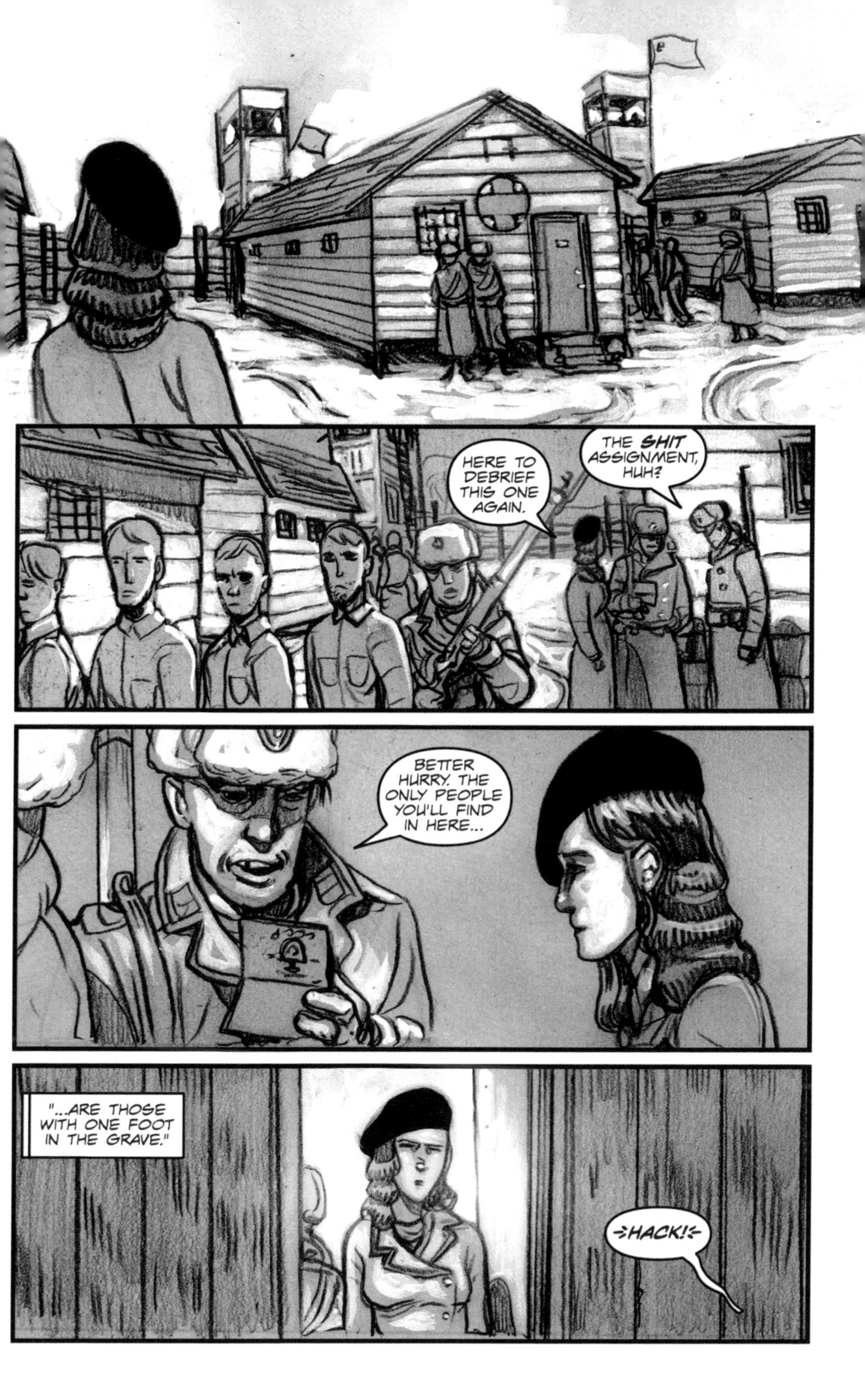
HERE TO DEBRIEF THIS ONE AGAIN.
THE SHIT ASSIGNMENT, HUH?
BETTER HURRY. THE ONLY PEOPLE YOU'LL FIND IN HERE...
"...ARE THOSE WITH ONE FOOT IN THE GRAVE."
HACK!

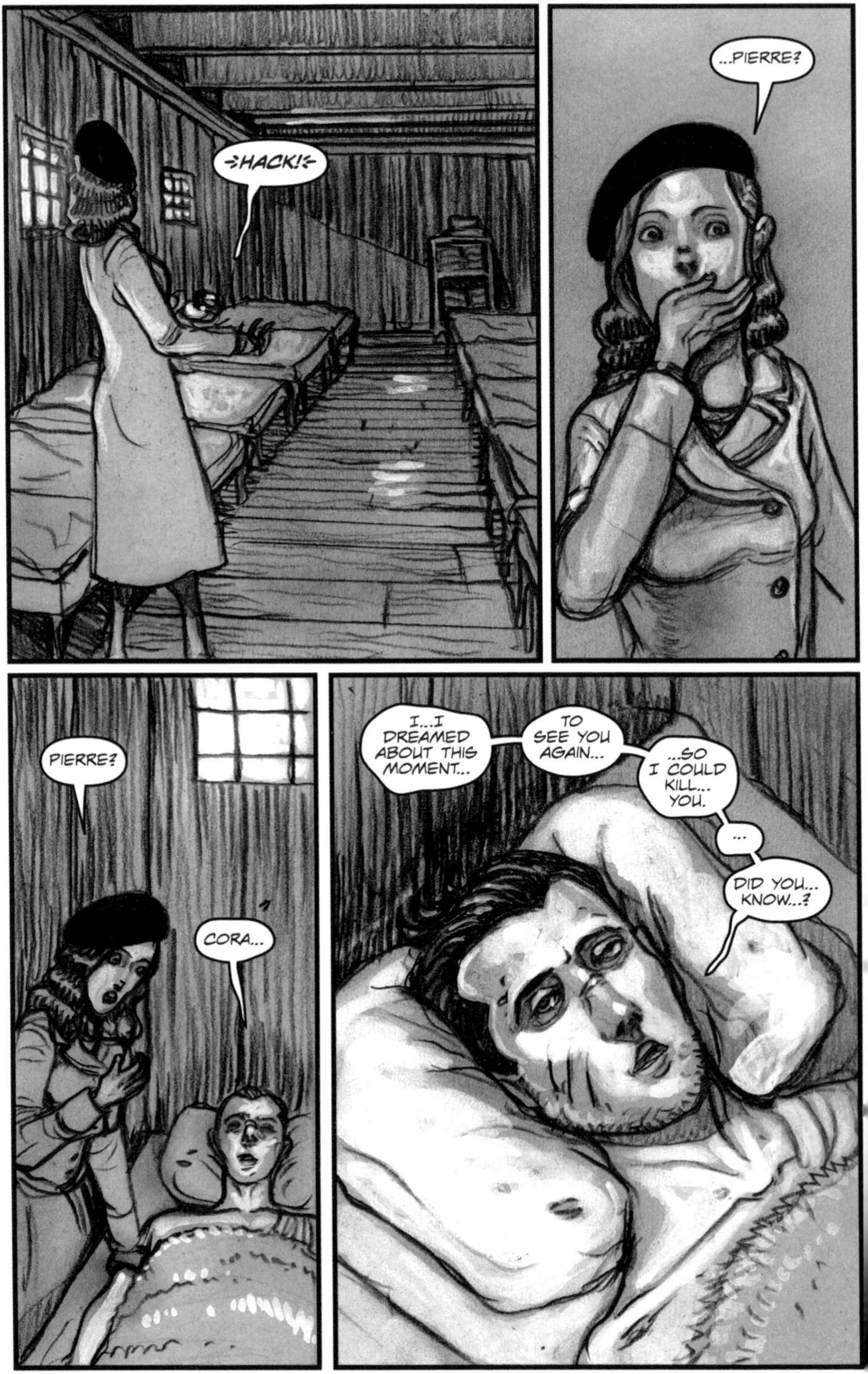
HACK!
...PIERRE?
PIERRE?
CORA...
I...I DREAMED ABOUT THIS MOMENT...
TO SEE YOU AGAIN...
...SO I COULD KILL... YOU.
...
DID YOU... KNOW...?

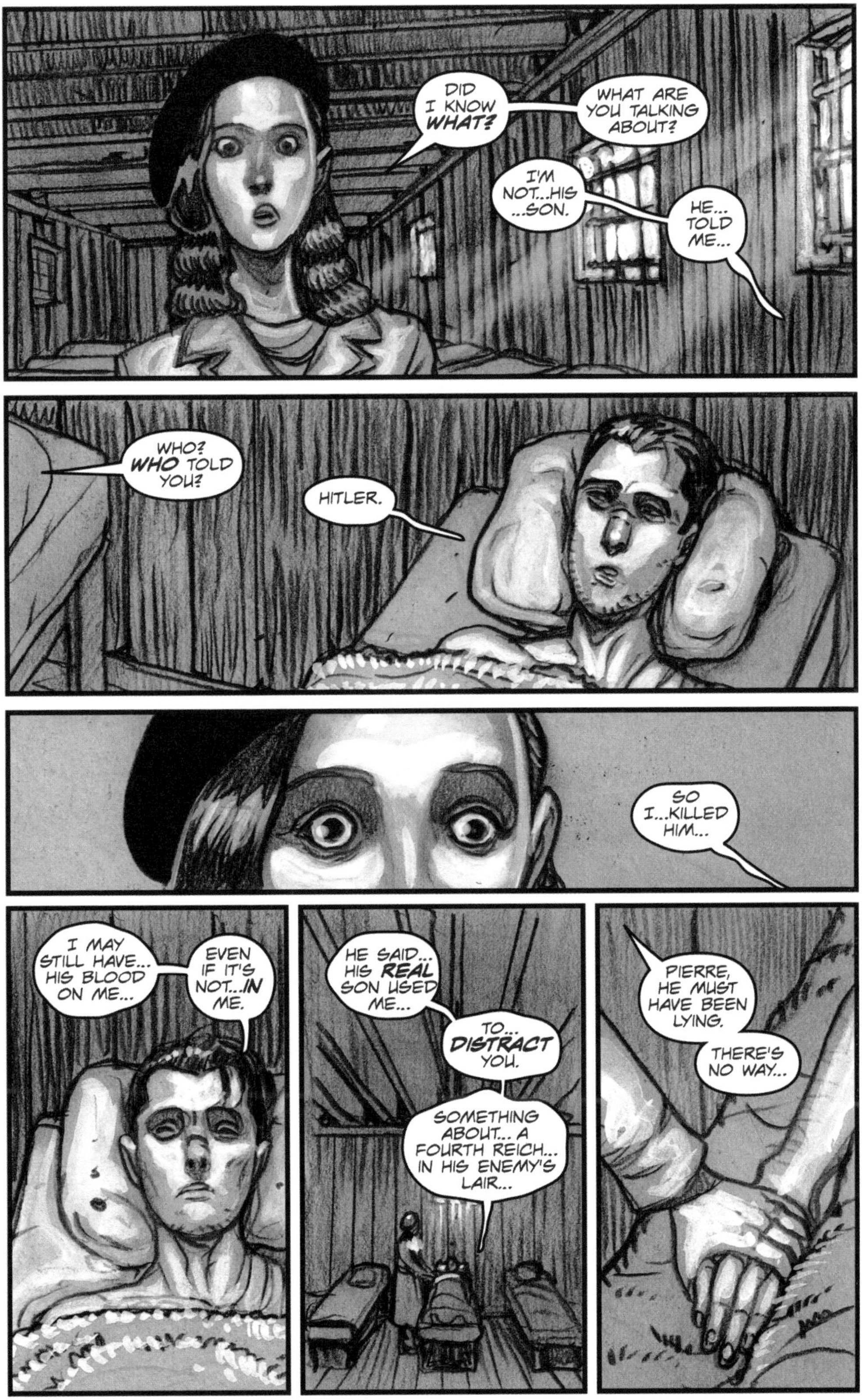
DID I KNOW *WHAT?*
WHAT ARE YOU TALKING ABOUT?
I'M NOT...HIS ...SON.
HE... TOLD ME...
WHO? *WHO* TOLD YOU?
HITLER.
SO I...KILLED HIM...
I MAY STILL HAVE... HIS BLOOD ON ME...
EVEN IF IT'S NOT...*IN* ME.
HE SAID... HIS *REAL* SON USED ME...
TO... *DISTRACT* YOU.
SOMETHING ABOUT... A FOURTH REICH... IN HIS ENEMY'S LAIR...
PIERRE, HE MUST HAVE BEEN LYING.
THERE'S NO WAY...

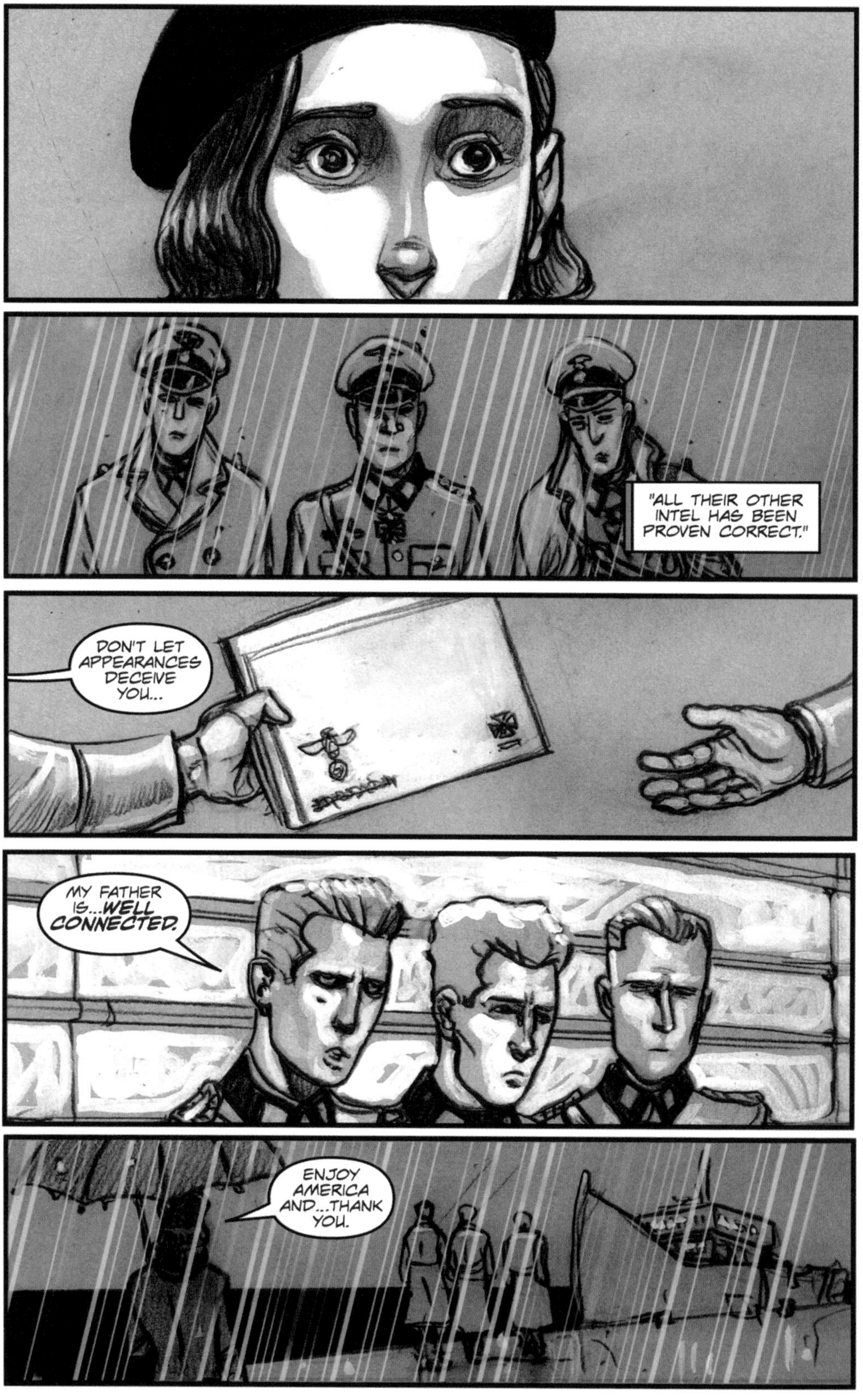
"ALL THEIR OTHER INTEL HAS BEEN PROVEN CORRECT."
DON'T LET APPEARANCES DECEIVE YOU...
MY FATHER IS...**WELL CONNECTED.**
ENJOY AMERICA AND...THANK YOU.

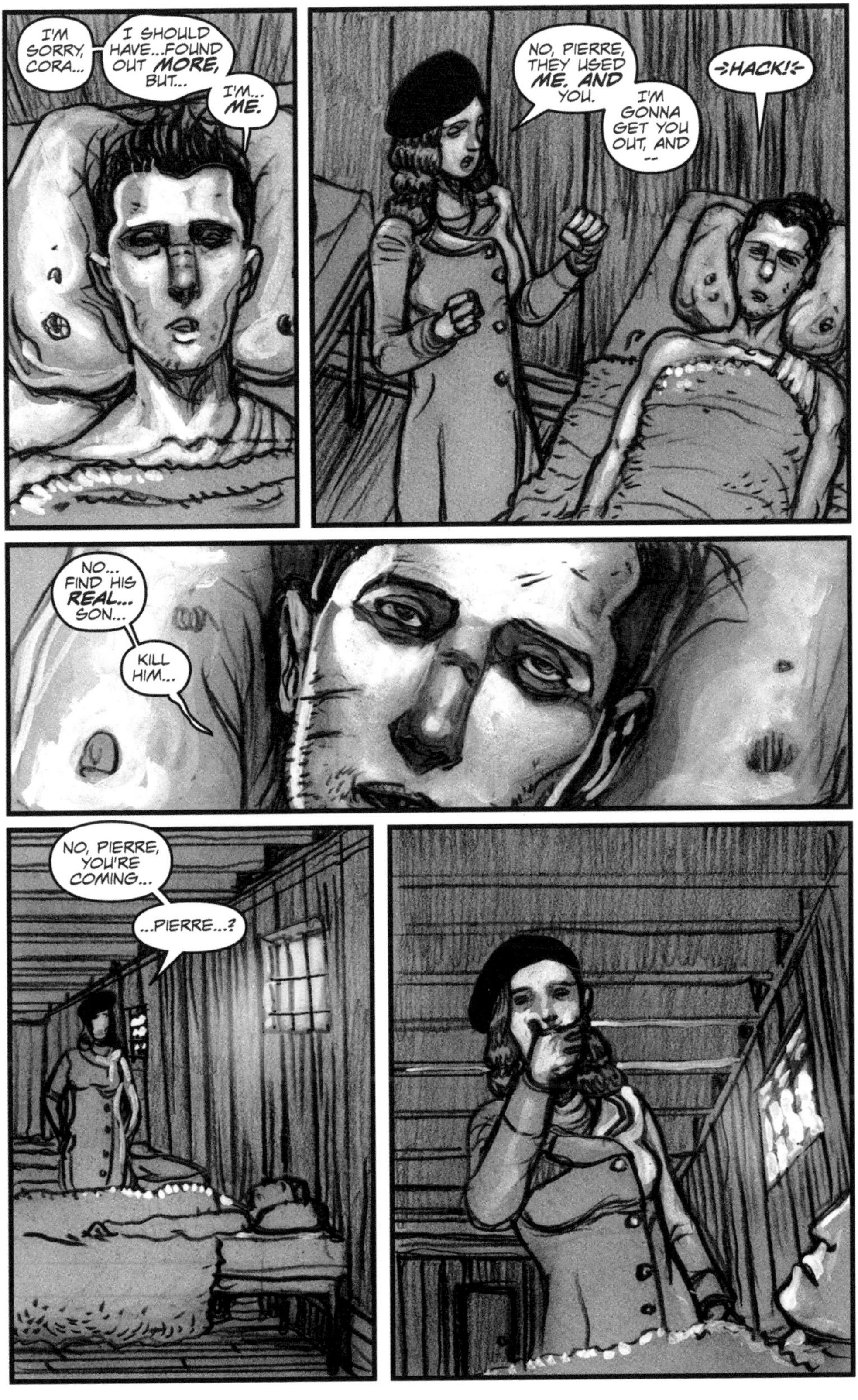
I'M SORRY, CORA...
I SHOULD HAVE...FOUND OUT MORE, BUT...
I'M... ME.
NO, PIERRE, THEY USED ME. AND YOU.
I'M GONNA GET YOU OUT, AND --
HACK!
NO... FIND HIS REAL... SON...
KILL HIM...
NO, PIERRE, YOU'RE COMING...
...PIERRE...?

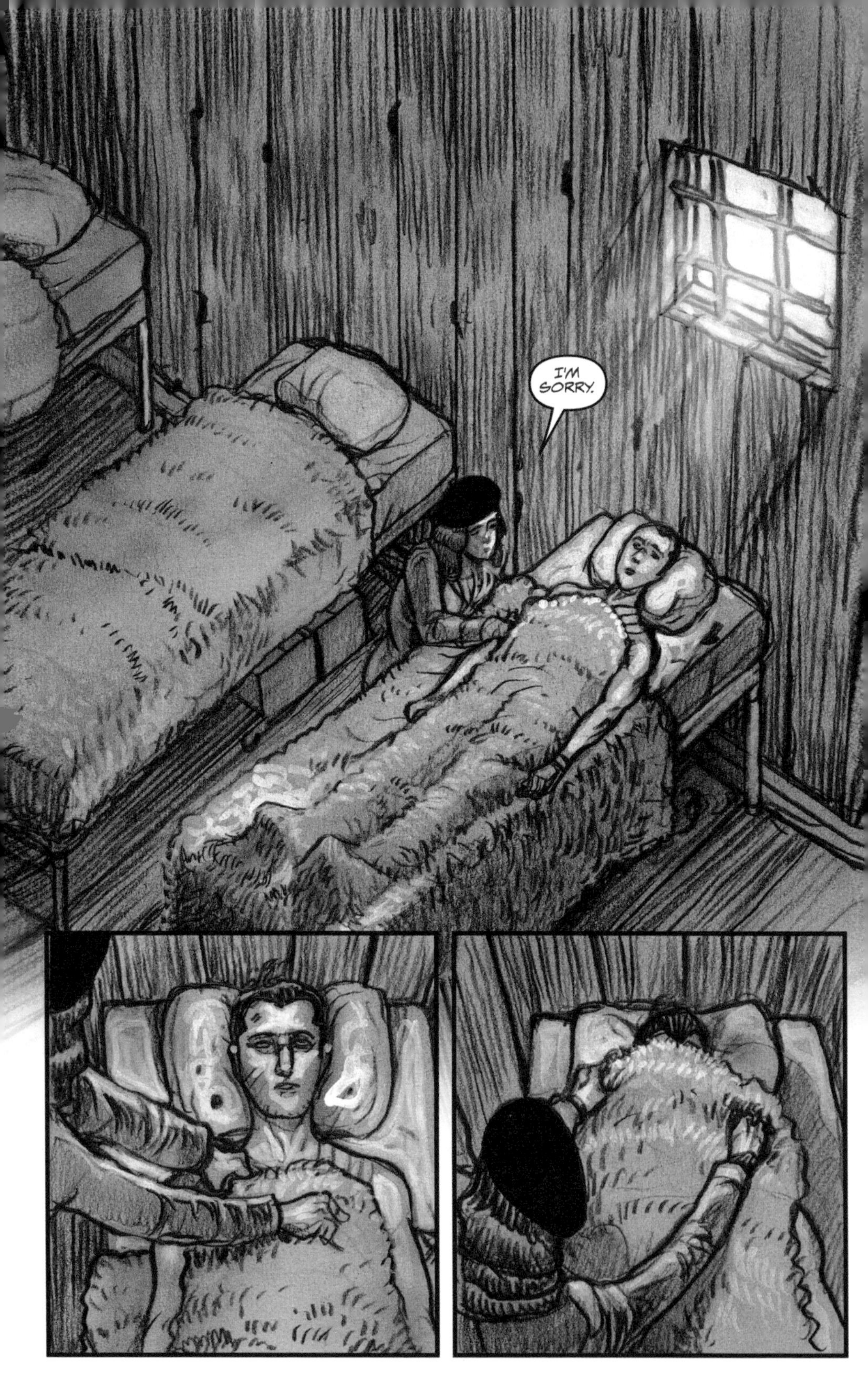
I'M SORRY.

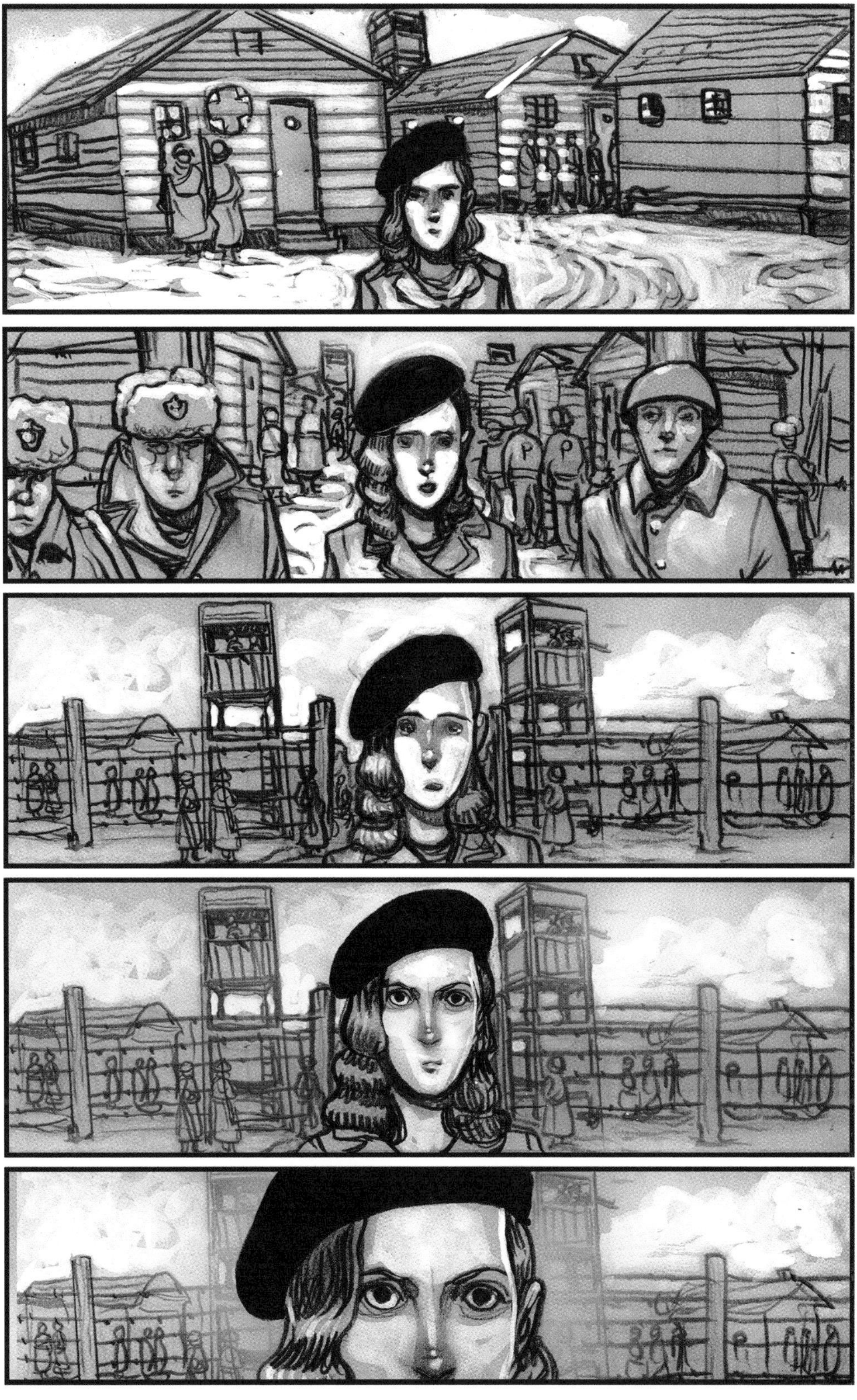
17
15

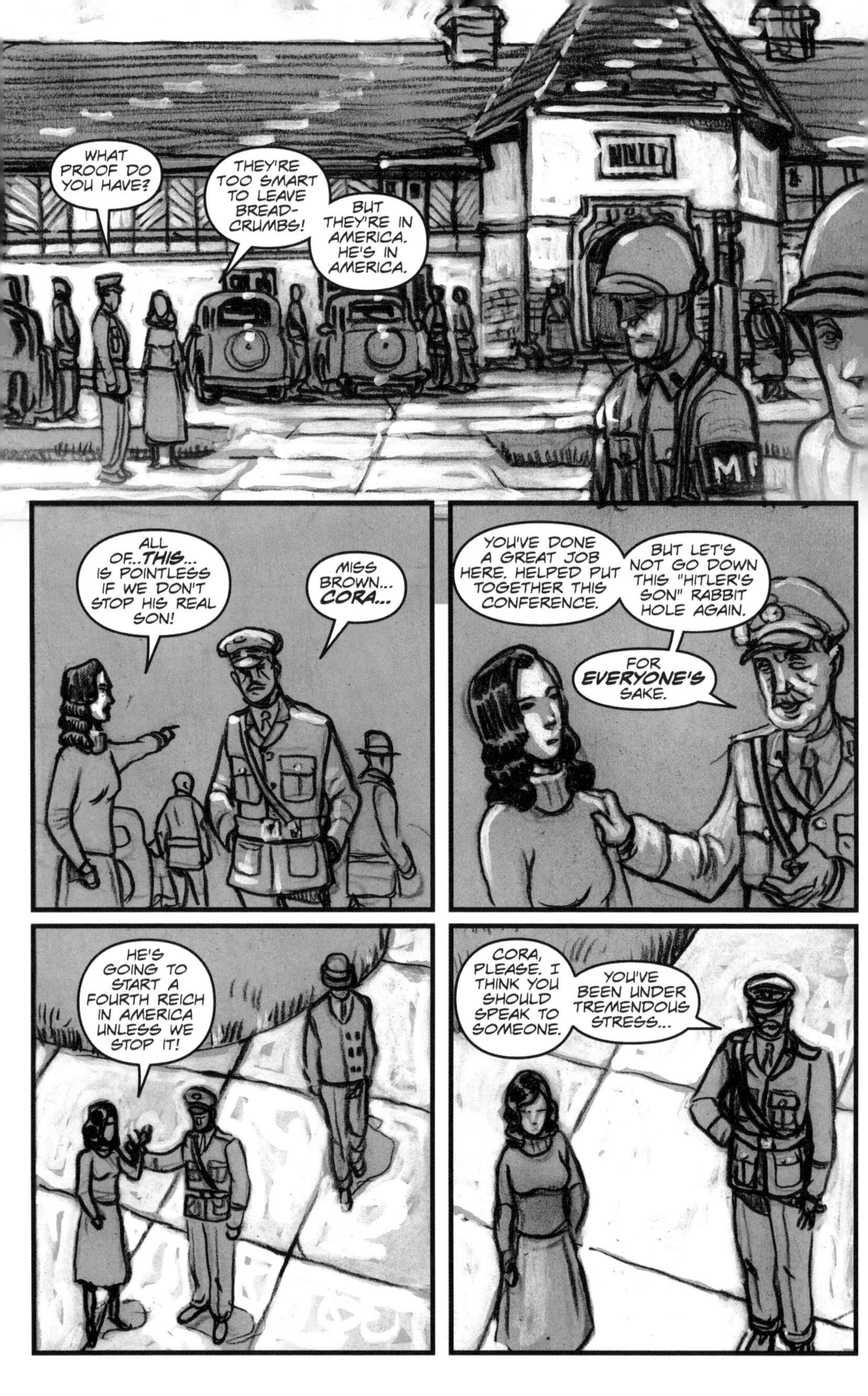
WHAT PROOF DO YOU HAVE?
THEY'RE TOO SMART TO LEAVE BREAD-CRUMBS!
BUT THEY'RE IN AMERICA. HE'S IN AMERICA.
MP
ALL OF...THIS... IS POINTLESS IF WE DON'T STOP HIS REAL SON!
MISS BROWN... CORA...
YOU'VE DONE A GREAT JOB HERE. HELPED PUT TOGETHER THIS CONFERENCE.
BUT LET'S NOT GO DOWN THIS "HITLER'S SON" RABBIT HOLE AGAIN.
FOR EVERYONE'S SAKE.
HE'S GOING TO START A FOURTH REICH IN AMERICA UNLESS WE STOP IT!
CORA, PLEASE. I THINK YOU SHOULD SPEAK TO SOMEONE.
YOU'VE BEEN UNDER TREMENDOUS STRESS...

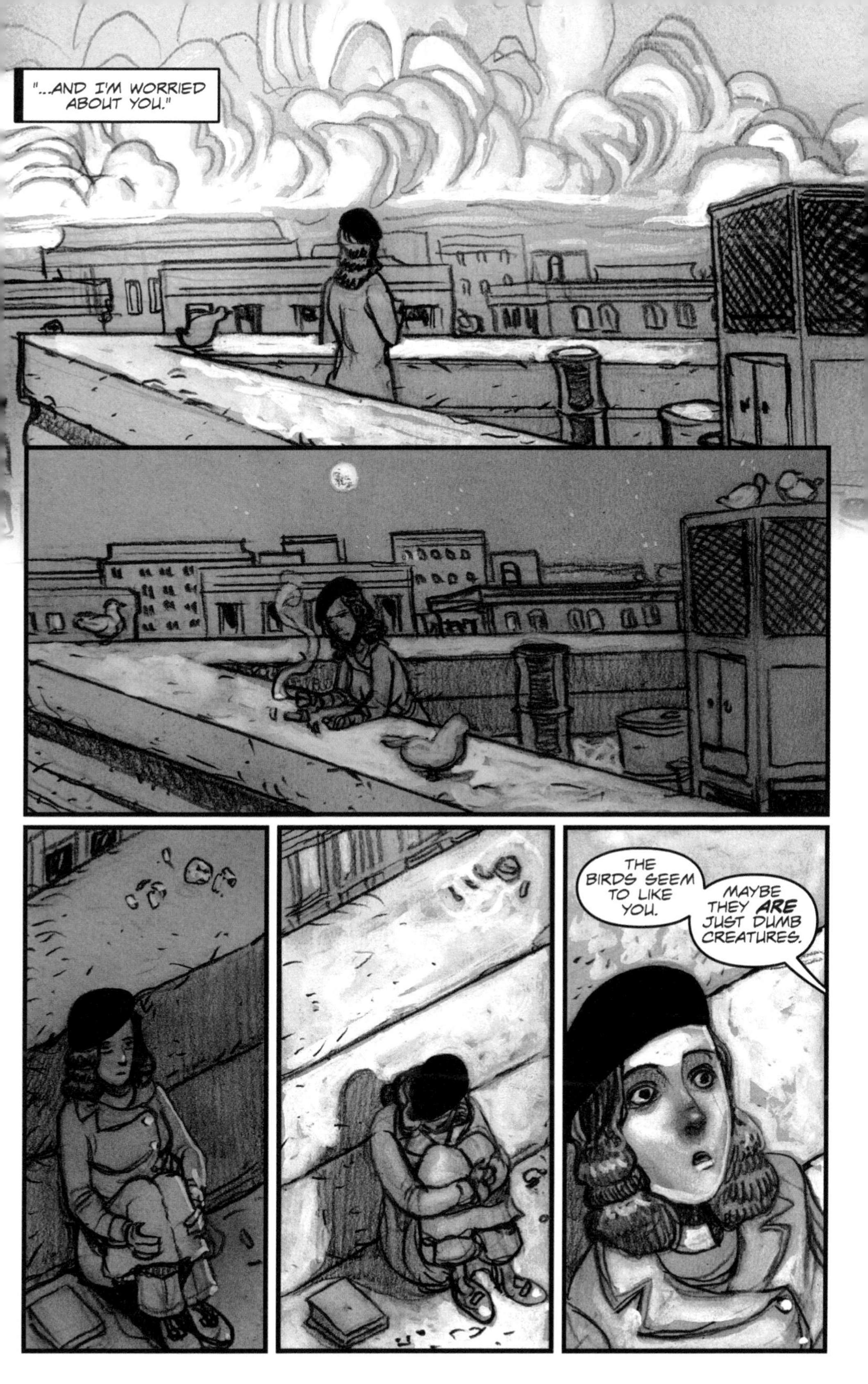
"...AND I'M WORRIED ABOUT YOU."
THE BIRDS SEEM TO LIKE YOU.
MAYBE THEY ARE JUST DUMB CREATURES.

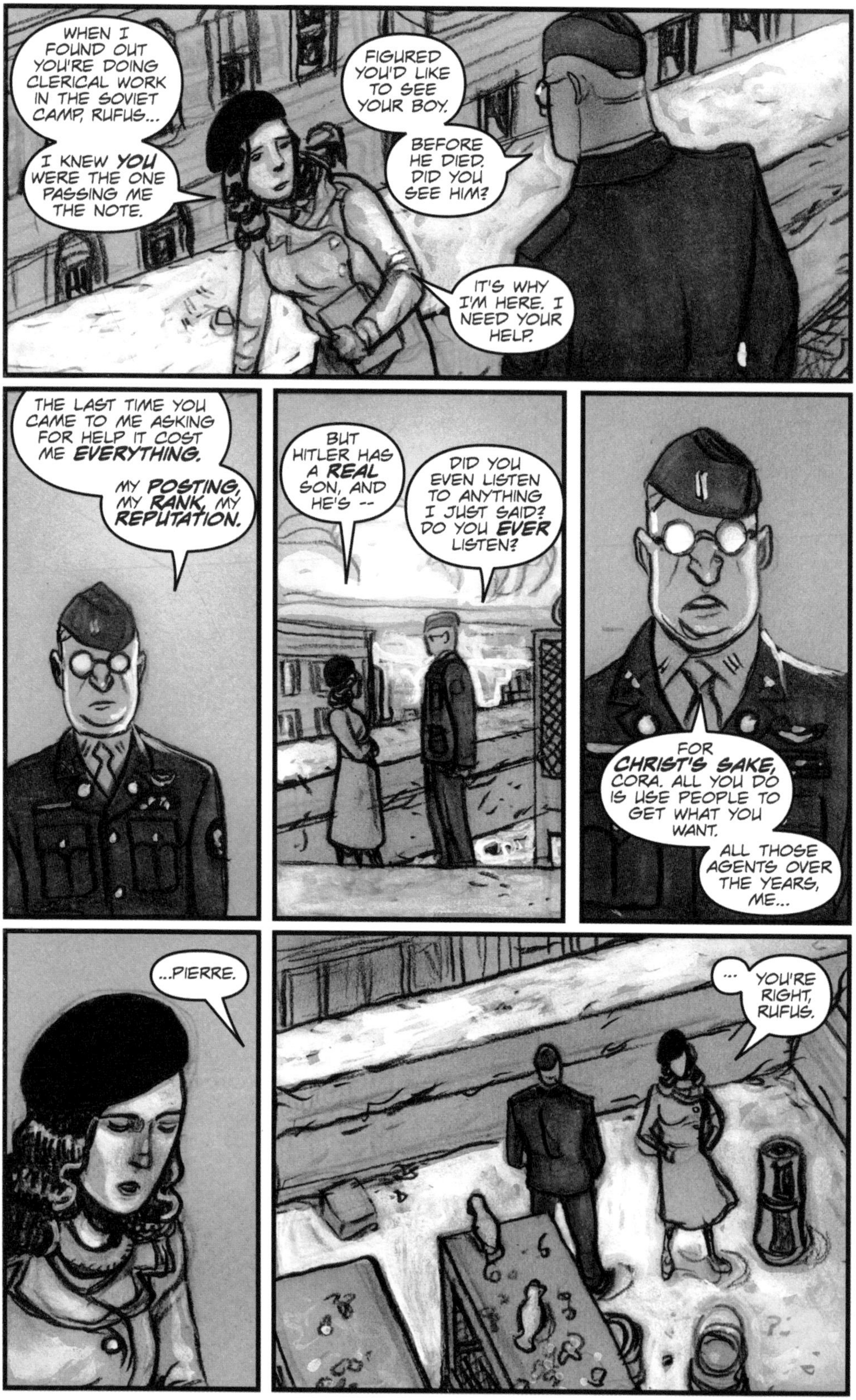
WHEN I FOUND OUT YOU'RE DOING CLERICAL WORK IN THE SOVIET CAMP, RUFUS...
I KNEW YOU WERE THE ONE PASSING ME THE NOTE.
FIGURED YOU'D LIKE TO SEE YOUR BOY.
BEFORE HE DIED. DID YOU SEE HIM?
IT'S WHY I'M HERE. I NEED YOUR HELP.
THE LAST TIME YOU CAME TO ME ASKING FOR HELP IT COST ME EVERYTHING.
MY POSTING, MY RANK, MY REPUTATION.
BUT HITLER HAS A REAL SON, AND HE'S --
DID YOU EVEN LISTEN TO ANYTHING I JUST SAID? DO YOU EVER LISTEN?
FOR CHRIST'S SAKE, CORA. ALL YOU DO IS USE PEOPLE TO GET WHAT YOU WANT.
ALL THOSE AGENTS OVER THE YEARS, ME...
...PIERRE.
...
YOU'RE RIGHT, RUFUS.

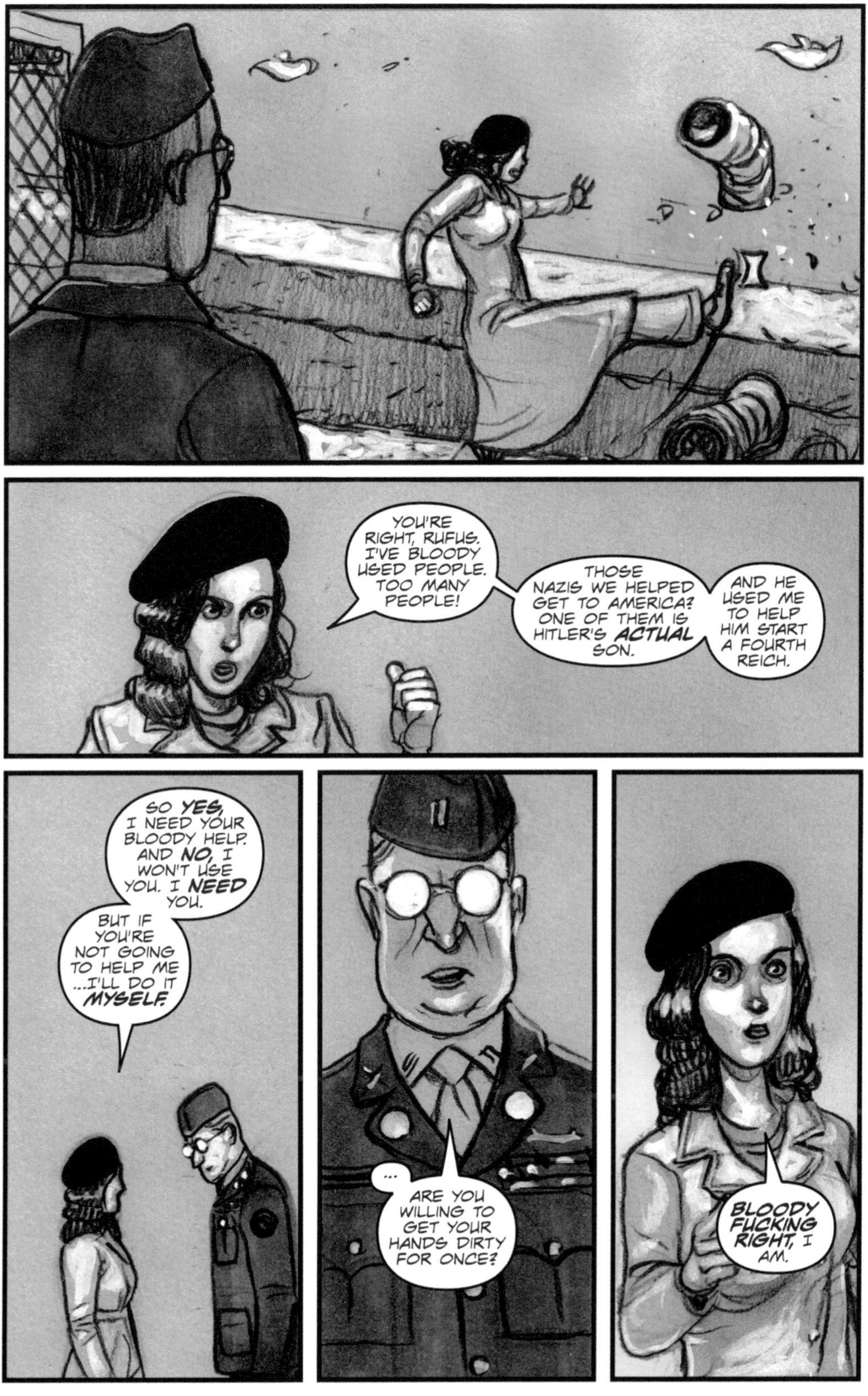
YOU'RE RIGHT, RUFUS. I'VE BLOODY USED PEOPLE. TOO MANY PEOPLE!
THOSE NAZIS WE HELPED GET TO AMERICA? ONE OF THEM IS HITLER'S ACTUAL SON.
AND HE USED ME TO HELP HIM START A FOURTH REICH.
SO YES, I NEED YOUR BLOODY HELP. AND NO, I WON'T USE YOU. I NEED YOU.
BUT IF YOU'RE NOT GOING TO HELP ME ...I'LL DO IT MYSELF.
... ARE YOU WILLING TO GET YOUR HANDS DIRTY FOR ONCE?
BLOODY FUCKING RIGHT, I AM.

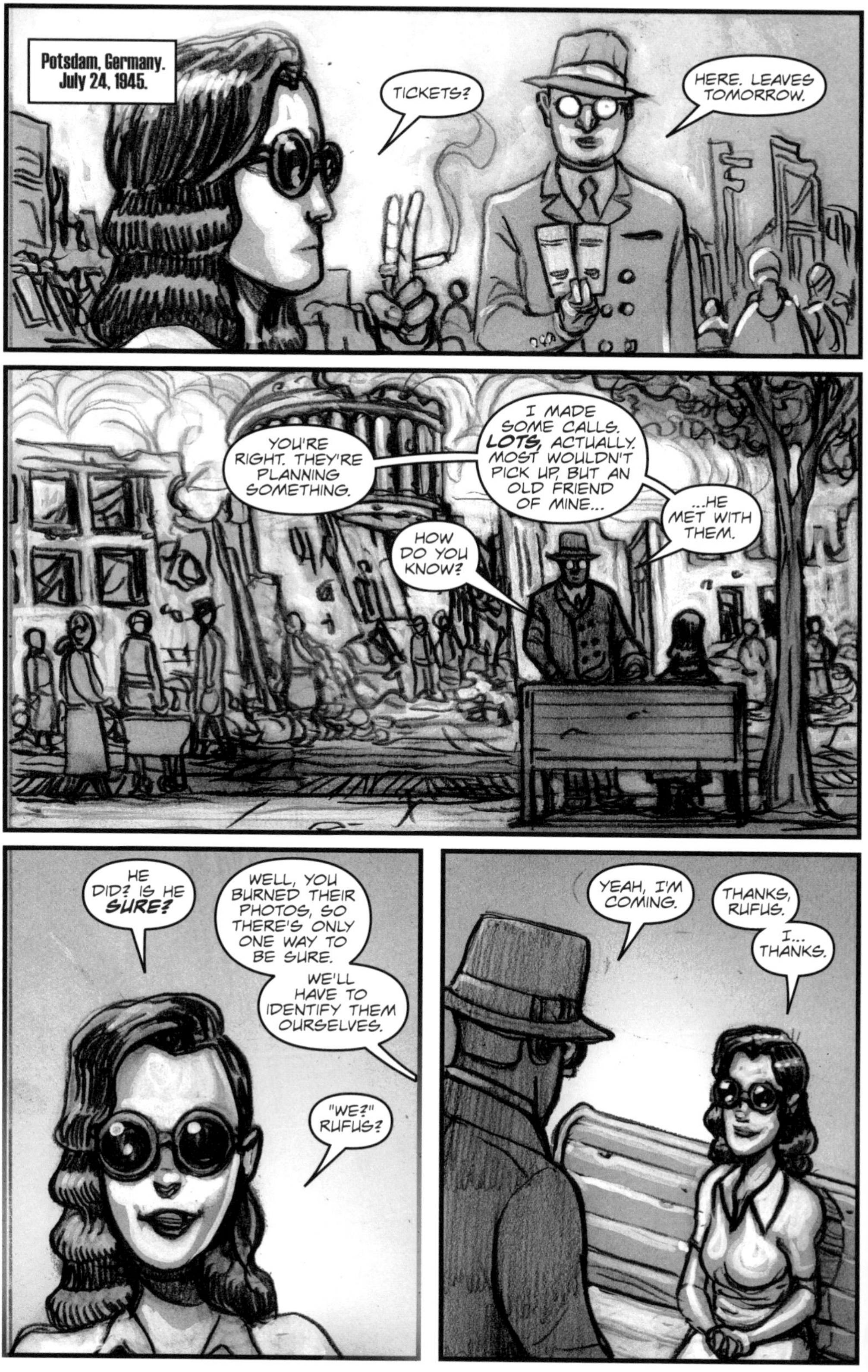
Potsdam, Germany. July 24, 1945.
TICKETS?
HERE. LEAVES TOMORROW.
YOU'RE RIGHT. THEY'RE PLANNING SOMETHING.
I MADE SOME CALLS. LOTS, ACTUALLY. MOST WOULDN'T PICK UP, BUT AN OLD FRIEND OF MINE...
HOW DO YOU KNOW?
...HE MET WITH THEM.
HE DID? IS HE SURE?
WELL, YOU BURNED THEIR PHOTOS, SO THERE'S ONLY ONE WAY TO BE SURE.
WE'LL HAVE TO IDENTIFY THEM OURSELVES.
"WE?" RUFUS?
YEAH, I'M COMING.
THANKS, RUFUS.
I... THANKS.

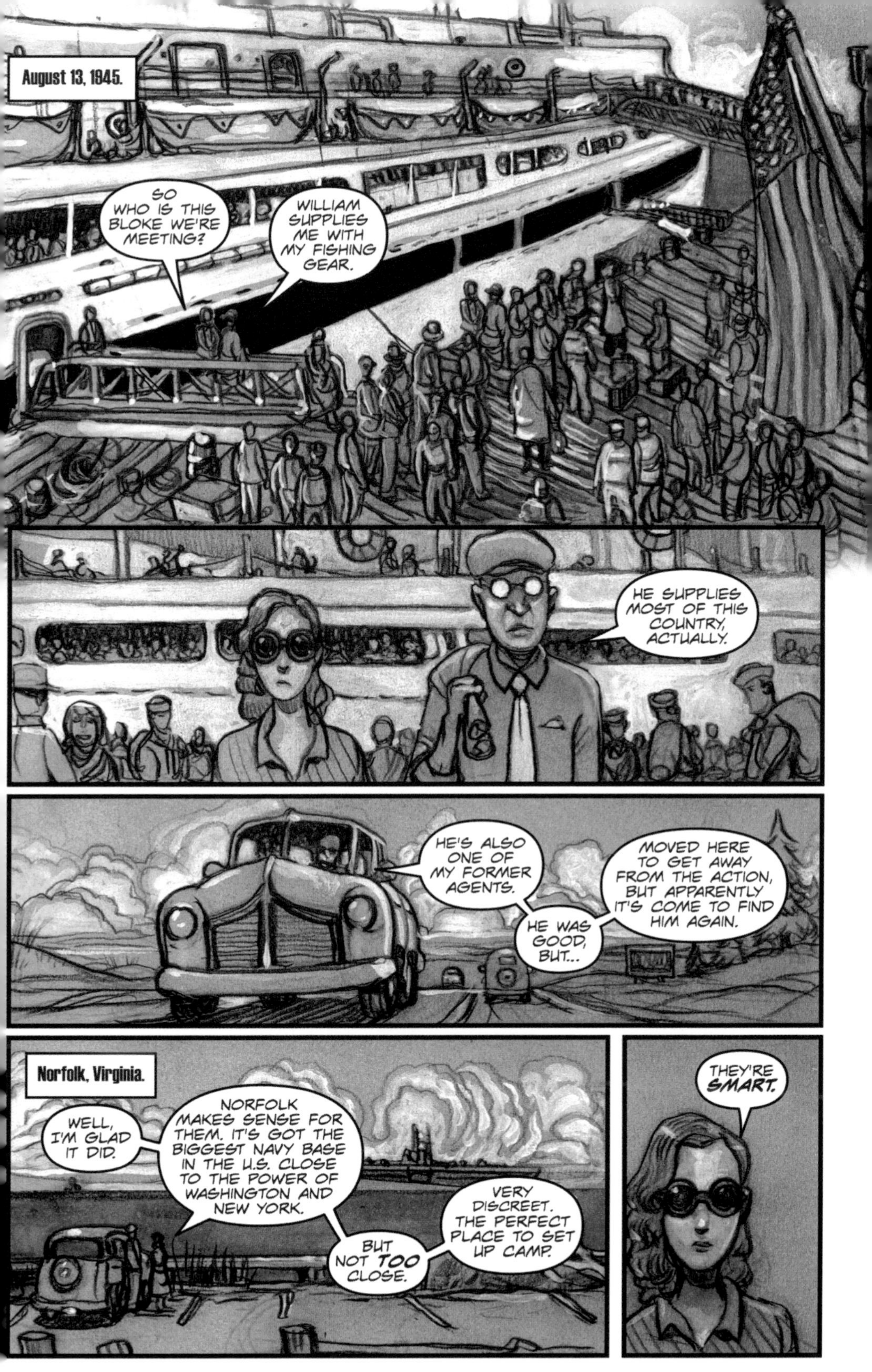

August 13, 1945.
SO WHO IS THIS BLOKE WE'RE MEETING?
WILLIAM SUPPLIES ME WITH MY FISHING GEAR.
HE SUPPLIES MOST OF THIS COUNTRY, ACTUALLY.
HE'S ALSO ONE OF MY FORMER AGENTS.
HE WAS GOOD, BUT...
MOVED HERE TO GET AWAY FROM THE ACTION, BUT APPARENTLY IT'S COME TO FIND HIM AGAIN.
Norfolk, Virginia.
WELL, I'M GLAD IT DID.
NORFOLK MAKES SENSE FOR THEM. IT'S GOT THE BIGGEST NAVY BASE IN THE U.S. CLOSE TO THE POWER OF WASHINGTON AND NEW YORK.
BUT NOT TOO CLOSE.
VERY DISCREET. THE PERFECT PLACE TO SET UP CAMP.
THEY'RE SMART.

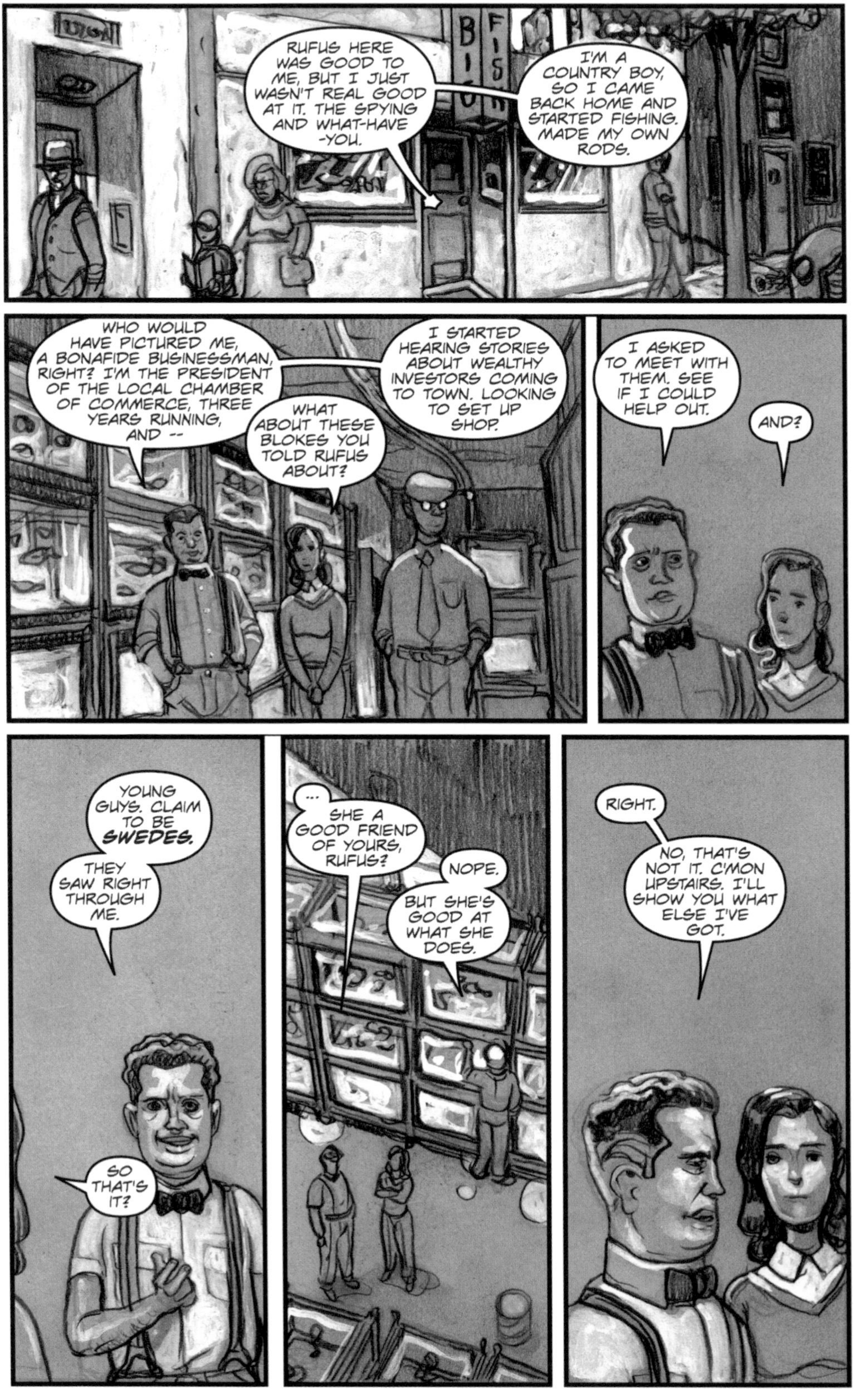
RUFUS HERE WAS GOOD TO ME, BUT I JUST WASN'T REAL GOOD AT IT. THE SPYING AND WHAT-HAVE -YOU.
I'M A COUNTRY BOY, SO I CAME BACK HOME AND STARTED FISHING. MADE MY OWN RODS.
B FIS
WHO WOULD HAVE PICTURED ME, A BONAFIDE BUSINESSMAN, RIGHT? I'M THE PRESIDENT OF THE LOCAL CHAMBER OF COMMERCE, THREE YEARS RUNNING, AND --
WHAT ABOUT THESE BLOKES YOU TOLD RUFUS ABOUT?
I STARTED HEARING STORIES ABOUT WEALTHY INVESTORS COMING TO TOWN. LOOKING TO SET UP SHOP.
I ASKED TO MEET WITH THEM. SEE IF I COULD HELP OUT.
AND?
YOUNG GUYS. CLAIM TO BE **SWEDES.**
THEY SAW RIGHT THROUGH ME.
SO THAT'S IT?
...
SHE A GOOD FRIEND OF YOURS, RUFUS?
NOPE.
BUT SHE'S GOOD AT WHAT SHE DOES.
RIGHT.
NO, THAT'S NOT IT. C'MON UPSTAIRS. I'LL SHOW YOU WHAT ELSE I'VE GOT.

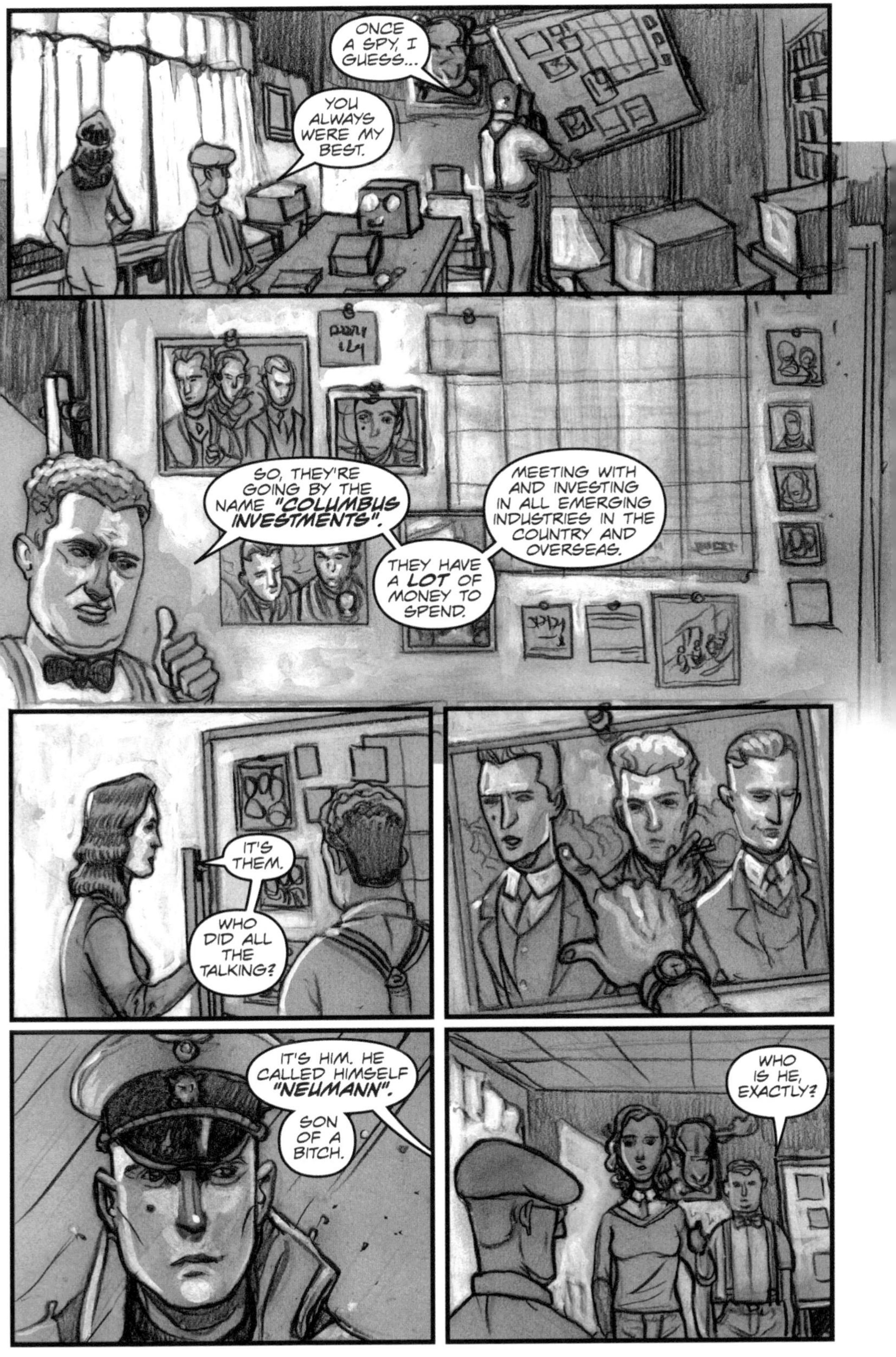
ONCE A SPY, I GUESS...
YOU ALWAYS WERE MY BEST.
SO, THEY'RE GOING BY THE NAME "COLUMBUS INVESTMENTS".
MEETING WITH AND INVESTING IN ALL EMERGING INDUSTRIES IN THE COUNTRY AND OVERSEAS.
THEY HAVE A LOT OF MONEY TO SPEND.
IT'S THEM.
WHO DID ALL THE TALKING?
IT'S HIM. HE CALLED HIMSELF "NEUMANN".
SON OF A BITCH.
WHO IS HE, EXACTLY?

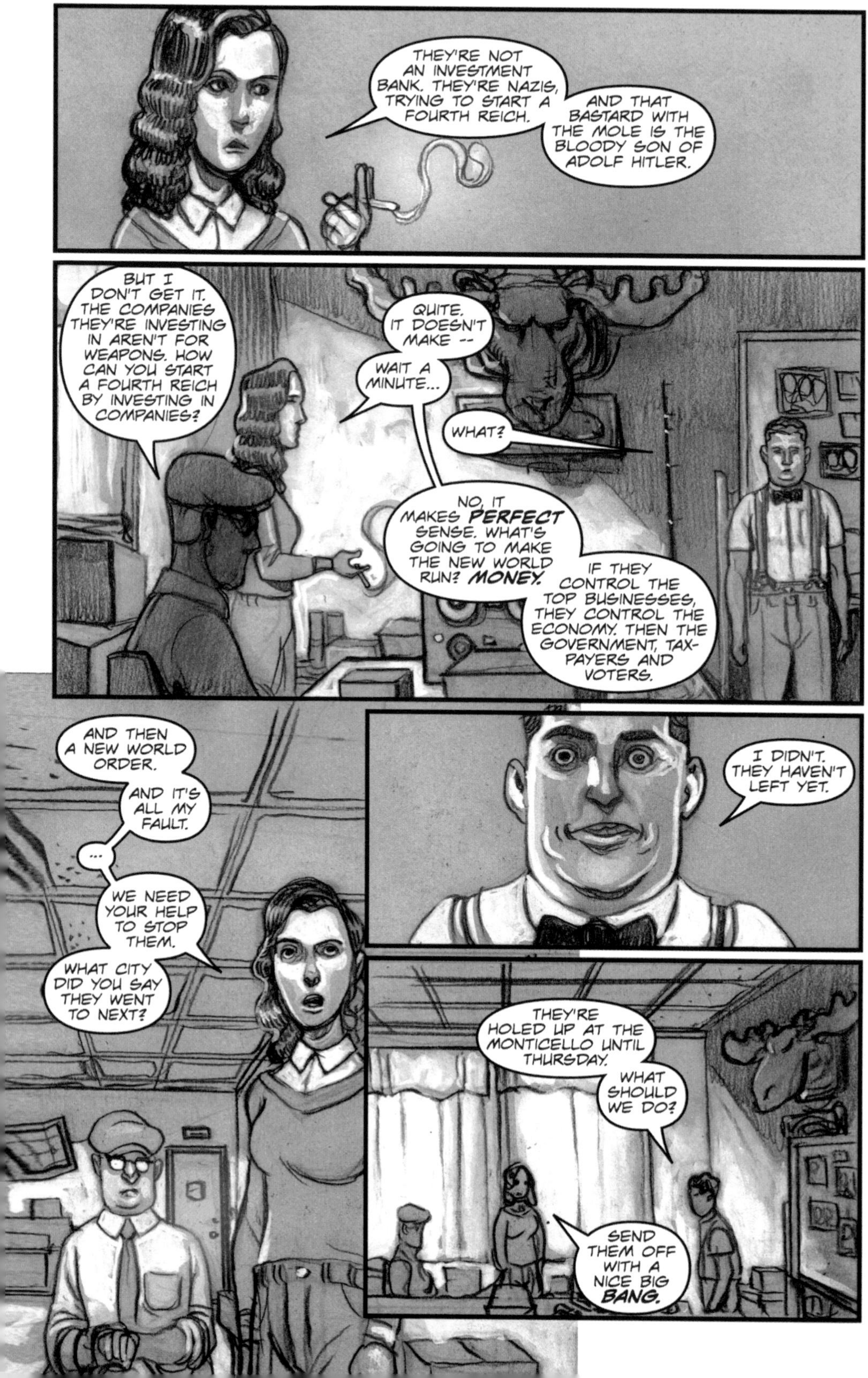
THEY'RE NOT AN INVESTMENT BANK. THEY'RE NAZIS, TRYING TO START A FOURTH REICH.
AND THAT BASTARD WITH THE MOLE IS THE BLOODY SON OF ADOLF HITLER.
BUT I DON'T GET IT. THE COMPANIES THEY'RE INVESTING IN AREN'T FOR WEAPONS. HOW CAN YOU START A FOURTH REICH BY INVESTING IN COMPANIES?
QUITE. IT DOESN'T MAKE --
WAIT A MINUTE...
WHAT?
NO, IT MAKES PERFECT SENSE. WHAT'S GOING TO MAKE THE NEW WORLD RUN? MONEY.
IF THEY CONTROL THE TOP BUSINESSES, THEY CONTROL THE ECONOMY. THEN THE GOVERNMENT, TAX-PAYERS AND VOTERS.
AND THEN A NEW WORLD ORDER.
AND IT'S ALL MY FAULT.
...
WE NEED YOUR HELP TO STOP THEM.
WHAT CITY DID YOU SAY THEY WENT TO NEXT?
I DIDN'T. THEY HAVEN'T LEFT YET.
THEY'RE HOLED UP AT THE MONTICELLO UNTIL THURSDAY.
WHAT SHOULD WE DO?
SEND THEM OFF WITH A NICE BIG BANG.

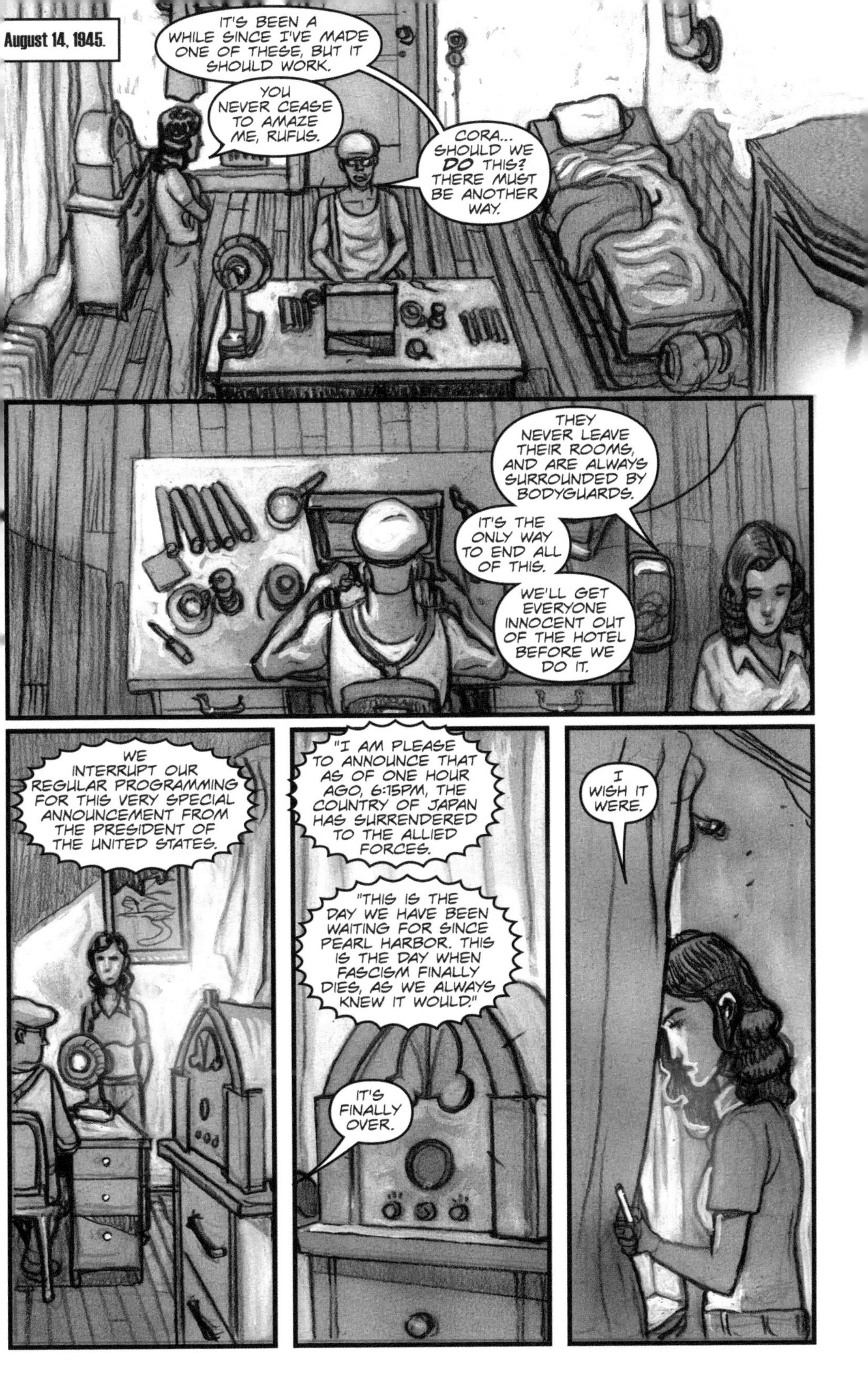
August 14, 1945.
IT'S BEEN A WHILE SINCE I'VE MADE ONE OF THESE, BUT IT SHOULD WORK.
YOU NEVER CEASE TO AMAZE ME, RUFUS.
CORA... SHOULD WE DO THIS? THERE MUST BE ANOTHER WAY.
THEY NEVER LEAVE THEIR ROOMS, AND ARE ALWAYS SURROUNDED BY BODYGUARDS.
IT'S THE ONLY WAY TO END ALL OF THIS.
WE'LL GET EVERYONE INNOCENT OUT OF THE HOTEL BEFORE WE DO IT.
WE INTERRUPT OUR REGULAR PROGRAMMING FOR THIS VERY SPECIAL ANNOUNCEMENT FROM THE PRESIDENT OF THE UNITED STATES.
"I AM PLEASE TO ANNOUNCE THAT AS OF ONE HOUR AGO, 6:15PM, THE COUNTRY OF JAPAN HAS SURRENDERED TO THE ALLIED FORCES.
"THIS IS THE DAY WE HAVE BEEN WAITING FOR SINCE PEARL HARBOR. THIS IS THE DAY WHEN FASCISM FINALLY DIES, AS WE ALWAYS KNEW IT WOULD."
IT'S FINALLY OVER.
I WISH IT WERE.

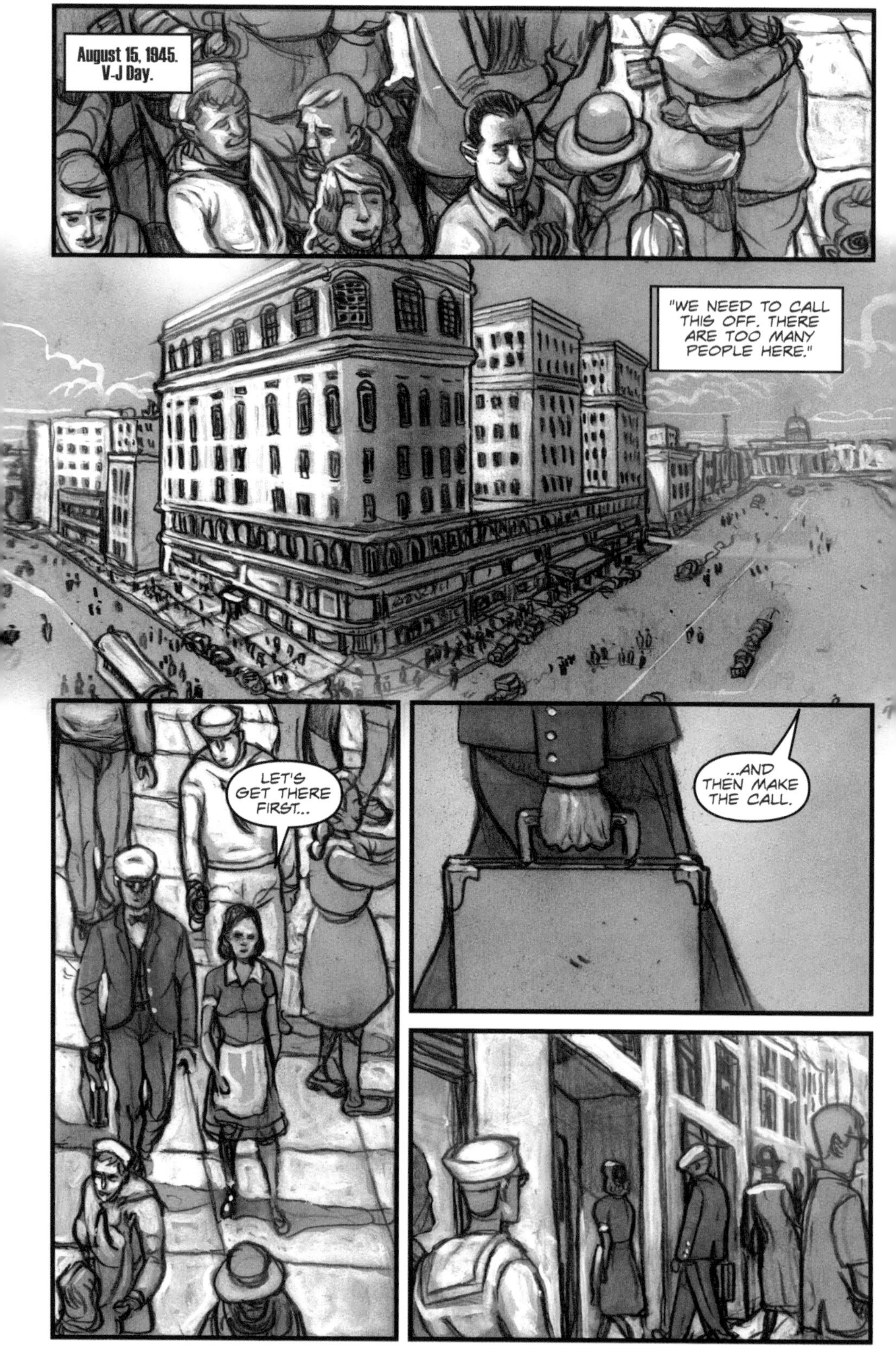
August 15, 1945.
V-J Day.
"WE NEED TO CALL THIS OFF. THERE ARE TOO MANY PEOPLE HERE."
LET'S GET THERE FIRST...
...AND THEN MAKE THE CALL.

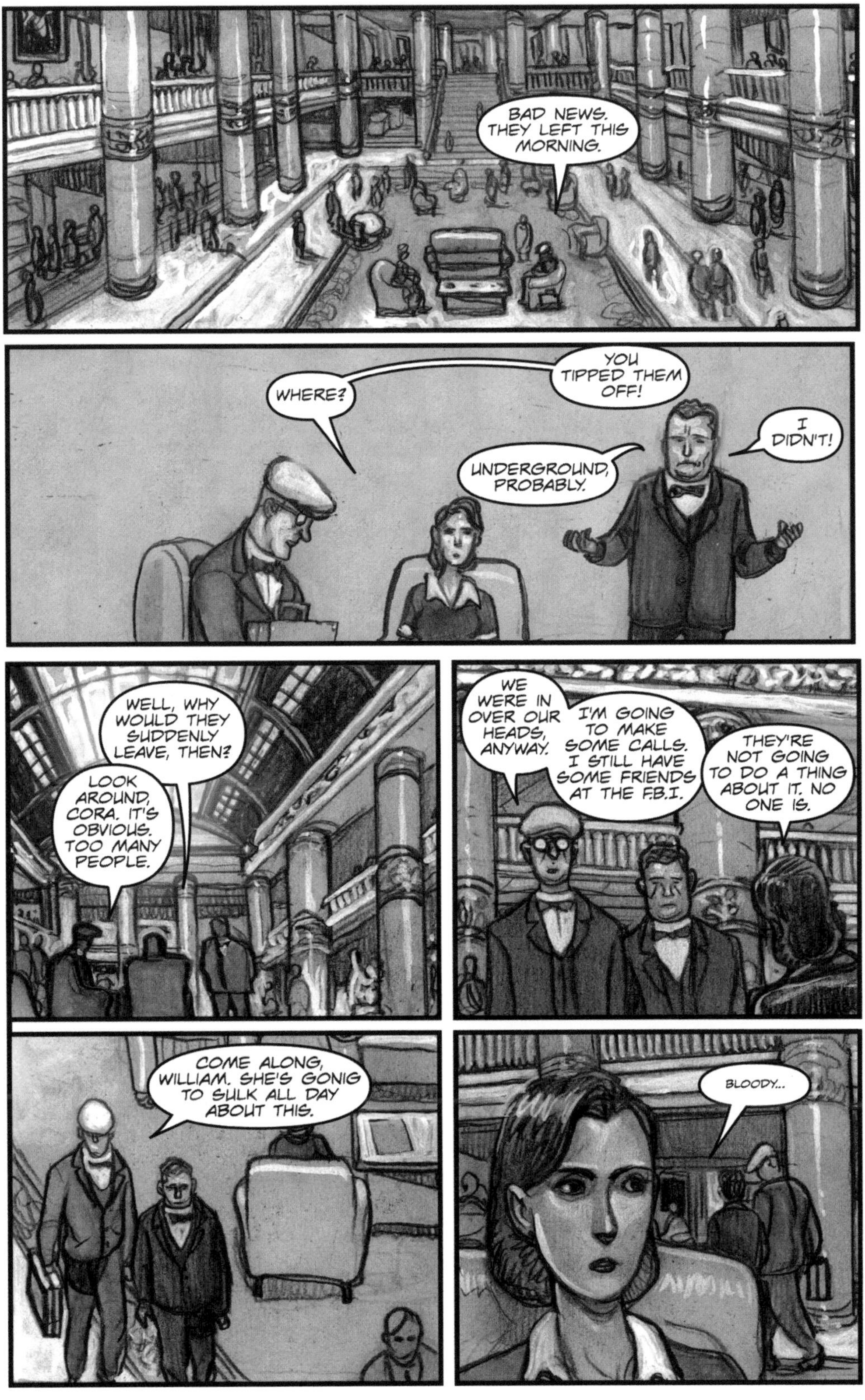
BAD NEWS. THEY LEFT THIS MORNING.
WHERE?
YOU TIPPED THEM OFF!
UNDERGROUND, PROBABLY.
I DIDN'T!
WELL, WHY WOULD THEY SUDDENLY LEAVE, THEN?
LOOK AROUND, CORA. IT'S OBVIOUS. TOO MANY PEOPLE.
WE WERE IN OVER OUR HEADS, ANYWAY.
I'M GOING TO MAKE SOME CALLS. I STILL HAVE SOME FRIENDS AT THE F.B.I.
THEY'RE NOT GOING TO DO A THING ABOUT IT. NO ONE IS.
COME ALONG, WILLIAM. SHE'S GONIG TO SULK ALL DAY ABOUT THIS.
BLOODY...

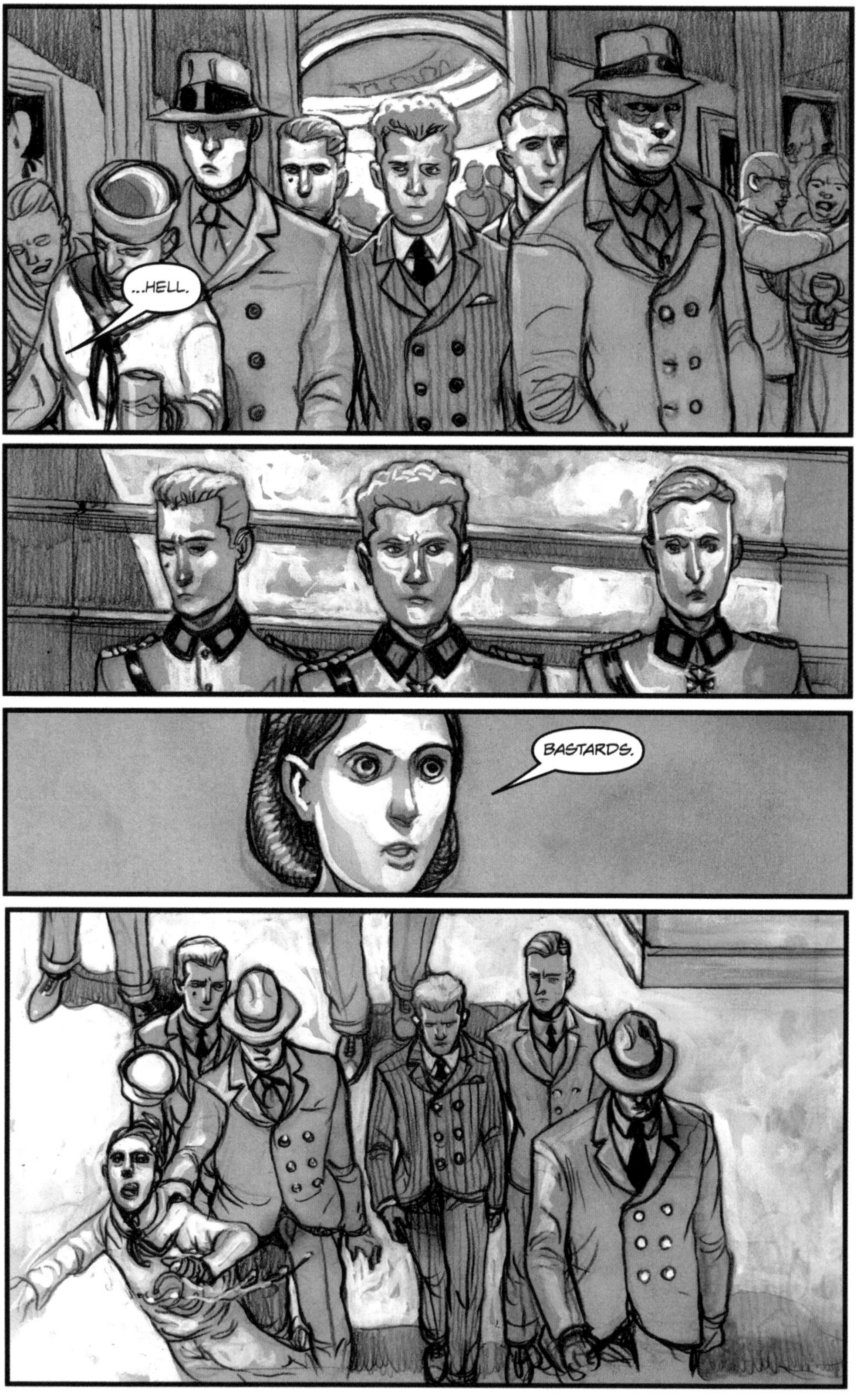
...HELL.
BASTARDS.

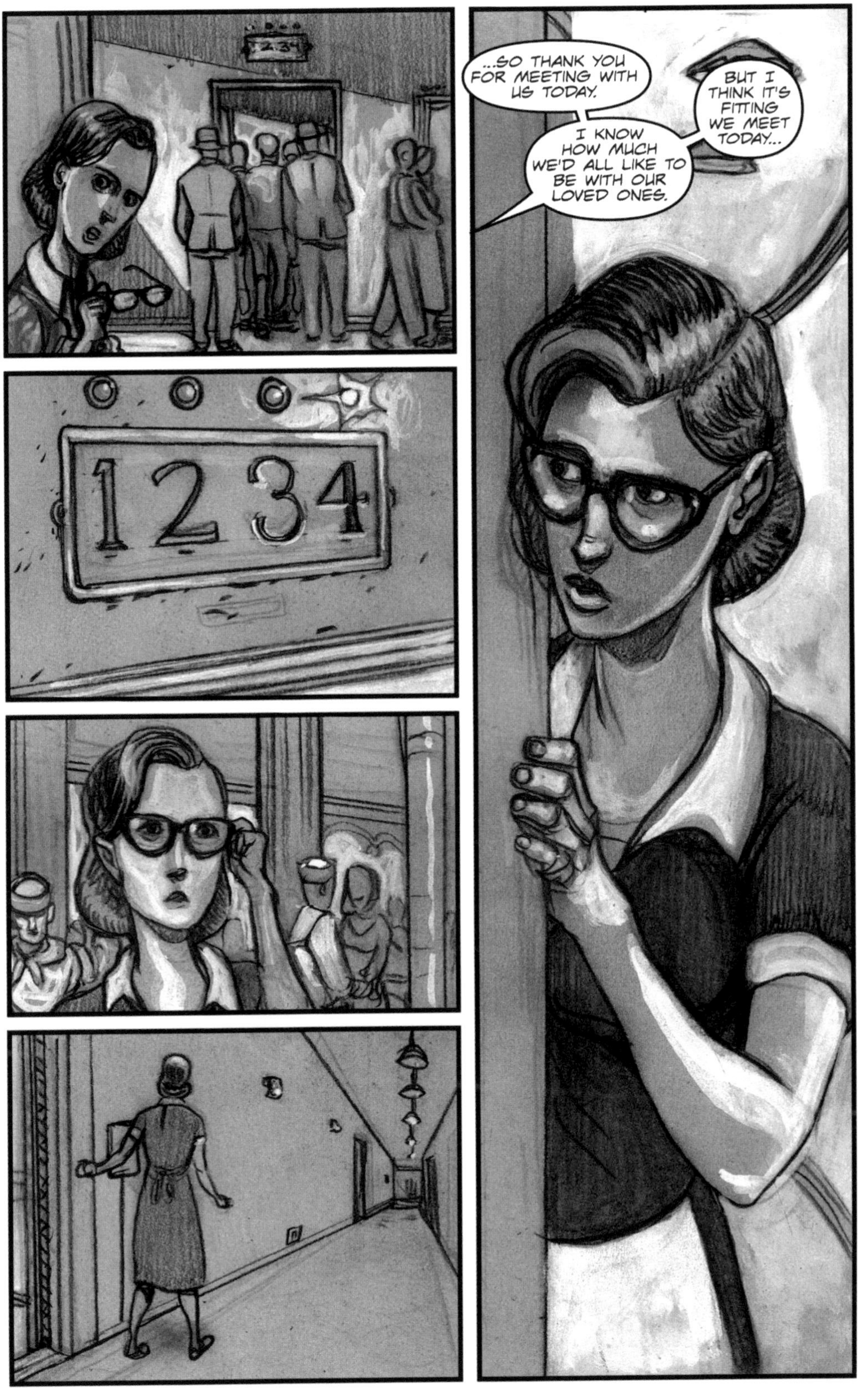
1234
...SO THANK YOU FOR MEETING WITH US TODAY.
I KNOW HOW MUCH WE'D ALL LIKE TO BE WITH OUR LOVED ONES.
BUT I THINK IT'S FITTING WE MEET TODAY...

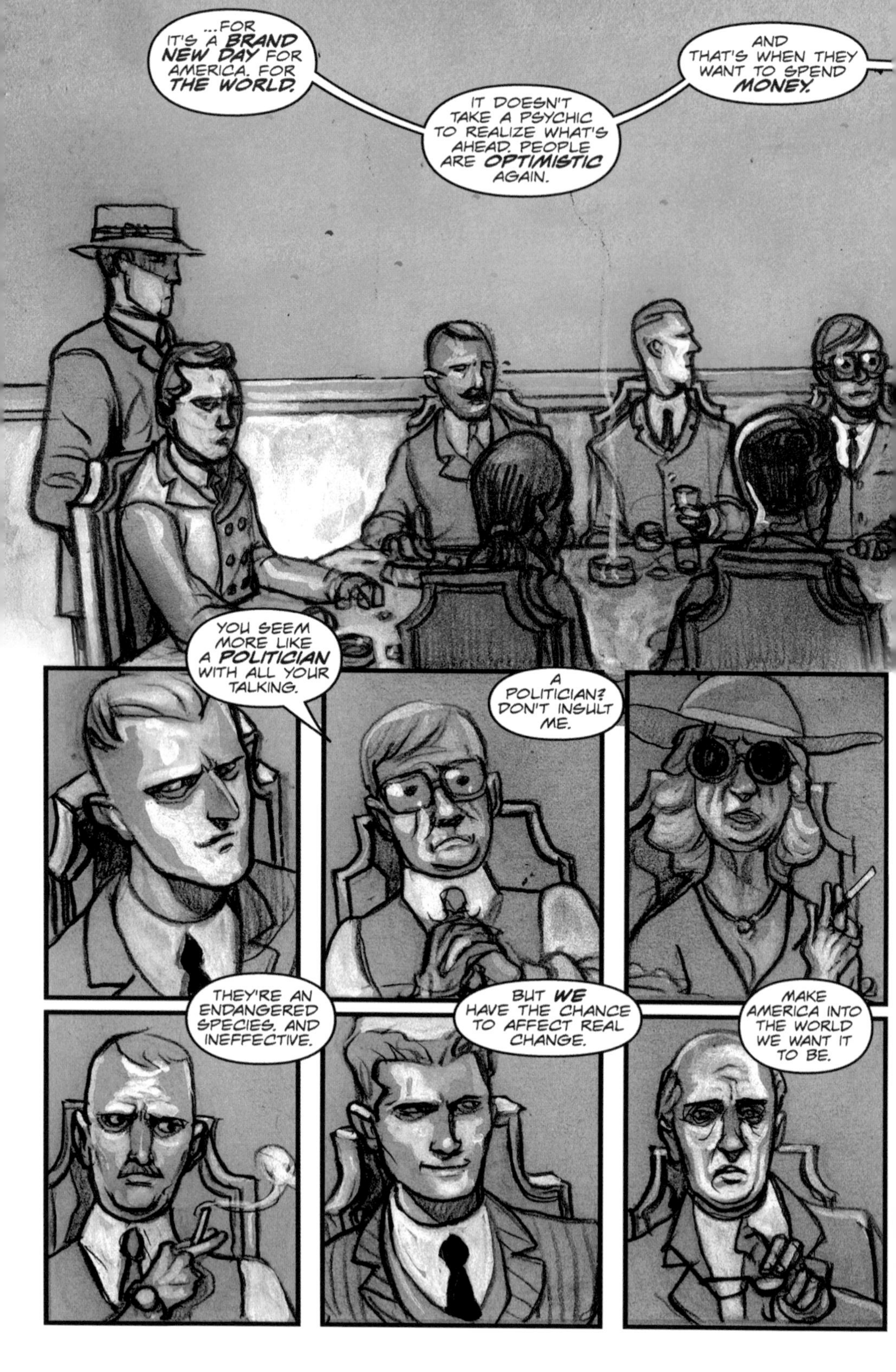
...FOR IT'S A BRAND NEW DAY FOR AMERICA. FOR THE WORLD.
IT DOESN'T TAKE A PSYCHIC TO REALIZE WHAT'S AHEAD. PEOPLE ARE OPTIMISTIC AGAIN.
AND THAT'S WHEN THEY WANT TO SPEND MONEY.
YOU SEEM MORE LIKE A POLITICIAN WITH ALL YOUR TALKING.
A POLITICIAN? DON'T INSULT ME.
THEY'RE AN ENDANGERED SPECIES, AND INEFFECTIVE.
BUT WE HAVE THE CHANCE TO AFFECT REAL CHANGE.
MAKE AMERICA INTO THE WORLD WE WANT IT TO BE.

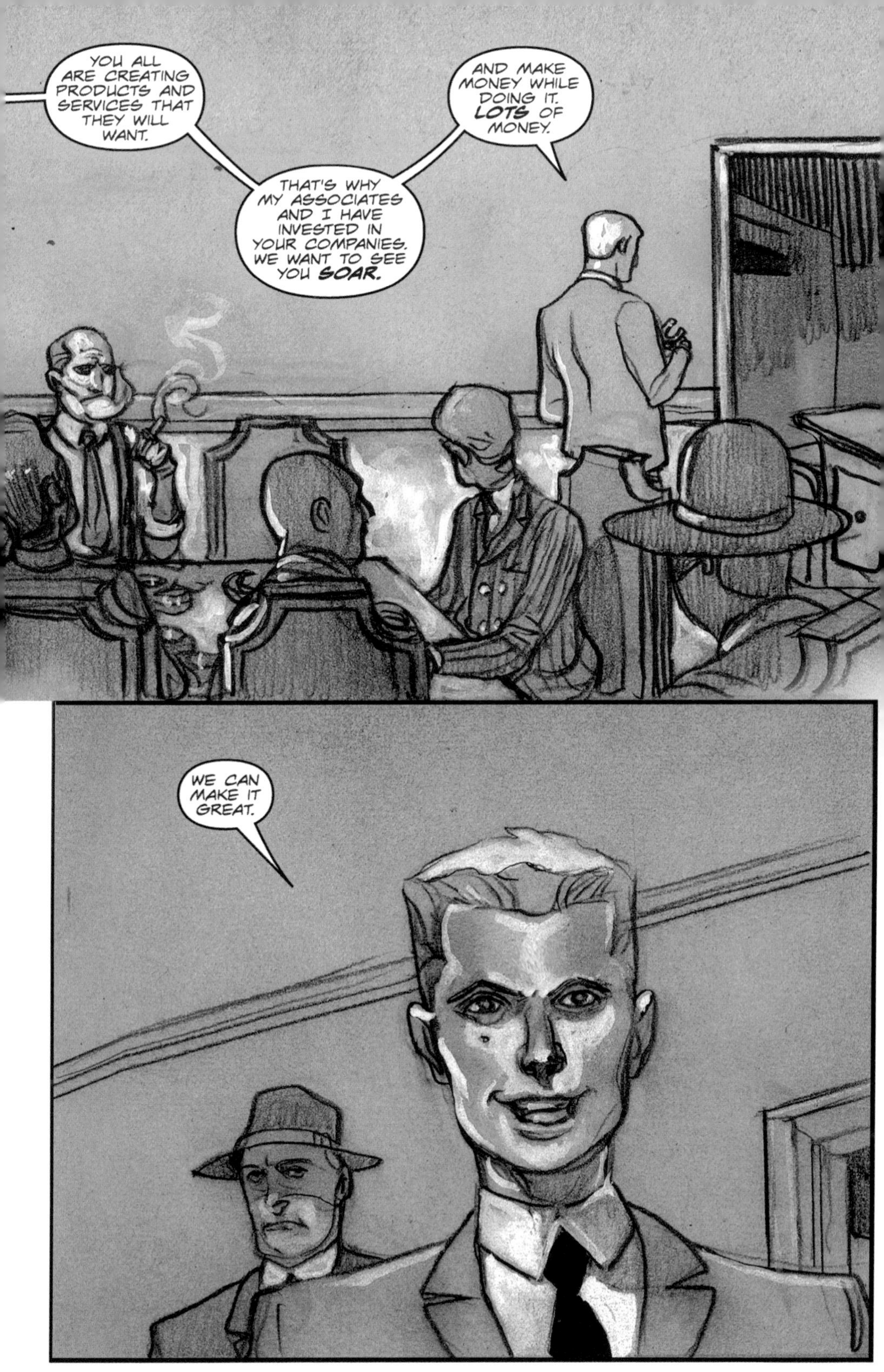
YOU ALL ARE CREATING PRODUCTS AND SERVICES THAT THEY WILL WANT.
THAT'S WHY MY ASSOCIATES AND I HAVE INVESTED IN YOUR COMPANIES. WE WANT TO SEE YOU SOAR.
AND MAKE MONEY WHILE DOING IT. LOTS OF MONEY.
WE CAN MAKE IT GREAT.

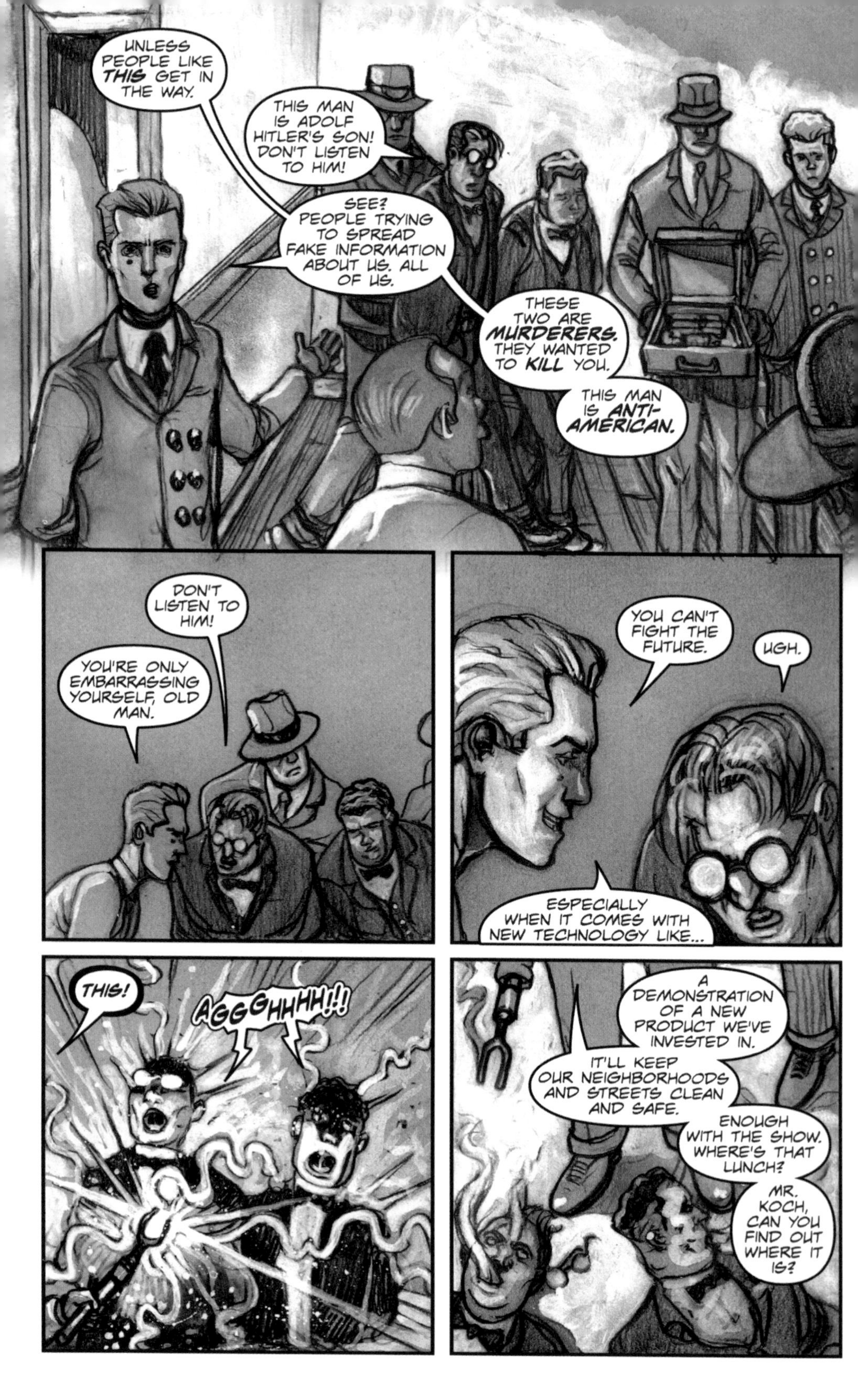
UNLESS PEOPLE LIKE THIS GET IN THE WAY.
THIS MAN IS ADOLF HITLER'S SON! DON'T LISTEN TO HIM!
SEE? PEOPLE TRYING TO SPREAD FAKE INFORMATION ABOUT US. ALL OF US.
THESE TWO ARE MURDERERS. THEY WANTED TO KILL YOU.
THIS MAN IS ANTI-AMERICAN.
DON'T LISTEN TO HIM!
YOU'RE ONLY EMBARRASSING YOURSELF, OLD MAN.
YOU CAN'T FIGHT THE FUTURE.
UGH.
ESPECIALLY WHEN IT COMES WITH NEW TECHNOLOGY LIKE...
THIS!
AGGGHHHH!!!
A DEMONSTRATION OF A NEW PRODUCT WE'VE INVESTED IN.
IT'LL KEEP OUR NEIGHBORHOODS AND STREETS CLEAN AND SAFE.
ENOUGH WITH THE SHOW. WHERE'S THAT LUNCH?
MR. KOCH, CAN YOU FIND OUT WHERE IT IS?

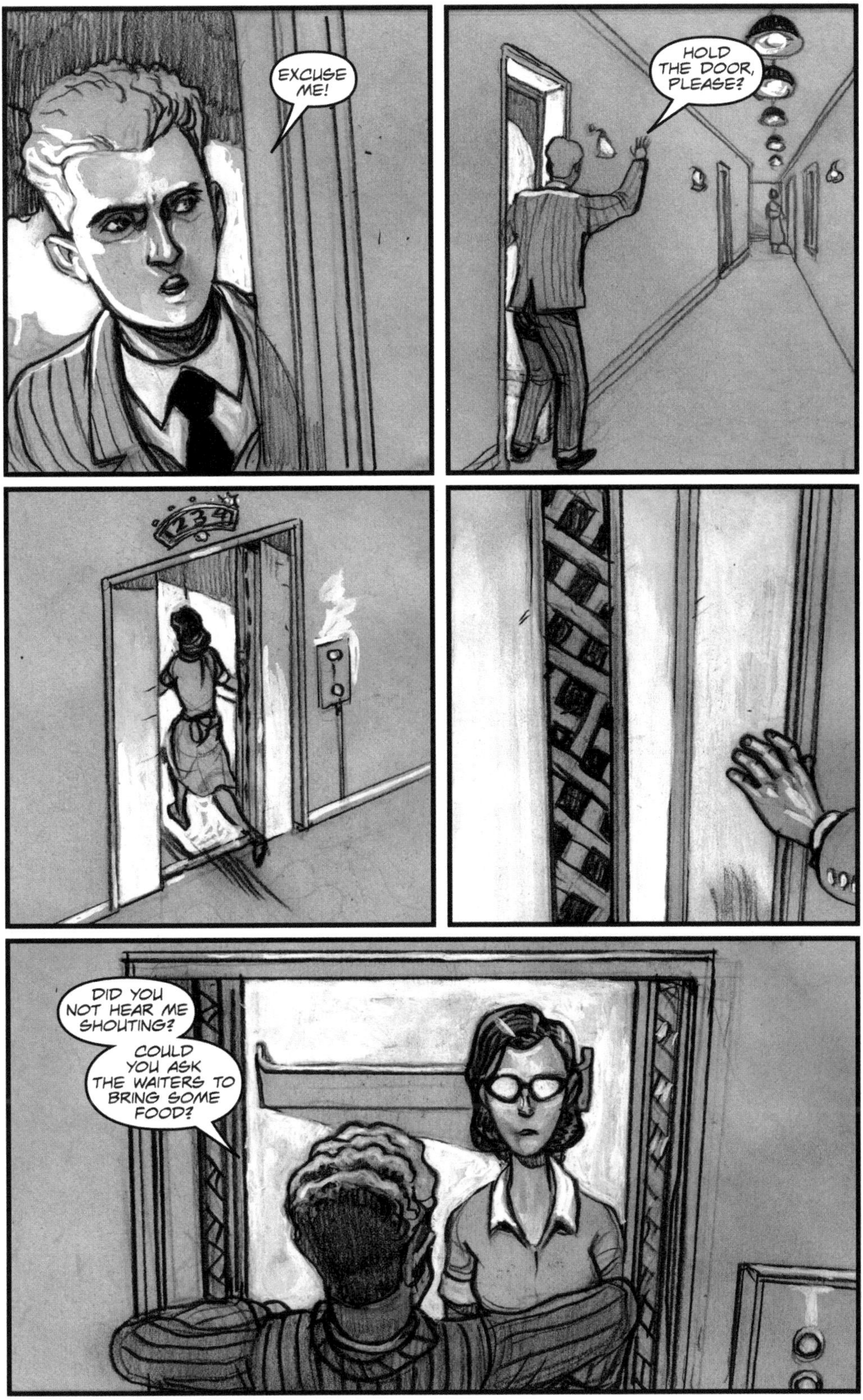
EXCUSE ME!
HOLD THE DOOR, PLEASE?
234
DID YOU NOT HEAR ME SHOUTING?
COULD YOU ASK THE WAITERS TO BRING SOME FOOD?

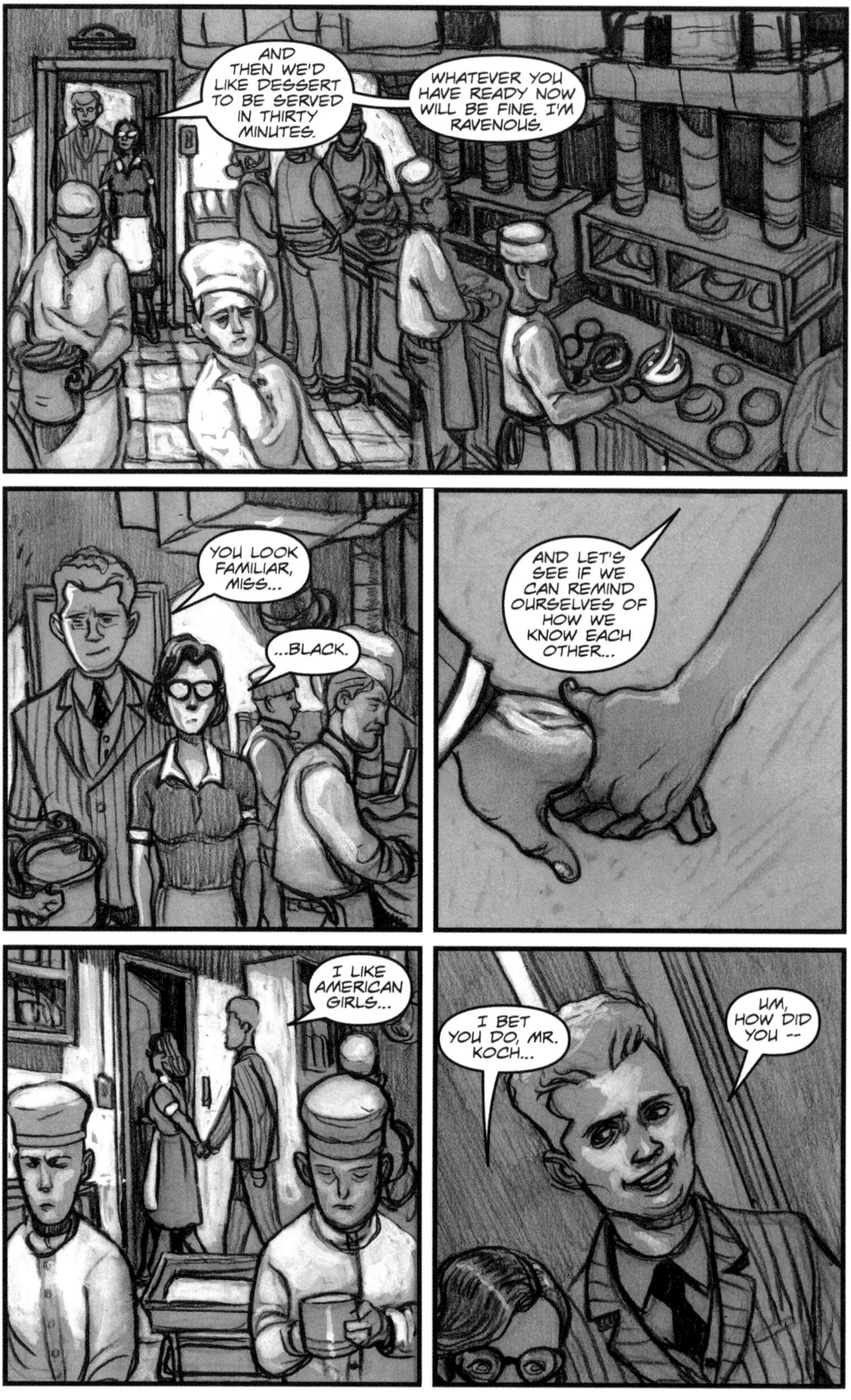
AND THEN WE'D LIKE DESSERT TO BE SERVED IN THIRTY MINUTES.
WHATEVER YOU HAVE READY NOW WILL BE FINE. I'M RAVENOUS.
YOU LOOK FAMILIAR, MISS...
...BLACK.
AND LET'S SEE IF WE CAN REMIND OURSELVES OF HOW WE KNOW EACH OTHER...
I LIKE AMERICAN GIRLS...
I BET YOU DO, MR. KOCH...
UM, HOW DID YOU --

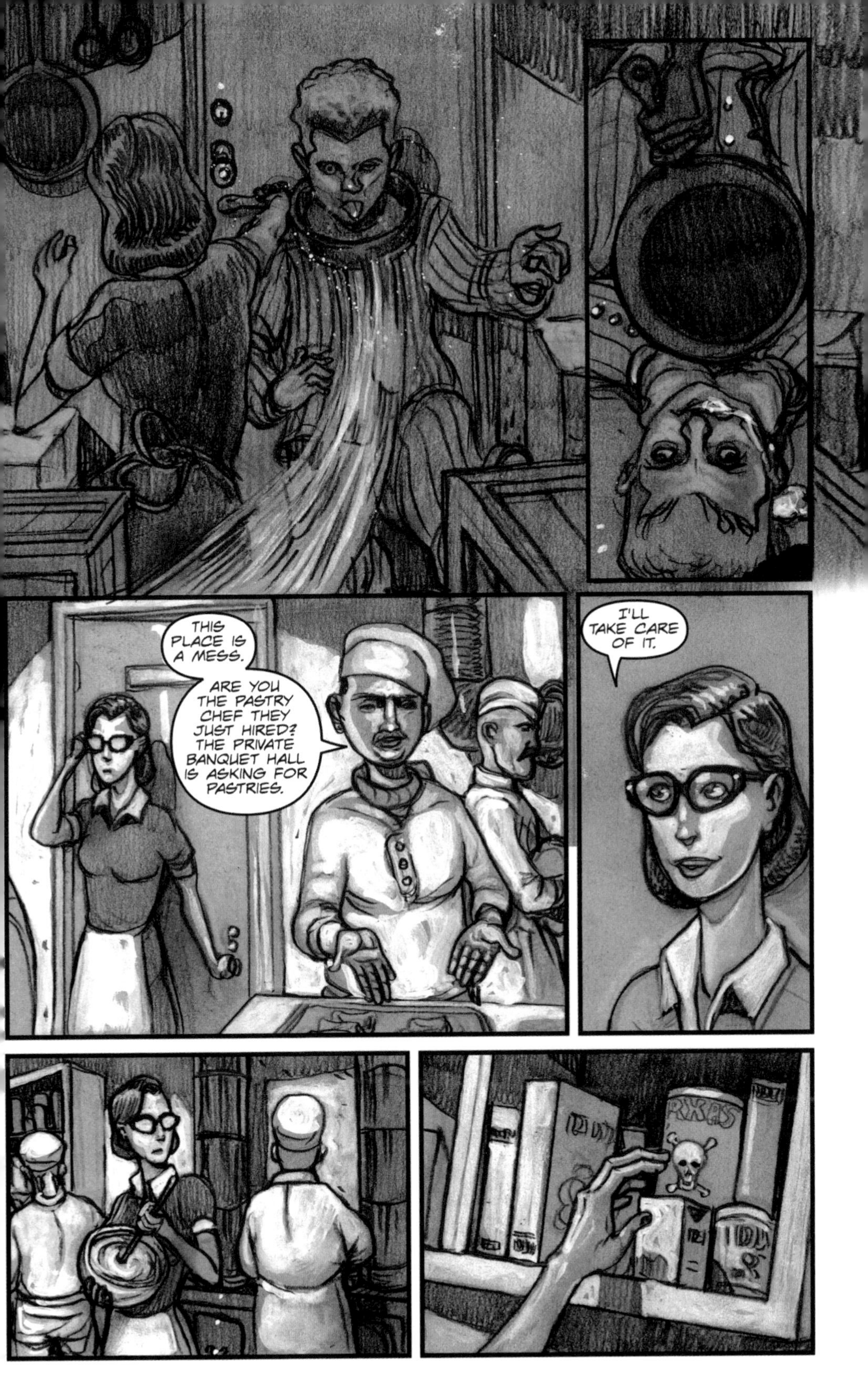
THIS PLACE IS A MESS.
ARE YOU THE PASTRY CHEF THEY JUST HIRED? THE PRIVATE BANQUET HALL IS ASKING FOR PASTRIES.
I'LL TAKE CARE OF IT.

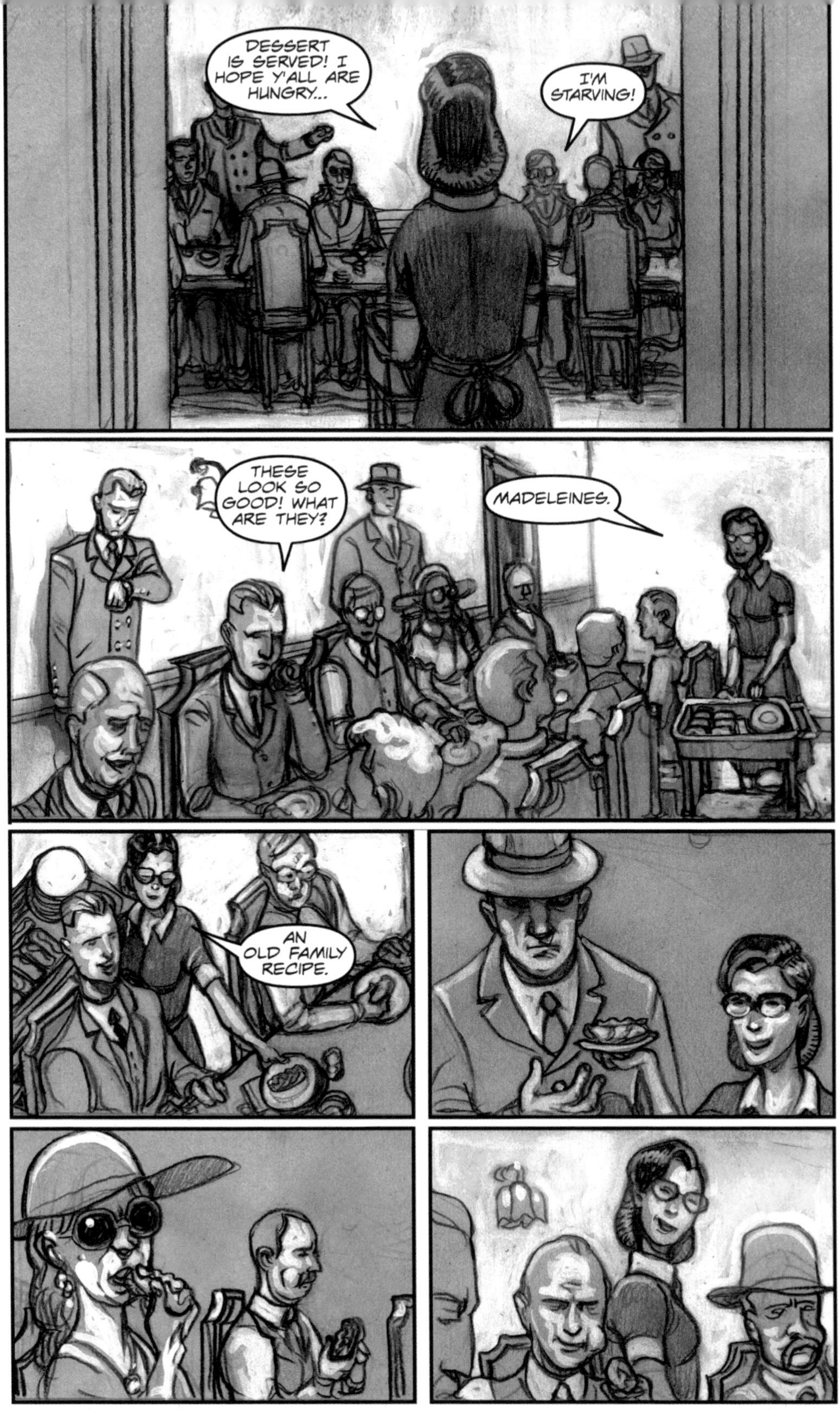
DESSERT IS SERVED! I HOPE Y'ALL ARE HUNGRY...
I'M STARVING!
THESE LOOK SO GOOD! WHAT ARE THEY?
MADELEINES.
AN OLD FAMILY RECIPE.

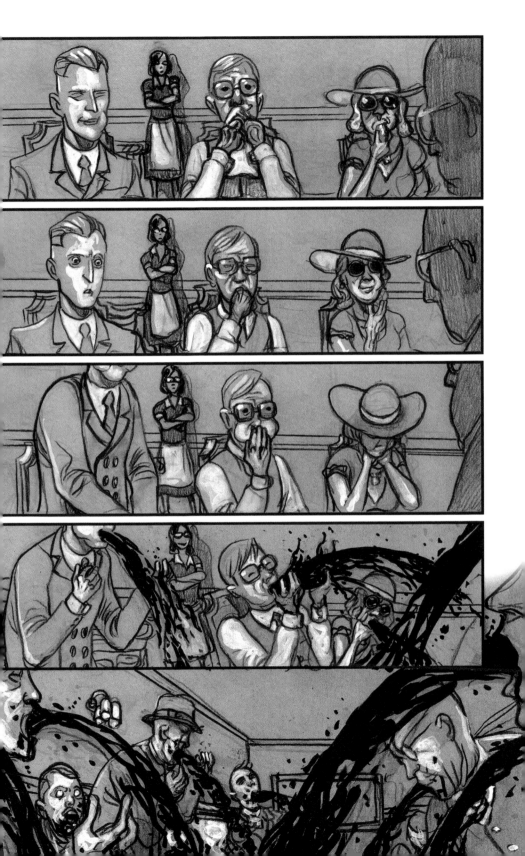

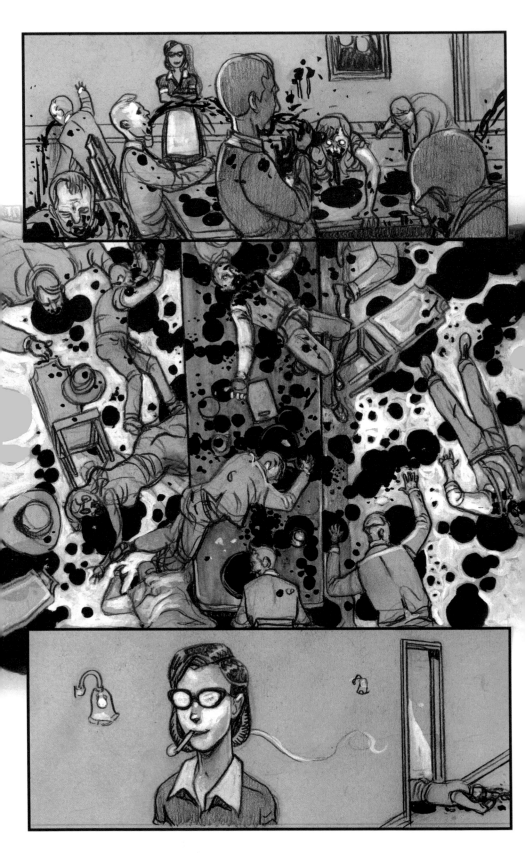

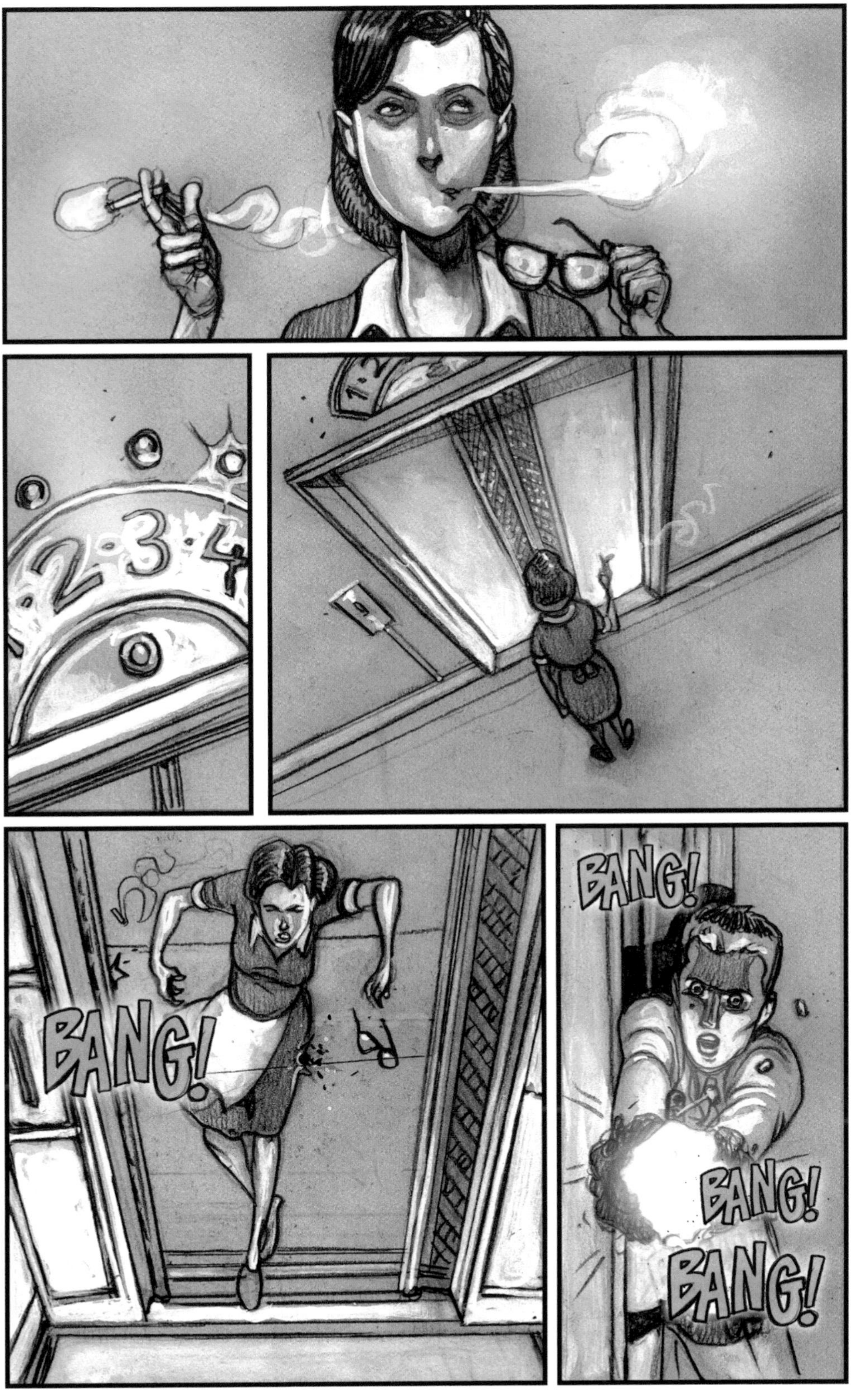
1·2·3·4
BANG!
BANG!
BANG!
BANG!

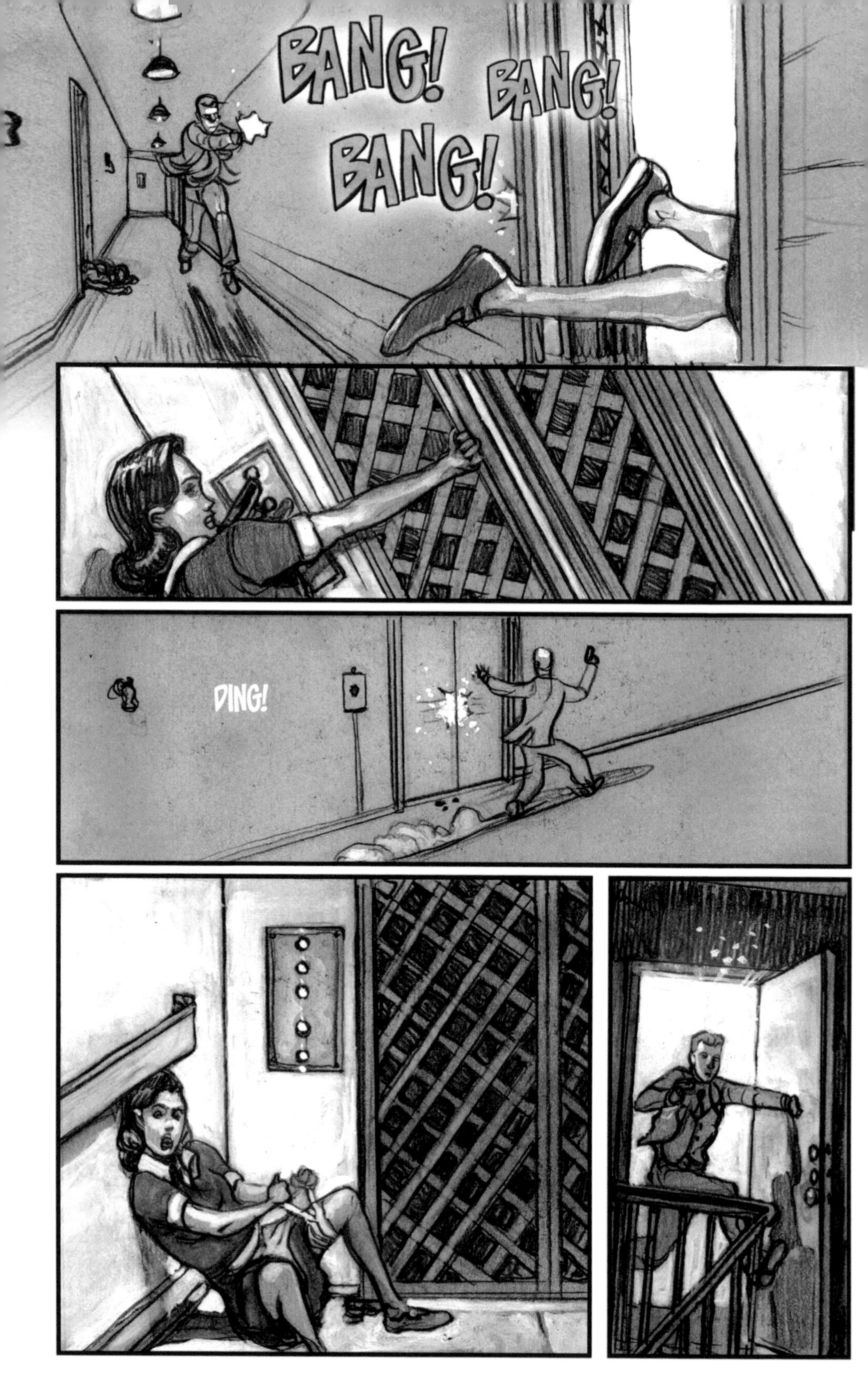
BANG!
BANG!
BANG!
DING!

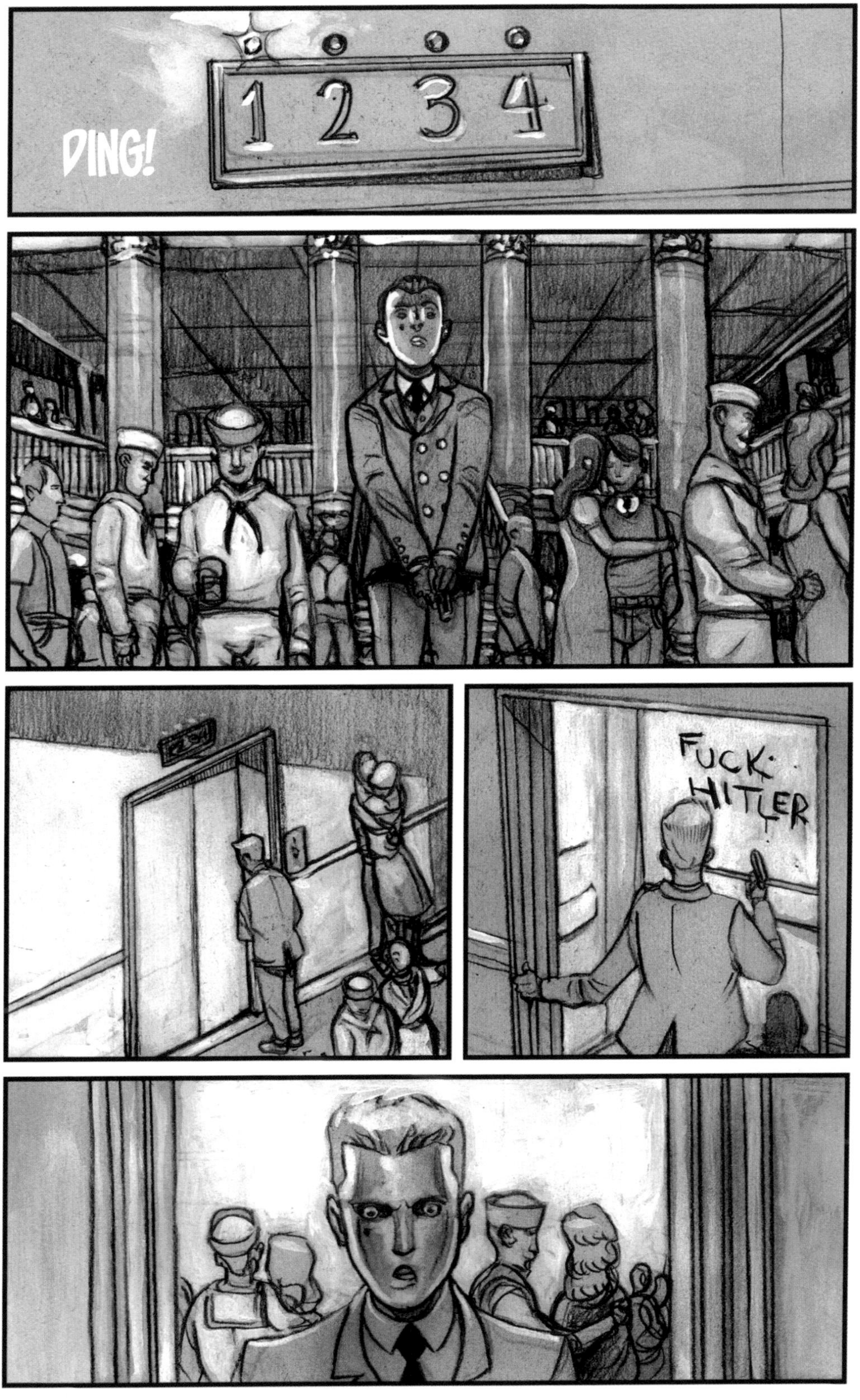
DING!
1 2 3 4
FUCK HITLER

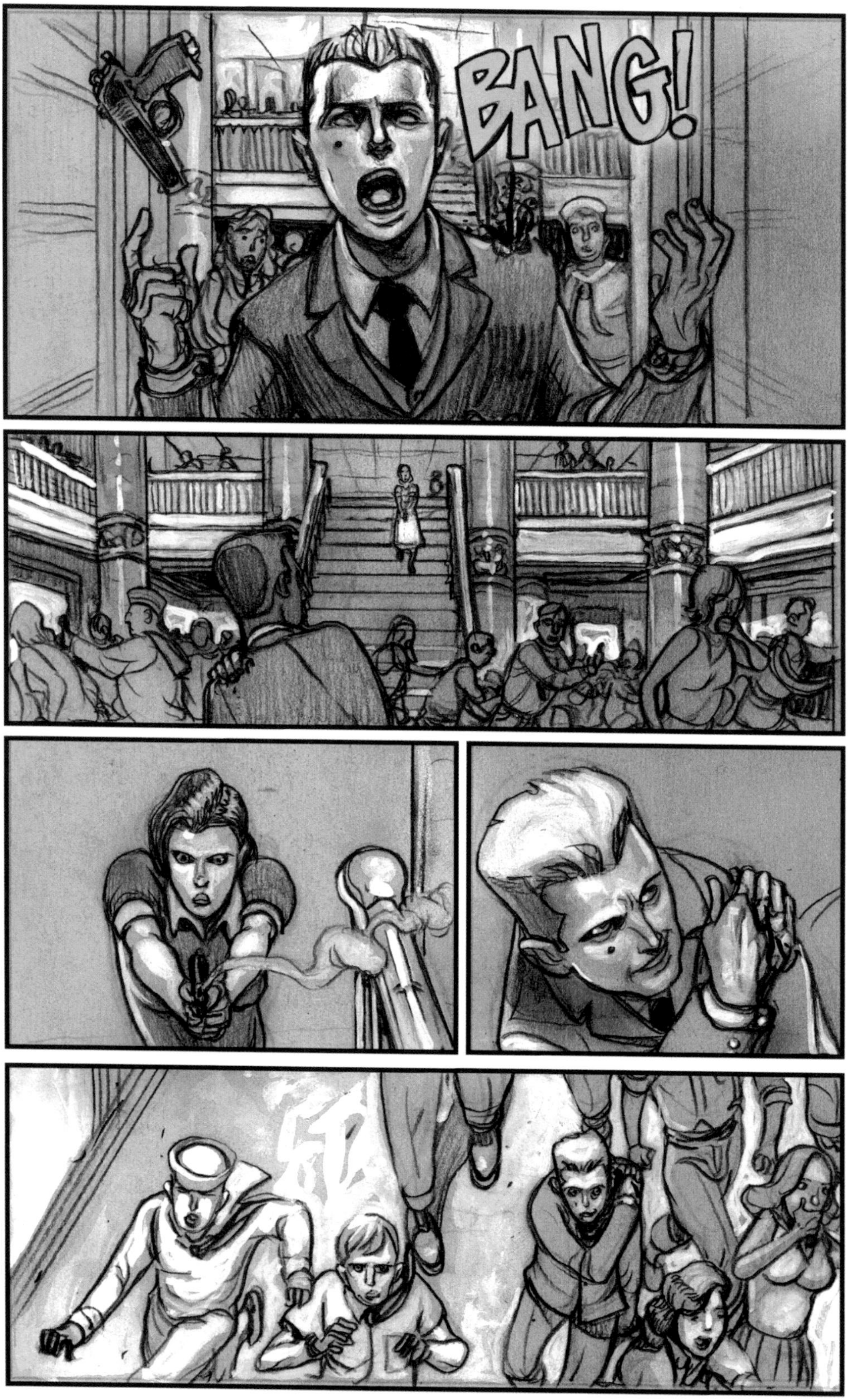
BANG!

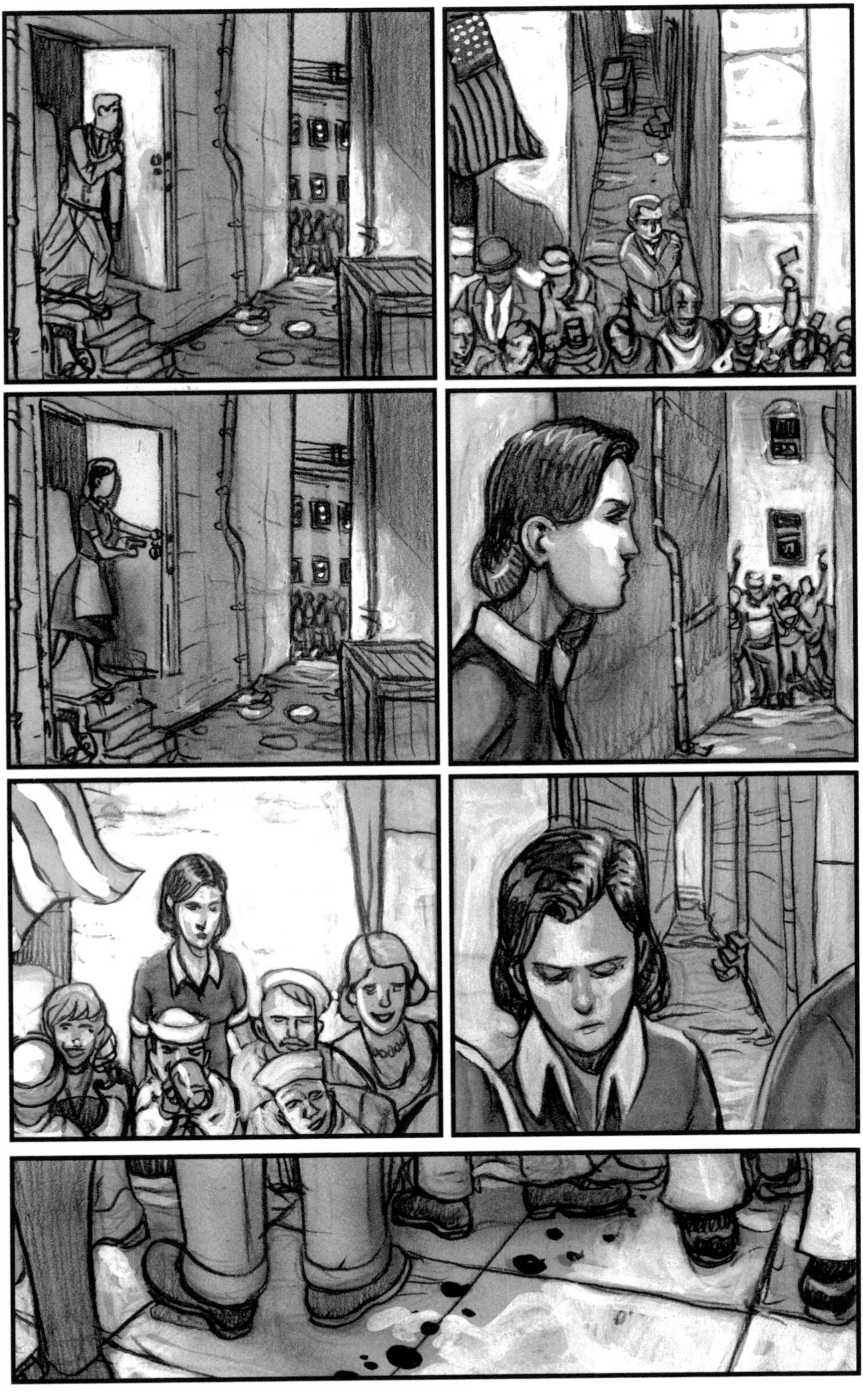

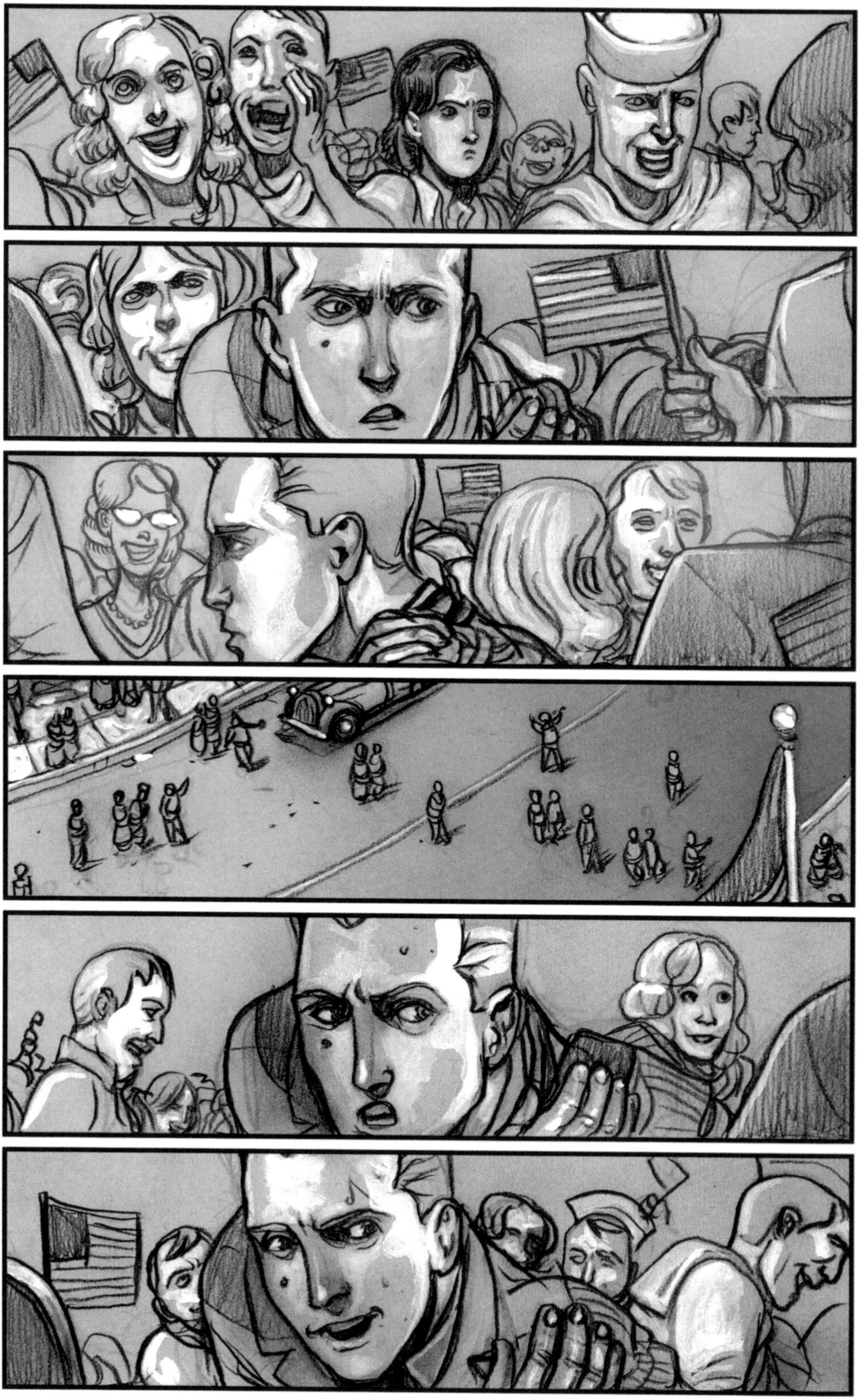

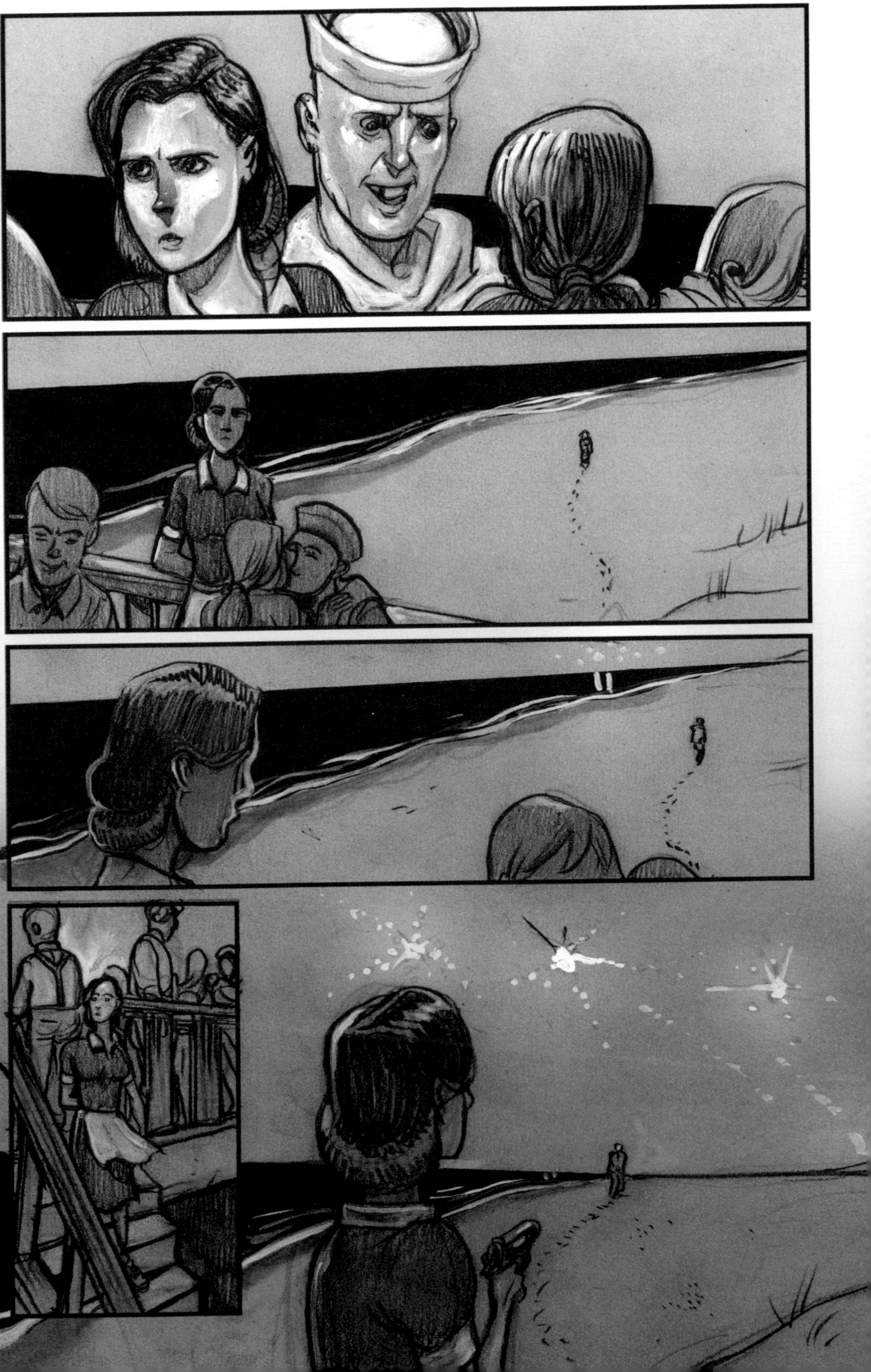

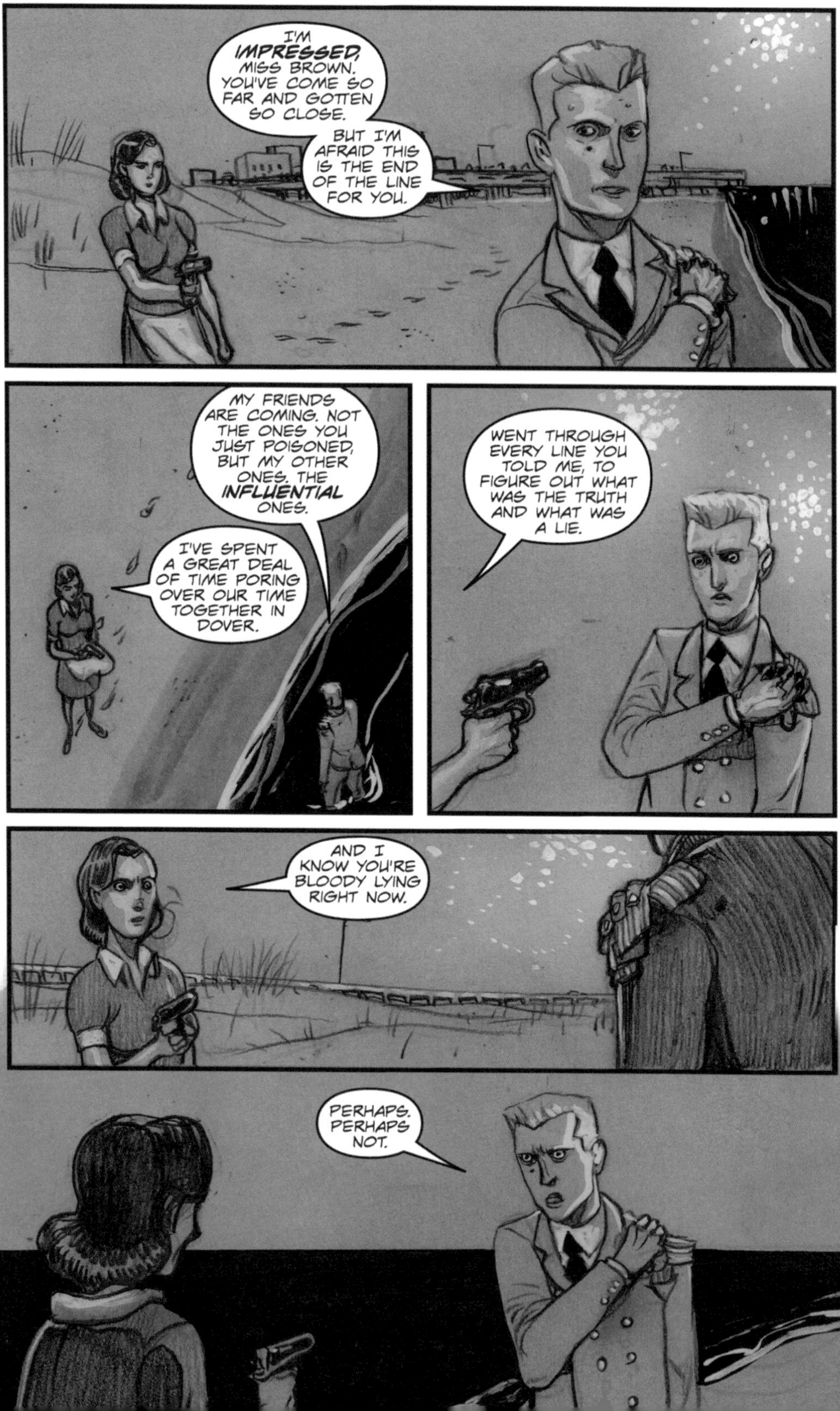
I'M IMPRESSED, MISS BROWN. YOU'VE COME SO FAR AND GOTTEN SO CLOSE.
BUT I'M AFRAID THIS IS THE END OF THE LINE FOR YOU.
MY FRIENDS ARE COMING. NOT THE ONES YOU JUST POISONED, BUT MY OTHER ONES. THE INFLUENTIAL ONES.
I'VE SPENT A GREAT DEAL OF TIME PORING OVER OUR TIME TOGETHER IN DOVER.
WENT THROUGH EVERY LINE YOU TOLD ME, TO FIGURE OUT WHAT WAS THE TRUTH AND WHAT WAS A LIE.
AND I KNOW YOU'RE BLOODY LYING RIGHT NOW.
PERHAPS. PERHAPS NOT.

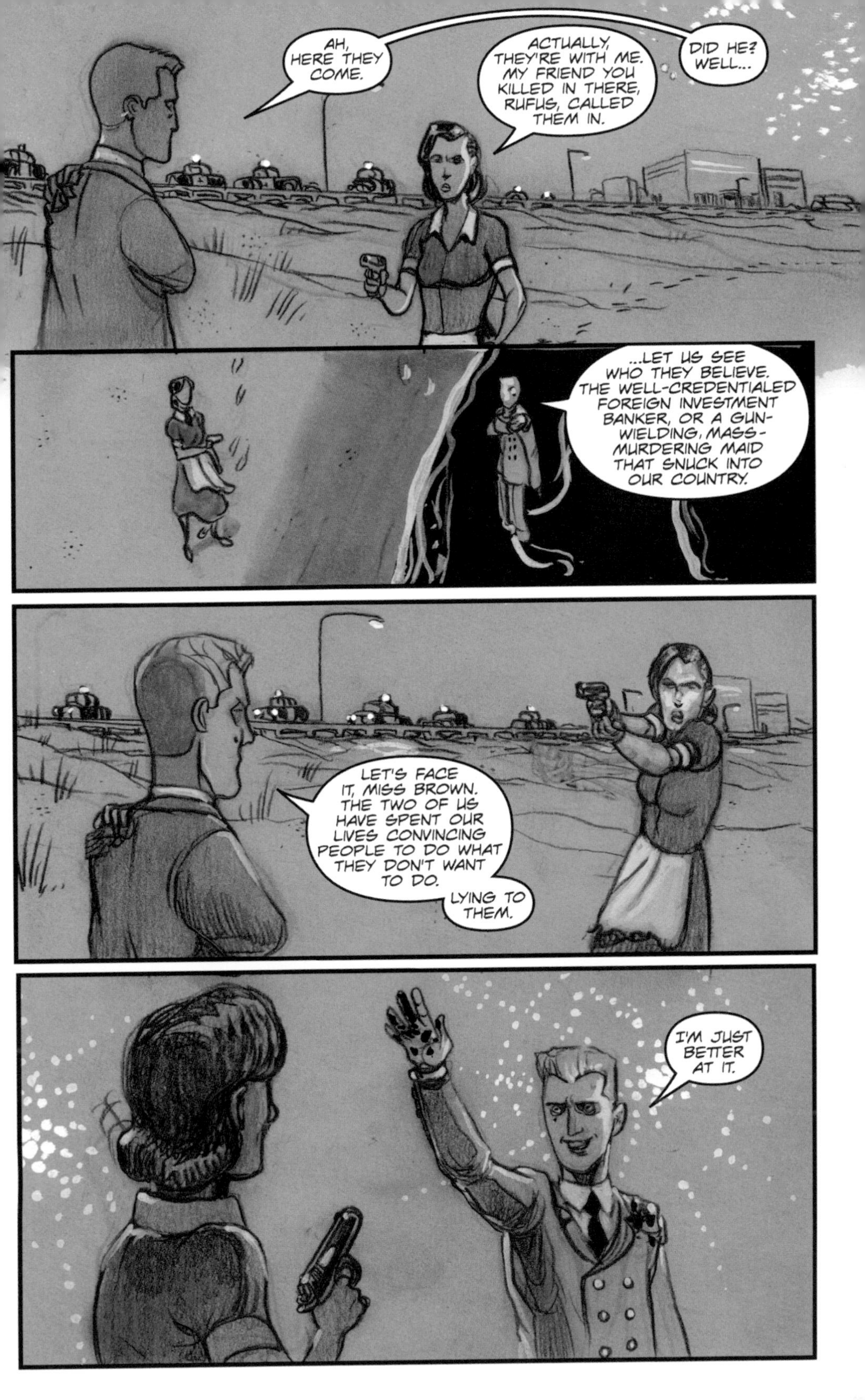
AH, HERE THEY COME.
ACTUALLY, THEY'RE WITH ME. MY FRIEND YOU KILLED IN THERE, RUFUS, CALLED THEM IN.
DID HE? WELL...
...LET US SEE WHO THEY BELIEVE. THE WELL-CREDENTIALED FOREIGN INVESTMENT BANKER, OR A GUN-WIELDING, MASS-MURDERING MAID THAT SNUCK INTO OUR COUNTRY.
LET'S FACE IT, MISS BROWN. THE TWO OF US HAVE SPENT OUR LIVES CONVINCING PEOPLE TO DO WHAT THEY DON'T WANT TO DO.
LYING TO THEM.
I'M JUST BETTER AT IT.

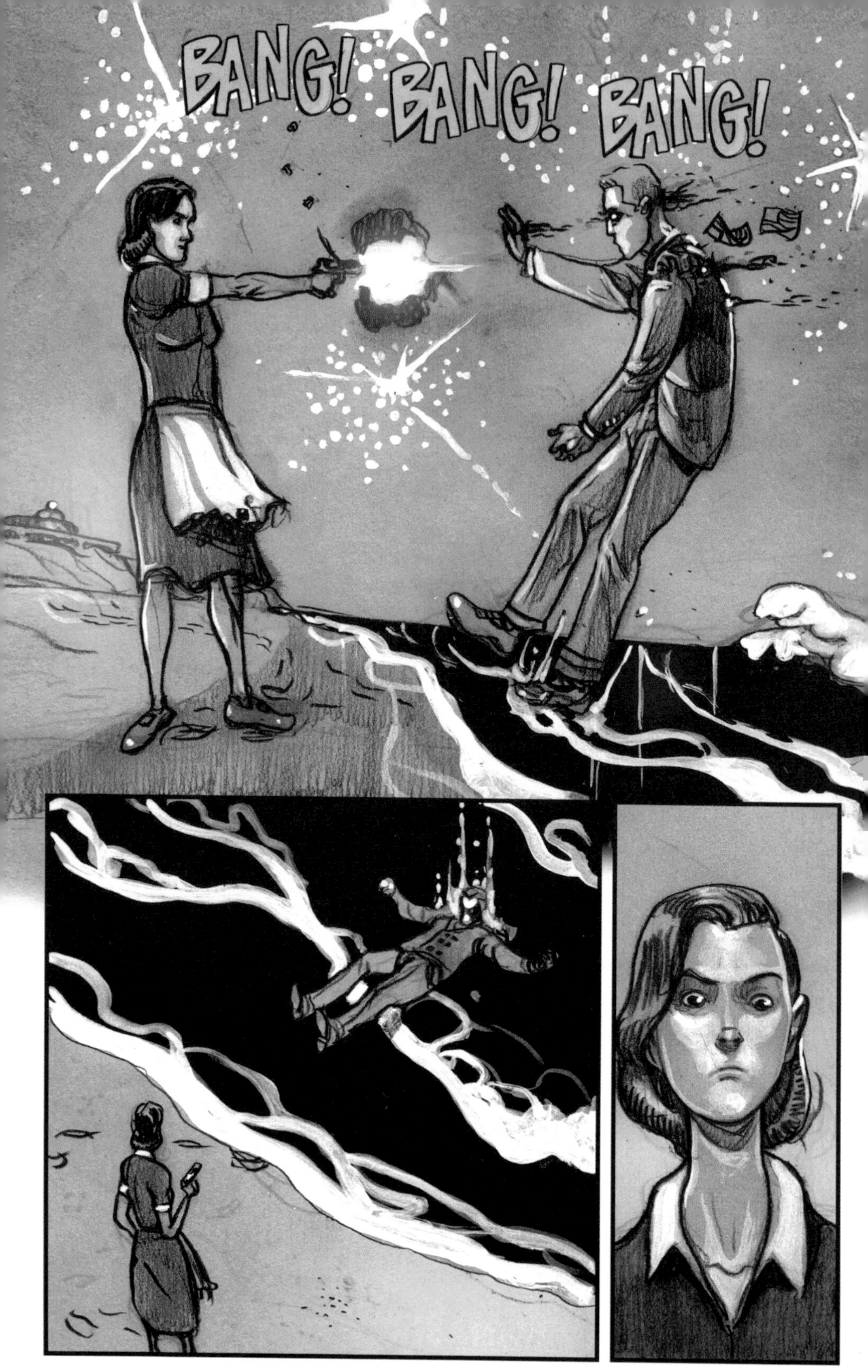
BANG! BANG! BANG!

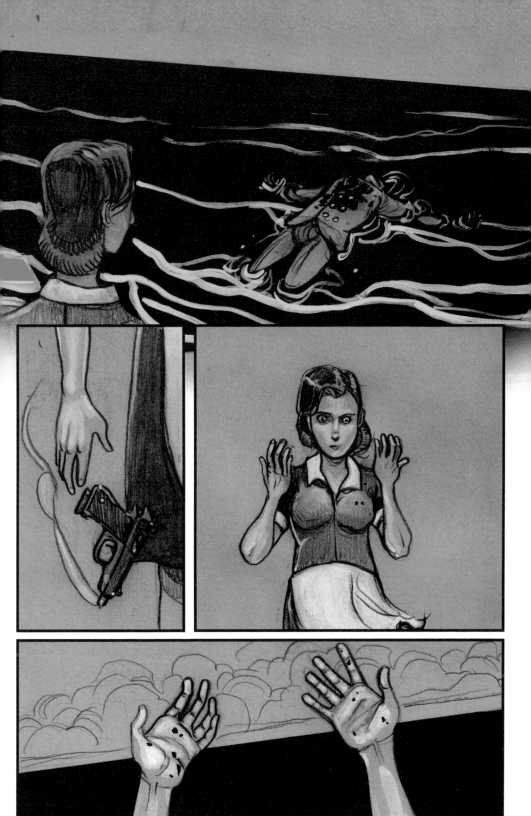

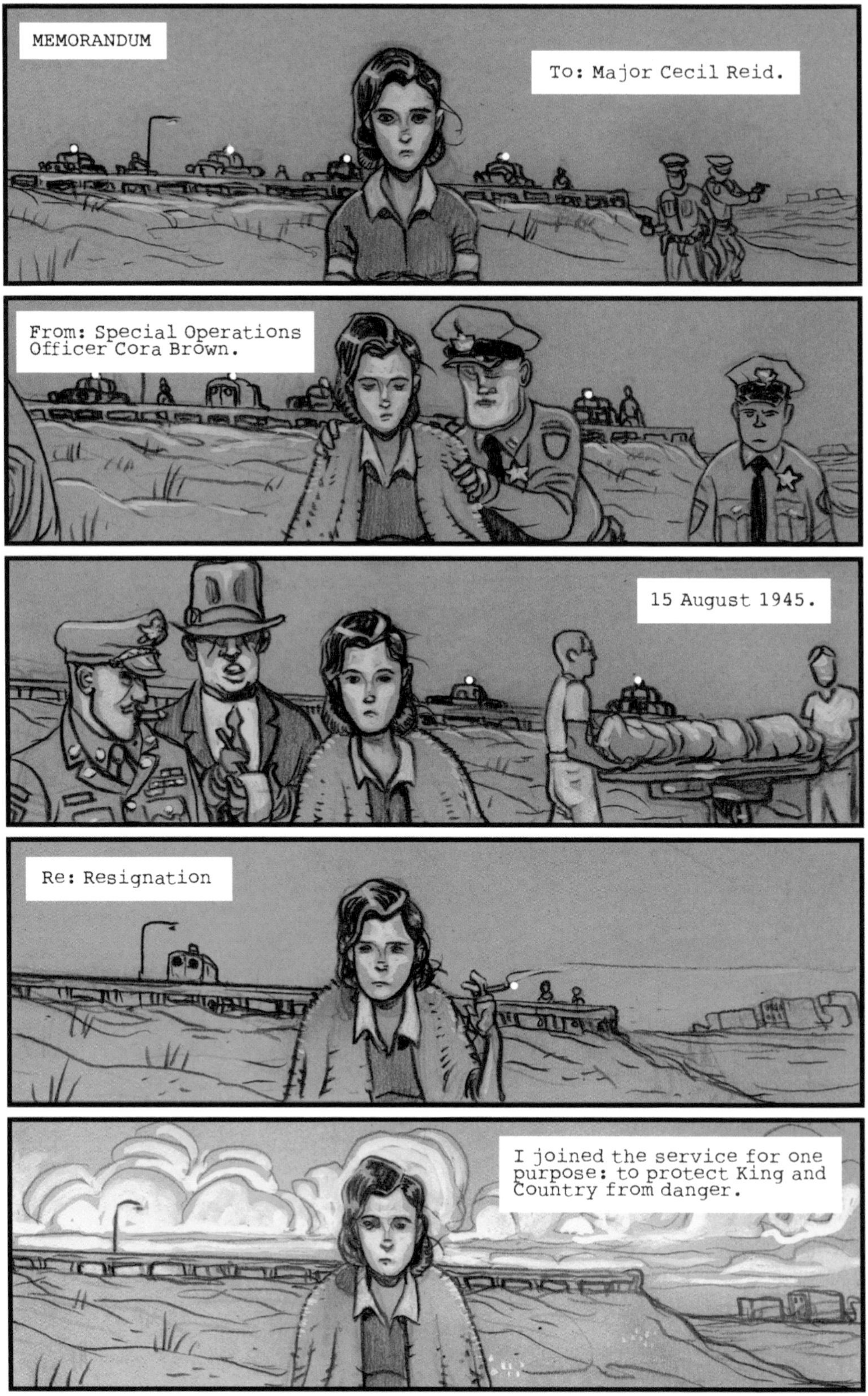
MEMORANDUM
To: Major Cecil Reid.
From: Special Operations Officer Cora Brown.
15 August 1945.
Re: Resignation
I joined the service for one purpose: to protect King and Country from danger.

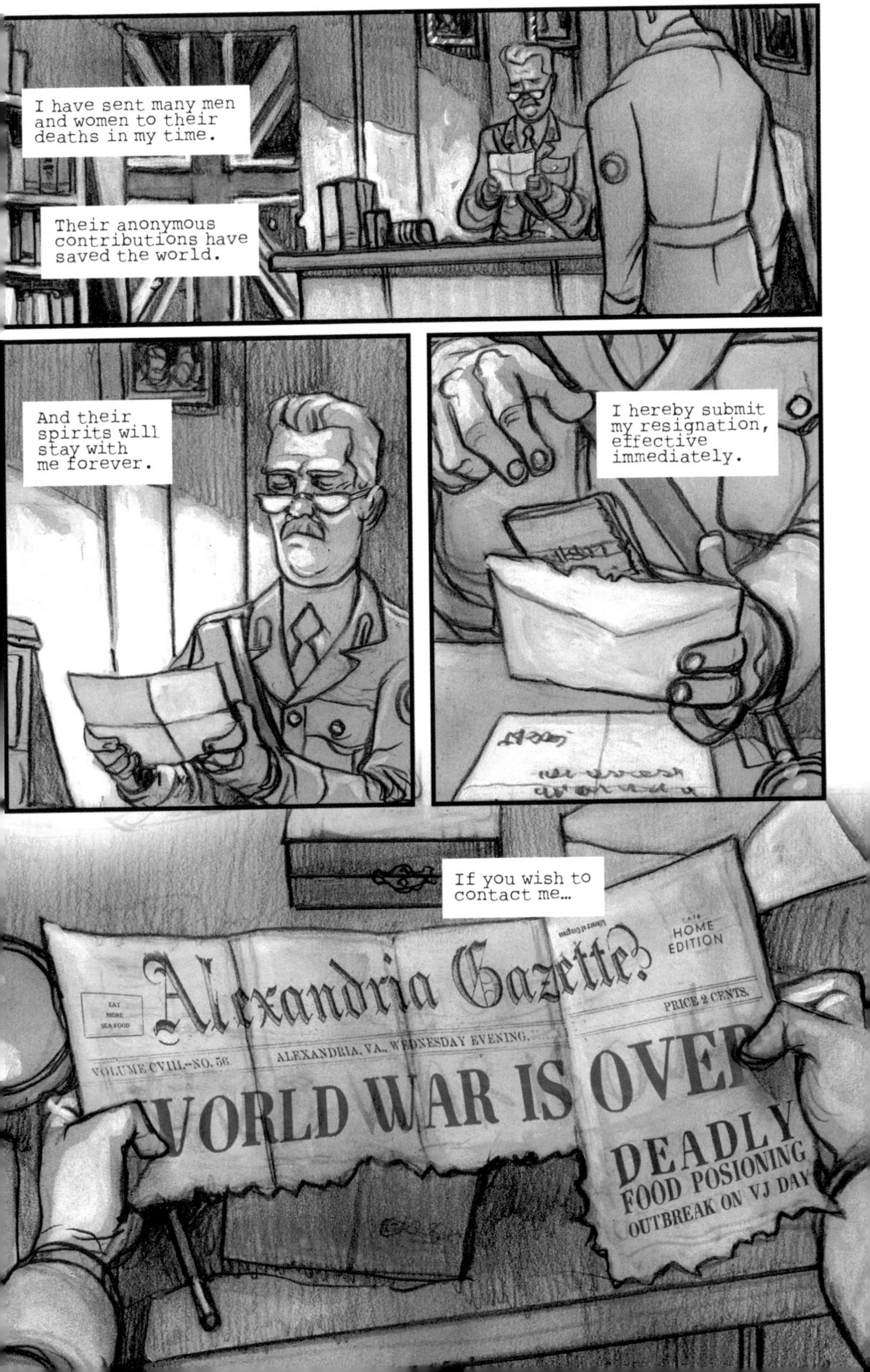

I have sent many men and women to their deaths in my time.
Their anonymous contributions have saved the world.
And their spirits will stay with me forever.
I hereby submit my resignation, effective immediately.
If you wish to contact me...
HOME EDITION
Alexandria Gazette
PRICE 2 CENTS.
EAT MORE SEA FOOD
ALEXANDRIA, VA., WEDNESDAY EVENING.
VOLUME CVIII.-NO. 56.
WORLD WAR IS OVE
DEADLY
FOOD POSIONING
OUTBREAK ON VJ DAY

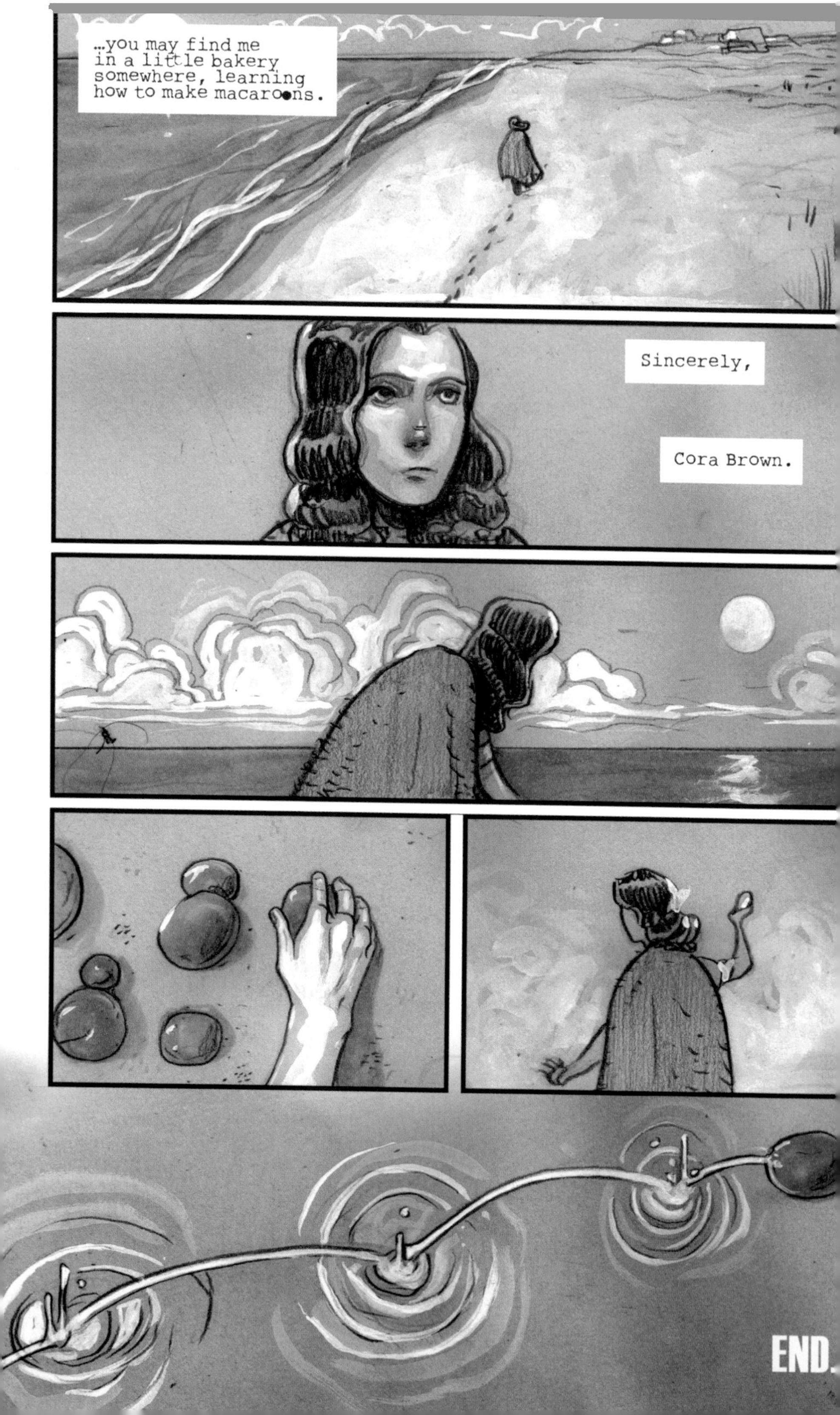
...you may find me in a little bakery somewhere, learning how to make macaroons.
Sincerely,
Cora Brown.
END.

ACKNOWLEDGEMENTS
"We few, we happy few, we band of brothers..."

There are so many people that have aided and abetted us in this battle against the world: Ansel Clarke for musing out loud about the story idea to Geoff Moore, Keith WTS Morris for his editorial assistance, Lyz Reblin for originally connecting Anthony and Jeff, Shawn Aldridge for his pinch-hitting on the galley edition, and Jeff McClelland for being a steely-eyed letterer with a strong disdain for a good night's sleep.

We would also be remiss to not thank everyone at Image Comics. It's a dream come true for all of us and we wish we could mention every person, but we know we're already tight for space. We'd also like to thank everyone at Diamond Comic Distributors for turning this into a success.

Anthony Del Col
would like to thank all of his family members but most importantly his own spy handler, his lovely and patient wife Lisa.

Jeff McComsey
would like to thank his wife Samantha for being a wonderful mother, amazing woman and for being extremely patient with Jeff while he was on his comics bullshit.

Jeff would also like to thank Michael Kitchen, Sir Alec Guinness, Roy Marsden and Ray Lonnen for entertaining him while he was on his comics bullshit.

Geoff Moore
would like to thank his family for inspiring him to create and tell stories, as well as all his friends for putting up with his never-ending what-ifs and over-explanations.

Jeff McClelland
would like to thank everyone willing to stand up and speak out.

And finally, we'd like to thank YOU for picking up this book and diving into an untold part of history...

SON OF HITLER

Art process:

Thumbnail 2"x3"

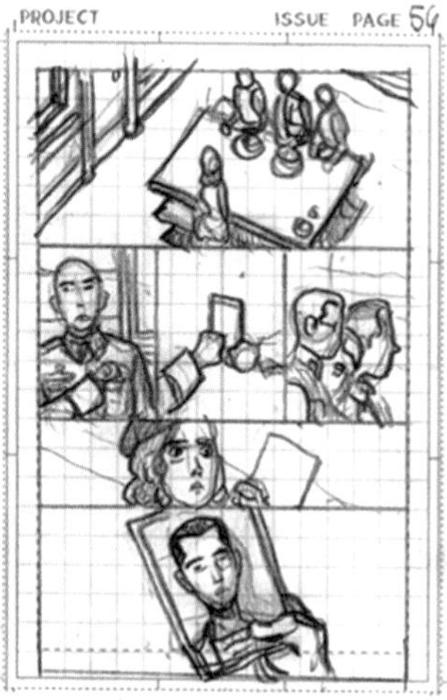
PROJECT
ISSUE
PAGE 54

THUMBNAILS:
I spend a lot of time on thumbnails specifically to make sure there's room for letters and speaking order is correct. At this stage, composition is the most important thing. I then scan my thumbs and work on top of an enlarged printout.

Pencils 10"x15"

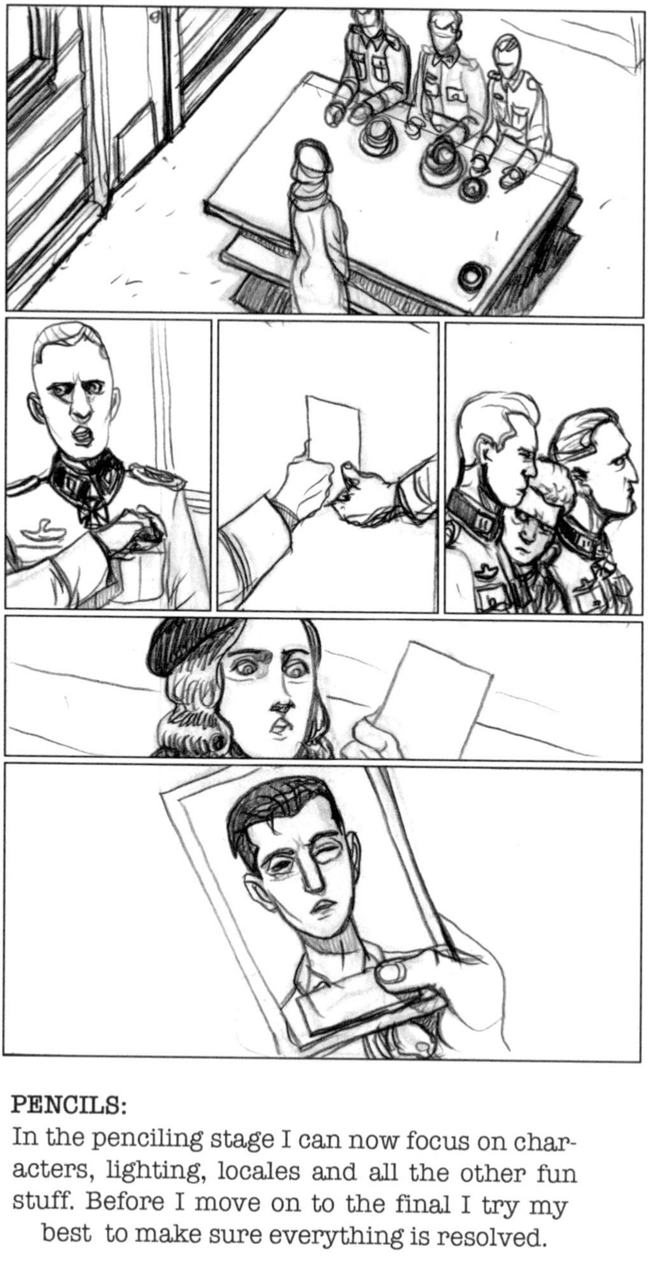

PENCILS:
In the penciling stage I can now focus on characters, lighting, locales and all the other fun stuff. Before I move on to the final I try my best to make sure everything is resolved.

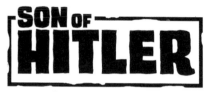

Scanned and cleaned up traditional painting.

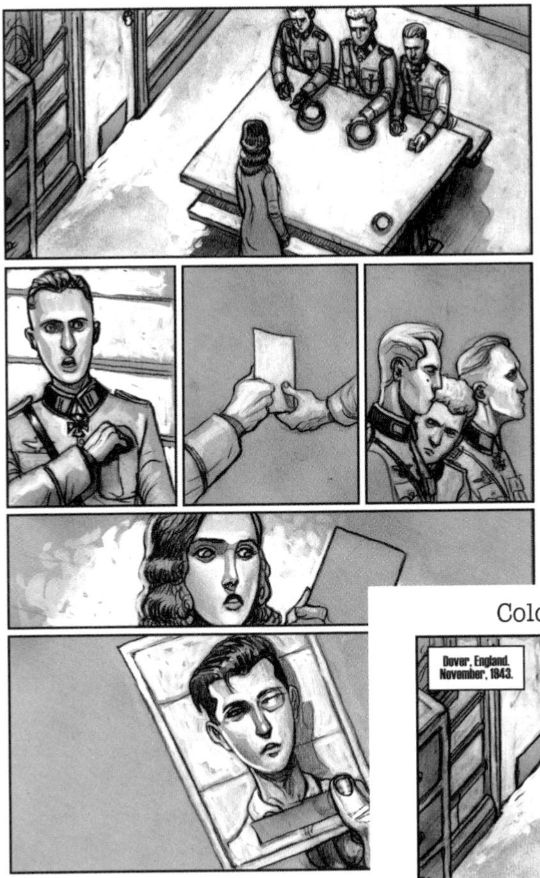

FINISHES:

Pages were finished in pencils then a non-waterproof white was used to render light areas onto the light gray paper.

I had a lot of fun working traditionally on these pages. Normally when inking you're using "spot blacks" to move the eye around the page.

This approach was more like using the paint to create "spot whites" to move the eye around the page.

Colored and lettered final page 6"x9"

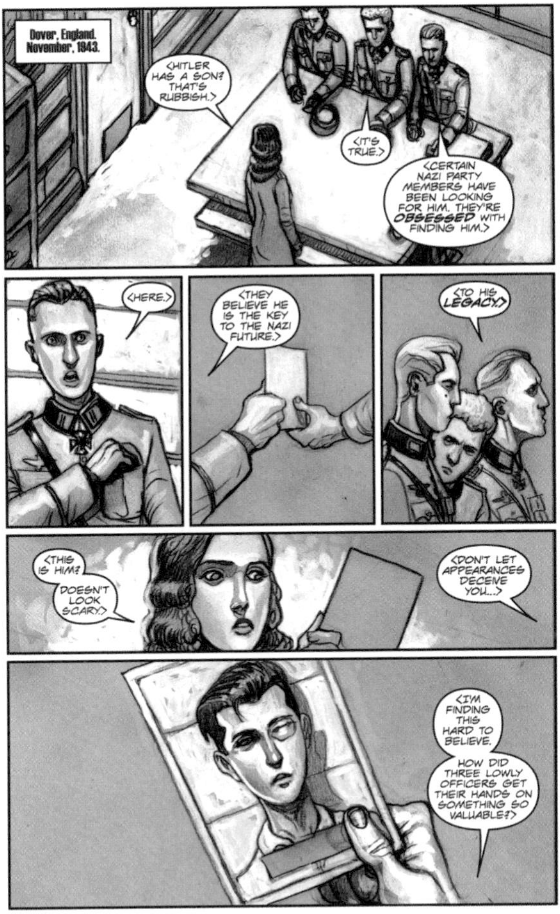
Dover, England.
November, 1943.
<HITLER HAS A SON? THAT'S RUBBISH.>
<IT'S TRUE.>
<CERTAIN NAZI PARTY MEMBERS HAVE BEEN LOOKING FOR HIM. THEY'RE OBSESSED WITH FINDING HIM.>
<HERE.>
<THEY BELIEVE HE IS THE KEY TO THE NAZI FUTURE.>
<TO HIS LEGACY.>
<THIS IS HIM?
DOESN'T LOOK SCARY.>
<DON'T LET APPEARANCES DECEIVE YOU...>
<I'M FINDING THIS HARD TO BELIEVE.
HOW DID THREE LOWLY OFFICERS GET THEIR HANDS ON SOMETHING SO VALUABLE?>

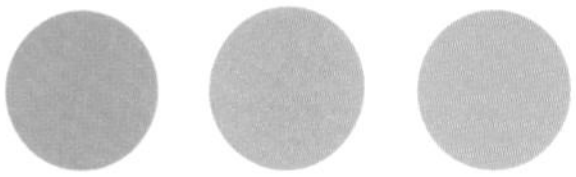

COLOR:

We always intended Son of Hitler to be a monochromatic book, and we knew we would use color for different acts. Throughout production we tried just about every color before settling on the above pallette.

When dealing with flashbacks or flash forwards, color allowed us to not just create a mood but also help keep the reader tuned in.

ANTHONY DEL COL (CO-WRITER)

Anthony is an acclaimed best-selling writer of comics, audio drama and television. His comic titles have included KILL SHAKESPEARE (IDW Publishing), ASSASSIN'S CREED (Titan Comics) and NANCY DREW & THE HARDY BOYS: THE BIG LIE (Dynamite), and his audio thriller UNHEARD: THE STORY OF ANNA WINSLOW was a #1 hit on Audible. Though a proud Canadian, Del Col lives in Brooklyn with his amazing wife Lisa. SON OF HITLER is his first title with Image Comics.

Follow Anthony on Twitter:
@anthony_delcol
or visit anthonydelcol.com

GEOFF MOORE (CO-WRITER)

Geoff is a Canadian hiding out in LA writing comics, developing kids' toys, designing games and creating podcasts, all to keep the world from figuring out he is a talentless hack.

Follow Geoff on Twitter:
@Theworkingnerd
(but he rarely posts).

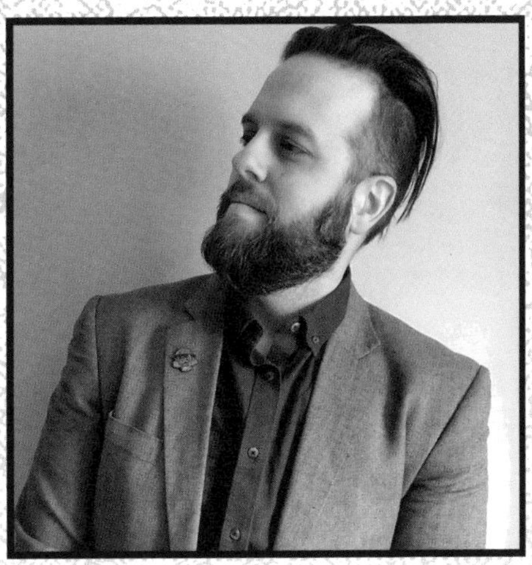

JEFF McCOMSEY (ARTIST)

Jeff is an American writer/illustrator (MOTHER RUSSIA, FLUTTER, HONCHO) working in comics for the past ten years. He is also editor in chief of the New York Times best-selling historical zombie anthology FUBAR, now into its sixth volume. Jeff and his family reside in the quaintly hip city of Lancaster, Pennsylvania. SON OF HITLER is his first title with Image Comics.

Follow Jeff on Twitter:
@jeff_mccomsey
Follow Jeff on Instagram:
@mccomseycomics

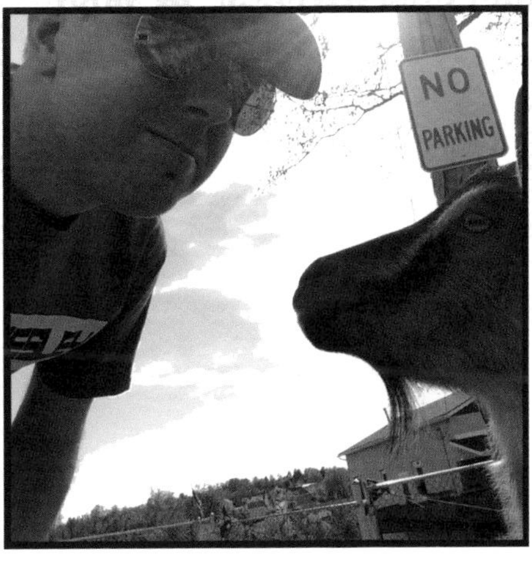
NO
PARKING

JEFF McCLELLAND (LETTERER)

Jeff McClelland writes comics. Well, he also letters. He lettered this book. It's a handy tool. Jeff currently writes THE TICK for New England Comics; he has also worked on THE FLUTTER COLLECTION for Dark Horse Comics, IMAGINARY DRUGS for IDW, and the New York Times bestselling FUBAR series for Alterna Comics. He wrote the graphic novel HONCHO with Jeff McComsey. The scourge of Pittsburgh, Jeff remains at large.

Follow Jeff on Twitter:
@jeffmcclelland

Pierre's Madeleines

Ingredients

4 oz (1 stick), plus 3 tablespoons unsalted butter - 2/3 cup sugar
1 cup all-purpose flour, plus 1 tablespoon, divided - 2 large eggs
1 teaspoon vanilla - Pinch of salt - 1 tablespoon lemon juice
1 tablespoon lemon zest - Powdered sugar (optional)

Directions

Melt the butter. Spoon 3 tablespoons of butter into a small bowl or cup and set aside. Let the rest of the butter cool slightly.

Prepare the dry ingredients and the wet ingredients in separate bowls. In a medium bowl, whisk together one cup of the flour and the sugar, and set aside. In another medium bowl, whisk the two eggs with the vanilla, salt, lemon juice, and lemon zest until the eggs are frothy.

Combine the dry and wet ingredients. Add the eggs to the flour. Using a spatula, stir until just combined. Add the 4 ounces of melted butter and continue to stir. It may take a minute for the butter to blend into the mixture but do not over mix.

Rest the batter. Cover the bowl with a plate (or plastic wrap) and place in the refrigerator to rest at least one hour and up to overnight.

Prepare the pans. Add the remaining one tablespoon of flour to the 3 tablespoons reserved butter and stir to combine. Using a pastry brush, brush the interiors of the shells with the butter-flour mixture so that they are well coated. Place the pans in the freezer for at least an hour.

Preheat the oven and fill pans. Preheat the oven to 350°F. Remove the batter from the refrigerator and one pan from the freezer. Fill each well in the madeleine pan with 1 tablespoon of the batter. Remove the other pan and fill in the same way.

Bake the madeleines. Check after 8 minutes and rotate pans. Check again 5 minutes later. The madeleines should be browning around the edges and puffed up a little in the middle.

Cool and dust with sugar. Remove the madeleines from the oven and let cool for 2 minutes. Dust lightly with powdered sugar and serve.